GUARDIAN OF CHAOS

NYX FORTUNA—BOOK ONE

MICHELLE MANUS

For Drew, as always.
Thanks for coming with me on this journey.

1

Nyx Fortuna was determined to leave Arizona, even if her head exploded. Literally.

The crossing from Tempe into Mesa brought on a splintering headache—not *quite* a migraine—and though her vision doubled as she climbed the steps onto the Greyhound bus bound for Billings, Montana, she felt an overwhelming sense of accomplishment at making it to a seat midway down the aisle.

Last time, she'd passed out on a bench and missed her boarding call.

She hugged her backpack to her chest, ignoring instructions to place the carry-on bag beneath the seat in front of her. No one would notice. No one ever noticed much of anything Nyx Fortuna did.

Once, she'd walked right past the ticket clerk at the movie theater and he hadn't even tried to stop her. The guilt had eaten away at her for the entire one-hundred and fifteen minutes of *Thor*, until she was forced to admit she wasn't made for a life of thievery, and paid for a ticket after the fact.

The twisted brand of luck that could have turned her into a world-class thief also made it impossible to hold down a job, what with her employers barely noticing when she came to work, or otherwise forgetting who she was altogether. She'd stayed afloat for a while, but the eviction notice stuffed in the bottom of her backpack said she was four months overdue on rent, and whatever curse dogged Nyx's heels apparently could not compete with a landlord out twenty-seven-hundred dollars' worth of rent.

Nyx closed her eyes and envisioned the stabbing railroad spike of pain in her brain turning into a gentle caress. It didn't work. In fact, it seemed to make the pain worse.

She opened her eyes and saw a young woman, maybe nineteen, shuffling down the aisle, eyes searching for a vacant seat. Precisely two seats were left on the bus—the one next to Nyx, and one at the far back next to a grizzled old man who stank of tobacco and cheap vodka. His head leaned back against the seat, eyes closed and lips partially open, a sliver of drool trailing out the corner of his mouth.

The girl saw the empty seat next to him and cringed. She didn't look at Nyx or the unoccupied seat next to her, though she stood only two feet away.

Nyx blinked past the pain and strung a few words together. "You can sit here."

The girl turned in Nyx's direction, confused, as if she'd heard someone speak but couldn't place the voice. Her eyes landed on Nyx, lighting up for a moment as they spotted the empty seat. Then her eyes glazed over, gaze slipping away as if Nyx and the row she sat on had been cut neatly from existence. Resigned, she made her way to the back of the bus and the old man.

Nyx slumped in her seat, regretting it immediately as her head hit the seatback and spikes of pain flared through her skull. She shifted uncomfortably. The climate control in the bus was too warm, sweat creeping through the thin fabric of her shirt.

In the seat across from her, a man wrapped his jacket tighter around himself and rearranged the scarf about his neck. Nyx envied his ability to wear sweater and scarf. Native Arizonans might find sixty-five degrees in December positively frigid, but

Nyx hadn't donned a long-sleeved shirt the entire time she'd lived here.

Makes a girl want to know where the hell she's from. Or even who the hell she is. But Nyx had given up trying to figure that out years ago. Back then, she'd had the mental energy to force doctors to recognize she existed long enough to explain her situation. She had stopped explaining it after the third time one suggested she stay overnight for observation. She'd had the feeling that stay would be in a ward one could not voluntarily leave.

The bus rumbled out of its idle with a jolt that reverberated through Nyx's entire body. Despite the resultant spike in her migraine, she felt relief. She was leaving.

Nyx didn't know what was waiting for her in Montana, save that it had to be better than whatever was here, and at least she wouldn't be sweltering in the heat nine months out of the year. She'd first tried to leave on a whim a few years ago, back when she'd still had a little money. Reading too many internet articles on the importance of self-care had convinced her a day trip was just the thing to cure her problems.

She'd still had a car, then, and it had taken her several miles up the I-17 to figure out that her nausea and migraine weren't going to go away. She'd turned around and—wonder of all wonders—her physical ailments had decreased the closer she came to the Tempe border. Once she got into the city proper, they had disappeared altogether.

It had taken eight more attempted day trips to convince her that her physical problems were a direct result of trying to leave her geographical location, and that had been enough to create a full-blown obsession. After all, if the location itself had this effect on her, then maybe it was possible her memory issues, and the fact that no one noticed her, were tied to the location as well.

Only passing out and nearly totaling the car had convinced her that the physical ailments weren't something she could overcome through her own willpower. Back then, it hadn't seemed worth the risk. Now... now she didn't have anything left to stop her from trying again.

No home. No family or friends or lover who would miss her. She didn't even have a dog because she wasn't selfish enough to get one when she couldn't even take care of herself.

The bus chugged along toward its stop in Phoenix, and Nyx's relief at moving gave way to the customary panic that seized her whenever she got too far from whatever residence she currently called home. Her hand went to her throat, pulling the chain of her necklace from beneath her shirt, reassuring herself of the pendant's presence.

She studied the sphere of four overlapping rings: one platinum, one onyx, one copper, and one indigo. The pendant flared with warmth, curling into her touch. She closed her fingers around the sphere and calm replaced panic as she slipped it beneath her shirt.

The necklace was another link in a very long chain of things she hated herself for, but she couldn't help it. She'd *promised*, promised the person who had been the only bright spot in the last handful of years, that she would always keep the necklace close to her, keep it safe.

Nyx Fortuna always kept her promises.

Midway into Phoenix the nausea set in, a full-body flu-like ache close on its heels.

No one noticed her discomfort, though the sweat poured off her in rivulets, and she eventually understood that the low moaning sounds she heard were of her own making. Even when the blood started to pour out her nose, and she had to grab a shirt from her backpack to staunch the flow, no one looked at her.

No one noticed.

Her vision blacked at the corners of her eyes. She fought through it with the panic of a wild animal certain that if it fell asleep, it would not wake again. And Nyx Fortuna discovered that she might have *thought* she was willing to die in the name of freedom, but she wasn't.

The bus slowed as it pulled into the Phoenix station. Nyx choked back a mouthful of blood and shoved to her feet, grasping the seat in front of her as her vision exploded in a multitude of bright lights. She took a deep breath and fled.

The bus's other occupants remained calm and bored, not even a blink from the bus driver as she forced the doors open. She tripped on the exit steps, the knee of her threadbare jeans ripping and her bare skin grinding into dirty asphalt, a fresh pain blending with the old ones. She rolled to her feet and stumbled six paces away from the bus before she fell back on all fours, retching up blood and acrid bile.

The pain in her head morphed into opposing pressures. The inside felt as if her brain was swelling up, and the outside felt as if it was locked inside a slowly tightening vise.

She was going to die.

It hit her with stunning clarity. She was too disoriented to know which direction Tempe lay in, even if she'd had the strength to start crawling there, which she didn't. In a few seconds she would pass out. No one would see her, no one would call an ambulance, and that would be that. Her entire life dwindled down to her blood-soaked corpse on a bus station parking lot.

Her vision reduced to a pinprick of sight and her head, impossible to hold up any longer, hit the ground.

A blast of icy air hit, startling her back to consciousness, the sudden cold a balm against the pain that swelled in her body. Groggy, she looked for the source of the frigid wind, and found that her hands rested six inches from a narrow dirt lane.

It cut impossibly through the bus station, both there and not there, overlapping the reality she knew. The first few feet of the lane were bare, after which old oaks, maples, and cedars lined both sides, the leaves of the former two in full autumnal colors. Most of those leaves had fallen off the trees, creating a blanket of multi-colored red and yellow hues on the ground.

Nyx stared at the leaves that covered the winter-dead grass.

Through them, she could still see the paved parking lot of the bus station.

It was as if two images on a computer screen had been laid on top of each other, and she couldn't tell which was real.

She squeezed her eyes shut and counted to ten. Then, she counted to ten again, for the sake of thoroughness. When she opened her eyes, she still saw the dirt lane. It looked so inviting, and the cool air blowing from it promised relief.

She crawled forward two inches and the nausea abated. Two more inches and the blood quit dripping from her nose. She stretched out her fingers, the tips just brushing the dirt, and the pain in her head vanished entirely.

Mad. She had gone utterly, raving mad.

She yanked her hand away and stumbled to her backpack. Pain roared through her head, more intense than before. The blood that had ceased dripping from her nose returned as a flood, joined by a trickle of red from her ears, and her stomach heaved with an insistence that clenched every muscle in her abdomen.

Nyx's fingers fumbled, found the straps of her backpack. Grasping the only possessions she had left in the world, Nyx threw herself onto the dirt lane. Pain fled her. Lying on her back, looking up at an overcast gray sky, she felt clear-headed, almost relaxed.

She rose to a sitting position, but though she braced for it, no wave of nausea drowned her. Her vision of the bus station beyond the lane was hazy, as if she viewed it through a cloud of dust or smog. People walked past, boarding buses or departing them. None noticed the dirt path, or the woman sitting on it.

Nyx turned away from the bus station and looked beyond. A quaint wooden street sign proclaimed her to be on Wayfarer's Way, and far off down the lane she could just make out a cabin, the building beckoning to her with a physical pull.

She stared at the thick forest that lined both sides of the rural dirt lane, then twisted to look back at the bus station. The two could not possibly coexist—the ancient forest alongside the barren desert metropolis.

They could not, and yet they did.

A foot away, the world waited as it always had, unchanging and unfeeling. She was not certain she would miss it. She *was* certain that it would not miss her.

If she had gone mad—and for some inexplicable reason she was not quite certain she *had*—did it matter? She felt alive, as she had not in years, and the cold air that bit through her thin shirt was comforting, as was the rustle of leaves as wind swept through the trees. She closed her eyes and breathed deeply, taking in sweet forest air devoid of the city pollution only a few feet behind her.

Nyx made up her mind even before she opened her eyes and turned away from the bus station.

"Well, Alice," Nyx muttered, settling her backpack firmly onto her shoulders and setting off down Wayfarer's Way, "we are officially down the rabbit hole."

2

The air smelled of damp and a trace of moss, and a little of the smoky scent from chimneys that always made Nyx feel like true winter had come. The farther she walked, the less apparent the city became, until eventually she could no longer see it when she looked over her shoulder.

The world had given way entirely to the ancient forest.

The lane ended at a two-story cabin. It had a well-maintained, green-shingled roof and a covered porch area complete with wooden bench swing. In front of the building sat a small stone fountain in the shape of a griffin. Water gurgled from the griffin's beak, pooling at its feet in a shallow basin.

Hanging from the porch roof on two black-linked chains was a wooden sign etched with the words, "Between the Lines Bookstore and Coffee." In smaller letters underneath were the words, "We do not discriminate based on species, planet of origin, or amorous orientation."

Well, at least the place has a sense of humor.

Nyx rose on her tiptoes and then rolled back onto her feet, completing the see-sawing action several times. Though freezing, she found herself unable to go inside. Now that she was *here,* in front of the building, the weight of the ancient forest pressing comfortingly upon her, the entire affair was too strange: the trees, the cold, the snug-looking cabin bookstore.

She was stressed. She was, no doubt, having some sort of psychotic break.

Maybe I already had one. Maybe that time I passed out at the station in Mesa I just snapped and right now I'm sitting in a padded cell in a straitjacket. Did they still put people in straitjackets?

In the event that hadn't yet happened, she needed to avoid it. She should go home—for the remaining two days she had a home—and rest. When she woke up in the morning she would laugh at this memory.

She turned to leave and caught her reflection in one of the cabin windows as she did. She stopped, staring at the image in the window, feeling a bit like Dorian Gray looking at his painting and discovering minute differences in what he saw before him and what he remembered.

Her black hair, too fine and flyaway to be truly manageable even at the best of times, hung dull and lifeless, brushing the tops of her shoulders in a discarded style that suggested she had ceased caring how it looked, even to herself. Her silver-gray eyes were as dull as her hair, matched only perhaps by her olive skin's apparent disinterest in perking up her features. Pinched lips suggested she hadn't smiled in quite some time. Worse than all of it, though, was the defeated slump of her posture, the drooping shoulders.

She pulled a spare shirt from her backpack and wetted it from her water bottle, using the makeshift washcloth to clean the remaining bits of blood from her face. She brushed her hair back from her eyes, smoothing it as best she could. Then she straightened her shoulders, walked up the four porch steps, and opened the cabin door.

Inside, the air was pleasantly warm, and she spotted a small fireplace in the corner, crackling sleepily. To her left stood a spotless, stainless steel bar, atop which sat a sleek manual espresso machine exactly like the one at the coffee shop she'd worked at in undergrad. No one appeared to be manning the bar.

"Hello?"

No one answered her tentative call, either, so she stepped into the room that adjoined the coffee bar, looking for any signs of another person. Bookshelves, arranged in serpentine formations, filled the room. The books were mostly science fiction and fantasy, though she found smaller sections on mystery, science, mythology, outdoor survival, and the occult.

They were all sections she read, and a brief perusal of the books showed she had either read them, wanted to read them at some point, or currently found them interesting. Nyx began to have a very bad feeling. The feeling intensified when she walked up to the fireplace at the end of the room and found a cozy gray papasan chair nestled nearby.

She had always wanted a cozy papasan chair, in gray. She loved fireplaces, and books, and coffee. Furthermore, she loved cabins and woods and the onset of winter. She loved absolutely everything about this place, right down to the color scheme and choice of wall décor.

It would be easy, so easy, to stay. To simply curl up in that papasan chair with a book and a latte and read until her problems were distant memories.

Unfortunately, she had read enough books to know this desire was *not* a good thing. Either she really had crossed into some otherworld and had walked into a space specifically designed to lure her in, or this was all a figment of her imagination.

The sensible explanation was that she'd passed out and wandered into a pleasant place in her own mind where her life was finally peaceful and comfortable and filled with all the things she'd always wanted. Maybe her body had sustained enough physical damage she'd slipped into a coma, and this place was her brain's response.

If she *was* in a coma, the idea of her body slowly rotting away in some hospital over the years until she finally died, well, that wasn't how she wanted to go. And if she was inside someone's carefully designed trap, well, that wasn't how she wanted to go either.

Both scenarios pointed to one solution: leave.

She took a careful, deliberate step away from the fireplace. Then another, and another. Instead of getting easier, moving became more difficult with each step, as if the room had a physical hold on her. Ten steps later, she'd broken out in a sweat and her breath was coming in harsh pulls.

She paused to rest and that was when she heard it: a low, deep thrumming that traveled into her bones and set her heart to beating in time with it. If she'd thought it difficult to leave the library, *not* responding to the call of that noise was impossible.

Her feet answered almost of their own accord, taking her out of the library and into a short hallway. The noise grew deeper, stronger, drawing her down the hall, through another doorway and into an odd, hexagon-shaped room. The walls mimicked the forest scenery outside, and set into the center of the room were six silver posts, each four feet in height. Floating atop each post was an orb that wasn't quite black, but something more galaxy-like.

Each post formed the corner of a smaller hexagon set into the center of the room, the floor between them shining with the same galaxy-like material as the orbs. It was there, in the epicenter of the hexagon, that the thrumming issued from. It pulsed in her ears, in time with her heartbeat, a crescendo of noise that pulled her inexorably forward, until she found herself crouched at the edge of the invisible line between two posts.

Her hand reached out involuntarily, brushing the strange, cosmic material of the floor. Liquid coolness spilled through her, an infinite expansion beginning in her chest and moving outward, as if the entire world was unfurling inside her.

In that instant of connection, she knew that this was no fever-dream brought on by a coma. This wasn't insanity. What it *was* sang in her veins, her blood, her bones, as if she was made for it and it for her: *portal*. She hovered over a *portal*, and the song it sang promised it could take her to a thousand different worlds.

Hands landed on Nyx's shoulders, yanking her back with bruising force. She skidded across the floor, and tumbled to a stop four feet back from the posts.

What the hell?

A woman stood to Nyx's right, gray hair framing her face in tight curls. Her dark skin was blanched with either fear or anger, her body trembling, and she looked directly *at* Nyx, as if she wasn't having any trouble recognizing that Nyx existed.

That *should* have mattered. The sudden presence of another person should have mattered. But the portal's call had not dimmed, and even as her rational mind tried to fight it, she found herself lunging for it again.

The woman's hands clamped down on her wrists with bruising strength. Thick scars encircled her wrists and a tattoo of a dolphin stretched across one forearm.

She gave the hexagon a severe look.

"Stop that."

The thrumming dimmed.

"I said *stop*."

Power crackled through the room, like an electric current, and the thrumming ceased. The pull of the portal vanished and Nyx collapsed, feeling as if she'd been brought to life only to have it ripped away from her again.

The woman shook her. "And you. I'll thank you to explain how you got in here and what you did to my Arrival Gate."

"I—" Nyx licked her lips, tried to think, to breathe, to do *anything*. Arrival Gate? "What the hell *is* this place?"

The woman's eyes narrowed. "Where are you from, girl?"

"From?" Nyx repeated stupidly.

"Yes. Where do you come from? Or are your wits so addled you can't answer?"

"Arizona. I—" She didn't get another word out. The dolphin

tattoo on the woman's arm began to *move*. It peeled itself off the woman's skin, dissolved into a blur of color and slid down, traveling to where the woman's hand gripped Nyx's arm.

Nyx yanked her arm back, but it was as if the two of them were welded together. Even when the woman uncurled her fingers with a sad smile, Nyx couldn't pull away from her. The mass of ink slid onto Nyx's forearm, shifting shape and color, stretching into various images—a horse, a wolf, a mountain lion —shifting faster and faster, until Nyx could no longer make out what each image was before it disappeared again.

The entire room crackled with power, the air filling with words that came from everywhere and nowhere, a chant made of ancient, primal syllables. They penetrated Nyx down to the bone, until the whole of her being vibrated with them, and on some instinctual level she understood what they were: a binding. Understood it, because it felt as if some vital part of her had been physically tied to the ground she stood on—to the building, and to the lands surrounding it.

The room spun, cycling faster and faster, shapes and colors blurring together, indistinct of one another. A fierce ache filled Nyx, so strong she thought it might break her. Through the chaos of pain and color a shadow flickered at the edge of her vision. Then the shadow vanished, the colors calmed, and the room settled.

The ink on her forearm resolved into a black griffin, its wings and claws tipped with silver.

Whatever force held Nyx and the other woman together vanished and they stumbled apart. Nyx stared at the tattoo on her arm in horror. It felt *alive*. She clawed at it, trying to peel the raised ink from her skin. Any time she succeeded in pulling a corner up it simply slipped from her grasp and readhered to her flesh.

The woman's hand gently covered Nyx's, halting her efforts.

"It won't come off, dear."

"What is it? What is this place? What are you?"

A breeze swept through the windowless room, the deep thrumming noise returning as the black floor of the portal began to swirl between the silver posts. It still called to Nyx, her every instinct telling her to move into that hexagon and *go*, but the call was tempered by the tattoo on her arm, by the binding that said she belonged *here*.

The woman glanced at the portal, a frown creasing her forehead. A figure emerged from the cosmic floor, as if the portal were an elevator bringing the individual up from below.

"I don't have the time to explain. Had the choice been given to me, I would have done things differently. But the choice wasn't mine, so I'll simply tell you what the last Guardian told me.

"This Station will seem a haven at first. I know I kissed the ground and thanked the gods for it when I stumbled in here." She rubbed the scars around her wrists. "But even a haven, if you are given no choice in staying, will eventually become a prison.

"When that day comes, you may petition for a replacement, and one will be sent." The woman smiled at her. "And you will tell your successor some version of what I am telling you now."

The figure in the hexagon had fully resolved, though they wore a cloak so deeply hooded Nyx couldn't make out any of their features. They held out one hand to the woman and she took it, stepping onto the cosmic platform. The floor swirled and the two began to sink down.

"Wait! You can't just leave me here. I don't understand any of this."

"The bond can't fully settle until I go, and with an Arrival in two hours, you'll need it to. The Avatar will explain everything."

They were half sunk into the floor now and Nyx's panic rose the farther they disappeared. The woman's words looped in Nyx's head: Avatar, Station, Guardian, Arrival. Words she understood the definitions of, but which held no contextual meaning for her at present.

The cosmic floor was up to the woman's shoulders when she said, "Oh, I almost forgot. I hired an assistant for the Station. Her name is Evra. Perhaps she can help you adjust."

Then the floor swallowed over the woman and the hooded figure, the cosmic depths swirling a final time before settling once more into a solid state.

Nyx was alone.

3

Nyx stared at the space where the woman had disappeared, but try as she might, she couldn't will the portal to bring her back. Then she turned and ran, winding through the bookshelves, past the coffee bar, and out the front door with a running leap she fully expected would clear her of both porch and stairs.

Instead, Nyx tumbled to the ground next to the portal.

"Oh, this is so *not* happening."

Nyx leapt to her feet and trotted out of the room, following her previous flight pattern back to the front door. This time, she opened it cautiously, peering out. *Porch*? Check. *Porch-swing*? Check. *Foresty-trees and griffin fountain beyond porch*? Check and check.

Slowly, she inched one foot out. It touched wooden flooring and relief flooded her. Laughing, she stepped outside, let the door close behind her…and found herself standing once more in the portal room.

Nyx tried the front door six times before searching for some other means of escape. She discovered a small office past the bookshelves in which she found a door looking out onto a picturesque back porch. It was, in fact, everything Nyx had ever wanted in a back porch, right down to the papasan chair, grill, firepit, and view overlooking a burbling spring.

She wanted nothing to do with it, but perhaps she could escape through it.

Nyx stepped onto the back porch… and returned to the portal room. She tried the back door three more times, four windows, and the front door once more before accepting what she'd known ever since the weight of the tattoo had settled into her: she was trapped.

Exhausted, she stumbled into the library and slumped into the fireside papasan chair, irritated to find it was precisely as comfortable as she'd always imagined one would be.

"Are you finished with the dramatics?"

Nyx jumped bolt upright out of the chair, but her terrified scan of the room did not reveal the speaker.

The speaker cleared his throat. "Ahem, over *here.*"

Nyx followed the voice to the coffee table. Atop it sat a small griffin, no larger than a cat. Perched upon his beaked eagle's face was a pair of silver-rimmed spectacles, which ought to have made him look ridiculous, but didn't.

Nyx opened her mouth. Nothing came out. She closed, opened, and tried again to a similarly spectacular lack of effect.

The small griffin rolled his eyes. Nyx firmly believed eagles' eyes were not capable of rolling. She also firmly believed griffins did not exist and were not the size of house cats. But in the last hour she'd almost been hypnotized into jumping through a portal, watched another woman disappear through it, and discovered she could not leave a building by any physical means.

She had hit her mental quota for astonishment.

"I am the Avatar of this Station, currently in the form of a griffin." He said it in the manner of a sandwich-shop clerk reciting a special, "Welcome. Today the ham on rye is only four-ninety-nine."

Huh. "You're tiny."

"I prefer the term *compact*." The griffin bristled, chest and feathers puffing, lion's tail flicking. "Honestly, you think you want a full-size griffin in here? They're as big as draft horses. How am I supposed to navigate these bookshelves if I'm as big as a draft horse?"

He peered at her, head cocked, clearly expecting an answer.

"I don't know."

The griffin continued to stare.

"I'm sure you made an excellent choice being sma—"

The griffin's glare turned murderous and while those claws might be small, Nyx was betting they would rip out her jugular just fine.

"—er, *compact*."

The griffin's feathers smoothed. "We Avatars pride ourselves on making the best choices for our Stations and Guardians. As such, it is my duty to remind you that you have only—" He dug into his feathers with one talon and drew out a pocket-watch on a silver chain. "Fifty minutes left before the first Arrival. I must recommend you begin familiarizing yourself with the Operations Manual immediately."

"Right." Operations Manual. Sure. "See, the thing is, I need to go home. It's been a long day, I'm pretty sure I'm on a hallucinogenic trip, and I don't think you're real. No offense."

Glasses-wearing, pocket-watch-carrying, talking griffin? What diseased part of her subconscious had cooked *that* up?

Probably the part that thinks he's adorable.

"Besides, people are expecting me. They'll miss me if I don't get home."

"No, they won't." The griffin let out a world-weary sigh. "If you had anyone waiting, anyone at all who would miss you or care that you're gone, you wouldn't be here. Guardians find their Stations when there's nothing left for them in their previous lives. That's how it works. And until you're ready to accept that, and the responsibility you've taken on, the Station won't allow you to leave.

Do you understand?" The griffin peered at her intently, beaked face pushed forward.

Did she understand?

"No, I don't understand. I don't understand any of this. Everyone keeps throwing out words like Station and Guardian like I'm supposed to have any idea what the hell that means and I just want…"

"What?" The griffin cocked his head.

She wanted to go back to an hour ago when the cabin had seemed like the most inviting, perfect place in the world.

"A drink," she said, instead.

Nyx found the espresso bar fully stocked, and for a few blissful minutes she lost herself in the familiar routine of steaming milk and pulling espresso shots. She added three pumps of Irish cream into the mug and tried and failed not to wish for a slug of Bailey's to add to it.

She finished pouring the latte and turned to find a bottle of Bailey's on the counter. It was dusty, like it had been in storage for years. Nyx considered it before deciding that being drunk right now was a really bad decision. She bypassed the bottle and could have sworn the griffin let out a sigh of relief as she did. He was perched on the back of a barstool, looking for all the world as if small griffins casually hanging out in kitchens was an everyday occurrence.

Nyx stared at the slightly lopsided latte-art heart in her cup, his words echoing in her head. *If you had anyone, anyone at all who would miss you…*

The despondency of earlier that morning came back, a flush creeping slowly up her neck. It would be so easy to slip underneath that surface of despair and let go.

The crazy part was, she didn't feel like she was crazy. Every piece inside of her felt like it was home. Maybe it was just that for the first time in years, people had actually spoken to her. The woman. The griffin. She was so starved for connection she'd have talked to a lamppost if it had had the inclination.

Logically, none of this made sense. But she'd lived her life logically, even when it came to trying to sort out the mess of her missing memories and the way people forgot she existed, and where had that gotten her? It had gotten her to nearly dying in a bus station with people walking right past her.

There was a reason her favorite books had always been fantasy. Because her life, her problems, were fantastical. She'd wanted to believe in magic, because magic seemed the only thing capable of explaining the way people's gazes slid right off her. But she'd never found any evidence that it actually existed, until now.

She ran her hand over the tattoo on her arm. It didn't hurt or bleed like a new tattoo should, and the ink was raised, more like an embossing than anything else. If it wasn't magic, if the binding tugging at her wasn't magic, she didn't know what was.

So, no, logically none of this made sense. But it felt more right than anything else in her life ever had. Perhaps irrationality needed to have its day.

"I don't really think I'm crazy," she said softly.

The griffin, perched next to her on the stainless-steel counter, gave an approving dip of his beak. "Good. That makes things less difficult."

"So, umm, if I'm not crazy, what *is* this place? Where am I?"

"You are still, technically, on Earth. This is a Waystation. It exists in what we call Earth Between. Think of it—" He paused, considering. "I suppose in the terminology popular today you would consider it a parallel dimension. It overlaps a portion of Dead Earth."

Nyx frowned. "Dead?"

"Non-magical. The majority of inhabited planets—"

"There's intelligent life on other planets?" Nyx squeaked.

He rubbed the side of his head. "This is what I get for not having to induct a new Guardian in over a hundred and fifty years. I'd forgotten how tedious it is.

"Yes, as you will discover firsthand very soon, there are a

number of inhabited planets. Most of them took a predominantly magical approach to progress. Earth took a primarily technological one. It caused somewhat of a rift in the foundations of your world, which is why magic, though it can *exist* in Dead Earth, is reduced to a fraction of its impact there. Here, in Earth Between, magic is as prevalent as it is on the other planets."

"How many?"

"How many what?"

"Inhabited planets."

"I'm sure there are a number we don't know about, but that are connected to the ley lines? One-hundred and seven."

Nyx swallowed. One-hundred and seven. *One-hundred and seven* planets with intelligent life on them. Scientists would lose their shit. Well, no, on second thought, they would just think she had lost hers and ship her off to a mental institution.

"Ley lines. That's the portal in the other room? Where the woman disappeared? Is she okay?"

"Sena is fine, and yes, a ley line connects each planet, allowing travel between them, and each culminates in a Waystation. Each Station has a Guardian—that's you, now that Sena's retired—and it is the Guardian's job to ensure travelers to your Station have the appropriate documentation to be here."

"I'm glorified passport control?"

The griffin blinked. "If what I've read of airline travel is accurate…yes, I suppose you could think of it that way. It isn't your only duty but it's the one most pertinent at the moment as your first Arrival is in—" He consulted his pocket watch. "Approximately forty-five minutes."

"Arrival? People are coming here from other planets? In less than an hour?"

"Precisely. Which is why I suggest you begin familiarizing yourself with the Operations Manual, and save further questions on the nature of the universe for later." His eagle's gaze surveyed her with a critical air. "Though for stars sake, you cannot be taken seriously in your present condition."

Nyx glanced down at herself. She'd cleaned up as best she could, but her shirt was still covered in dried blood, the knees of her jeans were torn, and she smelled...well, she *had* vomited.

"I do not suppose you would wear a suit?" he asked.

"A suit?"

He sighed. "I thought not. Change into these." A clean pair of jeans and a new shirt, both of which looked nearly identical to what she already wore, appeared next to him. He glanced at her again and a hairbrush and a tube of deodorant appeared as well. "There is a bathroom down the hall on the right. Don't tarry, we have a lot of work to do."

4

Nyx changed and cleaned up in the bathroom, and told herself that she could do this. Being a Guardian was a job. She was good at jobs, even if she couldn't get a good one. She was good at learning new things. And though what Sena had said about havens and prisons lingered in the back of her mind, all Nyx could really see was the former.

Sena *and* the Avatar had noticed her—spoken to her. She would probably have welcomed an actual prison if it came with that connection. Here, she had a purpose—she just needed to live up to it.

She walked back out to the cafe, where the Avatar waited.

"Okay. Where do I find the Operations Manual?"

"Follow me." The griffin launched into the air, flying lazily, and Nyx followed.

"So, what do I call you?"

"I am the Avatar of this Station."

"Yes, I know, but what's your name?"

He gave her a blank stare.

"What did the previous Guardians call you?"

"Avatar."

Nyx couldn't imagine saying, "Good morning, Avatar."

"I'm going to call you Griff."

She followed Griff into the portal room. A podium stood off to one side and Griff landed atop it, his tail curling around him.

"Griff. It's not terribly original, is it?"

Nyx shrugged and took a sip of coffee. "I could pick something else, if you like. Or you could."

"*No.*" The griffin's wings flared out. "No. Griff is nice. I like it."

Nyx looked at him. "Have you really never had a name before?"

A flicker of sadness passed across his face and then disappeared. "Once, perhaps. But I am an Avatar, now. We were created to do the Guardians' bidding. We were not meant for names."

"That sounds lonely."

Nyx approached the podium. A thick sheaf of papers held together by a binder clip rested atop it, covered in a thick layer of dust. She picked it up and swiped her hand across it to reveal bold printed letters that read: Operations Manual.

"For something that's supposed to hold the secrets of this uber-secret Station it doesn't look like much."

"You're very particular, aren't you? At this rate I'm going to be rearranging the place for years before you're satisfied." Griff reached out and tapped the sheaf of papers with one talon.

Brown blossomed in the center of the paper, spreading toward the edges. Nyx yelped and dropped the bundle. It landed on the floor with a thump, its transformation from a stack of grubby papers into a very fine, leather-bound book complete.

"I made it nicer for you and your response is to throw it on the floor?"

"Umm, sorry," Nyx mumbled. "I'm not exactly accustomed to magical transformations."

She picked up the manual. Embossed on the front were the words, "Operations Manual. Station 27. Current Guardian: Nyx

Fortuna. Location: Earth Between." Around the words was the picture of a griffin, beak touching tail to form a perfect circle.

Griff blinked. "Is it more to your liking?"

She sensed a hesitance in the question, a need for approval, and she shook off her own surprise and said, "It's beautiful. Thank you, Griff."

Impulsively, she reached out and gently stroked his wing before opening the book and reading aloud.

"Okay, here we go. One, all travelers must be recorded in the Station's Arrival/Departure Log. Great." Nyx looked around and found a drawer at the bottom of the podium. She opened it and drew out a clipboard, attached to which was a single sheet of paper which had Arrival/Departure written at the top.

Nyx scanned the columns on the log sheet. Name. Species. Homeworld. Documentation. Reason for Travel. Expected Duration of Stay, If Applicable. Arrival/Departure.

"Species?"

"You didn't think there were over one-hundred planets and only one species of intelligent life, did you?"

"Well, no, but—"

"Plenty of other planets evolved humans, too, but just as many didn't. Try not to stare."

Don't stare. Right. Focus on the job. "Where do I find more log sheets? This one's full."

"Tear it off."

Nyx tore off the filled sheet. The clipboard replaced it with a blank, pristine log sheet.

Okay, no denying it, that was cool. "What do I do with this one?" She held up the filled sheet.

"Drop it."

Strange being the order of the day, Nyx did as instructed. The paper floated down, touched the floor, and disappeared.

"Where does it go?"

"The Archives. I can show them to you later, if you like."

Because she was the kind of nerd to whom the word 'archives' sounded fun, she said, "Yes, that would be lovely."

She returned to the Operations Manual.

"Two, ensure that all travelers possess appropriate documentation. Any travelers not possessed of such documentation must return to their homeworld immediately."

Continued reading provided Nyx with an exhaustive, if completely incomprehensible, list of what constituted proper documentation. She had only just begun to feel like she had a grip on this, and had moved on to the next section, when the by-now familiar thrumming noise returned to the room.

"I think you'd better skip to the section on Station Arrival preparation."

Nyx flipped through pages furiously until she found the section.

"Five minutes prior to Arrival, turn on the containment field and check that it is in functioning order. The containment field prevents any un-cleared travelers from exiting the portal room and can be activated by pressing the Guardian's seal to the corresponding mark by the Portal Bay exit door. Guardian's seal?"

"Left hand."

Nyx looked at her left hand and found she now wore an old-fashioned black ring, like those used to seal letters. It, too, bore the likeness of a griffin. She walked to the doorway. On the wall next to it was a circular griffin painting, alike in size to the griffin on her ring. She pressed the ring to the miniature painting. The doorway filled with the kind of low buzz Nyx associated with electric fences, and a blue field filled the doorway.

Suitably impressed, Nyx returned to the manual.

"Field is in good operating condition if the color is blue and there are no visible breaks in the field's façade." Nyx gave the field a once-over. "Okay, good. After turning on the containment field, check all anchoring posts, ensuring they are in a fully upright position with no lean, and all connector orbs are spinning smoothly."

Nyx walked the six pillars that formed the hexagonal portal, and had only just completed the inspection when a form, covered in cosmic black ooze, emerged in the center of the portal.

Nyx ran, manual in hand, to the podium and tugged anxiously on Griff's left wing.

"Stop that," he scolded, "you'll pull out my feathers."

Nyx looked down and saw two feathers fluttering to the floor. "I'm very sorry, but what the hell is happening?"

"Your first traveler has arrived. They will not be able to hear you until the ley dust sloughs off, but once it does, get to logging. The longer travelers are stuck on the ley line the less pleasant they tend to be."

As if on cue, the cosmic ooze—ley dust, Nyx supposed— drained off the form to reveal a six-foot-tall woman with blue skin. She was impossibly slender, reminding Nyx of Meg from the cartoon Hercules, blue skin aspect notwithstanding, and the fact that her eyes were pure black from lid to lid.

The woman stepped out of the portal as if she were a wealthy heiress exiting her limousine. She did not take notice of Nyx until she approached the podium, at which point she frowned.

"You look very young."

Nyx gaped, too stunned by the impossibility of blue skin and the hauntingly ethereal tones of the woman's voice to muster any intelligent reply.

Griff had no such hang-ups. He pecked Nyx on the hand, *hard.*

"Oh, yes. New hire, you see." Jolted out of immobility, Nyx looked at her log sheet. "Name?"

The blue lady blinked. "Andreidorina Maat-Korvin Harmodicea the Fourth. How old *are* you?"

Nyx wrote down A-n-d. "Umm, twenty-five. Would you mind spelling that for me?"

"Twenty-five? And you're the Guardian? You cannot be serious."

While it was true that Sena had appeared to be in her late sixties, surely there wasn't an age requirement for being a Guardian. Obviously there wasn't, as Nyx now was one.

"Yes, last Guardian retired quite abruptly. Spelling of the name?"

Andreidorina Maat-Korvin Harmodicea the Fourth pursed her lips, pulled out a passport-sized notebook, flipped it open, and slapped it on the podium.

Nyx slid it closer. In most respects it *was* a passport. A photo of Andreidorina headed the page, and Nyx spotted her name next to it. The document was not written in any language Nyx recognized, though the script looked similar to hieratic. Logically, it should be unintelligible to her, but Nyx found she could make out the important bits just fine.

Shaking her head, Nyx copied the name in tidy script. Looking at the next two categories on the sheet, species and homeworld, Nyx breathed a sigh of relief to see both items on the passport as well. She wasn't sure she could have asked them aloud with a straight face. She filled in *Siren* and *Oceana*, respectively.

Behind the blue lady another form rose in the portal, ley dust crumbling off.

Okay, so far, not so bad. Now, acceptable documentation.

Obviously the passport thing was the documentation, but how was she supposed to know if it was *acceptable* documentation? Did Waystations require two forms of picture ID? Signature from the homeworld president? Travel-agent stamp?

Nyx smiled at the woman. "Pardon me for a brief moment while I confer with my Avatar." She slipped off the chair and pulled Griff close to the doorway, dropping her voice to a whisper. "How am I supposed to know if the documentation is in order?"

She tried to keep the anxiety off her face—years of retail experience had taught her customers pounced on insecurity like jackals on wounded animals. They'd never done it to her personally, of course, as they tended not to notice her, but she'd watched it happen enough times to coworkers.

The blue lady tapped her foot, looking bored. The person Nyx had seen shaking off ley dust a few seconds ago lined up behind the blue lady, already looking impatient.

"Flip to the pages in the back, you will see several blank pages. Some of those will have stamps on them. Touch your ring to an empty space. If it leaves a stamp, the document is valid."

"Great. I'll ask you how *that* works later."

A third form rose in the portal.

"How many people do you expect will be arriving tonight?"

"Likely between one-hundred and one-hundred and fifty."

Nyx clenched her teeth and closed her eyes, watching as a make-believe version of herself ran around screaming, breaking things, and generally going insane. Then she opened her eyes and straightened her shoulders. "You can create anything within the Station, right, that's how Avatarism works?"

"I do not believe Avatarism to be a word, and the Station needs to have the raw ingredients within it, but yes, within reason."

"Good, in that case I need refreshments, a *Line Starts Here* sign, and a better pen."

Griff blinked. "What kind of refreshments?"

Nyx glanced at the growing—and growing odder—cluster of beings in the room. The fact that a man with tentacles for hair and a six-foot-tall cat-looking creature standing on two legs could also be standing next to someone who looked entirely human was exploding her brain into tiny bits. She was apparently more ready to accept alien-looking aliens than she was ready to accept human aliens.

"Are cookies universally liked?"

"I believe so."

"Then get me a mix-platter, chocolate chip, sugar, and peanut butter."

"Yes, ma'am." Griff disappeared.

Nyx plastered a smile on her face and walked back to the podium, thoroughly wishing she had a pair of glasses to push up the bridge of her nose. Customers always took a person who was pushing up her glasses more seriously than a person who was not, and who furthermore had no glasses at all.

"I'm so sorry for the delay."

"Is there a problem?"

"Not at all." Nyx flipped to the first page in the document with stamps, found a blank space and touched her ring to it. A circle with a griffin inside appeared on the page. Nyx put a checkmark in the documentation box. "Reason for travel?"

Andreidorina Maat-Korvin Harmodicea the Fourth looked down on Nyx as if the Guardian were a very special breed of stupid.

"The festival." Though she did not iterate the words, her tone added, *Of course.*

Nyx wrote *Festival* in the appropriate box. "Expected duration of stay?"

"Two weeks."

Nyx filled that in, marked an A in the Arrival/Departure box, and handed Andreidorina her document back.

"Thank you for your patience. Enjoy your trip and—" It was at that moment Nyx realized she had no signs pointing to the front door, and no one to lead customers through the store to the exit. But she was beginning to catch on to how things worked around here and, hoping Griff was paying attention and wouldn't let her look like an idiot, she smoothly finished, "— follow the yellow brick road to the exit."

Holding her left hand out in the direction of the room's one door, Nyx snuck a glance at the floor. She was relieved to see a bonafide yellow brick road on the ground, snaking off in the direction of the store's front door.

Nyx hid a grin. She'd been kidding about the yellow brick part, really, but she couldn't deny it had a certain classic hilarity to it. Did people from Between read *TheWizard of Oz*?

The blue lady walked off, a haughty jaunt to her step, passing easily through the containment field.

Directing her attention back to the center of the room, Nyx saw Griff levitating a large silver serving platter piled with cookies, and a *Line Starts Here* sign. A water dispenser with disposable cups appeared in one corner of the room, and over a dozen people now milled about the small area.

"Thank you so much, Griff." She grabbed the sign out of the air and placed it just to the right of the podium. Clearing her throat, she addressed the crowd. "I apologize for the delay in getting started. If you could all please line up along this side, starting here," she indicated the sign, "in order of arrival and in such a manner so as not to impede new arrivals. Complimentary refreshments will be circulated by the Station's Avatar." She indicated Griff. "Water is available in the back. Please have your documentation ready to expedite the arrival process."

A small amount of grumbling went through the crowd—now up to eighteen individuals—but they assembled as asked, and the cookies seemed to appease at least a few of them.

The next traveler slid up in the portal and shook off cosmic goo. Once clear, he cocked his head slightly, as if listening to something. Straining her ears, Nyx could just make out a recording of her voice listing instructions to the newest arrival. Genius. She mouthed Griff a *Thank you* and turned to the next arrival, a man who would almost be Earth-human-looking if it weren't for the fact he stood nine-feet tall and had shoulders like a semi-truck.

Nyx stole a sugar cookie from Griff's platter and soldiered on. She settled into a rhythm of asking for name and documentation first, copying all of the written information before moving on to the verbal questions.

The line of people kept growing, and though the room never appeared to grow any larger, if Nyx began at the front of the line and shifted her gaze from person to person to the back of the line, she always counted far more people than could actually fit into so small a space.

Time flew by, and Nyx lost count of how many log sheets she filled and tore off, dropping them to the floor to disappear to the mysterious archives. Her hand cramped from writing and she was covered in ink stains. If she ate another cookie, which she really wanted to do, she was going to collapse and fall into a sugar coma.

A troll-looking individual approached the podium and handed her his documentation. She wrote down *Granite Shale* under *Name* and *Troll* under *Species*.

The troll squinted at her. "How old's you?"

"It really isn't polite to ask a lady's age, you know."

Everyone wanted to know how old she was. Apparently, no one took a young Guardian seriously. Nyx had initially tried to pass for her early thirties, but after the fortieth time she'd been asked, she'd simply stopped answering the question altogether. If she answered, people either gaped at her in disbelief, tutted at her in disapproval, or tried to walk all over her.

The first was annoying, the second degrading, and the third downright infuriating. However, if she didn't answer, each traveler became far too busy trying to reason out a guess of their own to cause her any real problems.

Two hours later, hand cramping and patience no longer anywhere to be found, Nyx stamped the final traveler's document. He was an odd-looking fellow whose documentation had listed him as an employee of an international package delivery company, and he had hefted his bag—the delivery package, apparently—impatiently while she checked him in.

Nyx watched him leave, listening to the silence of the room. The thrumming of the portal had long since ceased, and Nyx took this to indicate no more travelers would arrive.

As soon as she heard the clang of the front door opening and shutting, showing the messenger out the door, Nyx dropped both clipboard and pen and sprawled out on the concrete floor, moaning in pure hedonistic pleasure as a series of pops and cracks went through her spine.

Griff fluttered down next to her, close enough his feathers just brushed one out-flung hand. "You did very well."

Nyx opened one eye. "*Well?* I had no idea what I was doing, I think my hand's going to fall off, and sugar cookies are slowly eating away the lining of my stomach."

"I do think you should have stopped after the fifth."

"Yeah? You might have mentioned it."

"You seemed busy."

"You don't say?" Nyx thought she might never again rise from the floor. "What's this festival they all kept mentioning?"

With the exception of three individuals—an elf visiting family, a harpy trader on an acquisitions trip, and the aforementioned package delivery man—everyone was here for the bloody festival.

"The Solstice Festival. Betweeners are very concerned with the changing of the seasons."

"Why? Is the Winter Court coming into power?" Nyx only half-meant it as a joke. Not all of the species she'd recorded that night fell into what she knew of Faery mythology, but a majority of them had.

Griff shook his head, his eyes taking on a distinctly scholarly tint. "Not exactly. The Winter and Summer courts were abolished centuries ago when the Fae joined with the other non-Earth races and the All Council was formed to govern the ley lines between the planets. But most of the Fae still have strong ties to Winter and Summer, and those with heritage on Earth like to come back for the festival."

Nyx rolled onto her side, propping herself on her left elbow. "You're telling me I started on the busiest week of the year?"

Griff dipped his beak. "Essentially."

"If I ever see Sena again, I'm inclined to give her an earful."

"That might be a little unfair, as she had no more control over the situation than you. Unlikely, too, as she will in all probability be long-dead before a new Guardian comes to this Waystation to relieve you of your duties."

"Cheery. Speaking of Sena, didn't she say she hired an assistant? Evie, or something like that?"

"Evra. And yes, Evra is late. I am beginning to worry."

Nyx shrugged. She didn't know what the protocol for late assistants was, and wasn't sure she cared. Four hours ago, an assistant sounded heavenly. In her current, exhausted state, the arrival of an assistant sounded like exchanged pleasantries and paperwork, which, coincidentally enough, sounded like one of Dante's circles of hell.

"Evra. Sounds like a stick-thin model who wears pinstripe suits and her hair's always in a bun."

The thrumming, beating noise of the portal began again. Nyx whimpered, silently pleading to any available and benevolent gods that this did not herald the start of a second wave of travelers. The mere thought of lifting a pen brought forth shivers of terror.

"I very much doubt that is what she looks like."

"Why?"

"Because *that* is Evra." He pointed his wingtip at the portal.

A six-foot-two blonde bombshell stood in the portal, though she wasn't the sort of bombshell one would ever mistake for a debutante or trophy wife. She had plaited her pale blonde hair close to her skull and her eyes sparked a fierce, Nordic blue. Muscles rippled along every inch of a body clad in black combat gear, feet sheathed in black boots that went up past her knees.

Her left hand clutched a black duffel bag that, gauging by the subtle strain of muscle along the woman's arm, Nyx guessed to weigh at least fifty pounds.

None of this, however, was the most interesting piece of the woman's ensemble. No, that honor definitely went to the blades —plural—covering her like adornments. Nyx spotted at least three daggers, a longsword hanging from a hip sheath, and in case that wasn't enough, the hilt of a short sword protruded above her right shoulder.

Honestly, who carried *two* swords? If they were both one-handed weapons, maybe she could see it, sure.

But Nyx had always had a fascination with weaponry and consequently knew that, contrary to what some badly-written television scenes would have people believe, longswords absolutely were a double-handed weapon.

Pushing herself up to a sitting position, Nyx tried unsuccessfully not to stare. "*You're* Evra? The assistant Sena hired?"

The blonde warrior looked down at Nyx as if she found something about the black-haired Guardian particularly troubling or distasteful.

"I am Evra Al-Daemon. I apologize for my late arrival. The Station on Scythia had an issue with its Guardian being available to fulfill its planned Departures."

Evra looked around. Not finding what she was looking for, her attention returned to Nyx. "Where is Sena?"

"She retired. About five hours ago. I'm her replacement. Name's Nyx."

Nyx stood and held out her hand. Evra glanced at it but she did not take it. Maybe handshaking was not a universe-wide thing.

"My agreement was to work for Sena. If she is no longer here, then my contract is null."

Evra stepped back into the portal, ley dust circling around her ankles. Nyx had the distinct impression she looked *frightened*, then discarded the thought. A woman like Evra wouldn't be frightened of anything in this room.

"Actually, it is not," Griff said.

The thrumming noise cut off and the ley dust slunk from Evra's ankles, slipping back to reform the cold, smooth floor surface.

Evra turned, eyes flashing. "Allow me to leave."

Nyx shrugged. "I didn't do it."

Evra's eyes fell on Griff. "What is the meaning of this, Avatar?"

Nyx bristled. "His name is *Griff*."

"You *named* your Avatar?"

Nyx crossed her arms. She liked Evra less and less by the second. "He is a person. People have names."

Griff looked like he wanted to crawl into a hole and die of embarrassment. He covered his discomfort by reaching up with one taloned appendage to remove his spectacles and then furiously polishing the lenses on his feathers.

He finished cleaning his spectacles, returned them to his face, and met Evra's eyes. "Your contract states you owe one year's service to the Guardian of Waystation 27. This is Waystation 27, and Nyx is its Guardian. Your salary is paid in full, as per the terms of the agreement you signed. The salary is non-returnable and, as I am sure you are aware, the contract is incapable of being voided by anyone but Sena.

"Will you go back on your word?"

Nyx suspected, by the manner in which Evra's jaw clenched and the way she stared at Griff like her eyes could spit venomous snakes, that going back on her word was not something the woman took lightly.

When Evra spoke, it sounded like she was talking around spikes in her throat. "It seems I was mistaken about the terms of the agreement. I will, of course, fulfill them."

Evra turned to Nyx, a muscle along her neck twitching, eyes as cold and distant as the galaxy Nyx supposed she came from.

"Have you need of my services this night, Guardian?'

Nyx blinked. She had need of Evra's services hours ago when the place was swamped with travelers and Nyx had no idea what she was doing.

What the hell would I have her do now? Sweep the floors? Make tea? Alphabetize the books?

"No."

"Then kindly direct me to the lodging provided in my contract."

Griff answered smoothly, saving Nyx from the embarrassment of having no idea what to say. He'd been doing that all evening.

"Exit to your right. You will find a staircase. Yours is the room to the right, upstairs. Here is your key." Griff slipped a talon into his feathers and drew out an old-fashioned key on a cord of rawhide.

Evra took the key and walked past them both without another word. Nyx heard her boots on the stairs, then a *thwump* as a door slammed shut above.

Nyx chose her next words carefully. "Not that I'm ungrateful to you for handling the situation, but couldn't you have just let her go? It doesn't appear she likes us very much and her attire doesn't really scream *assistant*."

"Technically, yes. But I am not wrong about the terms of the contract, and the contract is self-enforcing."

"Meaning?"

"Meaning it is a magically-binding contract, and if I let her go it would afflict her with fever delusions resulting in a slow and painful death unless she returned to this Station and fulfilled her obligations."

Nyx whistled.

"I did her a favor by reminding her, and she knows this. She is simply not pleased with the circumstances."

Already feeling like Griff was a friend she'd known since childhood, Nyx didn't guard her speech. "I can't imagine working with her for a year. She looks at me like I'm something she wants to scrape off her boot. And the way she talked about *you*, as if you're a thing."

"I am an Avatar," Griff said, gently. "Your treatment of me as a full-fledged individual is unusual, especially at such an early stage in our partnership."

Nyx reined in her anger, not at Griff, but at whoever, long ago, had made him believe he didn't have rights.

"I've known you for less than six hours, Griff, and I already know what kind of person you are. You're a *good* one. You breathe and talk and eat. You like people and dislike them. You don't *like* being treated dismissively.

"I don't even think all of those things are *necessary* conditions for someone to qualify as a person, but they are certainly *sufficient*. Why can't you see that?"

Griff ducked his beak. "You can't imagine what I can and can't see. What I *have* seen. And so I ask you, do not make me long for something I cannot have. The longing is more painful than the acceptance of what is."

Nyx bit her tongue on the arguments she wanted to make. Aloud, she said only, "You *are* a person. Someday, I'll prove that to you." She stuck her hands in her pockets. "Do you have any suggestions about Evra?"

"Give her time," Griff advised. "She is young, and she is an Amazon. Amazons are…"

"Haughty?" Nyx suggested. "Arrogant? Self-involved? Rude?"

A muscle twitched at the corner of Griff's beak. Nyx thought if he had lips they would be curled in a lopsided smile.

"I was going to say *difficult*. She will come around. But she must come to terms with this on her own, first."

Nyx sighed. "Yeah, well, I guess I know the feeling."

5

In the kitchen, Nyx found a variety of teas. She selected a smooth chamomile, poured water into a stainless-steel kettle, and set it on the burner to heat. She leaned back against the counter, humming contentedly while the kettle heated.

As she waited, she noted that the kitchen was an odd hybrid of personal and industrial. Everything was made of stainless steel, which lent the place a feeling of industrial cleanliness, yet certain things—like the traditional gas-burning range and the full-size refrigerator—gave it the feel of a more personal space.

Her stomach rumbled, as good of an excuse as any to investigate the contents of the fridge. Milk, orange juice, eggs, bacon, a container of grapes, your basic package of American cheese, and a package of mozzarella string cheese.

Nyx broke off a branch of grapes, snagged a string cheese, and retreated to the counter with her haul. Griff returned from wherever he'd run off to after their conversation about Evra just as she shoved a fistful of grapes into her mouth.

He alighted on the counter and tucked his wings in, his tail curling around his back paws. "Ah, I see you've acquainted yourself with the kitchen. I stocked it with the basics, since you haven't thought about food enough since arriving to give me a clear idea of your tastes, but I can expand the variety tomorrow."

Nyx swallowed the grapes and hurried to remove a now-furiously whistling tea kettle.

"When should I expect the next Arrival?" She poured water over her tea bag and blew across the top of the cup. "Are there set times? Can people arrive whenever they want?"

"Most travels are booked at least one Earth week in advance and those schedules are sent here. The bookers try to condense Arrival times to make things more streamlined, though emergency travels can be booked for the right price. Such travelers are given to understand that they may be stuck on the ley line for some time, if the Guardian on the destination end is out, but that doesn't mean they aren't cranky when you do get around to letting them through."

So, they're pushy and it's still my fault. Apparently the customer service industry was consistent galaxy-wide.

"What do I do when there aren't Arrivals?"

Griff shrugged, a casual movement that made varying shades of earth-toned feathers ripple in hypnotic waves. "Whatever you want. Run the shop, if you like—you can choose your own hours. Betweeners often shop in Waystations, usually for the novelty of it."

Nyx yawned, a great gaping action that resulted in the sharp pop of her jaw. "Well, if I make my own hours, we'll open at nine. But I'll probably be downstairs by eight." It was a delightful feeling, knowing she had somewhere to be in the morning.

"Very well." Griff opened his mouth, then shut it.

"What?"

"Pardon my saying so, Miss Fortuna—"

"Oh, please, call me Nyx."

"Nyx." Griff rolled the name around in his mouth. "Pardon my saying so, *Nyx*, but you seem to be taking this all much better. Have you accepted it, then?"

Nyx swirled the tea bag around in her cup. "Well, either it's real, and I'm home, or… or it's *not* real, and my life goes back to the way it was." She shivered and wrapped her hands around the cup, taking comfort in its warmth.

"When will you know which it is?"

Nyx stared at the stainless-steel counter and answered Griff with words she had once spoken to someone else. "The morning will tell. Illusions, for me, never last past sleep."

What Griff answered her, Nyx couldn't have said. She was busy hearing a different answer from across the years: *Then don't go to sleep.*

She'd taken the advice, then, because she hadn't wanted it to end. But illusions always ended, even if they took a couple years to do it.

She wasn't nineteen anymore.

"Griff, there's something I need to know."

"Ask. If I have the answer, it is yours."

"You said Guardians are chosen when they have nothing left in their former lives. I can't remember anything from before I was eighteen." Despite how frequently Hollywood liked to use it, she'd learned that kind of full-onset amnesia was rare. So rare, in fact, that no one had actually believed she had it. She swirled the tea bag in her cup and chose her next words carefully.

"Is this—the Station, the All Council, are they the reason I can't remember?"

Griff's eagle face approximated a frown. "No, Nyx. The Station's magic draws people who already have few ties with their former lives, but it does not create that existence for them. I'm sorry, I didn't know about your condition."

Nyx smiled to cover the ache in her chest. She would have been angry if she'd learned this place had taken her memories, but at least it would have given her an answer. At least she wouldn't still be wondering who she was and what was wrong with her.

"You don't remember anything?"

Nyx shook her head. "Damnedest thing. The first morning I can remember I woke up with a letter taped to my hand. It said the apartment I was in was paid in my name for the next year, gave me my ID and social security card and stuff, and told me I had a scholarship to Arizona State.

"I thought it must be a joke at first. That I had friends or something who'd given me a temporary memory-loss drug and were having a good laugh at me. Only no one ever showed up to laugh."

I should know. I waited until all the food ran out. Then I waited another two days, anyway.

"You never found out who wrote the letter?"

"No." Nyx gripped the tea mug so hard her knuckles bleached white. "And that's what makes it so bad because *somebody knows*. Somebody out there knows who I am, but—" She broke off, shook her head again. "I remembered all sorts of day-to-day things right away, you know? What I liked and didn't like. I went to school on that scholarship and I got really good grades in classes and stuff, and it was never that hard. I must have taken a lot of martial arts growing up. I can think of six ways to incapacitate a man in under ten seconds off the top of my head, but I can't even tell you my parents' names."

Nyx hadn't had anyone to tell the story to in so long that the words kept flooding out of her mouth. "Whoever wrote that letter knows. They *know* who I am, and they just left me there to wake up alone. Who does that to a person? How did this even happen to me? The doctors I could get to listen to me didn't even believe I had amnesia."

Predominantly because her type of amnesia didn't really exist in medical terms. Though a common enough plot device in fiction, her extensive research on the subject had led her to understand that people didn't just lose their personal identities and retain everything else about their lives. Sometimes a traumatic event caused temporary loss of identity but, well, she'd hardly define the last seven years as *temporary*.

"And now I'm here, and this is all so weird, and I just thought, maybe…" She trailed off, sniffling.

"Maybe it was magic?" Griff asked gently.

Nyx nodded.

"I am hardly an expert on every form of magic, Nyx, so I won't tell you that it's impossible. But it is not something I have ever heard of before."

"Right." Nyx straightened, setting the tea mug down on the counter and smiling brightly. "Well, it would be a shame to lose a good mystery. Do you know where I sleep?"

"Nyx, I—"

"It's okay, Griff. Really, it is. I've lived with it a long time." *Long enough that I stopped looking for answers, until today.* "It's nice just to have someone to talk to who doesn't think I'm crazy."

Griff nodded, but he looked unconvinced. "Your room is across from Evra's, up the stairs and to the left."

Across from Evra. Of course.

"I arranged everything as best I could. Our bond is still new, though, so I can't see everything. Please let me know if you would like something changed."

He's so painfully eager to please, Nyx thought. *I was like that, once.* "Whatever you've done, Griff, I'm sure it's perfect."

Impulsively, she leaned forward and kissed him on the cheek. Or whatever passed for a cheek on the eagle's head of a griffin.

"Goodnight, Griff."

"Goodnight, Nyx."

She carried her tea upstairs, deciding to focus on the positive. Like how she had always wanted a spiral staircase and now she had one. At the top, she opened the door to her room and fumbled for the light switch. Grinning, Nyx looked around at her room. Nothing about it was particularly lavish, which suited her. The room itself was maybe twelve feet by eight, and the floors were dark ebony. Aside from the bed and a small ebony nightstand—complete with ornate, antique lamp—the room was largely empty.

Four barren bookshelves of the same wood as the nightstand scattered themselves against various walls, presumably to be filled at her leisure. At the foot of the bed stood a chest of color to match the rest of the room's furniture. She opened it and found a stack of blankets and an extra pillow. She extracted a crocheted blanket of soft green yarn and placed it on the bed.

Then she turned and sat on the chest, unzipping her backpack. She almost zipped it back up and put it in the chest with all its contents still inside, but the sweats and T-shirt she liked to sleep in were in the bag, and to get to them she'd just have to deal with *it*.

She reached inside and pulled out the small canvas painting, running her fingers over the thick brushstrokes. The skies in the scene were gray and overcast, the waves of the sea choppy as painted ships pulled into harbor. She hadn't really *looked* at the painting in over a year, not since she'd moved into the studio from which she had so recently been evicted, and while she had left most of her remaining possessions in that forlorn place, she had not been able to leave the painting behind.

She had told herself when she'd taken it with her that she would sell it somewhere, but as her fingers brushed gently over the canvas, and memory assaulted her with indelicate grace, she knew she never would have parted with it. How could she have given away the one thing she had left from the only person who had ever been able to remember her?

Closing her eyes, Nyx saw a flash of green eyes and blond hair, remembered her fingertips resting on a cold gray door. Ordinarily, she had found the gray of that door soft and inviting, but on that particular day it had stood harsh and unwelcoming, hanging open a quarter inch, a coldness emanating from the apartment beyond that had nothing to do with the temperature.

Inside, the apartment she had spent so much time in stood empty, everything gone. Counters bare, furniture gone, clothes gone. Not even a mote of dust left, only the painting on the wall.

It was the only thing she had ever given him. It was the only thing he had left behind.

She remembered it all, then, as she had not allowed herself to do in years. Her hand, as it so often did when she thought of him, went to the chain around her neck, to the pendant that rested close against the warmth of her skin.

It responded to her touch, seemed almost to nestle against her. She had always thought its response to her was in her head. But now, looking at where she was, knowing what lay beyond the borders of their planet, Nyx wasn't so sure anymore.

Exhaustion tugged at her eyelids and she stood, tucking the painting away in the heavy chest. She changed into her sweats and T-shirt, turned out the lights, and wrapped the soft green blanket around her. As she drifted off to sleep, it occurred to her that though her amnesia stayed on, the curse that had followed Nyx her entire adult life did not appear to have followed her here.

Griff had not, *yet*, had any difficulty remembering who she was.

6

S unlight played on the backs of Nyx's eyelids. She groaned and rolled over, burying her face in the pillows, but it was a half-hearted groan. She felt like something was missing, and it wasn't until she realized the missing piece was her usual feeling of morning dread that she also realized she was *not* in her studio apartment.

She jumped up, untangled herself from the soft green blanket, and noted that a new pair of jeans and a clean shirt had been laid out on top of the chest at the foot of her bed. Both articles of clothing were black—at least the place knew her colors.

A quick search led her to the bathroom which, though small, didn't skimp on the amenities. The silver-gray walls matched the bathmat, rug, and plush towels, and the shiny black tile floor flowed seamlessly to comprise the shower walls and floor as well.

She showered quickly, even though the excellent temperature and water pressure promised the hot water wouldn't run out for some time, and the fancy showerhead had at least fifteen settings she really wanted to try.

Don't want to be late on my first day.

Downstairs, Evra sat in the kitchen. The short sword was

once more strapped firmly against her back, and several daggers were still in evidence, but she'd ditched the longsword.

Nyx checked her watch: six-thirty a.m. If she had hoped to have a quiet morning to herself, it clearly wasn't meant to be.

She took a deep breath and walked in.

"Morning, Evra."

She half-expected Evra to don a confused expression and ask Nyx if they had met before. Nyx had spent all of her remembered life being so far beyond the notice of everyone around her that it seemed impossible Evra *should* remember her.

But Evra did not ask. She made a grunting noise that might or might not count as an acceptable reply on whatever far-off planet she hailed as home. Her eyes, sleepless and a little puffy, followed Nyx's path to the espresso machine.

The Amazon had a plate of grapes in front of her, and though she methodically picked the grapes off their stems, she never ate them.

"You don't really seem like a grapes-for-breakfast kind of woman." Nyx spoke the words casually as she tamped ground espresso beans into a portafilter and began pulling shots.

She looks like the kind of woman who eats protein six meals a day.

"Griff said you cook on that thing." Evra waved her hand in the general direction of the stove. "I don't know how it works. We don't have them on Scythia."

"Mmm." Yet Evra was smart, Nyx thought, and probably could have figured it out.

Or she already knows, and she's just messing with me.

"I'm sure Griff could show you how everything works."

"I certainly offered." Griff alighted on the counter next to Nyx.

So Griff remembers me, too. It's enough to give a girl a heart attack.

She contemplated her newfound ability to be remembered as the crema rose to the tops of the two espresso glasses. She flipped the lever and poured the shots into a mug of hot water, blew across the top and took a cautious sip.

Not a half-bad Americano, considering how out of practice I am.

Evra glared at Griff, her eyes promising she wanted to wring his eagle-neck. Nyx stepped closer to him, a streak of protective instinct roaring through her.

Evra straightened in her chair and crossed her arms.

"I cannot cook." She spoke the words as if admitting to some great moral failing, the shame of which was on par with treason or familial disloyalty. At the same time, she braced herself, as if daring Nyx to comment on her admission of inadequacy.

Nyx took another swallow of coffee, considering. "Well, fortunately for you, I can. Do you like coffee?"

I'm stuck with her for a year. May as well try to get along with her. Haven't had to do that in a while.

The amount of difficulty people had remembering her varied from person to person, and she'd met one—only one—who had been immune to it entirely. But that person was several years gone. Remembering him again, after looking at that stupid painting last night, only sent an ache through Nyx's chest.

Especially since she was beginning to suspect her malady had magical origins. If someone had been immune to it entirely, well, what did that *mean*, precisely?

"I like coffee," Evra replied, cautious. "Why do you ask?"

Rather than answer, Nyx pulled the shots for a second Americano and plunked the drink down in front of Evra, who stared at the mug like it contained an exotic poison.

"Here's the deal. If I'm cooking, you're doing the cleanup."

Evra wrinkled her brow. "Can't your Avatar do it?"

"Of course, I would be happy to—"

"*Griff* is not a servant. I trust the task isn't too difficult for you?"

Evra bristled. "Of course not."

She bristles a lot. Like a porcupine all puffed up to fend off a lion.

"Good. Then we have an agreement."

Nyx fried up bacon and eggs, tossed a couple pieces of bread into the toaster for good measure, and divvied up the food onto plates. Griff flipped a piece of bacon into his beak and swallowed it whole. Nyx blinked, trying to discern how so large a piece of bacon had disappeared so quickly down so small a mouth.

Then Evra asked the question Nyx had been dreading.

"What are my duties here?"

Nyx choked on a mouthful of dry toast and reached quickly for her coffee. "Well, ah, there are…that is, I'm sure there are several things around the shop that could use—"

"You don't have any idea, do you?"

Ah, there it is, that pleasant, contemptuous tone I was missing.

"None whatsoever. What capacity did Sena hire you in?"

"She hired an assistant." Evra looked as flustered as Nyx had moments ago.

Nyx smirked. "You don't have any idea, do you?"

Evra's lips twisted into what could be either a smile or a snarl, depending on interpretation. "None whatsoever."

"You took a job where you have no idea what you're supposed to—" Nyx broke off as the sound of humming drifted from the portal room. "Griff, I thought we didn't have any Arrivals on the books."

"We don't."

Nyx ran for the portal room, a panic in her gut she couldn't quite explain. She slid to a stop a foot away from the silver posts, her heart skittering behind her chest. Black cosmic ooze bubbled up. A small silver box was ejected onto the floor, and the space between the six posts reformed into a hard surface.

Nyx squatted next to the nearest post, not quite willing to touch the small cube. Each side was inscribed with a different rune. The ones she could see from her current vantage point included an ankh, a Celtic cross, and a lunar symbol Nyx couldn't identify as belonging to any particular religion or tradition she was familiar with.

A fluttering of wings and a stomping of boots heralded the arrival of Griff and Evra. Griff looked normal, even if his glasses were slightly askew. Evra stood with her feet spread a little wider than hips-width apart, short sword in one hand, knife in the other.

Nyx looked up and down the blades with an appreciative envy she was careful not to let show on her face.

Best not to let her know I like her taste in weaponry.

"I don't think we'll be needing *those*."

Evra flashed a grin, the first genuine one Nyx had seen.

"No, not for a missive." Evra flipped the sword back into its sheath with the ease and accuracy of constant practice. "But I prefer caution."

Nyx indicated the cube. "That's a missive? Who sent it?"

"The All Council." Evra's tone added, *Don't you know anything?* Her lips, pressed into a thin line, indicated this missive was not good news.

Nyx pressed her palms to her temples and applied pressure. "Why do I insist on staying here with the crazy?"

"Did you say something? You are mumbling."

"Never mind. Who is this All Council and why are they sending me missives?"

Evra made a strangled sound in the back of her throat. "You do not know what the All Council is?"

"No, Evra, I don't. If I did, I wouldn't have asked. So why don't you be a good little assistant and give me a history lesson?"

Evra stared at her with a look that could have been disdain or slight indigestion. Perhaps both. Then she crossed her arms and leaned against the wall, settling in. "You are the keeper of knowledge, Avatar."

"His *name*—"

"Is Griff, I know."

"Then *use it*."

Griff cleared his throat, gave them both a look that made Nyx, at least, feel childish and properly scolded, and straightened his glasses.

"Long ago, when Earth was only just seeing the dawn of the age of man, planets in the far-flung galaxies already teemed with civilization. As these civilizations became aware of each other, the desire to travel between the planets arose. But these were not civilizations of science and technology, as Earth would one day become. These were civilizations built on magic.

"In order to connect the planets, the ley lines were created, making travel between the planets near-instantaneous. For a time, all was well, but unrestricted travel gave rise to dangers and darkness, and it was decided that all planets connected to the ley lines should share a single, governing body. Thus was the All Council born. As its first act, the All Council created the Waystations, giving each Station an Avatar who would forever be bonded to their Station's current Guardian.

"No longer could one simply jump on a ley line and travel, but one must seek the permission of a Station's Guardian to do so. Glorified passport control, as you said." The centuries-old storyteller tone dropped from Griff's voice on the last sentence, the change making Nyx smile.

Nyx nodded. "So the All Council is, like, the galactic governing body of the magical universe?"

"Do not sound so incredulous, Earthling, someone must be in charge," Evra said.

Several witty retorts leapt to Nyx's tongue, but she swallowed them down.

You are an adult, she told herself, *you can act like one.*

Nyx turned back to the cube, eyeing it with newfound suspicion. "Is it normal to get a missive from the All Council?"

Is it too much to ask for it be a very fancy welcoming letter?

Griff shuffled his paws, resettling and curling his tail around himself. "Their security and PR team sends out monthly newsletters on the latest in travel and safety, but I've never known them to send a message to a specific Guardian directly."

"Oh."

Great. Then, *Of course the All Council has a newsletter and PR team.*

"And we're certain this isn't a newsletter?"

"The newsletters look like newsletters," Evra said. "*That* is a recording inside a security box designed to open and play for one person only."

"Of course it is."

Under different circumstances, Nyx would have found a box that would only open for her fascinating. She snatched it from the portal floor, foolishly afraid something might reach out and grab her back. The box warmed, as if her touch was a key.

She set it on the podium and the sides of the cube fell outward, settling flat on the podium's surface to reveal a golf-ball-sized sphere made of interlacing blue and silver strands of light. The sphere spun, faster and faster, until it topped out on speed, moving so quickly that the strands were no longer visible as independent pieces, the entire mass a blue-silver muddle.

A voice filled the room, as if the air itself had been wired for surround-sound. "Guardian Nyx. The All Council offers its commendation on your new appointment and wishes you a long, happy Guardianship on Earth. However, an issue has come to light and we must assign you a task of the highest urgency.

"When the bond passes from former Guardian to new Guardian, the Station is temporarily vulnerable, and a traveler may come through without a Guardian's authorization. As you received your bond, the criminal Morgen Drahl slipped through such a breach and into your world. You must apprehend him and relinquish him to the All Council.

"Until such time as this is done, we must suspend any travel to or from your Waystation. To aid you in your task, we have sent a gift. At the bottom of this box, you will find the chain Gleipnir. When Drahl is found, bind him with the chain, then place this box into the portal. It will return to us and we will send an Enforcer to collect Drahl.

"We put our faith in your ability, and trust you will resolve this matter satisfactorily."

The sphere stilled, the blue and silver strands turning dull. The box rattled, dumping the chain out before the sides folded themselves up.

Is it just me, or did that entire message sound more like a threat than a vote of supreme confidence?

"How exactly am I qualified to apprehend a criminal? I'm not a police officer. I have degrees in the humanities, for fuck's sake." Admittedly, she had a wealth of martial arts skills she didn't remember acquiring, but it wasn't as if this All Council knew that, right?

"You are the Guardian of this Station. Qualifications matter little. It is your duty to ensure travelers are legal, so it is your duty to find this one, who is not." The calmness of Evra's voice set Nyx's teeth on edge.

"How is this my responsibility? This Drahl slipped through a security glitch the Council knew about at a time when I had no idea what was going on."

I still don't know what's going on. She thought belatedly of the shadow she'd seen when her arm had been clasped in Sena's and the world had been spinning out of control.

Drahl, presumably.

"Fine," Evra said. "It is all very unfair. You may either cry about it or do something about it. I advise the latter because I guarantee the All Council is not going to take *it was not my fault* as an acceptable reason for failing to apprehend Drahl. Your choice."

Nyx wanted to strike the superior look off Evra's face, all the more so because the Amazon was right. This, apparently, came with the job. She liked the job, mostly, and wanted to keep it.

"Fine." Nyx did her best to mimic Evra's haughty, superior air and hoped she came even a quarter of the way there. "I'll do something about it."

"*Wonderful.*" Evra did the warrior equivalent of examining

her nails in boredom. She pulled a knife out of her hip-sheath and began cleaning nonexistent specks of dust off the blade.

Since Evra did not appear interested in being helpful, and Nyx didn't want to ask Griff anything in front of the woman and further reveal her own ignorance, she did what any self-respecting Guardian *would* do.

She consulted the Operations Manual.

It sat on the podium in all its leather-bound glory, still open to Arrival Procedures. Nyx flipped through forty or so pages with no luck, fervently wishing for a Table of Contents.

Griff cleared his throat. Loudly. Nyx looked up. Evra, who paid no attention to Griff's throat-clearing, had progressed from cleaning her knife to cleaning her fingernails *with* her knife. Griff caught Nyx's gaze, tapped his talons to his temple and then nodded at the manual.

Great, now we're playing charades.

Okay, so talon to the temple. Thinking? Okay, so thinking and an indication of the manual. She'd just been thinking about how she wished this damn thing had a Table of Contents when—

Griff cleared his throat.

Nyx got the hint and flipped to the beginning of the manual. Where previously the tome had only a blank page in the front, she now found a page labeled *Table of Contents* in elegant script.

Thank you, Griff.

She scanned the listings, the most promising one titled *Illegal Travelers*. Nyx flipped to page two-fifty-one and scanned the headings in the section. *Illegal Traveler Stopped by Containment Field*. No. *Traveler Refuses to Pay*. No.

Wait, the travelers were supposed to pay? Where had it mentioned that in Arrival Procedures? She'd logged a few hundred people in last night. If she now owed the All Council a small fortune, the joke was on them. She was broke.

She made a mental note to ask Griff about it later and continued scanning the headings until she came to a passage titled, Illegal *Traveler Beyond the Station.*

In the extraordinarily rare event an unauthorized traveler should make it past all Station securities, it is the responsibility of the Guardian to apprehend the traveler and restore order. Each Station maintains contacts with those most adept at aiding a Guardian—your Avatar can direct you to a reliable warlock capable of scrying the traveler. Keep in mind it is unlikely a traveler will venture out of Earth Between, as the lack of magic in Dead Earth is extremely disorienting to off-planet travelers.

Nyx looked up, frowning. "There's more of Earth Between than the Waystation?" She had assumed—mistakenly, it appeared—that the travelers she'd checked in last night were going to *Earth* Earth.

"How do you know so little about your own planet?" Evra slipped her knife back into its sheath.

"Seven *billion* people on this planet don't know anything about any of this." Nyx waved her hand, indicating the Station.

Evra sighed. "The Between exists in spaces parallel to those where your people live. It is invisible to those without magic or calling. The only reason a ley line was even *built* to Earth is because some few of your kin had power. But you are, and ever will be, a race of technology before magic."

Nyx rubbed at her temples. "Parallel spaces. Are you saying that for every mile of land on Earth there exists a mile of the Between?"

"Perhaps once there was so much. The Between, like the ley lines, had to be built, though the technique for doing so has long been lost. But the Between must be maintained by a constant influx of magic to continue existing.

"Travel to Earth has not been robust over the last few centuries so, as I understand it, the Between has shrunk to the city surrounding the Station. I believe isolated pockets of it still exist in some places where the magic of Earth was once strong."

"Okay. Okay, this is good. It means we have a fairly finite space where Drahl could be hiding."

"I doubt you will find anything about the Between to be finite."

Nyx flashed Evra a sardonic smile. "Your cryptic pieces of knowledge are definitely helping."

She returned to the section on illegal travelers.

Any weapons, materials, or supplies you may need can be obtained by your Avatar, or at a local armory, apothecary, or junk shop. The All Council approves and backs at least one of each type of shop near every Station to ensure the Guardian access to quality goods.

Note: Guardians may use any force necessary to retrieve and subdue an illegal traveler, and no space in the Between shall be barred to a Guardian on such a quest. Any damages to businesses or property of citizens of the Between shall be reimbursed in full by the All Council.

Nyx reread the line on weapons. "Exactly what kind of criminal do you think Drahl is?"

Evra shrugged. Griff gave Nyx a look she suspected was meant to be comforting.

Great. "Is there any way to find out?"

"If he was arrested by the All Council he should be in the Intergalactic Criminal Records."

"Great. Do I have access to those?"

"Your Ava—"

Nyx shot Evra a warning glance and the warrior smoothly transitioned.

"Griff should be able to locate those for you."

"I would be happy to do so." Griff leapt from his perch atop one of the portal's silver posts and flew out the door. He turned in the direction of the library, Evra trailing him.

Nyx hesitated for a moment, staring at the box and chain on

the podium. Something about the chain's name bothered her, like she'd heard it before. She picked it up carefully, reverently, marveling at the thinness of the chain, a slenderness that in no way indicated any weakness.

She drew the chain through her hands and it caressed her skin, its metal running through her fingers like silk ribbon.

Chain like ribbon. Gleipnir. *Holy fuck.*

She grabbed the chain and ran after Griff and Evra. Nyx overtook them halfway through the library, running at full speed.

They turned to see what the noise was, Griff looking concerned and Evra looking amused as Nyx skidded to a halt next to them. Nyx held up the chain, its silver links shining brilliantly even in the library's soft light.

"Is this *the* Gleipnir? You know, forged by dwarves, the only chain in all the land the Asgardians could find to bind the Fenris wolf?"

"I believe so." Evra looked, as usual, quite calm while explaining things capable of blowing Nyx's very Earth-centric mind.

"The *Asgardians* are real? Thor? Odin? *Frost giants*?"

Evra's brow wrinkled, then smoothed out once more. "Ah, I forget you have your own stories here. Asgard is a planet connected to the ley lines. Thor and Odin and such did exist in the distant history of that world, though they were not gods, only talented warriors and magicians. I believe Ragnarok is an Earth creation entirely. The Fenris wolf was uncontrollable, and so was bound by Gleipnir until his death, upon which the chain was freed. The Asgardians gave the chain to the All Council, when it was founded, as a sign of goodwill."

"And the All Council just loans out rare items?"

Nyx ran her hands over the chain in disbelief. If myth proved accurate, the dwarves had put things into the making of this chain that could never be returned to Earth, not the least of which were the sound of a cat's footfalls and the roots of a rock.

Nyx didn't know if she believed in such magic, but she knew Gleipnir was precious.

"No, they do not." Evra looked at the chain, her eyes worried. "The All Council must want Drahl very badly to have given Gleipnir to an untested Guardian."

Nyx stared at the chain. It was finer than a necklace chain, and even though it was fairly long Nyx could still fit it in the pocket of her jeans.

"Show me the records."

Griff led them through serpentine stacks of books, past the fireplace and into a hallway formed by two rows of bookshelves where Nyx found herself staring at…a wall.

Unless the records are in with the scifi books, I'm not sure what we're doing here.

Griff coughed gently, drawing Nyx's gaze down. Carved into the hardwood floor, in painstaking detail, was a griffin inside a circle. The outer edge of the circle was segmented, formed from four interconnecting puzzle pieces.

"It takes both Avatar and Guardian to open."

"Tell me what to do."

Griff hesitated, his gaze falling on Evra. "Are you certain you wish to bring her with us?"

Evra stiffened.

"I do not say this to insult your honor, Amazon, only to make Nyx aware of the risks. I have not had need of showing this room to a Guardian in centuries. Sena, for all her time here, did not even know it existed. It contains many objects of power." To Nyx, he said, "If you are going to bring someone inside, other than myself, you must be willing to accept the dangers such a choice brings."

Nyx looked at the Amazon. Evra carefully studied the shelf over Nyx's right shoulder, giving no indication she was aware of the scrutiny.

I don't even like her.

To be fair, Nyx didn't really know her, which was an excellent reason not to take her into the super-secret place Nyx knew nothing about.

But I'm stuck with her for the next year. And if I'm tracking down a potentially dangerous criminal, she's just the person to have with me.

"She can come."

Surprise flitted across Evra's face, then was gone.

Griff didn't argue with Nyx's decision. She wondered if that was because he trusted her judgment, or if it was because he was her Avatar. *Could* he disagree with her? Refuse to go along with a choice she made? How deep did the Avatar bond run?

"A drop of blood will do, then."

"Seriously? Blood magic?"

"Blood is very difficult to fake," Evra said, her tone contemplative. She offered Nyx a dagger.

Nyx took it and pricked her finger. The blade slid through her skin with hardly any pressure, and a fair amount more than one drop of blood fell onto the carved symbol. Griff pecked at his talon, adding his own contribution.

Well, now that they'd all been properly barbaric...

The carving drank in the blood. It issued a snicking noise before it swung inward on invisible hinges, opening like the hatch on a submarine to reveal a metal ladder leading down into what Nyx presumed to be the basement.

"I'm never going to be bored here, am I?"

She meant the question rhetorically, but such subtleties were lost on Evra.

"I shouldn't ever think a Guardian would be *bored*. My dagger?"

Nyx wiped the dagger clean on her pants, handed it back to Evra, and looked down. From above, the ladder disappeared into impenetrable darkness. She shrugged and descended the ladder, expecting to climb down for quite some time. She was therefore surprised to find her feet stepping onto firm ground after only ten rungs.

Evra descended next, bringing along her usual positive

energy. "Why, for stars' sake, are we standing down here in the dark?"

Nyx clenched her teeth. She had never before understood how characters in books simultaneously spoke and clenched their teeth, but Evra brought the skill out in Nyx effortlessly.

"Because I don't know where the light switch is."

A fluttering of wings announced Griff's arrival. "It's here."

Light flooded the room. Nyx blinked rapidly, adjusting from absolute darkness to full light.

They stood in a four-by-four space that contained the ladder, the light switch, and a door. The door's only adornment was a small circular griffin the size of her ring, like the one in the portal room she'd used to activate the containment field.

Nyx pressed her ring to it and the door swung open. She moved into the adjoining room, the previous room's light spilling over the threshold. She'd meant to look immediately for a new light switch, but stopped short. The near darkness of the new space was illuminated in random places by pieces of glowing light.

To her right, a blue orb of light glowed and spun but never shifted from its place. Directly ahead of her a tall, cylindrical green glow illuminated the glass cylinder that contained it. Other patches of light glowed throughout the room in various shapes and containers, reminding Nyx of nothing so much as a mad scientist's lair.

Without bothering to look, Nyx reached over to where she expected a light switch to be and flicked one on. Light came, not from overhead lightbulbs, but in the manner of dawn creeping over the horizon and spreading light through the land. Nyx looked around, but she couldn't find the light's source.

"Umm, Griff? What exactly *is* this place?"

Objects lay everywhere, in no particular order or organization, some of them ordinary, like a nightstand or a jewelry box, others strange and disturbing: a staff covered in vines that looked alive, twisting and writhing; a sword inlaid with lapis lazuli that had an iridescent sheen to it; a charred skeleton sitting in a chair as if it were a lazy frat boy kicked back on a couch, legs spread wide. The only thing it was missing, Nyx thought, was a red Solo cup in its skeletal hand.

"This is the Station's Den. A Guardian's duty also entails policing the use of magic in the area immediately surrounding the Station. Frequently, a Guardian must confiscate magical items that are being used inappropriately, or which shouldn't be in the hands of the general populace at all. When that happens, these items are brought to the Den."

"So you're telling me everything in here is potentially dangerous?"

"Yes."

"Huh." Nyx nodded at the skeleton. "What's his deal?"

"*She* is the skeleton of a now more-or-less extinct race of beings that fed off the blood of others. I think you call them vampires, on Earth. At any rate, though the soul has moved on, the skeletons can hold a bloodlust for a few centuries after death, so I would take care not to bleed on her."

Vampires. Of course. And everything in the room is dangerous.

Nyx stepped away from the vine-covered staff that was propped against the wall. Was it her imagination, or were the twisting vines starting to peel themselves off and reach for her? "So I take it you're going to tell me the Records are on the far side of the room?"

"Where else?" The griffin had a mischievous glint in his eyes.

I swear he's actually enjoying this. "All right then, lead the way. Evra, don't touch *anything*."

"Do you presume I need to be treated as a child?"

Sledgehammer, Nyx thought, *to my head. All of my problems, over.* "I mention it because you keep staring at that blue orb over there like a debutante ogling a diamond ring."

Evra's brows drew together and a single crease formed between them. "What is a debutante?"

Sledgehammer. To my head. "Never mind. Just keep those twitching hands to yourself, all right?"

Evra's hands were indeed twitching, fingertips tapping against her thighs. She stilled them as Nyx's gaze fell on them.

"As you wish. I will touch nothing. We can cross the room now, yes?"

"Follow me." Rather than fly, Griff trotted along on all fours, taloned front claws clacking, back lions' paws following silently.

"If these items are so dangerous, should they not be better protected?" Evra's voice held its typical mixture of curiosity and disdain.

"We may not have armed guards, Amazon, but the contents of this room are quite secure," Griff answered.

"What are the protections?" Nyx asked, now curious as well.

"The removal of any item from this room will lock down the Station completely. No leaving the building through either doors or portal until the item is returned."

"Has that ever happened before?"

"Once. We had a necklace here that bewitched anyone who looked at it for too long. A former Guardian did just that, becoming so enamored of it that he took it out and up to his room. Didn't mind a bit he couldn't leave or that none of the travelers could come through, on account of all he wanted to do was stare at the thing."

Behind Nyx, Evra's tone turned thoughtful. "How was the situation resolved?"

"After the Station had been locked down for three months the All Council decided to step in. They built the Stations, so they are able to enter one that is locked down. They forcibly reclaimed the necklace and had me return it to the Den.

"Poor Alist." Griff shook his head. "He was never the same after that. We had a new Guardian within a year, and Alist died of longing soon after. Never lost the yearning for that infernal device."

"If the items here are so dangerous, why does the All Council leave them in the Stations? Why not take them?"

"I suspect they would like to, but the Dens are, strictly speaking, not under their control."

"Then whose control is the Den under?"

"The Station's." At the confused look on her face, Griff said, "Think of the Stations like sentient buildings. A Station's Den and the contents within it *belong* to the Station. What a Station claims as its own, it is unwilling to part with."

On that ominous note, Nyx resumed their trek, her line of sight catching on the floor underneath her feet. She stood on an ornate wrought-iron grate about two feet wide that ran the length of the room. But what really caught Nyx's eye was what flowed *beneath* the grate. Pure golden liquid—at least it *looked* like liquid, though lighter, less viscous—ran beneath the grate like a river. It shifted and flickered, carrying at once a hundred different shades of gold and bronze.

The river mesmerized Nyx, taking her breath away. She squatted and put her hand flat against the grate. The golden stream called to her, thrummed in her veins, like the call she had felt in the portal room.

"Is this…"

"The ley line," Griff confirmed.

"It's beautiful."

"It is, yes. The magic composing the ley lines is ancient and rare. It calls to people, hypnotizes, and if you do not maintain control, you can become lost to it forever. That is why no one untrained is allowed to travel the lines without a guide."

Nyx turned to Evra. "Can you travel the lines without a guide?"

"I can."

"Would you teach me?" Nyx, misinterpreting the hesitation on Evra's face, added, "I'd pay you, of course. I'm not difficult and I pick things up quickly." The river underneath beckoned.

How wonderful would it be to ride those lines? To actually travel to another *planet*?

Evra hesitated, then said quietly, "Guardians are not allowed to travel the lines, even with a guide."

The excitement building in Nyx died, a flame guttering out before it had been given a true chance to burn.

"Oh. Of course."

"I am sorry, Nyx. I thought you knew."

And Nyx thought the woman really *was* sorry, because it was the first time Evra had ever used her name.

"It's fine. Are we close to those records, Griff?"

"They are just here." Griff turned down an aisle formed by two rows of bookshelves and stopped at the end shelf. "It's the bottom-most right volume."

Nyx found the volume in question easily, an enormous black tome with the single word *Records* written in gold lettering down the spine. She wiggled it free of the surrounding volumes, setting adrift a great cloud of dust.

Coughing, Nyx waved her hand, clearing the air.

"When was the last time anyone *looked* at this thing?"

"I believe three or four centuries ago," Griff answered with earnest sincerity.

Nyx held the book in front of her, skeptical. "And yet it's supposed to have information on a man arrested *recently*?"

"Every copy of the Records updates itself to contain all changes made in the Primary Records Book."

Nyx cocked her eyebrow. "Instantaneously?"

"I believe there can be up to a ten-minute delay, depending on the distance between the Primary and the copy."

"You mean this thing's hooked up to the magical equivalent of the Internet?"

"What is this Internet?" Evra asked.

Nyx sighed. "I'll show you sometime. I have this odd feeling you're going to love World of Warcraft."

"What world?"

"Never mind."

Seeing no available table she couldn't be reasonably certain wasn't cursed, Nyx sat down on the floor and spread the book open on her lap.

"How is this organized?" *Please say alphabetized by last name. Please say alphabetized by last—*

"Chronologically. Each arrest is entered under the day it occurred."

So not *quite* as great as the Internet. "Any idea when this guy was arrested?"

Griff and Evra shook their heads.

"That's what I figured." Nyx bent her head to the book and began searching.

Evra watched her for a full five minutes before she cleared her throat.

"Whatever are you doing?"

"Trying to find the record on Drahl?"

"Obviously. Why are you going about it like that?"

"Like what?"

"Reading the entries."

"Do you have a better suggestion? You said it's chronological and no one knows when he was arrested, so…"

Evra leaned over the book and spoke, enunciating carefully. "Entry, Morgen Drahl."

The pages of the book flipped, moved by an invisible hand, and landed on a page with Morgen's name at the top.

"You two just let me fumble my way around for five minutes?"

"I try not to be overbearing," Griff said, at the same time Evra answered, "It was amusing."

Nyx glared at Evra. "Does everyone know how the Records work?"

"No. I had occasion to access them while working in my mother's employ."

"And you came to work here because…?"

Evra met her gaze and maintained perfect silence.

Right. Nyx read the entry on Morgen.

Morgen Drahl —**Arrested on suspicion of being complicit in treason and attempting to aid one who would steal from the All Council.**

Update—Released on lack of evidence. Grounded permanently from traveling the lines. Violation of this order will result in immediate removal to the Arkadian Prison Planet.

Nyx stared at the page, willing the entry to continue. It did not. "That's it?"

"What were you expecting?"

"Oh, I don't know, information that might actually help us find him? Age. Height. Hair color. Description of any identifying marks or tattoos." *I have watched way too many detective shows.*

Evra's face brightened. "On that issue, the Records can do better." She touched her finger to Morgen Drahl's name and spoke clearly, "Identification."

The ink on the pages swirled, blurring together and rearranging to form the full-length portrait of a man with dark skin and long black hair woven into multiple slim braids that were pulled back at the nape of his neck. His eyes were a brilliant, flirtatious brown and Nyx thought he looked more like the good-natured mischievous type who played practical jokes on his friends than the type to commit treason.

But what do I know? History's proved me a terrible judge of character.

On the right page was a close-up of Morgen's face, along with a description of his height and weight—five feet eleven inches tall, one-hundred and eighty pounds, fit. There was also a close-up of the inside of his left wrist—it looked like a tattoo had once been there but now she saw only burned flesh, like a brand had been used to blot out the former mark.

"Now *that's* something to go on. Griff, the manual said you might know a warlock? Someone who could track this guy?"

"I know of an individual who should be able to do the job."

"Great. Let's go."

As they walked back to the ladder, Evra's gaze fell once more on the glowing blue orb, a deep longing in her eyes. Nyx wondered if it had a hypnotic effect, like the necklace Griff had spoken of, but she didn't mention it. Something in the set of Evra's shoulders told Nyx the Amazon wasn't in the mood for prying questions.

7

"What do you mean you're not coming?" Nyx stood next to a little wooden sign declaring that she would soon be entering *Earth Between. Population: 85,000*. Griff had stopped a few feet prior.

"I cannot. The Station's grounds end here, Nyx, and I am bound to the Station."

Nyx ran her fingers over the tattoo on her arm. "Aren't *I* bound to the Station, too?"

Griff dipped his beak. "Not as tightly as I. Now go on." He urged her on with a wave of his wing. "Find Drahl and come home."

Home. The word sent a thrill through her, even if Sena's words and Griff's geographical limitations troubled her. *Home*. She couldn't remember ever feeling like she had one.

"Are you certain you need to bring that?" Evra asked, indicating Nyx's backpack.

"Yes," Nyx answered, more confidently than she felt. No way was she telling Evra that at this exact moment, her backpack felt like a security blanket, one she was loath to be without. Also, it had energy bars, in case she got stranded. The wary part of her still wasn't entirely certain about the safety of going out into unknown, alien-inhabited territory.

Ahead, that territory sprawled before her, painting the land-scape in shapes and colors. Unlike the assembly-line houses of Tempe, the structures here conformed to no single model. Some rose in triangular shapes, pointing to the sky like miniature pyramids of lilac-reflective stone, while others burrowed into hillsides or rose straight up, small towers in their own right.

Other structures were more familiar—log cabins, stone ranch-style houses, even a few geodesic domes which were, if not necessarily normal, at least known. Admittedly, when Evra had referred to Earth Between as a town, Nyx had envisioned a quaint village of medieval-style homes with only a few thousand inhabitants at most.

"How am I supposed to find Morgen Drahl in all of *this*?"

"By finding the Warlock." Evra gave Nyx a helpful push to get her started walking. "And you will not find the Warlock by standing around gawking."

"I am not *gawking* at any—is that a castle?" Nyx stopped, pointing at a stone structure in the distance. It sat on high ground, easily ten times the size of the surrounding houses, if not more.

"That is most certainly not a castle." Evra looked at Nyx as if she feared the Guardian was perhaps a couple horses shy of a two-cart team.

"Well, fine, so it's not a *castle* castle."

"The distinction being…?"

"So it's missing the moat and the drawbridge and such, but come *on*. It's massive. It's got towers and turrets and stone stair-ways and…you're really going to tell me it bears *no* resemblance to a castle?"

Evra sighed. "It's the manor house of Lord Beauregard, if I recall the travel guide correctly. He is infamous in the greater worlds for his extreme paranoia. Thinks the Kumir are going to come after him at any moment and keeps a retinue of armed guards on hand at all times."

"The Ku-what?"

"Kumir," Evra repeated. "They are relentless and highly-skilled mercenaries. They contract out to anyone willing to pay the exorbitant price for their services, and once they accept a job they will not stop until it is finished, no matter how many of them are killed."

"They sound like real cheery folk. And this Beauregard thinks the Kumir are out for him personally?"

"Yes. As I said, paranoid. Hence the armed retinue. He is also," Evra conceded, "fond of architecture in the classic castle style."

Nyx nodded in satisfaction. *Definitely a castle*. She could just *see* a dragon perched atop one of those towers. "Hey." She elbowed Evra in the side. "Are dragons real?"

"Not that I am aware of."

"Oh." Nyx's face fell, then brightened as a new thought occurred to her. "What about unicorns?"

"*No*. Are you going to pester me with asinine questions all day or are we going to see the Warlock?"

"Fine, fine." Nyx started walking, muttering, "Thinks *I'm* crazy for asking about dragons and unicorns, but talks calmly about warlocks and interplanetary travel through magical portals."

Once in the city proper, it took Nyx and Evra half an hour to reach the shop. This was about fifteen minutes longer than it should have taken, because Nyx couldn't help stopping every ten feet or so to stare at something new and wonderful.

There had been the blacksmith on the edge of town, the blows of her hammer pounding out a new sword as sweat beaded and dripped down her neck despite the chilly outdoor temperature. Nyx wanted to watch her work, watch the sword take shape, but Evra had urged her on.

Next came the tall, thin woman with gray hair and mottled

skin, promising to cure what ailed her with this or that potion. Nyx hadn't actually intended to buy anything—she recognized a con artist when she saw one—but the luminescent liquids glowing in the small vials tucked into the woman's traveling case held such beauty she half-wanted to buy one anyway.

Evra slapped Nyx's hand down and bared her teeth at the woman in a feral grin that had her and her luminescent vials scurrying for the proverbial hillside. After that, Nyx didn't stray far from Evra's side. They passed shops selling armor and weapons, clothing and travel gear, each one not wholly unknown to her in idea, but so many shades removed from what Earth had to offer that they became new and exotic.

"Whatever it is, just ask," Evra ordered.

"What?"

"If your brow furrows any more it will cleave in two."

"I guess I'm just wondering why people live here?"

"People have to live somewhere."

"Well, yeah, but..." Nyx paused, trying to figure out what she was even trying to ask. "People come here to visit Earth, right?" What was the term Griff had used for world outside Earth Between? "Dead Earth?"

Evra made a noise of ascent.

"So if people from other planets were going to live here, wouldn't they just live there?"

Evra gave Nyx another one of *those* looks. "For anyone who has grown up on a magical planet, I am told that entering Dead Earth is extremely uncomfortable. Most can't stand it for longer than an hour or two.

"Earth is a tourist destination, Nyx. Like most tourist destinations, people want to come here and stay in comfortable, familiar surroundings—" Evra indicated Earth Between, "—and pretend they are experiencing a different culture.

"Most of the people who live in Earth Between make their living off that—*they* go into Dead Earth and bring back the technological curiosities the tourists want to see. They run excursions for those willing to step across the boundary and see it for themselves."

"Eighty-five thousand full-time residents seems a bit large for a tourist-only town." At the look Evra gave her Nyx said, "What? I'm just trying to learn about the place I'm going to be living."

Evra sighed. "Earth Between is...quiet. No one important comes here—why bother, when it has such a small land area that anyone would be willing to live in? Certainly no one with significant magical power comes here. It's a good place to disappear. To start over."

"Is that why *you* came here?" Nyx had been trying to puzzle Evra out all morning. The Amazon was so confident. Everything about her screamed capable and lethal and, well, none of that screamed Assistant to the Guardian of the Most Boring Station in the Known Galaxy.

"We're here," Evra said, rather than answer.

Secretly, Nyx had been imagining the Warlock's shop as a dusty hut where they would have to peel cobwebs from the front door just to get inside and, upon entering, would encounter all manner of strange things, at least one of which was certain to be a large, slimy toad.

Instead, she stood before a disappointingly modern building. It was sandwiched between a bakery and a tailor's shop, its front consisting mostly of large glass windows too darkly tinted to see through.

Written on the windows in elegant, cursive script were the words, *The Warlock. All Council Approved Spells, Enchantments, and Potions. Herbs, Fresh and Dried. Supplies. Family Owned Since 1492.*

Nyx stared at the script, frowning. "The people who come here, they're from all over the galaxy, right?"

Evra nodded.

"Then why can I read and understand everything here? Surely... surely not everyone learned English just to come here?"

Evra laughed. Nyx thought it had a nice, chime-like quality to it when brought on by amusement rather than derision.

"No, they didn't. Translator spells are soaked into every inch of the Between. Everyone present will hear and read everything as if it is in their native language."

Feel sorry for the poor sot who got tasked with that *job. Can't deny it's useful, but…* "Is it possible to hear what it's really like? Just for a minute?"

"You can override the spell's effects. You have been hearing English up to now because it is what you expected to hear. Close your eyes and ask for reality, and that is what you will get."

Nyx closed her eyes, letting the expectation of English fall away. At first, nothing happened. The conversations around her still flowed, still made sense. But maybe that was because she had never stopped listening to them. She focused inward, a quick, centering meditation that shut out the surrounding noises. Within that quiet center, she let her expectations fall away.

Then she opened her eyes. The script on the Warlock's shop scrawled across the glass in graceful swirls and loops, the lettering elegant but not recognizable to Nyx *as* lettering. To her ears, the world had exploded into a multitude of sounds, garbled together and yet wonderful.

The couple standing in front of the tailor's shop, tall and willowy and blue-skinned, spoke in rolling, lilting cadences that threatened to hypnotize and take her breath away. Six feet from them a woman exited a bakery, bread in hand, chattering happily to her friend in a language reminiscent of Mandarin.

Excited, she turned to Evra. "Say something."

Evra cocked an eyebrow. "Like what?"

Nyx frowned, understanding every word. "You learned English."

"How very self-centered of you. No, I didn't." She tapped the underside of her right wrist, where a circular tattoo of various symbols rested. "If a person travels frequently, the expense of a personal, permanent translator is well worth the cost. Only the major cities on each planet can afford to spell for translation, so if you plan to go outside of them it pays to make sure you can understand and be understood on your own."

Nyx barely heard the explanation. She was too busy staring at the tattoo. The achingly familiar tattoo. Her hand went to the pendant around her neck of its own volition, and the sphere pulsed comfortingly against her hand.

She'd always thought its little flashes of warmth were in her head. Now that she knew magic was real, now that she was staring at a tattoo identical to one she used to trace on someone else while she drifted off to sleep—

No. She dropped the pendant. Its pulsing *was* in her head, and Evra's tattoo wasn't identical to that other one. She was remembering it wrong, seeing a connection where there wasn't one.

"Is something wrong?"

Evra stared at Nyx with that slightly condescending expression that indicated she was once again worried about Nyx's sanity or competency. Or both.

"No," Nyx lied. "Everything is fine."

8

Though the outside of the shop made it clear this was a modern establishment with equally modern standards of hygiene, Nyx was nonetheless disappointed at the lack of dust and disarray. It looked like any store she might walk into in Tempe, items stacked neatly on shelves, priced and labeled.

She was amused, as they approached the un-manned register, to see a selection of candy bars neatly placed in a basket. The sign above them read: *Earth Dessert Bars. Delicacy. Twenty Universals.*

She elbowed Evra, dragging the taller woman's attention away from an exceptionally old Swiss Army knife that had garnered the full Evra eyebrow raise of skepticism.

"What?"

"Does your translator thingy do currency?"

"No. Why?"

"Just wondering if that is reasonably priced."

Evra frowned at the candy bars. "I couldn't really say. I *can* tell you I could buy an entire meal with an actual dessert for around the same price."

Assuming that food was not exorbitantly expensive in the Between, Nyx decided to roughly equate three universals to three US dollars for the sake of her sanity, in which case she was actually staring at a Snickers bar priced at twenty bucks.

Dragging her gaze from the candy bar collection, Nyx spotted a desk bell on the counter and rang it.

"I implore you to let me handle the communications," Evra said.

They waited until Nyx was considering breaking her rule of never ringing for assistance twice when a tall, auburn-haired woman with light brown skin stepped out of a back area. Feathers dusked the auburn mane, and something about the organic way they moved and flowed with the woman's hair, as if they had volition of their own, made Nyx think the feathers were a part of the woman rather than an adornment.

The woman's hazel eyes flashed with barely restrained anger. Not, perhaps, the best sign in someone one had come to ask a task of, though Nyx thought she would be angry, too, if she bore this woman's bruises. They ran the sides of her face in deep, purplish splotches, and a gash sliced the left side of her nose.

Despite the marring of her face, she was beautiful, and did not look much older than Nyx. Her beauty lay not only in her features, but in the way she carried herself, as if the bruises *didn't* matter.

Evra shot Nyx a look indicating any mention of those bruises would not be well-received, and stepped up to the counter.

"Good afternoon, Warlock. My friend and I were hoping to engage your services."

"What manner of work?"

"We need to locate someone."

The Warlock stiffened and her tone took on an icy chill. "I do not offer those kinds of services."

"But you do have the capability?"

The Warlock didn't budge. "I am afraid I must ask you to leave." She turned and strode to the back.

"Wait," Nyx called. When the woman stopped, Nyx hurried on. "You see, I just took over the Guardian position at the

Waystation. I'm really new at everything here and I guess someone got through the portal without authorization, and now the All Council expects me to find them, and really I've got no idea what I'm doing, except the Station's manual said you could help, and so—"

"*Nyx,*" Evra whispered, tone sharp.

Remembering Evra's request to do the talking, Nyx fell guiltily silent.

The Warlock turned, arms crossed, inspecting Nyx carefully. "You are the new Guardian?"

"Yes?" Nyx's wavering tone turned it into more of a question than she would have liked.

"Let me see it, then."

"See what?"

"The Guardian mark." The Warlock used the same tone Evra often used when talking to Nyx, the one that said, *My God, you're an idiot,* in subtext.

It took about five seconds for Nyx to realize that "Guardian mark" referred to the griffin tattoo, and another ten seconds for her to shrug off her backpack and slip out of her coat. She held her left arm out over the counter.

The Warlock stepped forward, hand streaking out with impressive speed to grab Nyx's wrist. Her fingers traced the lines of the tattoo. A tingle of something no doubt magical in nature zinged through Nyx's arm. Hopefully it wouldn't kill her.

As abruptly as she'd grabbed Nyx, the Warlock let her go. "So, you're the new Guardian. You're much younger than I expected."

"Yeah? You're much younger than I expected the All-Council-approved Warlock to be." The retort flew off Nyx's lips before she could stop it, and were it not for the fact she had *some* pride left she would have clapped a hand over her impertinent mouth.

At least I didn't tell her I was expecting a wizened old hag with warts. Small miracles.

The Warlock looked embarrassed for a moment but quickly smoothed it over. "You need to locate an unauthorized traveler?"

Nyx nodded.

"I will need a picture of the individual you're looking for, as well as any personal details you can recall. My fee is a flat one-hundred universals."

Again, Nyx wasn't positive on the conversion rate, but that seemed expensive. "Is there a Guardian discount?" She'd meant it half as a joke, but no one seemed to find it funny. Evra elbowed her in the ribs, hard, and the Warlock took on the expression of a teacher dealing with a difficult student.

"You will not find many Warlocks willing to perform such a spell at all, and of the ones who would, I can guarantee their rates are at least triple what I named."

Right, Nyx thought, *Guardian discount has already been applied.*

It was then that Nyx realized she had another problem entirely. "Say, Evra—"

"Forget it. I don't carry that amount of money around."

"You don't have any money with you? You came to hire a warlock's services and you didn't bring a form of payment?"

Nyx sighed. "I forgot to ask Griff if I *have* money."

Wasn't it his job to make sure she didn't wander off unprepared?

"Who is Griff?" The Warlock now looked thoroughly confused.

"He's the Station's Avatar."

"You *named* your Avatar?"

"That is what *I* said." Evra looked altogether too vindicated for Nyx's taste.

Nyx's gaze fell on the bowl of candy bars. "Do you ever trade goods for payment?"

"Depends on the trade."

Nyx unzipped her backpack and rummaged through it. "I noticed you're selling candy bars. You have a good market for that sort of thing? Earth food?"

The Warlock nodded. "When I can get it. Not many people are willing to cross the line between our two worlds to retrieve it. The tour guides can't be bothered most of the time."

"Yes, that's what I suspected," Nyx said, as if she had any idea what the Warlock was talking about. She pulled out one of the energy bars she'd packed for her trip. "Now, the candy bars are interesting, I'll give you that, but at the end of the day, they're still just dessert. *These* are far more useful."

"What are they?" The Warlock, like any experienced haggler, kept any excitement off her face and out of her posture, but a definite glint of interest flickered in her eyes.

"They're a type of nutrition bar. Humans use them to help recover from strenuous activity or keep their energy up, build muscle. See, the candy bars are just a novelty, and people pay twenty for them. *These* are actually useful *and* novel. I'd say you could get at least thirty out of them."

The Warlock wanted to say yes. Nyx could practically feel it.

"They are certainly interesting," the Warlock admitted. "But what do they taste like? I'll get a sell out of the idea, but I won't get any repeats if they taste awful."

Swallowing her fears, Nyx did what any good salesperson would do, despite her limited supply of product. "Why don't you try one? On me. There are several flavors, but this one is my favorite."

Nyx opened the vanilla almond bar, broke it in half and gave part to the Warlock and part to Evra. The Amazon did her part, biting in and appearing suitably impressed without going overboard.

The Warlock chewed thoughtfully, swallowed. "They are… interesting. I will give you twenty-five each, as that is what I will be selling them at. If they do well in the future and you are looking for a straight sell, I will pay half that."

"Deal." Nyx counted out four bars and handed them over.

"Let me get my tools." The Warlock and the energy bars disappeared into the back of the store.

Once alone, Evra eyed Nyx with new interest. "I had no idea you were a hawker." A faint note of disapproval tinged her voice.

"I am an opportunist," Nyx clarified. "I do what I have to do to get what I need."

"In that way, you and I are not so different, I suppose," Evra mused.

Before Nyx could reply that, no, they were really not alike in any way that she could comprehend, the Warlock swept back into the room, a large copper bowl in one hand, a notebook and two packages of herbs in the other.

The Warlock filled the bowl with water. Nyx was a little disappointed it wasn't wine, or holy oil, or blood, or something equally esoteric and occult-like.

"What are those?" Nyx pointed to the herbs.

"Do you have to know everything? She is like a child," Evra confided to the Warlock.

Nyx took it in stride. "I was born with an insatiable curiosity."

"Oh? Is that what your mother told you?"

"Don't remember her." Nyx shrugged off the look Evra gave her and turned back to the Warlock. "So, what are those for?"

"They are to help focus the spell, direct it. Rosemary for clarity, eyebright for vision." The Warlock tore a scrap of paper off the notebook, wrote *Week's End Day* on it, and dropped it into the bowl as well. At Nyx's questioning look, she explained, "For grounding us to the present. No point in seeing the past."

"You can do that? See the past?"

"I can see a piece of an individual's past, sometimes of a place's. But it is never much, and I never decide which piece to see." The Warlock laughed. "Why, are you thinking of making another trade already?"

Nyx shook her head. "No, I just—there's something I would have liked to know, that's all."

The Warlock made a noncommittal noise and held out her hand. "Picture."

Evra produced a copy of Morgen's photograph from the Records.

The Warlock took it and her face turned white.

After a few seconds, her voice soft, she said, "I'm sorry. I cannot find this person for you."

Evra, whom Nyx suspected had very limited supplies of patience, had apparently exhausted those fragile reserves. "We had a deal—"

Nyx hushed the Amazon with a look. The Warlock was obviously terrified. Her hands shook, goosebumps spreading up the pale flesh of her arms.

"What happened?"

The Warlock did not answer.

"Does it have anything to do with how you got those?" Nyx kept her voice low and soothing, like she would if trying to comfort a frightened animal, and indicated the Warlock's bruises.

The Warlock touched her fingers to the bruises running up one side of her face. "I can't."

"If this is connected to the man we're looking for, then whoever did this is directly interfering with an investigation sanctioned by the All Council." Nyx racked her brain, trying to remember all the rules and laws she had dug up in the past twenty-four hours. "That means Evra and I have the authority to take that person in. Now, I know I don't look like much, but come on, *she's* pretty scary." Nyx pointed at Evra.

That, at least, got the Warlock to smile.

"We can help."

The Warlock lifted her eyes from the photograph. "I believe you would try. I do not think you can." But she stood anyway and, still holding onto the picture, beckoned them to come around the counter. They followed her through a door, down a short hallway and up a flight of stairs that let out into an above-shop apartment.

They entered a small kitchen, very much the opposite of the stainless-steel one back at the Station. This kitchen felt cozy and lived-in. A small but organized stack of dirty dishes sat next to the sink awaiting a wash. The countertops were a pale yellow Nyx would have curled her nose up in disgust at had she encountered them in a hardware store but they looked nice here, matching as they did the yellow lace curtains in the small kitchen window.

It matches her, Nyx thought, looking at the Warlock, *and that makes it beautiful.*

"This space is warded. No one can listen here. Tea?"

The Warlock's hands trembled as she filled a yellow teakettle with water, but she was calmer than she had been downstairs, evidently taking comfort from familiar surroundings.

They had just settled into seats around a small white table when the door burst open and a dark-haired woman in flowing black silks stepped in wielding twin honest-to-gods scimitars.

Evra was on her feet in an instant, her own knife in hand, and Nyx feared it would come to bloodshed before she had any clue what was happening. Then the Warlock was on her feet, hands on the woman's wrists, turning her attention away from Evra.

"I am fine, Diana, these people had nothing to do with it."

Diana's gaze never left Evra, obviously judging her a more pressing threat than Nyx.

"Then what are they doing here?"

"This is Nyx," the Warlock said, carefully. "She's the new Guardian."

Diana looked at Nyx, skepticism dominating her face.

"And this is her assistant, Evra."

Diana's gaze followed Evra's every move as the Amazon slowly slipped her knife back into its sheath.

"Nyx, Evra, this is my wife, Diana."

Nyx swallowed, wishing Diana would put the scimitars away, and found a smile. "It's a pleasure to meet you."

Diana ignored Nyx. She turned back to her wife, tilting the Warlock's chin up with her free hand, tracing the bruises on her face. "Who did this to you?"

"I was about to explain that. It has to do with someone they're looking for. Put the swords away and I'll tell you."

"They're scimitars," Diana corrected, but she sheathed the weapons. Then she took the Warlock's face in her hands and kissed her.

Nyx looked away, swallowing a hint of sadness. It had been a long time since anyone had kissed *her* like that. Like the world would end if that kiss didn't happen, like the kiss could somehow prove the depth of love two people felt for each other, could ensure that nothing would break that love.

Diana broke the kiss, then pulled out a chair for the Warlock. The Warlock sank into it gratefully and began pouring jasmine tea into delicate floral-patterned china cups, as if her lover hadn't just barged in, blades out.

Then again, maybe for her it wasn't that unusual.

Nyx took the cup of jasmine tea handed to her, blowing across the top to cool it.

The Warlock wrapped her hands around her own cup and said, "I don't know that it will be much help, but I will tell you what I know." She took a sip of her tea, collecting her thoughts. "A woman came into the shop last night as I was locking up. I told her I was closing, but she insisted she needed to purchase a service.

"I told her if it was quick, I would do what I could. When she said she wanted me to find someone for her, I refused. Told her I didn't traffic in that sort of thing and asked her to leave. That's when five more of her walked in the door."

"Kumir." Diana breathed the word like a reverent curse. She hadn't taken a seat at the table and she stood behind the Warlock, her fingers gently massaging her wife's shoulders.

The Warlock nodded. "I had never seen one before, much less six. But I can tell you that all the stories, they don't come half-close to the truth of it. They can hold up a façade of emotion when they need to, like that first woman did, but when they let it drop? It's like staring into an abyss. The fact they're all identical makes it that much worse."

Identical? Evra had said the Kumir were mercenaries but she hadn't mentioned the identical part. Nyx could imagine twins, sure, triplets, maybe. But six identical women? An entire race?

"What exactly *are* the Kumir? I mean, I know they're elite soldier-for-hire, take-any-job types," Nyx said at Evra's look, "but *what* are they? They're all identical? How is that even possible? How many of them are there?"

Evra and the Warlock shared a look before the latter said, "No one really knows. They have only been around for thirty years or so. At least, that's when the stories became widespread. As to how they all look alike? It's anyone's guess. Some people think they use glamouring spells, but it would be too much physical strain to keep that up during a battle, and besides which, there are tells. I didn't see any evidence of glamour when they were in my shop.

"No one really knows where they come from, or where they go when they are not on a job."

Nyx frowned. "How do people hire them, if no one knows where they are?"

Evra let out a sigh of such long-suffering that Nyx was tempted to punch her.

"Why they choose clueless Earthlings for the Guardian post on this planet, I will never know." She turned to Nyx. "You hire the Kumir the same way you do anything illegal in this galaxy. Through the Shadow Market."

"So, they did this to you?" Nyx lifted her hand, indicating the Warlock's bruises. Knowing the Kumir were responsible, she wondered if the rest of the Warlock's body was as bruised as her face.

"Yes, when I wouldn't help them. But I am no fool. The Kumir have no regard for life. If I did not help them, they would simply kill me and use my death to convince someone else to help them. So I told them I would do it. I couldn't fake the test, but I could lie about the results. I thought it might buy me enough time to run before they figured out I had lied and came back for me."

Diana's hands tensed on the Warlock's shoulders. "I never should have left you alone."

The Warlock patted Diana's hand. "My love, if you are afraid to ever take a trip without me, neither of us shall have any sort of life." Turning back to Nyx, she said, "The man they were looking for, it is the same person you have asked me to find. It is the same photograph, actually."

Evra and Nyx shared a look.

"That photograph came from the All Council arrest records. How did the Kumir get their hands on it?"

Evra's lips compressed into a thin line. "It would have come from their employer. Whoever hired the Kumir has access to the same records we do."

"Does that help us any?"

"Not really. The list of people with access is selective, but not so selective it would be feasible to investigate them all."

"Okay." Nyx turned back to the Warlock. "You told us downstairs that you couldn't find this guy. What happened when you did the spell?"

"Everything and nothing. I performed the spell correctly. The magic flows, as it always does, but I could not see him. Could not see anything." She smiled, ruefully. "It took a long time to convince the Kumir of that. I think I only convinced them because they knew that if I was going to lie, well, I would have just *lied*."

"And they just let you go?" Evra asked, a frown wrinkling the smooth skin between her eyebrows.

"I think they thought I might be useful again. I really don't know."

Evra made a noncommittal sound, but she did not voice whatever it was that was bothering her.

Nyx's mind was engaged with a different problem. "Why couldn't you find him? Is that normal?"

The Warlock shook her head. "There are precautions a person can take to keep from being scried—potions, charms. But even then I should be able to *see* him. It would just be hazy, and I wouldn't be able to tell where he was.

"This… this was like running up against a wall. I couldn't see *anything*. I don't know of anything that can do that."

It was a few moments before Evra spoke, her voice distant. "The All Council's Enforcers can."

The Warlock appeared to have trouble choosing between several questions, but the one that came out was, "How?"

"Scrying relies on touching the mind of the person you are searching for, yes?"

"Yes. When a warlock scries, we see the person through *their* eyes."

Evra nodded. "Enforcers are trained to keep their minds partitioned, compartmentalized. They are conditioned against psychic attack and coercion." Evra looked up, met the Warlock's eyes. "I assure you, the walls Enforcers put up around their minds would keep hell itself out. You have nothing to be ashamed of."

And what Enforcer did you know, to make you so bitter? Nyx wondered. Aloud, she said, "So you think our ley line jumper is an Enforcer?"

"No. I think he *was* an Enforcer. In fact, I am nearly positive." She slipped out the picture of Morgen Drahl, pointed to the inside of the left wrist. "His Enforcer mark would have been here. How his wrist looks now? That is about how it would look after they burned it off him."

Nyx's throat turned dry and scratchy. She took a swallow of

tea, but it did nothing to soothe the dryness. "And, uh, ex-Enforcers, they would be difficult to apprehend and turn over to the proper authorities?"

"Quite difficult."

"But you are certain you can handle it?"

"No fight is certain, but I am confident."

"How confident?"

"I spent much of my life training under an Enforcer, so quite confident. And before you ask a single question more, know that I will not be answering it."

Turning to the Warlock, Evra dipped her head in a manner that was half bow, half deferent inclination. "Thank you for your help, Warlock. We will not intrude further upon your time."

"I'm not sure I was much help at all," the Warlock smiled, "but you are welcome."

"If you ever need anything," Nyx offered, "please let us know." She couldn't help but feel the bruises on the Warlock's face were somehow *her* fault.

The Warlock turned speculative. "Actually, if you wouldn't mind, there might be something you *could* do for me. For us." The Warlock reached up to take Diana's hand.

Diana seemed to know what the Warlock meant. Her face turned hard and she said, "I am certain the Guardian has better things to worry about."

"It can't hurt to *ask*, Di. Or are you too proud to have her know our problems?"

Diana looked away, but she didn't protest any further.

"We're trying to have a child."

"Oh. I see." Nyx did not see how she was going to be of help in that department.

"There are methods to help couples like us have children, but they require an egg from both partners and..." The Warlock trailed off, looking up at Diana.

"And they won't work for us, because I'm sterile," Diana bit off.

Evra frowned. "A skilled healer should be able to correct that. Most of them won't even charge for that particular service."

"A healer can't fix me because a healer broke me in the first place," Diana growled. "Scarred me past the point of ever fixing me again."

Evra rose to her feet in a flash, hand gripping the hilt of her long knife. "Tell me this healer's name. I will drag him before the All Council myself."

Diana stared at Evra, as if she couldn't quite believe someone had felt the need to leap to *her* defense. Then she threw back her head and laughed, a rich, guttural sound that made her seem much softer. "I admire your fire, Amazon. And I assure you, could the healer responsible have been made to pay, I would have made him. But he belongs to the Kormadin royal family, and so will never pay for anything."

Evra looked long at Diana, examining her from head to toe. Then she exhaled softly, her eyes widening. "You are Dianara Kormadin."

Diana inclined her head.

"I'm sorry." Nyx cleared her throat. "I, um, I'm still really new to this whole more than one planet thing. I'm afraid I don't know what that means."

Evra gave Nyx her you-really-don't-know-anything look. "The Kormadin family rules the six most important merchant planets in the universe. They are one of the ten wealthiest empires and though they are theoretically not above the law, it would take an army to make them bow to it."

Nyx frowned. "But then, if you're a Kormadin, why would their healer do something like that to you?"

Diana smiled. "Because my parents ordered him to. Because I am a Kormadin no longer. I am afraid my dear parents have a rather antiquated mindset. When I refused to marry a man they'd chosen for a political alliance, when I told them I would never marry *any* man, they disowned me. They knew I had no personal interest in claiming their empire, but inheritance laws are a tricky beast in our corner of the universe, and they didn't want to risk the possibility that I could have a child who might one day try to claim it. So they ensured I couldn't have one."

"I'm sorry."

"It was quite some time ago. I am past it."

Nyx didn't know if you could ever really be past your parents disowning and sterilizing you for being who you were, but didn't think saying so would make the situation any better, either. "But there's something else you can try? Something I can help with?"

"There is a healer here who does experimental work. He has had some success in helping couples conceive when one partner is sterile, he calls it a pairing spell. It can be dangerous, so he requires any couple petitioning for it to seek approval from a governing body. We had planned to petition this sector's Council representative, but that would take months, maybe even years. But a Guardian's approval would fulfill the requirement, too."

"What do I need to do?"

"Just sign a consent form." The Warlock leapt from her seat as if she were terrified Nyx would change her mind before she could find the form. She opened a kitchen drawer and drew out a long ream of paper, hurrying it over to the table.

Nyx looked it over, but it appeared to be nothing more than a standard release of liability form. She signed at the bottom of the page. If her signature could help them, it was the least she could do.

The Warlock stared at the signature for a moment, then carefully folded the document. "Thank you."

"I hope it works out for you." She glanced at her watch. She'd spent more time here than she'd intended. "Thank you for your help, and I'm sorry about the Kumir. We should get going, though. Fugitives to catch, and all that."

As if I apprehend fugitives every day.

The Warlock nodded and walked them downstairs, waving

away Diana's attempts to escort her with a well-placed, "I'm not made of *glass*, Di, I can walk to the door on my own."

On the threshold, Nyx stopped. "Oh, I almost forgot to ask, what's your name?"

"*Nyx*." Evra's outrage crackled in her voice. She did not quite grab Nyx by the ear and scold her, but it was a near thing. "Apologize immediately."

"For what?" Nyx momentarily forgot the Warlock's presence —she only saw Evra scolding her for the millionth time that day. All right, well, maybe it was only the thousandth. Nyx crossed her arms, defensive. "It's not like I asked her to strip naked and dance a jig."

This brought a short bark of laughter from the Warlock, reminding Nyx of the other woman's presence. Evra, not nearly as amused, scowled. "It might be less offensive if you had."

"I just asked her her *name*."

"Exactly."

The Warlock stepped in, placing a hand on each of their arms and ending what could otherwise have been a very long, pointless argument. "It is all right, truly."

The Warlock's graciousness finally turned on Nyx's guilt-center. "I didn't mean anything rude by the question. I didn't mean to cause offense."

The Warlock laughed, a musical, water-chime sound that made the world seem a shade less dark. "It is all right, Nyx, you are far too ignorant of what you have done to cause offense."

"Can I ask exactly what I *did* do?"

The Warlock smiled. "There are many people within a city such as this whose profession is warlock. But there is only ever one who is *the* Warlock and allowed to be called as such. It is a great honor, a sign of respect and achievement. I am that Warlock in Earth Between.

"To call that Warlock by her name, to even ask for her name, is considered a sign of disrespect, that you think she is not worthy of the title Warlock."

"Oh." It seemed to be Nyx's word of choice for the day. "I'm very sorry. I think you're a wonderful warlock." At Evra's glare, Nyx amended, "*The* Warlock."

"Apology accepted. Truth to tell, I am not overly fond of titles, especially from people I should like to some day call my friends. My name is Ankira. I would be honored if you used it."

"Thank you, Ankira."

9

Nyx was surprised to find the sun still up when she and Evra stepped outside. Rationally, she knew they hadn't spent *that* much time at the Warlock's. Outside of rationality, or perhaps directly between it, Nyx felt like years had passed, and the world she now walked in was not the same one she had walked in earlier.

"So what do we do now? Go back to the Station? Do some more research?"

My first real assignment as a Guardian and I've got no clue what I'm doing. With the Warlock unable to scry Drahl, she had no idea how to find him. *I'm not a detective.*

"Now, we prepare to run like hell." Evra said this in an even tone while smiling and steering Nyx over to a vendor of hand-made jewelry which the Amazon, to all casual observers, appeared to be fascinated by.

Were it not for the tension in Evra's fingers, placed lightly on Nyx's elbow to steer her to the jewelry stand, Nyx would have thought she'd heard the Amazon wrong.

Nyx smiled pleasantly and picked up a bracelet carved with symbols she didn't recognize. She turned it over in her hand, pretending to scrutinize every detail. "Run where? From what?"

Evra lifted a ring and began trying it on different fingers. "I feared the Kumir might have stayed behind when they couldn't get what they wanted out of the Warlock."

Only Evra, holding a necklace up to Nyx's neck, which was really a clever excuse to put a vise-like grip along her jawline, kept Nyx's head from whipping around to scan the area for a pack of identical women.

"How many?"

"At least twelve."

"I don't suppose you feel as good about your chances of taking on twelve Kumir as you do about one ex-Enforcer?"

"No."

Nyx swallowed, then uttered a question she had never previously imagined she would have occasion to ask, though it always sounded interesting enough in films. "Are we going to die?"

The pause following this question, in addition to the set of Evra's lips, was not comforting.

"Not immediately. They will want to find out if we know where Morgen Drahl is."

"So what's the plan?"

"Run. If we can make it back to the Station, the defenses there will keep the Kumir out."

Nyx didn't bother asking what those defenses were. She was more focused on another problem. "It's around three miles back to the Station. That's a long way to bet on our being faster than them." Or on them not having projectile weapons.

"Do you have a better suggestion?"

A structure in the vicinity caught Nyx's gaze. She gauged the distance and put it at roughly one mile. "Actually, I do."

"Then use it," Evra growled. "We are out of time."

A second before Evra upended the jewelry table, Nyx finally spotted the Kumir. They had surrounded the marketplace and were closing in on her and Evra in a tight circle.

Evra's act of destruction caused the perfect distraction. Well, that, and the wickedly long knife she pulled out of her hip sheath. People bolted in all directions in the busy square, jostling Kumir and citizens alike. Those who recognized the Kumir for what they were literally ran screaming in the opposite direction.

Nyx grabbed Evra's hand and took off running for the eastern path leading out of the marketplace square. Evra liberated her hand almost immediately, and once she caught on to the general direction they were going, she doubled her pace.

Nyx struggled to keep up with the Amazon and wondered how the hell she had ever thought she was in shape. Up until this exact moment, she'd been proud of coasting her way through six-mile runs every few days, taking the exercise at a leisurely ten-and-a-half minutes per mile and never feeling any particular motivation to push the speed or distance any further.

She very much regretted that lack of drive at present. Already, her legs were getting that heavy, leaden feeling in them, and they had only covered half the distance they needed to. Evra had to be clipping along at a six-minute-mile, her shoulders back, legs flying beneath her as if they were a machine independent of her body.

Nyx gritted her teeth and pushed forward, sucking down air in painful, irritating gasps further complicated by her nose's annoying habit of thinking that because *she* was running, it should be too.

A quarter-mile flew by and they reached the point Nyx had feared: a long, steep hill. Evra took the hill with ease, her steady pace unwavering. Nyx tore after her with effort, digging into the ground as if the earth had personally offended her.

They crested the hill, their destination a mere agonizing four-hundred-feet away.

"*This* was your big plan?" Evra's voice sounded completely even and normal despite the absurd pace, even managing to convey hints of disdain.

In that moment, Nyx hated her more than ever. "Well yours,"

gasp, "*sucked*." Deeper gasp. "Just be glad," two gasps, "the gate's" gasp, "open."

"*Glad*? We will be lucky if he does not chain us in the dungeons and torture us."

"He's got dungeons? *Neat*." On that cheerful thought, Nyx put all the willpower she had into a final burst of speed and she and Evra ran into the courtyard of Lord Beauregard's castle.

They made it ten feet inside the gate before a contingent of guards, wearing all black and face masks that showed only their eyes, blocked their paths. Skidding to a stop, Nyx was profoundly grateful to not be running anymore, even though she knew her calf muscles would seize up any second.

Evra looked fresh and alert, like she'd just stepped out of a luxurious day spa. Nyx would have glared at the Amazon if she hadn't been too busy trying to breathe around freshly cracked lips, or battling to contain the legion of snot coming out of her nose.

The guard remained interested in them for roughly one-point-five seconds. Then Evra said, "Kumir," and said aforementioned Kumir came running through the gates.

Around Nyx it was as if the world, previously locked in a standstill, burst into motion. The guards drew their swords. Evra drew her short sword and a long knife, and Nyx would bet she was wishing for her longsword right about now. Come to think of it, Nyx was wishing for one right about now. Or, well, *any* weapon.

For a moment, Nyx stood suspended, a point of stillness in the chaos. She watched Evra whirl and lunge, sword and knife spinning, defending, slashing. Nyx watched as a Kumir fended off two guards, the movement of the three fighters hypnotic, dance-like, until the Kumir ran her sword through first one guard, then the other, and the dance was ended.

A sick flash of heat swept through Nyx, the kind that chilled her and yet made her break out in a sweat at the same time. As Nyx watched, the Kumir raised her leg and placed a booted foot on the chest of the guard whose stomach her sword was stuck through. Without ever losing her balance, the Kumir kicked the man off her sword.

He fell to the ground, enough consciousness left to break his fall with one hand, the other clutching at the gaping wound in his stomach. He didn't manage to break his fall much, and Nyx wondered if he felt the pain of it, or if all attention was focused on the pain in his abdomen.

The books and movies, they don't prepare you for death like this.

Then she didn't have time to think anymore because the Kumir who had felled the two guards advanced on her, and the sounds of battle told Nyx no one was coming to save her.

She was, she hoped, not entirely out of her depth. She had kept up on martial arts lessons the last few years, when she could afford it, building on what must have been extensive lessons in her childhood. She didn't hold the actual memory of those lessons, but her body remembered the teachings, and she'd slipped into various classes with ease. She'd even had a boyfriend a few years ago who trained with her, and he had been skilled enough to teach her quite a few interesting things.

The Kumir advanced and Nyx cast about for a weapon. A guard lay dead a few feet to her left. The sword in his limp hand was broken, but two metal rods in a case along his leg caught her eye. They were the same diameter as a bo staff but only a foot and a half or so in length.

Nyx backed toward the body slowly, her eyes never leaving the Kumir. She didn't have to work very hard to mimic a frightened creature backing away from a predator, but her timidity kept the Kumir from advancing too quickly.

Nyx pretended to stumble into the body, bent down and yanked the metal rods from the dead man's case. A portion of each rod was roughened and grooved to provide a better grip, and Nyx slipped her hands to the correct holds, taking up a defensive stance.

The expression on the Kumir's face changed from cool arrogance to murderous rage. She did not break into a run but she advanced quickly, her sword coming up.

Nyx sidestepped away from the body, giving herself room to move. When the Kumir's first strike came, Nyx blocked the sword's blow with the rod in her left hand. The blow jolted all the way down into Nyx's wrist, further through her entire arm.

She almost dropped the rod, recovered. She met the next blow, prepared for the force this time, and didn't falter. Her world narrowed to the fight, methodically blocking swings of the Kumir's sword. She gave ground steadily, more interested in keeping the sword away from her than in maintaining any specific piece of ground.

She recognized her mistake when she realized the sounds of other battle were far away. The Kumir had maneuvered her away from any help, around a copse of trees where no one would notice her unless they already knew she was there.

Looking through the trees, Nyx saw a second contingent of guards arrive, joining ranks to fight against the remaining Kumir.

By the time they put them down and Evra notices I'm missing, I'll be dead.

Nyx kept up her rhythmic line of defense, but she was faltering. The Kumir's blows were wearing her down, and the Kumir knew it.

Instinct told Nyx to change the flow of the fight, and it took no conscious effort to drop one rod and take the remaining one in both hands. She blocked the next strike and moved into the blow this time instead of away.

She used the closer proximity and the better leverage it gave her to bear down on the Kumir's sword. When the Kumir's hold wavered, Nyx used the rod to twist the sword in a clockwise motion, putting all her strength into a quick *flick* of her wrist that ripped the sword out of the Kumir's hands.

The sword did not go flying a great distance, as it often did in the movies, but rather clattered to the ground about three feet away. Just close enough for Nyx to wonder what would happen if the Kumir got her hands on it again.

She didn't intend to find out.

She went on the offensive, bringing the bar in her hand to bear on the Kumir ruthlessly, hitting all of the vulnerable places on the woman's arms she knew should render them all but useless, and when the Kumir stopped raising her arms, Nyx delivered a barrage of blows to the Kumir's legs that dropped the mercenary to her knees.

Nyx grabbed the sword and lunged. She never felt the impact of sword hitting flesh. She looked down. The sword's tip rested gently against the hard leather of the Kumir's shirt.

I can't do it.

She had seen death a hundred times in films, read about it hundreds more in books. But she had never *really* seen it before today, before this very Kumir had plunged her sword into a man's chest and shoved his still twitching body off her blade like it was an irritation.

The memory of it filled her with rage, a sick heat that made her hand, holding the sword, tremble. This Kumir had killed a man today. Had probably killed many more in the past. Would kill Nyx without hesitation.

None of it mattered. Nyx couldn't bring herself to run the sword through, and the Kumir knew it. The mercenary batted the sword aside. Nyx wasn't prepared for the swing that followed—the Kumir's limbs should have been useless for another minute, at least—and the sword clattered from her hand.

The Kumir lunged, coming up with a knife.

Instinct took over again. She deflected the blow, grabbed the Kumir's wrist and turned it inward on the woman. The Kumir's lunge threw her weight onto Nyx, and when it did, it forced her down on her own dagger.

Nyx fell, the Kumir landing on top of her, Nyx's hand still wrapped around the Kumir's wrist, warm blood spilling over her hands. The look on the Kumir's face was one of surprise.

Nyx scrambled out from under the Kumir, rolled onto all fours and vomited. Her sides heaved, arms shaking, until she had nothing left to choke up but bitter yellow bile. She gave herself that moment and then, remembering where she was, what was happening, she leapt to her feet only to realize the battle was over, the air hanging still and quiet.

A hard knot formed in Nyx's throat. *Evra. What if she—*

Not quite able to go right out and just *look*, Nyx peeked through the copse of trees. Heart in her throat, Nyx looked for Evra. It took her a bit to find the Amazon, mostly because she ended up only being about six feet away, hidden completely from view on the other side of a large oak tree.

Nyx was alerted to the Amazon's presence by an occurrence Nyx had never expected—the sound of Evra's laughter. It was deep and throaty, exactly what one would expect from a warrior.

Nyx peeked out, not far enough to be seen, but enough to see.

Evra stood next to one of the castle guards, the only part of him visible beneath his uniform's mask a pair of warm brown eyes. They were talking about the battle, going over moves.

"I have never seen anyone suicidal enough to attempt Serpent's Strike in the midst of *three* attackers." The guard's tone was playful, mischievous.

Wait, was that the sound of someone brave enough to *flirt* with Evra al'Daemon?

"It is only suicidal if you do not know what you are doing." Evra's tone sounded suspiciously light and of good cheer.

"Perhaps you could give me a few pointers then, lady Amazon."

"Well, you do seem as if you need them."

Nyx restrained a groan. Was that the sound of Evra *flirting back?* Nyx was spared any further trauma by the arrival of a second guard.

"Lord Beauregard wants you back on perimeter patrol. Make sure there aren't any more of them around."

"Yes, Captain." The flirtatious guard turned back to Evra,

brown eyes sparkling. "You know where to find me if you want to give me those pointers, lady Amazon." He turned, trotting off at a brisk pace.

"Lord Beauregard would also like a word with you and your companion," the new guard said.

Evra sighed. "I suspected as much. We will—" She broke off, looking around. "Where is Nyx?" The cold fury in her voice had Nyx scrambling into sight.

"I'm right here."

"You are safe." Evra released her breath. "Did you hide during the entire battle or —" Evra's gaze caught on the blood covering Nyx's hands, the wet stain of it on her shirt. "Stars above, what happened?"

Nyx tried to explain, opening her mouth, but all that came out was a strangled noise. She turned sideways and pointed through the trees where the Kumir lay, unmoving.

Understanding bled into Evra's eyes.

"Your first?" she asked, voice soft.

Nyx nodded, not trusting herself to speak.

"She would have killed you in a heartbeat, Nyx. You did what you had to." Turning to the guard, "Take us to Lord Beauregard now, please."

"Of course."

Nyx followed Evra and the guard up a tidy gravel road, grateful to have something to focus on, to think of, other than what she'd just done. She took in the landscape, looking for bodies, for any signs of the battle at all, and found nothing save a few clods of overturned earth. She wondered about that, as they passed through two exceptionally large doors and into Lord Beauregard's castle.

10

The inside of the castle met all of Nyx's secret, inner-geek expectations. Smooth, black tile floors. Stone walls festooned with artwork that depicted battles, mythic scenes Nyx didn't recognize, and the occasional pastoral setting. Nyx even caught glimpses of a few family trees and crests.

The place was lit not with electricity or torches—though Nyx thought the latter perfectly acceptable for a castle setting—but glowing orbs the size of softballs. They hung in the air close to the ceiling, or at least Nyx imagined the ceiling must be up there *somewhere*, because she couldn't quite see it even though the orbs were very, very far up.

It was obvious that magic of some sort powered the orbs, and Nyx would have liked to ask what kind, only they had traveled in silence thus far and the way their footsteps echoed in the vast halls did not invite inquisitive chatter.

It took them five minutes to reach their destination, during which time Nyx was certain they went in more than one circle, the guard intentionally leading them down unnecessary passageways in an attempt to confuse them.

It worked. Nyx had no idea where they were and could only hope Evra was immune to such tactics of confusion.

The guard halted in front of an elaborately carved door of deep ebony wood. He knocked once but didn't wait for a reply. He swept the door open, ushering them inside.

"Lord Beauregard, these are the two trespassers you asked be brought to you."

Nyx wasn't quite sure what she had expected to walk into—throne room, dungeon, interrogation room—but she certainly had not expected to walk into an executive office. Or, what an executive office would look like if done medieval-style.

Shining black stone floors, impressive wall-to-wall bookshelves filled with matching leather tomes. Fur area rug and a hulking desk carved of the same ebony wood as the door. And what office was complete without a tastefully displayed human skull on the fireplace mantel?

"Thank you, Borden, I will handle it from here."

That voice—a rumbling like water going over a fall, powerful and yet hypnotically soothing at the same time—belonged to the man seated behind the large desk. He was as large as his booming voice indicated he ought to be, and well-muscled despite the crow's feet beginning to creep in around his eyes. He had close-cropped salt-and-pepper hair that matched a neatly trimmed beard, and skin far darker than the ebony-wood desk.

The different facets of his presentation—his facial expressions, the set of his jaw, the ease with which he held himself, the light twinkle in his eyes—contradicted each other, making his age impossible to guess. He dressed much like his guards from what she could see—black shirt and she suspected black pants as well, though the desk hid them.

Something about him struck Nyx as familiar, though she was certain she had never seen him before.

Borden gave a dip of his head and exited, closing the door behind him. Lord Beauregard studied them in silence for fifteen or so seconds, which felt more to Nyx like fifteen or so minutes. Then he steepled his fingers atop his desk and leaned back in his chair.

"So. You are the two responsible for leading a contingent of Kumir onto my grounds."

It wasn't precisely a question, so Nyx didn't answer. She felt far too much like a teenager in the principal's office—or how she imagined it felt like, since she couldn't actually recall such an occasion—and she didn't care for the experience. Beside her, Evra also remained silent.

Lord Beauregard continued. "Obviously, the Kumir were chasing you. Am I to assume you ran onto my grounds by accident and not that you intentionally led hostile parties onto my lands?"

He knows —has to know—we didn't come here by accident. "Well, not *exactly*."

"Oh?" The twinkle in Beauregard's eyes let on that Nyx had given the correct answer so far. "What, exactly, then?"

"It's, umm, sort of a long story."

Lord Beauregard spread out his hands. "I am quite at my leisure and I do enjoy a good tale."

Okay, then. "I'm not sure where to start."

"I find the beginning is usually best," he answered with a wry smile.

"Right, the beginning." *As if I know where that is.* "Well, yesterday when I woke up, I didn't know anything about magic or ley lines or intelligent life on other planets but somehow I ended up the Guardian of the Waystation here." Nyx paused, needing some sign of encouragement if she were to continue.

"Yes, I hear that's how it happens with this Station more often than not. So. *You're* the new Guardian." He leaned forward, peering at her with interest, gaze scrutinizing the tattoo on her left forearm. "You are quite a bit younger than I would expect but that's the mark, no doubt, and Sena *was* getting on in years. Please, continue."

"Sure. Well, this morning I got a message from the All Council saying this fugitive, Drahl, had traveled illegally through the lines, and it was my responsibility to apprehend him. So we went to see the Warlock about locating Drahl, only the Kumir had already been to see her about locating the same guy, and he's apparently un-locatable by magical means.

"Anyway, the Kumir must have been watching the Warlock's place because Evra spotted them in the market square after we came out. Then they converged and we, ah…"

"Ran here?" Lord Beauregard supplied.

Nyx nodded. "I saw your castle on the way in and Evra mentioned you were well-versed in the Kumir and so I thought, where better to run than towards someone who keeps armed guards trained to deal with Kumir?"

"Well-versed. How very politic of you. Most people just call me paranoid."

Nyx swallowed and did not mention that paranoid *had* been the word Evra used.

"It's been at least a decade since anyone has been bold enough to come onto my grounds without invitation, and you with Kumir in tow, no less."

"I'm very sorry for any inconvenience we caused. I would be happy to pay reparations for any damages caused, or—" Nyx broke off, remembering a Kumir shoving a man off her sword. Her voice broke down to a whisper. "How—how many people died?"

Lord Beauregard dipped his head. "Three."

"Oh." Her stomach made a disquieting flip. *If I hadn't been involved, if I hadn't led the Kumir here, no one would have died.*

Nyx's stomach heaved again but a room like this was too nice to vomit in. She choked on bile and forced it down, trying to think of something, anything, else.

"Is that the first time you've seen death?" Beauregard's voice was not unkind, and the waterfall sound of it was soothing when he spoke at quieter volumes.

Nyx managed a nod. A co-worker a few years back had died in a car crash—Cynthia, three car pile-up on I-10—but Nyx hadn't *seen* it. One didn't see death in this day and age, not really, not unless you were a soldier or a medical worker or a mortician. And if you hadn't seen it, Nyx thought, you couldn't understand.

Beauregard sat up, his expression distressed and his voice gruff. "All right, listen attentively because I do not usually give warm speeches and I am only going to say this once. What happened was not your fault."

Nyx's lower lip trembled and her eyes brimmed with water, both of which she refused to acknowledge, even when the water spilled down her cheeks.

"Every man or woman who joins my guard does so because they have lost something to the Kumir. Lost enough that they do not have anything left they care about outside of these walls. For any one of them, a chance to take out Kumir is one they would be angry to have missed.

"If you hadn't led the Kumir here, my guard and I would have sought them out as soon as we knew they were in the area. We have our own watchdogs, we would have been informed."

Nyx sniffed. "But I didn't know any of that. And I led them here anyway."

"Yes, you did. And if you had not, if we had had to seek them out, how many innocent people would have been caught in the mix? People who did not choose to go up against the Kumir, people who know nothing about fighting? Your choices may have been quickly made, and you may not have had all the facts, but your choices did save lives. That is the most the people of Between can ask from their Guardian."

Nyx drew a deep breath through a nose once again displeased with her. She *had* led the Kumir here because she knew the castle guard was formed exclusively to battle Kumir. It made them the most rational choice, people who had already decided to take the risks involved in such a career. If it didn't erase the guilt she felt, perhaps it could still lessen it.

She swiped at her face, met Beauregard's gaze and nodded.

"Thank you. If there was any damage to the grounds I'd be happy to—"

Beauregard waved a hand dismissively. "Do not concern yourself with reparations, I have no need of money. What I do have is a vendetta. If you would like to repay me for the help of my guard, tell me about the Kumir."

Nyx looked to Evra—she *liked* Beauregard, but she wasn't sure how the laws here worked, how much she was allowed to tell people. Evra dipped her head in a barely perceptible nod.

"I don't really know anything else. Just that the Kumir are searching for the same man we are."

Beauregard rubbed the short beard beneath his chin, his eyes downcast.

"Lord Beauregard—"

"Please, call me Jim."

Jim? A name like Lord Beauregard and his first name is Jim? Hope it's at least short for James. "Jim, then. Do you know why the Kumir were after our man?"

"Hmm?" Beauregard looked up from his desk. "No, I'm afraid I do not."

But you know something, she thought.

"I can tell you the Kumir do not hunt a person they have not been hired to find."

Nyx frowned. "The All Council charged us with finding Drahl. And if he's wanted for treason, who else would be interested in finding him?"

"Who else, indeed?"

Evra bristled, speaking for the first time since they had entered the room. "Surely you are not suggesting the *All Council* hired the Kumir to retrieve Drahl?"

"Of course not." Beauregard paused, watching Evra relax, and added, "The Kumir do not take retrieval contracts, only kill contracts."

"The *Council* is not in the business of putting kill contracts on individuals they have already tasked a Guardian with apprehending, and the Council most certainly would not hire *Kumir.*"

"No, the Council would not," Beauregard agreed. "Not when they have Enforcers willing to follow their orders without question. But an individual Council member with something to hide? Well, he or she just might."

Evra stepped forward, shoulders taut. "Careful, *Lord*, what you speak of is borderline treasonous in its own right."

Far from looking intimidated—and Nyx would have been cowering in a corner if Evra were looking at *her* as she looked at the castle lord—Beauregard looked intrigued. His gaze swept over Evra from head to toe, cataloging features until something clicked. "Ah. You would be one of Moriana's daughters, then. The eldest?"

"What would you know about my mother?" Evra's voice had a low, dangerous quality to it.

"I used to know her quite well. Not like *that*," he added, when Evra's eyebrows rose alarmingly high.

He tapped the inside of his left wrist where a tattoo—seriously, did the magical universe have tattoos for everything?—displayed an E followed by a series of numbers. It had a line through the middle, like a typed strikethrough.

"We were in the same initial unit." He smiled. "Before she became the legend she is today. Ask her, some time, how the individual members of the Council handle their personal business. If she is willing to answer you—and I suggest you make sure she is damn drunk before you ask—*then* you may come back here and pass judgment on me for my accusations."

Evra held Beauregard's gaze, a muscle ticking along her jaw. She never replied, and after he had blinked three times she looked away.

Suspecting nothing good would come out of Evra's mouth if she were to speak, and sensing they had gotten all the information they were likely to get, Nyx decide it was time to leave.

"Thank you for your help, Lord Beauregard," Nyx said.

"Jim."

"Right. Jim. We should be heading back to the Station."

"Of course. I will have Borden escort you to the gates. You are welcome to visit again under less dire circumstances. A Guardian should have good relationships with the people of Between, and I can introduce you to some you might find useful."

"I would appreciate that. Thank you."

Beauregard nodded. "Show this to the gate guard should you choose to visit. It will ensure they let you through." He flipped her a coin.

She fumbled, caught it, trapping the coin against her stomach. It was gold with a burning house on one side and crossed swords on the other.

"What we have lost," Bearegard said. "And why we fight."

"Who did you lose?" Nyx asked softly.

Bearegard was silent until Borden arrived at the door with a second guard. "My wife. I lost my wife." He stood and gestured to the door. "Borden, please escort our new Guardian and her companion to the gate.

"Jackson," he said to the second guard, "please bring my newest recruit to see me."

11

Nyx made it out of the castle and off the grounds by paying attention to details of the landscape and determinedly not thinking about the person she'd killed. When they entered the market square, the wreckage of their flight from the Kumir distracted her, filling her with guilt.

Yes, she and Evra had been running for their lives, and trying to prevent anyone else from getting hurt, but they'd still caused a great deal of property damage that Nyx had no way to pay for. Several merchants stopped cleaning when they entered the square, and one finally gathered her courage and approached Nyx, her eyes on the Guardian tattoo.

"Is the Station going to cover the damages for this?" She sounded a little nervous, but determined, and she asked loudly enough for everyone in the square to hear.

Nyx started to say that she had no idea, but then she remembered reading something in the Operations Manual that morning about investigative damages being covered.

Act like a Guardian, she told herself. *Pretend you know what the hell you're doing.*

"Of course. If everyone who suffered a loss could please form a queue?" She pulled a pen and notebook from her backpack and took down everyone's names, leaving them with instructions to bring an itemized list of damages by the Station later. She didn't know if that was the proper way to handle this, but since she really *hadn't* had any training, she didn't care.

She didn't even care if the merchants took advantage of her ignorance and price-gouged her on the whole affair. They *had* suffered a loss and it was, presumably, not her money being used to reimburse them. And if it was, well, she didn't care too much about that, either.

Once they were finished, and she had nothing more to distract her, the images of the dying Kumir woman invaded her mind. She continued to hold it together until they got out of the city, but she only made it a quarter of a mile down the path to the Station before the remembered copper-scent of blood, the heat of it spilling over her hands, had her darting off the path. She fell to her knees behind some bushes and vomited again. She didn't have anything left to throw up, dry-heaving as silent tears leaked out of her eyes.

Gods, that image.

She closed her eyes, clenched her teeth. Little by little, she pushed the memory away, burying it deep in her mind beneath layers of ordinary reality. The feel of the dirt beneath her hands, the sharp scent of dried pine needles. She rocked back onto her heels, the cool, late-afternoon breeze playing at the tears on her face. She wiped them away, opening her eyes to see something covered in black cloth: Evra's knees. Nyx traveled her gaze up to Evra's face, finding a mix of expressions she couldn't accurately identify.

"Are you all right?"

Nyx wiped the back of her hand across her mouth, swallowing against the gritty taste of leftover bile. "No."

Evra stood, silent, a wrinkle worrying the space between her eyebrows.

Nyx wiped her mouth with the back of her hand. "Are *you* all right?"

"Something is bothering me."

Nyx waited.

"You killed a Kumir. You should not have been able to do that. Council Enforcers have fallen to Kumir and they have some of the best training in the universe."

Nyx shrugged. "I got lucky. She probably underestimated me."

"No doubt she did." But the wrinkle didn't leave Evra's face.

"Whatever it is you're thinking, you may as well just ask."

"Very well. Luck or no, defeating a Kumir would require years of training. You claim to be from Earth. From what I have read of the place, there is not much emphasis on hand-to-hand martial skills. Is there something you are not telling me?"

Great, she thinks I'm an alien. But underneath her inner sarcasm, Evra's worries dredged up some of Nyx's own.

"I claim to be from Earth because, as far as I know, I am."

"As far as you know?"

"Yes."

"Explain."

"I can only remember the last seven years."

"You have amnesia." Evra's face could have been in the dictionary next to the word "skeptical."

I can't blame her. "I guess you'd call it that. I woke up in an apartment I didn't recognize. I found a note telling me it was mine, paid for the next year. It told me my name, my bank account information, and where I was going to college. It didn't tell me anything else."

"You are telling me someone knew you would wake up without a memory and they left you a note that mostly only explained your financial situation?"

Did I think she looked skeptical before? "Believe me, I know how it sounds. Nobody knows me. I even Googled myself but there's literally nothing on me."

"Googled?"

"It's a way of searching for information. I should have been able to find *something*, but I couldn't. As for how I could kill a Kumir? I don't know. I just *know* how to do stuff like that.

"So if you're asking if I'm not from Earth... I don't know. Maybe I grew up here, maybe I grew up hopping ley lines and tossing magic around, but I can't tell you, because I *don't know*."

Evra studied Nyx, eventually letting out a long breath. "I am sorry. The lack of such knowledge must be difficult to live with."

Nyx shrugged and resumed walking when Evra did. "Hasn't been the greatest. But being here, at the Station, that's been... better. And who knows? If I didn't grow up here, maybe one day I'll walk into Earth Between and run into someone who recognizes me. Take Beauregard, for example. Something about him seemed very familiar."

Evra shot Nyx a sideways glance. "I had the same thought when we met him."

Both Nyx *and* Evra thought Beauregard looked familiar... Nyx stopped walking again as the probable reason occurred to her. "Say, Evra, if you were a wanted fugitive being hunted by the Kumir, and you came to Earth Between, where the man most equipped to fend off the Kumir happens to live, where do you think you would go first?"

"To that man, I suppose. But why would Beauregard help Morgen Drahl? Unless..." Evra trailed off, putting the two-and-two of both her and Nyx finding Beauregard familiar together. "They're related."

Slow, dramatic clapping sounded from Nyx's left and a man stepped out of the forest shadows, brown eyes sparkling with mischief.

"*Very* good."

Nyx recognized the eyes and the voice of the guard who had flirted with Evra at Beauregard's castle. Only now he wasn't wearing a mask.

Morgen Drahl bowed with a flourish. "Not everyone sees the resemblance."

Nyx pulled Gleipnir from her pocket. Evra slipped her sword free. "What are you doing here?"

"Turning myself in out of the goodness of my heart, obviously." He ran his gaze down the length of Evra's sword and raised an eyebrow. "Ladies, there's no need for violence. I'm only here to do the right thing." To Evra he added, "But if you want to rough me up a little on the way in, I won't complain."

Nyx and Evra shared a look. "Why would you turn yourself in *after* you illegally jumped planets?"

"Ah, so glad you asked, little Guardian. I am only wanted at present *because* I rode the lines illegally and I did *that* to find you."

Nyx dropped Gleipnir. She retrieved it hastily, trying not to look completely incompetent as she did. "Why on Earth would you be looking for me?"

"Ah, why in the *universe*, more accurately. But perhaps we could get inside before we talk about that?"

Nyx glanced uncertainly at Evra.

The Amazon lifted her chin. "Tell us what your interest in Nyx is, or we are not taking you anywhere."

Morgen lifted his eyebrows, one side of his perfectly full lips quirking up. "Let me make sure I heard correctly. You're refusing to arrest me as leverage to get me to tell you what you want to know?"

Well, when he puts it like that…

Nyx crossed the three feet to Drahl and looped Gleipnir around his wrists. As it occurred to her she had no means to tie a chain together, the end link closest to Morgen's wrist fused itself to another link midway through the chain, forming an unbreakable loop. Nyx tugged on the long, free end experimentally—the length of chain around Morgen's wrists drew tight, and his hands and wrists pulled together with a snap.

"Holy stars beside us, is that Gleipnir?" Far from looking properly captured, Morgen looked fascinated.

Nyx ignored him. She also ignored Evra's pointed glare, the

one that said, *You shouldn't have done that without talking to me first.*

She was tired of talking. It was time to get something done. Why had he said he could help? Why had he claimed he'd come here for her?

"At least take his damn sword," Evra muttered.

"You're the assistant," Nyx shot back. "Why don't you *assist*?"

"Assistant?" Morgen asked as Evra grumbled and walked over to him. "I'm dying to know how an Amazon becomes a Station assistant."

"If I don't tell you, will you *actually* die?" Evra asked, a little too much enthusiasm in her voice.

"No, but if you kiss me, I might. Want to try it and find out?"

Morgen was apparently immune to the venom Evra's glares produced. He was dangerously close to *smiling* the entire two seconds it took Evra to unbuckle his sword scabbard and remove it.

Evra stepped back and waved the sword at Nyx. "Let's go."

Nyx tugged on the chain, pulling Morgen behind her. He seemed far too enthralled with Gleipnir to mind. His long stride meant he was more or less walking beside her as opposed to being dragged along, and even the sword Evra kept pointed in his direction didn't keep him from looking more like a happy-go-lucky sidekick than a prisoner.

He brought his wrists up close to his eyes, studying the fine links of the chain. "The All Council actually thought I was worth giving *Gleipnir* to an untested Guardian. I'm touched. I might actually be tearing up."

"Check again," Evra muttered. "I am sure you will find it is just the wind."

Nyx frowned, of which she seemed to be doing a lot lately. "Shouldn't the Council have mentioned he had a relative living here?"

Morgen looked from Nyx to Evra. When Evra just shook her

head, Morgen raised his hand, like a kid in history class, the look on his face every bit of, *I know, I know, ask me.*

Nyx sighed. "Yes?"

"The Council has no idea Beauregard's my uncle. Strictly speaking, my uncle went a little nuts after he lost his wife. Went through a dozen name changes and hopped so many planets it even took *me* a year and a half to track him down."

"Uh-huh. And I suppose it's just coincidence he happens to be on this planet?"

Morgen grinned. "Not a chance, little Guardian. I sort of asked him if he wouldn't mind hanging out on Earth Between for a few years, in the eventuality I found myself in my current straits. He's rich and bored and he had nothing better to do."

Right.

"Speaking of lineage," Morgen said, turning his attention to Evra, "Uncle says you're Moriana's eldest daughter? That is *intense.*"

Evra turned a withering a stare on him. "Your point?"

"Simply wondering if you adhere to the Amazonian tradition that all potential paramours seek your mother's approval before asking you on a date. Not that I wouldn't do it, of course, but that woman is scary."

This time Evra's lips twitched in amusement. "I could not care less about my mother's approval. However, the very notion of you approaching her in that regard is so foolish that were you to do it and survive the attempt, I might be impressed enough to take pity on you."

"Seriously?" Morgen perked up. "If I ask her, you'll go on a date with me?"

"There wouldn't be enough of you left to date."

Interested at this peek into Evra's life, Nyx turned to Morgen. "Exactly how scary would you say her mom is?"

"Let me put it this way, they don't call her the Mother of Demons for nothing."

"You have actually met my mother and are insane enough to voluntarily approach her?"

"Not insane. Motivated."

"When did you meet her?" Evra asked, voice carefully neutral.

"Ah, my third month in the Enforcer academy. She was that year's specialist trainer." He shivered. "She focused on minimalist survival."

"Did she drop you in the deserts of Arasann for a month?"

"No. The forests of Doren for two."

"Consider yourself lucky. When I was twelve, she left me to the mercy of the Shifting Seas."

"For how long?"

"Six months, give or take a few days."

"It took her six *months* to come get you?" Nyx couldn't hide her incredulity. "When you were *twelve*?"

"Oh, she never came for me," Evra replied brightly. "Six months is just how long it took me to earn a place on the Bored Baron's pirate ship and scrape together enough resources to find my own way home."

Morgen fanned himself. "Marry me," he demanded.

"No."

"Why not? I'm a charming, educated, well-traveled individual. And, if I might say so, dashingly handsome."

"You are a wanted fugitive of the All Council, you have betrayed those who trusted you, and you appear to have no remorse for your actions." She frowned. "And we just met."

Morgen sighed, dramatically batting his eyelashes. "The wanted fugitive thing really is a *big* misunderstanding."

Nyx held back a giggle. She wasn't supposed to find their newly apprehended fugitive funny. Did the Operations Manual have a section on that? Something like, *Seven Easy Steps to Loathing Your Prisoner*?

She shook her head, gave up, and laughed.

12

A shift in atmosphere became apparent the closer they drew to the Station. The skies hovered above, dark and thick, fat drops of rain and sleet falling from heavy clouds. The temperature dropped at least twenty degrees between one step and the next and thunder crackled above, a long, pealing cry that shook the ground beneath their feet and sent shockwaves through the air.

Evra stopped and looked back to where, twenty feet behind them, the afternoon glowed bright and sunny. "What in the stars is going on?"

"It's Griff." Nyx felt a twinge shudder through the Guardian tattoo. "I think—I think he's worried about me." Nyx couldn't say how, but she *knew* Griff was causing the storm, could feel his concern in the tattoo's uneasy writhing.

"Who is Griff?"

Evra looked in the direction of the Station, squinting against the sheets of rain and sleet. "He is the Station's Avatar."

"You *named* your Avatar?"

"*Yes*. For the love of these stars everyone keeps talking about, I named my Avatar. He's not a thing, he's a *he*, and if everyone doesn't stop commenting on it, I'm going to punch one of you."

A rush of wind blew, its strength brutal. It drove Nyx to her knees and Griff landed before them with a force that sent vibrations through the ground.

Griff was *large*. Gone was the housecat-sized griffin, replaced by one the size of a tank. Gone, too, were the spectacles and pocket watch. He was also pure black from tail to beak. The massive griffin lowered his head down to hers, each great eye the size of a bowling ball.

"Are you all right?" His voice boomed, shaking the earth and trees, and the breath of his words blew her hair back from her face.

Nyx winced. "I'm fine. I think I might be deaf now, and I'm soaked through and all," *and I killed a woman today*, "but I'm fine."

Her word was not quite enough for Griff, who prodded her with a beak the size of her torso until he became convinced she would not break. Inspection complete, he settled back on his haunches, folding his wings along his sides.

The rain slowed to a drizzle, the light now gloomy but not the dark of full-storm it had been moments before.

"I see you have captured the line-jumper."

"Er, sort of."

Griff peered at Drahl intently. "But he is not the danger I felt you were in."

"No. There were… Kumir."

A griffin's eagle-nostrils could not flare like a horse's, but Nyx thought they would have were it possible. "That is cause for concern indeed. Come inside and we will sort this out."

Nyx followed him back to the Station, relieved. Funny, how she found it rankling when Evra told her what to do, but comforting when Griff did. Maybe it was the fur and the cute paws, or the enormous wing he stretched out above her as they walked back, shielding her from the continuing drizzle of rain.

As soon as the door closed behind them, Evra spoke. "We should put Drahl in the Den. It is the most secure location."

Nyx hadn't thought quite that far ahead, but she had to admit it made sense. "Agreed. Griff?"

The Station's Avatar returned to his normal, bespectacled size and led them through the Station, back to the Den's trapdoor. Drahl remained in a cheery mood the entire journey, yapping like a child on vacation rather than a prisoner en route to a holding bay.

"This is fantastic. Do you know how many people actually get to *see* a Guardian's Den? Hell, half the Guardians don't even know they *have* a Den. I mean, I got to see a lot of places as an Enforcer, but a *Den*…"

Griff glanced at Morgen's sword, which Evra still held. "Either leave that here or put it on. If you drop it in the Den, the Den will claim it."

Nyx took the sword from Evra and buckled it on. The process felt oddly familiar, as if she'd done it often at some point in her life. The sword belt was, predictably, far too wide for her, but she made do with the last hole punched into the leather. The weight was… comforting.

Griff flew into the Den and Nyx descended behind him. At first, she worried about keeping hold of Gleipnir, but as she descended it was obvious that the chain lengthened to make the process move smoothly, for Drahl followed her down without her ever feeling a tug on the chain.

She found the light switch with ease this time, illuminating the four-by-four of space at the bottom of the ladder that Nyx was beginning to think of as the "landing bay." She pressed her ring to the door opposite the ladder and it swung open obligingly.

Inside, Nyx paused a moment before hitting the next light switch, taking in the glowing neon shapes and swirls in the darkness. The room filled her with a sense of euphoria. Every item here felt hidden, secret, and they called to Nyx. Secrets and mysteries had always held sway over her, and if given half an opportunity she suspected she could stay down here for days on end, learning each item's past.

"Nyx?" Morgen's voice. Soft. "Some things are even more intriguing with the lights on." The mischievous tinge to his voice was still present, yes, but why did he sound as if he understood precisely how this room made her feel?

Nyx hit the light switch. "Griff, is there a suitable chair in here that will neither harm Mr. Drahl nor help him escape?"

"The silver one in the corner should do nicely."

The chair in question managed to be both ornate and harsh, cold silver metal gleaming around cruel filigreed designs, not a speck of dust on it despite the many years it must have waited down here.

Without knowing quite why, Nyx held out her hand. Heat flared through the Guardian tattoo and the chair slid across the room, its back coming to rest against her outstretched palm.

Morgen, eyebrows raised, whistled. "Is that a Guardian thing or a *you* thing?"

Nyx ignored him. She was supposed to ignore prisoners when they asked her things, right? She was quite certain that was somewhere in Prisoner Law 101.

She would like to say she deposited Morgen in the chair, but he settled into it of his own accord, watching with interest as silver manacles sprang from the chair legs, trapping his ankles. Nyx wound Gleipnir around the bottom rung as well, pleased when the chain adhered itself to the metal, pulling tight so Drahl's bound hands were pulled down between his legs with only a centimeter or so of mobility.

"Is this really necessary, little Guardian?"

"I generally find the people who ask that are the ones waiting to escape at the first opportunity."

"Tied a lot of men up, have you?"

"No. I've read a lot of books."

"About tying men up?"

"What? No, that's not what I—" Nyx broke off. *He's stalling.* "You said you were looking for me. Why?"

Morgen sighed. "Do we have to play this game?"

"What game?"

"The one where you pretend you aren't a Hidden and I pretend I don't know?"

"Holy stars," Evra breathed.

"I have to admit," Morgen continued, "I'm a little disappointed. I thought Hidden were supposed to have a practically hypnotizing effect on people but I don't feel the slightest inclination to do whatever you tell me to." He shrugged. "Maybe it's my heritage."

Nyx finally found her voice. "What is a Hidden and why do you think I am one?"

It was Evra who spoke.

"Many centuries ago, at the dawn of the ley line construction, five families carried the talent for Hiding. Anything they wished to keep secret would be hidden from both physical and magical search. To my knowledge, nothing a Hidden has chosen to Hide has ever been found. They were the keepers of our greatest and most dangerous artifacts."

Nyx managed to make her throat work. "Were?"

"The Kumir have hunted the families into near extinction. Nyx, I was skeptical about your missing memories but this—this could explain things."

"Missing memories?" Morgen asked.

Nyx ignored him. "How?"

"We don't really know the limits of what a Hidden can Hide."

The subtext of what Evra was saying fell into place, and Nyx didn't like what it said. "You think my own *parents* did this to me?"

"Will someone please explain to the dashing fugitive in the room what the hell you're talking about?"

Figuring he wouldn't shut up until she did, Nyx explained.

"So, if I don't know anything about me, how do you?"

Morgen shifted uncomfortably. "I don't, really. I knew about your mother."

"Tell me." Nyx tried to temper the excitement coursing through her at the possibility of finally having answers.

"I don't know much, Nyx. Her name was Elena Fortuna. As far as I know, she was the last living Hidden. She disappeared twenty-six years ago. I, uh, guess you came along sometime after."

Not long after, given that timeline. *Elena.* She rolled the name over in her head, willing it to unlock something inside her, but it didn't.

"And yet," Nyx said slowly, "you said you came here looking for me. Not my mother."

"Right." If she'd thought Morgen looked uncomfortable earlier, he looked twice-so now. "The thing is, this isn't exactly what I was led to expect."

"Led to expect?" Nyx echoed.

Morgen squirmed. "You remember the whole suspicion of being complicit in treason thing? Well, I wasn't the only person accused, and there might have been an artifact of some importance involved. An artifact my buddy and I needed Hidden until we could, ah, retrieve it at the opportune moment and resolve this ridiculous treason accusation.

"He came here looking for your mother. He sent word he'd found you instead but I thought... well, I thought you *knew*."

A curious numbness spread through Nyx's veins.

"You have the wrong woman." Even as she said it, she knew it wasn't true. "I didn't know about any of this. I couldn't have Hidden anything."

The pendant, pulsing against her chest, said otherwise.

"You could, actually." Morgen looked faintly sick. "At its most basic level, all your ability requires is a promise. If you promised to keep something hidden, your ability would make it so. Even if you didn't know what you were promising."

He was wrong. He had to be wrong. Only it made too much sense. One person, *one*, in her entire remembered life had been able to see her before she came to the Between. She bit her tongue to hold back the prickling sensation behind her eyes, and remembered even though she didn't want to.

That night, lying tangled in bed, sweat-soaked and infinitely happy. He pulled something over his neck, slipped it over hers, settling the pendant against her chest.

"Promise me you'll keep it safe. It'll be a secret. Our secret."

Her fingers touching the entangled metal loops of the pendant, trembling, some innate instinct whispering that promises were always dangerous. "I don't know, I—"

"Promise you'll keep it hidden? Please?" His lips meeting hers. "I love you."

"I promise. Of course I'll keep it safe."

Waking up the next morning, every morning after, alone.

She hadn't misremembered the tattoo on his wrist, hadn't imagined it looked like Evra's translator spell. It had *been* a translator spell.

Her head spun and she couldn't get enough oxygen, her vision blacking at the edges like it used to whenever she tried too hard to think about her past. The room was too small, the walls closing in on her, and if she didn't get out *right now* she was going to suffocate.

"Where are you going?"

Nyx turned at Evra's voice, knew she must look half-wild. Evra. Evra was her assistant. She definitely needed assistance.

"Can you guard him?" She forced her rapid thoughts to slow down long enough to think. If she took Griff and locked the Den, Morgen couldn't escape. Evra would make sure he didn't get into anything dangerous. "Don't notify the Council yet. Griff, come with me. I'll be back. I just need to—"

She didn't know what she needed to. She fled. Morgen called after her but Evra's cold voice cut him off.

"Let her go."

13

Water pelted off Nyx's back, scalding hot. Her skin had long ago turned red as she sat on the shower's black tile floor, hunched over her knees, staring at the loops and whorls of the pendant held out in front of her.

How often had she thought it pretty? How often had she thought that if she had nothing else, at least she had this one piece of him, something that had belonged to him? Something he had cared enough to leave with her.

I promised to keep this, and then he was gone. She had wondered what happened to him so often over the years it had become a daily ritual. Make the coffee in the morning, wonder where Kaden was. Do the laundry, wonder if Kaden ever thought about her. Wash the dishes, make up some lame story that could explain why he'd just disappeared. Go to bed, imagine she'd wake up and he'd be there, explaining everything.

The pendant sent a little flare of warmth against her palm and Nyx trembled. She hadn't even asked what it was, hadn't wanted to ask, hadn't want to hear whatever story Morgen had to tell her. She wanted to go back twelve hours to when she'd woken up this morning feeling like something in her life was finally going right because she deserved it. Because she'd earned it. Not because of a power in her blood or a man it turned out she hadn't known at all.

She didn't *want* to hear the rest of Morgen's story.

But she needed to.

Nyx slid into clean jeans and a fresh shirt as a rustle of feathers announced Griff's entrance into her room. He landed on the bed, folding his wings and tilting his head to the side, looking up at her.

"Are you all right?"

Nyx smoothed a wrinkle out of her shirt, tucking the pendant beneath it as she did.

"I don't know." She walked to the sliding glass doors that let out onto a small wooden balcony, twitching aside the curtain to look out at the forest beyond. The storm had cleared, and she wished she could be as placid as the sky now was.

"Did you know?" she finally asked. "About what he says I am? About my mother?"

"Nyx...no. I would not have kept something like that from you."

"So it's not...it's not why I was chosen as the Guardian?"

"Is that what you're worried about? That you were chosen because of what you are?"

She shrugged. "Maybe a little."

"It is not the case. I told you part of it earlier when I said you were chosen as Guardian because you had no attachments in your old life. But that isn't all of it.

"The Station runs a constant spell that seeks potential Guardians. It searches for people with few attachments, but also for those with a disposition towards open-mindedness and fairness. When the time is right for the Guardian to change, the spell chooses the best of the potentials it has found and draws them to the Station.

"You were not the only person who could have become this Station's new Guardian. You were the Guardian the Station chose, and that is not because of what you are—it is because of *who* you are."

Nyx drummed her fingers against the glass, watching as a squirrel scurried up a pine tree, a weight lifting from her chest she hadn't realized she carried.

The Station was still hers. She could name, now, the fear she'd been carrying. The fear that what Morgen had said, what he *would* say, could take the Station from her. That she could be found unfit to be its Guardian.

It's mine. The truth echoed through her blood, in her bones. *It's mine, and no one is taking it from me.*

She watched as the squirrel disappeared too high into the tree to follow. "Griff?"

"Yes?"

"Thank you."

She turned to smile at him, her hand resting on the sliding glass door, and the explosion hit. A flare of power surged from the door to her hand, lifting her off her feet and tossing her across the room.

Her back hit the bed, the sharp corner of the bedpost bruising skin and muscle. Her arm twinged and twitched, from her palm all the way up to her elbow, like the time she'd accidentally grabbed an electric horse fence with her bare hand.

The Guardian tattoo flared angrily, power sweeping up her arm, pulsing behind her chest, thump-thumping like a second heart. Wind swept through the room, no mere draft or product of an open window.

She glanced back to the glass doors and *saw* the power arcing along the walls of the building, semi-solid sheets of blue light wrapping around the Station like a tight cellophane cover.

Griff alighted on the ground next to her. "Are you hurt?"

Nyx pushed herself to a sitting position, grateful to find nothing was broken. "Just my pride. What was that?"

"The Station is locking down. It will allow no one to enter or leave via either physical doors or the ley line."

"Why?"

A troubled shadow passed across Griff's face. "This response can only be triggered by someone removing an item from the Den."

"*Morgen.*"

Nyx gained her feet and ran for the Den's hatch, Griff following in her wake. "I thought they couldn't leave."

"They should not be able to. I am as much at a loss as you are."

How could he have escaped Gleipnir, the chair, and *Evra, and still gotten out of the Den?*

Nyx opened the Den's hatch and clambered down the ladder, Griff soaring ahead of her. She stumbled through the landing bay only to find that the scene that greeted her in the Den made little sense.

Morgen sat in the silver chair, Gleipnir wrapped firmly around his wrists, a grim look on his face. Evra was gone.

Nyx had the distinct sense something was missing from the room—*obviously* something was missing, since the Station was locked down—but what? She turned in a circle, recalling the things she had seen as they'd entered the room that morning.

There, by the door. A spinning blue orb, the one Evra had stared at so, was gone.

She was an idiot. Of course it was Evra. Evra, who had suggested they put Morgen in the Den in the first place. Evra, who had told Morgen to let Nyx leave. Evra, who had no real reason to become a Guardian's assistant, only Nyx hadn't questioned it enough because she'd been too busy trying to get a handle on everything that was happening to her.

"Where is she?"

Morgen shook his head. "That woman is crazy. I mean, she's wicked deadly and I may be in love with her and all, but she's *insane.*"

"Where is she?"

Morgen sighed. "I am supposed to tell you she is sorry for

what she is doing, but she has to do it for her sister's sake, and she'll be back. Mind you, I'm only serving as verbal messenger because she kissed me as payment to pass on the message, and holy *stars*, I will never want another woman as long as I live."

"*Morgen*. Where. Is. She?" The room itself took on Nyx's mood, darkening and sending echoes of her question reverberating off the walls.

Morgen's eyes widened. "You're a bit scary, you know that? Your girl took yon blue orb from over there, which just so happens to be the Opener of Doors, and went to the bloody Arkadian prison world."

Nyx blinked. "Griff?"

Griff fluttered down to land on a table beside her. "Arkadia is a small world—its land area is roughly twice the size of the Phoenix Metropolitan area. Atmospheric magic made the planet habitable, but it is not a place anyone would *desire* to live.

"Weather conditions are unpredictable on Arkadia, swinging from blistering heat to killing cold in areas only a few miles apart. Since it was deemed undesirable for general habitation, the All Council turned it into a prison planet. Only the most dangerous criminals are sentenced to Arkadia, prisoners the All Council has no intention of ever pardoning.

"The ley line into Arkadia feeds into an autonomous Station not operated by a Guardian. It only admits entrance to those the All Council implants with an opener spell, and that spell only works once. The Station allows no exit to anyone.

"In over five centuries of operation, no one has ever escaped Arkadia."

Nyx frowned, looking at the space where, an hour ago, the blue orb had rested. "And this Opener of Doors. That would get Evra into Arkadia without this All Council spell?"

"Theoretically, it should." Griff removed his glasses, polishing the lenses against his feathers. "More importantly, it will allow her to leave."

"Why would Evra want access to a prison world?"

"Excellent question." Morgen leaned back in the chair as far as Gleipnir would allow, his head tipped back. "I've no idea."

"You said she mentioned a sister?"

Morgen nodded. "She grabbed the orb and right before she patched into the ley line over there—"

"She did *what*?"

"How did you think she got out of here?"

"But the Station's locked down." She looked to Griff.

"Ah. It is. But the magic of the ley lines cannot be turned off, so to speak. Locking down the Station locks down access to the portal in the Arrival Room."

Nyx walked across the room, found the molten, golden river that ran the length of the room beneath its ornate, wrought-iron grate. A section of the grate had been carved and pulled out, leaving the river exposed. Accessible.

Its siren hum called to Nyx and begged her to touch it, to join it.

Nyx pressed the heels of her palms against her eyes.

"And you didn't think to mention this was possible?" Even as she said it, she knew the accusation was unfair. Neither of them had had any reason to think *Evra* would want to leave, and the triple protection of chair, Gleipnir, and Evra had made Morgen extremely low risk as well. Not to mention that he'd turned *himself* in.

"I'm sorry, Nyx. It didn't occur to me. Yes, the ley line can be accessed here, but entering the lines from an untried origin point is dangerous bordering on suicidal."

Okay, sort through the problem, she ordered herself. "You said she mentioned something about her sister? Griff, is there any way to search for Evra's sister? News articles? A way to contact her family?"

"I don't think that will be necessary. When Sena was considering hiring her she requested a full background from the All Council. I have the report in the Archives. Give me a moment." Griff closed his eyes, stretched his talons out as if he were reaching to retrieve a book from a shelf, and pulled a folder from thin air.

Nyx took it from him, frowning. "Evra said she owed Sena a debt, that that's why she'd ended up with this job."

Griff tilted his head sideways. "Evra requested the job. She said she had heard Sena was looking for an assistant and, though she wasn't, Sena was convinced that an assistant wasn't a bad idea. She hired Evra after the background report came through."

Nyx flipped open the report, wondering what such a seemingly unnecessary lie had to do with the most recent turn of events. *It made me trust her more. I believed she didn't want to be here, so I had no reason to wonder what she might* want *here.*

The report listed basic information first—height, weight, race, origin, birthdate, etc. Evra was one year older than Nyx. Her mother had previously worked as an Enforcer for the All Council—that explained the Amazon's staunchness on the subject of Enforcers and All Council loyalties—and her father was, of all things, a farmer. She had two siblings—an older brother, Horace, and a younger sister, Tamrin. The latter would be fifteen next month.

It only took a few pages to find out what had happened.

Ten years ago, Evra's mother had retired from the All Council's employ to found a private security firm. Evra and Horace both worked for their mother. On Evra's last job, she had received permission for Tamrin to come along in a shadow capacity.

The job was supposed to be low risk. Evra and Tamrin were hired as extra muscle on a prisoner transport to Arkadia. It should have been a simple drop and deliver. But the prisoner had been important enough to the right people, and those people attempted to hijack his transport right at the Arkadia Station's gates.

Fighting on a ley line landing sounded like utter chaos to Nyx, and all but four people involved had died. In the confusion, the prisoner's spell overwhelmed him and he was dragged through to Arkadia's Station. As he had slipped through the gates, he had grabbed Tamrin and pulled her through with him.

She relayed the information to Griff. She probably shouldn't be so free with information around Morgen, but it wasn't like he was going anywhere.

"I don't understand," Nyx said. "Why wouldn't Evra just ask the All Council to open Arkadia's Station to get Tamrin out?"

"I'm sure she did," Morgen answered. "I'm equally sure they refused."

"But Tamrin's *fifteen*. Why wouldn't the All Council—I don't know, send a team to retrieve her, or something?"

Morgen's mouth twisted bitterly. "Because if they let a team *in*, they would have to give them a way to get back *out*. And the chances of that way out ending up in the hands of free-roaming criminals on a planet full of free-roaming criminals would have been a risk they considered too high."

"She's a *child*."

"I know."

Nyx paced the floor, willing her boots to dig rivets into the stone tile, as if the physical manifestation of her anger would solve anything. "Without the Opener of Doors, we can't follow her? There's nothing we can do?"

She might be pissed at Evra, but she could understand why she'd done what she had. There was also the pesky fact that if Nyx didn't get the Opener of Doors back, her Station was potentially never unlocking itself. She didn't know what the overarching effects of that might be, but she was pretty sure it would get her Guardianship revoked.

"There might," Morgen said, slowly, "be another way."

Nyx halted and spun. Morgen's eyes met hers, all trace of mischief gone.

"What way?"

"You need to hear the rest of my story, first. You know I used to be an Enforcer, right?"

Nyx nodded.

"Do you know what the job is?"

"All Council's elite soldiers?"

Morgen laughed, a sound that held no joy. "Not a quarter of it, little Guardian, but good enough for this tale. Me and a friend, we joined up together. Thought it'd be great, you know? Adventure, saving the universe, glory and girls and all that. Just like the recruiting propaganda says.

"Anyway, we worked our way up through the ranks together, him and me."

"So what went wrong?"

"He did his job. He reported in early for a shift guarding the Council's Vault and found the Enforcer he was replacing out cold. That's when he saw Alastair, glorified member of the All Council itself, removing an item from the Vault."

"Doesn't the All Council have the authority to remove items from their own vault?"

"Yes, but only if all thirteen members of the Council are present, and the item coming out of that vault is not the bloody Harvester of Worlds."

The pendant gave a brilliant flare of warmth, as if recognizing its name. No. No, no, no.

"*Harvester of Worlds*?" she squeaked. "Please tell me that name does not literally correspond to what the item does."

"I…"

"Morgen?"

"I don't really know."

"How can you not know?"

"Look, the Harvester was supposed to be a myth, okay?"

"Then what makes you think I—" She broke off, not wanting to admit to Morgen or herself that she thought she had something called the Harvester of Worlds hanging around her neck. "That that's what Alistair was taking from the Vault?"

"Because that's what he called it? My friend triggered the building's alarms spells to shut everything down and called every Enforcer in the vicinity to his location. When Alistair saw his predicament he 'relinquished' the stolen item, so when the backup arrived my buddy was holding it and Alastair was shouting his fool head off about how the Vault had been broken into and the Harvester of Worlds had been taken.

"See, there's no way to verify who triggered the building's alarm spells. Alastair said he ordered the lockdown because an Enforcer was attempting to steal from the Vault. No one's going to believe an Enforcer over a bloody Councilor."

"So what did your friend do?"

"The only thing he could. He ran. Alastair didn't think he'd get twenty feet, much less escape. It's why he hadn't worried about handing over the Harvester. But my friend did.

"After he escaped, the Council put every Enforcer in the galaxy on his trail so he came here—Earth, where it was rumored the last Hidden family came to escape the Kumir.

"He didn't know what Alastair wanted with the Harvester, but he figured it was only a matter of time before he was captured. When that time came, he needed the Harvester to be safe. Hidden."

Nyx crossed her arms, leaning forward. "And what makes you so sure this story's the true one? How do you know your friend *didn't* steal the Harvester?"

Morgen ground his teeth. "Because *I'm* the Enforcer Alastair knocked out to get into the Vault."

"Then why didn't you say something? Clear your friend's name."

"I tried. But accusing a Councilor of treason is unheard of. I had no proof and it made matters worse that Kaden was my friend."

Nyx's heart sped up, beating fast in her throat. That name…

"Not only did the Council *not* believe me," Morgen went on, "they accused me of collusion and banned me from the force."

"How long ago was this?"

"Six years. He came straight here and I didn't hear from him for a while, and then it was just that he'd found you instead of your mother. He hid from the All Council for another two years after that. Probably could have done it longer, only they sent out an ultimatum over the Enforcer wave-lines to every planet: he could turn himself in and clear my name, or they would send me to Arkadia in his place.

"He's a good friend. He turned himself in."

"How do I—" Nyx's voice caught. She swallowed, tried again. "How do I know any of this is true?"

"Pocket inside my shirt. Left side. There's a picture."

Nyx slipped off the table, found the pocket and pulled out a picture of herself. She and Kaden had taken it down by Tempe Town Lake on the fourth of July, but no one else would know that. Half the picture was missing. All you could see of Kaden was his arm around her shoulders.

"He sent that to me right before he turned himself in. Said he'd gotten wind a Guardian shift was happening in a few years and I could slip through the lines, then. Find you. Try to clear our names."

Nyx ran her thumb across the picture. She was smiling like an idiot in it, so deliriously happy to have not been alone.

"Look, Nyx, it's not like Kaden and I had a lot of correspondence when he was here. I thought—I was under the impression you knew what you were getting into when you Hid the Harvester."

"It doesn't matter." It mattered. It mattered more than she cared to contemplate. It mattered to the level of every happy memory she possessed being a lie. She'd *told* Kaden she couldn't remember anything. She'd probably cried on his fucking shoulder about it and he'd let her, and the whole time he could have shown her *this*: Earth Between. He could have told her who she was, who her mother was.

He could have let her make a choice about whether to help him or not. But that would presuppose that he'd cared about her at all. She'd been a means to an end, nothing more, and when that end had been achieved, he'd disappeared.

"It doesn't matter," she repeated. "But I'm not giving you the Harvester." Stars knew she didn't *want* to hang on to something with a name like that, but every fiber of her being revolted at the idea of letting it go. The mere thought of doing so viscerally reminded her that she had promised to keep it.

"That's fine."

It was? "You came all the way here for the Harvester and it's fine that I won't give it to you?"

"Ah, well, the thing about that is, I don't really have Kaden's naïve beliefs that our names are clearable, so to speak."

Nyx groaned. "You came here for the Opener of Doors, the same as Evra. You only came here to go after *him*."

"Is that such a terrible thing?"

"No." Except, of course, where it made her the party being used. Again.

"So, you're fine with it if I go, then?"

Nyx stared at him. "Go where?"

"To Arkadia? Rescue my friend? Aid an extraordinarily hot Amazon?"

"Did I miss the part where there is a second Opener of Doors?"

"Ah, about that. See, the All Council doesn't bluff. When they were threatening to send me to Arkadia they actually implanted me with the opening spell. They didn't bother removing it when Kaden turned himself in because they grounded me from travel. See, the spell acts like a beacon, pulling me toward Arkadia whenever I'm on the lines. Makes riding them anywhere else *very* difficult.

"So I can get to Arkadia. I just can't leave unless I find Evra."

It took Nyx less than a second to make up her mind. "All right. Let's go."

"You believe me, then? That we're innocent?"

She liked Morgen. If she had to go with her gut, she'd say that, no, he hadn't committed treason. Admittedly, her gut seemed to be a terrible judge of character. But whether he was innocent or not, she didn't think he meant her any harm, and she was tired of things happening to her. Her memories, Kaden, the Harvester—even the Station—were things she'd had no control over.

It was time to take control.

"I didn't say that. I said we were going."

Morgen stilled. "We? No. No, no, no. *I* am going. Guardians aren't supposed to travel the lines and I am not taking an untrained Earthling to a prison world."

"Griff, what happens when a Guardian travels the ley lines?"

"I…I am afraid I do not know, Nyx. But I would accept the risk, to bring Evra and her sister back."

Nyx met Morgen's eyes. "We're going."

Morgen held her gaze. When he spoke, his voice was almost a full octave lower than usual. "No, I am going. You will let me out of this chair and bid me a fair journey."

Morgen's words wrapped around Nyx, a web of spun steel crushing in on her will, her thinking growing muddled. It made sense to let him go, didn't it? He knew Kaden, after all, and had experience traveling, and—

No. I have to find Evra. I have to get answers from Kaden. Morgen's not going anywhere without me. The spider's web of Morgen's words ripped, the influence of them spilling off her like rainwater from oiled leather.

She narrowed her eyes in a withering glare. "What was that?"

Griff alighted on Nyx's shoulder, staring at Morgen with interest. "He's half-Siren. He attempted to Influence you."

"Morgen?"

He shrugged, devil-may-care grin in place. "Can't blame a guy for trying."

"I can, actually. Fortunately for you, I still need you. So here's the deal. *We* are going. You can either take me with you or you can rot in this damn chair. Try to Influence me again, and I'll break your nose."

Morgen held out his hands, jangling Gleipnir. "The more the merrier?"

Nyx undid Gleipnir, frowning as she pocketed the chain. "Why do you talk like you're from Earth? Evra talks all stiff and foreign. Do you have a better translator spell or something?"

Kaden's speech patterns, too, had been different. She'd always just assumed he'd been born in another country, that English wasn't his first language. They'd never talked about it. Not that she hadn't wanted to, but the look on his face whenever she'd asked too much about his past…she hadn't wanted to ruin what they had.

They hadn't *had* anything.

"I took a lot of foreign language immersion courses. Other planets always have the best slang."

"And you chose English because?"

"Earth Between's Station is geographically located parallel to an English-speaking country?" The chair's silver manacles slipped loose, and Morgen stood, stretching. "Now, if we're going to Arkadia, the return of my sword might be in order."

Nyx hesitated.

"Little Guardian, if you can't trust me with a weapon, you definitely should not be going with me where we're going."

"Fine." She unbuckled his sword and gave it back to him.

"Griff, everything in here is dangerous, right?"

"Highly."

"Think you could point out what might be useful on a prison world?"

Morgen made a strangled, choking noise, his mouth agape.

Nyx rounded on him, hands on her hips. "What? The Opener has already been taken, what's the Station going to do? Lock itself down *again*?"

Morgen's jaw snapped shut. "You make a good point."

Griff flew down, settling on Nyx's shoulder. "I can suggest a few things. Just make sure you make it back with all of them. Otherwise, the Station won't unlock."

Nyx froze. "You aren't coming with us?"

Griff shook his head. "I am a part of the Station, remember? I cannot leave the grounds."

A lump formed in Nyx's throat but she worked around it. "Tell me what I should take, then."

Fifteen minutes later, Nyx was ready. She had a pack that never ran out of food or water, which was great, except "food" apparently only meant bread and cheese.

"It's like I'm in a Tolkien novel," she muttered.

"What?"

"Never mind." She had an assortment of other items as well, all of which came with individual warnings from Griff. Veritas: a knife which, if you drew the blood of a person onto its blade and asked said person a question, would indicate whether they were telling the truth. A bo staff made of a light metal that would return to its wielder's hand if knocked away in battle.

The knife had the unfortunate side effect of wanting to be fed, frequently, and might bite the hand that wielded it if that need was not accommodated. The bo staff could become permanently melded to its wielder's hand if used for too long. But it collapsed down to a mere foot in length when not in use and hung from a loop on her belt for easy carry, which was too neat to pass up.

How it shortened itself, she didn't know. It didn't have segmented parts, like a telescoping rod, which would have ruined its integrity as a weapon, and it seemed to weigh the same amount whether in its short or long form. The staff responded to its wielder's intent to choose its size, and Nyx kept lengthening and shortening it over and over again, trying to figure out how it worked.

Finally, Morgen took it away from her, collapsed it, and stuck it in her belt loop.

She frowned at him. "But I want to know how it works."

"Magic," he offered.

"That's like asking how nuclear power works and saying 'science,'" she grumbled. "It's technically true but it doesn't tell you anything."

Morgen shrugged. "If we had a week to take it apart and study it, I'd figure out how it works and tell you. But we don't, and also you wouldn't have a bo staff at the end of it."

"Fair enough." She quit messing with the bo staff and,

even though she would prefer not to use one, added a sword to her ensemble as well, albeit a non-magical one she had Griff pull out of the Station's armory.

The last thing Griff slipped into her pack was a long, crooked flute-like instrument. She noted Griff was quick to do so when Morgen wasn't paying attention. The Avatar leapt to her shoulder, speaking quietly into her ear.

"The instrument is a last resort. I advise you not to let Morgen know you have it, unless you find yourself in a situation you can't see your way out of."

"Why? What does it do?"

Griff hesitated. Finally, "It will amplify the Siren half of his abilities, allowing him to use them in ways he otherwise might not be able to. But it is a powerful object, and it has been alone for quite some time. If he takes it up, it may not want to let him go."

"I understand. Last resort only."

"And Nyx? Find Evra fast. The contract she signed here, it will view her leaving as a breach of that agreement. If the fever delusions have not hit her yet, they will soon. She will need you. *Both* of you."

"I'll find her, Griff. Don't worry." Nyx awkwardly gave him a hug, as best she could given his house-cat-sized state. He hesitated, then stretched out a wing, placing it gently around her shoulder.

Nyx settled the pack across her back and walked to the

opening in the grate, the siren call of the ley line humming beneath her feet.

"So, how do we do this?"

Morgen stepped up to the grate, booted feet next to hers. "This? This one should be easy. We jump in, relinquish control, and the opener spell pulls us straight to Arkadia." Morgen held out his hand. "*Your* job is not to let go of my hand. Don't want you getting lost to the chaos pockets."

"Right. Chaos pockets?"

"Don't worry about them. Hold on to me and you won't have an issue."

Her breath ratcheted up, nervous and excited, like the time Kaden had convinced her to go skydiving. Nyx took Morgen's hand. "What's it like?"

He closed his fingers tight around hers. "Like being unmade."

Nyx heard the wonder in his voice and thought maybe it wasn't *like* being unmade, maybe it *was* being unmade. Realizing that she thought she knew, in her bones, why Guardians weren't supposed to travel the lines.

She and Griff and the Station, they were integrated, bound. If she came undone, even for a brief span, what happened to them?

She opened her mouth to tell Morgen. To tell Griff.

Too late.

Morgen jumped into the molten river, pulling her with him, their hands locked tight. All thought fled her, all sense of time, of space, of *being*. Everything that *was* her, was the world, ceased to matter, and Nyx knew what it was like to be unmade.

It was euphoria.

14

Nyx existed in a rush of swirls and colors, present and yet somehow body-less. She had the sense of traveling thousands of miles, of moving at a speed both suicidal and incomprehensible. At the same time, she felt suspended, unmoving, floating in the essence of the universe.

Was that what the ley lines *were*? She couldn't see the line itself anymore, not like when it had been a molten river in the Den. Instead, the river enveloped her, golden mist kissing her face, cooler and sweeter than soft rain on a warm summer evening.

At the edges of the mist, pockets of color swirled and danced, hypnotic. Enticing. An energy emanated from them, a magnetism beckoning her to come, to join, to merge.

Nyx veered toward them, the desire to join them the only thing necessary to move in a place where she had nothing physical to push off of to change her course. The closer she came the faster the colors swirled, pulsing in response to her nearness. She broke out in a sweat despite the cool golden mist, her heart beating frantically as she reached out.

She found herself pulled up short of her goal, something—a hand on hers?—restraining her. Nyx thought it wrong she even *had* a hand. A body, any form at all, felt too constraining. But if she was going to free herself, to untangle her fingers from whatever held them, she needed to reconnect with her physical form.

At first it was nearly impossible, like trying to dexterously operate a limb that had fallen asleep. Gradually, she slipped back into herself, becoming aware once more of eyes and arms and legs and, *there*, fingers. She wiggled those fingers, struggling against the grip that entangled them until they were finally, gloriously, free.

She floated, untethered, drifting toward the pocket of colors, but her newfound reconnection with her body reconnected her with something else as well—her memories—and a specific memory, a warning, surfaced.

Your job is to not let go of my hand.

A jolt of adrenaline tripped her heart and Nyx fumbled for Morgen's hand, but he was too far, and slipping farther away every second.

The pulsing pockets of color ahead were no longer where she wanted to go, but they pulled at her relentlessly, reeling her toward them.

Panic set in and she flailed wildly. It made no difference. She hung suspended in a formless environment, nothing to touch, to grasp, to give her traction. Helpless, the pocket pulled her forward, her face brushing against the edges of swirling color. It felt rough but fuzzy against her cheek, a texture like dried moss, and it smelled of dank and mildew.

Chaos pockets, Morgen had called them.

I'll never find Evra, never help her find her sister. I'll never see Kaden again, for whatever closure that's worth.

She would never find out if being a Guardian was the role she would finally fit into, as she had begun to hope it was.

And Griff. Poor Griff. What would become of him if she fell into the chaos and never came out? If she remained here forever, perpetually undone?

Would he die? Or would a new Guardian simply take her

place, smoothing everything over? She couldn't know for certain, but she couldn't take the chance. Whatever Griff's story was, she hadn't had the chance to learn half of it, and he deserved more.

Maybe it was the bond—she'd known Griff all of two days—or maybe it was how comfortable she was around him, but Griff was *family*. And in the new world she inhabited, you didn't let family down because you were weak and fell into a chaos pocket.

Think, Nyx, if you can't push away from it physically, what can you do?

Nyx closed her eyes as the rough fuzz scraped harshly against her cheek, tiny needles pricking into her skin. She thought of how she'd pulled the chair across the room in the Den, simply by wanting it to move.

Now, more than anything, she wanted to move away from the chaos pocket. Back to Morgen. She put every ounce of will into that desire until it coalesced, bursting out of her, a force like a rocket knocking her backward through the ley mist.

Her back slammed into something solid. An arm wrapped around her in a bruising, viselike grip, and Nyx was grateful for the pain, grateful that she hadn't, yet, screwed everything up.

She settled into Morgen's grip, comfortable to remain there if it meant the danger of the chaos pockets was beyond her. Beautiful as the golden ley mist was, Nyx choked on relief when it disappeared, when her feet landed on solid ground and she stumbled out of Morgen's arms.

Relief gave way to confusion. She *felt* solid ground beneath her feet but she couldn't see it. All around her hung darkness, a complete absence of light. Her own body and Morgen's were all she could see. They glowed as if lit from within by halogen bulbs, the only brightness in an infinite span of darkness.

"Is this the Station?" Nyx's voice echoed, faded, disappeared.

"No. The Station's through that door."

Nyx turned in a complete circle, searching. "What door?"

"That one."

Nyx looked where he pointed, saw nothing. Morgen frowned.

"Take my hand."

Nyx did. As her skin brushed his, a door blossomed in her vision, stark and white, glowing as their bodies glowed in this space.

She squeezed his hand tight, asked the question she already knew the answer to, one she should have considered more before diving headfirst into outer space. "If we go through and we don't find Evra…there's no coming back, is there?"

"No."

Nyx took a deep breath. She'd already known that. If she'd jumped headfirst without thinking, that was her own damn fault. "Then let's find her fast."

She stepped forward and was pulled back almost immediately by Morgen's unmoving mass and the iron grip he held her hand in.

"And Kaden," he said. "We don't leave without Kaden."

Nyx choked on a laugh before it escaped her. *Does he think I could leave without him? Without knowing?*

Yet Morgen seemed to know nothing of her relationship with Kaden so it wasn't surprising, she supposed, that he would think she could leave him on Arkadia.

"We'll find him, Morgen. That much I promise you. But we find Evra first. Kaden's been here for years. Evra just arrived and the fever delusions are weakening her. She needs us first. Deal?"

"Deal."

She turned to him for the obligatory deal-confirming handshake. As she did, he caught sight of her right cheek. His eyes widened, free hand darting out to grab her chin, turning her face so he could see it more clearly.

"Holy stars, did you *touch* a chaos pocket?"

"I—I brushed one." She shivered, remembering the fuzzy prickling of her cheek against the mass. "Why? What's wrong?"

Morgen lifted Nyx's free hand to her own cheek. Her finger-tips brushed across her skin, passing over rough prickles, tiny thorns sticking up from her skin. They felt like stone rather than wood, and they arced in an odd spiraling pattern from her cheekbone down to her jawline.

They didn't hurt, but she had to fight against the fear-soaked adrenaline surging through her at the feel of something foreign in her body.

"Get them out."

"Nyx, I've never seen this before. I don't know what they are, don't know what will happen."

"I don't care, just get them out."

"Nyx—"

"Get. Them. *Out.*"

"I'll try." He pinched one of the small thorns between his thumb and forefinger—they stuck up bare millimeters from her skin and it took him a moment to get a good grip. When he did, he braced his free hand against her shoulder and *pulled*.

Nyx screamed.

Pain like battery acid burned through each neuron in her brain as they fired. She clutched her hands to her skull, curling into a ball and rocking as the fire raged inside her, from her skull down to her neck, her back, through the rest of her body until it finally, blessedly, burned out.

Trembling, she lifted her hands from her head. She felt a throbbing in her lips, brushed her fingers against the source. Her fingers came away wet with blood—she'd bitten clean through. Gingerly, she ran her fingers across the tiny thorns, found the space at the top where one was missing. The skin was smooth, whole.

Shuddering, she turned to Morgen. "Maybe—" Her voice caught. She cleared her throat. "Maybe we'll wait on the rest."

Morgen leveled her with a look. "Nyx, I have never heard anyone scream like that." His face told her just how many screams he *had* heard. "I am never doing that to you again.

Here." He thrust out his hand, the black thorn nestled in his palm.

Nyx shook her head. "I don't want it."

"Nyx, it feels *alive*. I don't think you should leave it here and I am *not* keeping it."

Nyx stared at the thorn a long moment before holding out her hand. Morgen tumbled the thorn into her palm. It hit her skin, warm, almost fever-hot, and pulsing. Her eyes widened and she sucked in a breath.

"See what I mean?"

It felt like part of *her*. "What are they?"

Morgen looked at her sideways. "No one has ever come that close to a chaos pocket and come back. I have no idea what it is. Nothing good, that's for sure."

Nyx swallowed and avoided considering what it meant to have particles of a mass with "chaos" in the title embedded in her skin. Carefully, she slipped the thorn into her pocket. "We'll worry about the rest of this later." She took Morgen's hand and the glowing door re-appeared.

Nyx tugged him forward. Two steps closer, three steps, and the glowing door swung open on silent hinges, the darkness beyond it a gravitational force that lifted them off their feet.

Nyx swallowed a scream, airborne, limbs and hair flying, and held onto Morgen's hand like it was her lifeline.

Darkness swallowed them whole.

15

Arkadia's Station pulsed around them, dark and weary. It pushed them towards the exit, a solitary door in the deep not unlike the one they had entered through moments ago.

The Station's power hummed in Nyx's bones, familiar and yet foreign. She felt the same power that resided in her own Station, only here it felt different. Raw, angry, exhausted. Hopeless. Tears welled behind her eyes but did not fall. Her heart broke for reasons unknown, tiny pieces chipping off and shattering.

As Morgen's hand reached for the door, Nyx caught sight of a pair of anguished yellow eyes. A pitiful, wasted creature huddled in the corner, visible only by the light of the door. It saw her looking and let out a whine, like and yet unlike a dog. Trembling with the effort, it stretched a paw—claw? Hand? She couldn't tell—for her.

Nyx moved toward it involuntarily, its pain calling out to her. No creature should live in darkness.

Then the door opened, pulling her through behind Morgen, and the sad-eyed creature slipped away. *Avatar*, Nyx thought. *Avatar with no Guardian. Alone. Helpless.*

Griff, I'm so sorry.

They passed fully through the door and the Station spit them out onto hard-packed dirt, harsh sun beating down from overhead. Fifteen sets of leering eyes greeted them, belonging to various unkempt and volatile looking individuals, several of races Nyx did not recognize, and every one of them armed with weapons ranging from clubs to shoddily made swords.

That was when Nyx realized what bored, enterprising individuals did on a prison planet. They waited for new arrivals.

Nyx let go of Morgen's hand, afraid someone in their welcoming party would notice and view it as a weakness, an attachment to exploit.

A tall, lean woman stepped forward, tattoos shifting along corded muscles. Her hair was a short-cropped affair, rust-colored like the little down feathers that grew interspersed between her hair follicles. She was one of the few in the party to have a sword. This, and the fact she was cleaner and better fed than her cohorts, bespoke her authority of the group.

She swaggered forward, right hand on her sword, a knowing sneer on her beak-like lips. "Well, we-ell, what do we have here? Two fine and well-fed looking new arrivals. Don't they just look *edible*?" She looked over her shoulder at her gang, who laughed and jeered in an all-too-rehearsed manner.

Nyx remained perfectly still and silent, because that was what Morgen did. Even when the woman stepped into Nyx's space, tilting Nyx's chin up and breathing rancid breath right into her face, she didn't move.

Nyx might be feigning calm but her heartbeat wasn't, and as if in response she felt a sharp sting from the thorns in her cheek, there and then gone. The stinging from the thorns was answered by a pulse of heat against her chest, and it took Nyx a moment to identify the source of that heat: the Harvester.

The thorns stung again, answered by a second pulse from the Harvester, almost as if…almost as if the two were *talking* to each other. The conversation kept up for fifteen seconds or so and then the thorns fell silent, refusing to answer the pulses from the Harvester until, eventually, the pulses tapered off.

She had the distinct impression that the thorns and the Harvester had decided to ignore each other out of mutual dislike. The anger that flooded Nyx in the wake of the thorns' stings and pulses, however, was something *she* could not ignore.

The woman let go of Nyx's chin. "You look a bit soft to be here, my pretty. What'd you do? Sleep with the wrong noble's spouse?"

Her gang laughed again, and the glances cast over Nyx's body had a feel to them Nyx liked not at all, further spurring the anger in her chest. The small tentacles cascading around one man's hands, so like the sleeves of a peasant top, began to writhe and twitch with excitement, making Nyx's gorge rise.

Nyx took her eyes off the tentacles, brought them back to the woman in front of her. She spoke, surprising herself when her voice rang out calm and authoritative, no trace of the fear within. "I'm looking for three people. Help us locate them, and we will leave you in peace."

The woman stared at her for a long moment. Then she laughed, a high, chirping noise, just like a bird's save for the chills it sent down Nyx's spine.

"Do you hear that, fellows? She and the pretty boy will leave us in peace." The woman stepped closer. "I'll make you a counter-offer. Hand over your weapons and any other items you might be carrying, and we'll consider sending you to work in the mines instead of selling you to the brothels."

Nyx curled her fingers over the sword hilt, a dark restlessness coursing through her veins. The thorns in her cheek flared in response and the restlessness grew, burning up behind her chest.

Morgen stepped forward, hands out in a peace-keeping gesture. "Now fellows, let's not make any rash—"

"You can have our weapons," Nyx interrupted him, calmly, "if you can take them."

Morgen sidled back to her side. "Nyx, what in the stars' names are you doing?"

Nyx shrugged. "Getting in a fight." *Isn't it obvious?* "They were never going to let us go."

"You don't know that. I *am* half Siren, I can—" Morgen took his eyes off the welcoming mob long enough to really *look* at Nyx. His face lost some of its color. "Nyx, this isn't you. Think. You wouldn't normally act like this."

She laughed. "You met me a few hours ago. You don't know anything about what I would normally do."

"Hey." The bird-woman's voice rang out, sharp, and she backed away a few steps. "What's wrong with you, girl? You sick or something?"

"What's she talking about?" Nyx's voice came out clipped and irritated.

"Look at your hand."

Nyx looked. The veins along her arm and hand on her right side stood out in black lines beneath her skin. *What the hell?*

"The chaos thorns, Nyx. I think they're affecting your judgment."

Nyx took a deep breath, staring at the black veins, a moment of clarity sliding through her. *I just challenged a gang of prison inmates to a fight. Morgen's right. I need to calm down.*

"Hey, girl, I asked if you were sick." The bird-woman picked a rock from the dusty ground and hurled it, hitting Nyx on the forehead, drawing a bright well of blood.

Nyx snarled and fury blossomed in her chest. Every fiber in her being begged to pull the sword from her hip. The small logic left in her reminded Nyx of blood gushing over her hands, of the dying light in the Kumir's eyes.

So she let go of the sword hilt and pulled the metal bo-staff from its loop. It extended to full size and she gave an experimental twirl in front of her, grip sure and natural.

Morgen cursed and pulled his own sword free. "I really don't think you should have hit her, lady."

The roar building in Nyx's throat loosed and she charged the bird-woman, staff spinning.

"Oh, what the hell," Morgen muttered. He flipped his sword up with a practiced grace and dove into the rising fray behind Nyx.

16

Nyx kept the staff spinning, dipping and striking when opportunity arose, her muscles singing in sheer pleasure. Black fire thrummed in her veins. Whenever fatigue crept in the fire burned it out, keeping her strong, and she lost track of the number of people her staff put down.

A pot-bellied man who reeked of a month's worth of uncleaned stench charged her, his sword raised in a sloppy over-hand strike. Trained warrior he was not, but he was well over six feet and two hundred pounds, and the sheer force of the blow Nyx blocked should have driven her to her knees.

Instead, the shoddily made sword met Nyx's staff and shattered, leaving the man staring at the broken blade. Nyx swung the staff up in a controlled strike to his head. It hit his skull with a satisfying crack and he went down, though it took three more strikes to make him *stay* down.

A strangled cry, behind her. Nyx pivoted. The bird-woman ran at Nyx, fury written on her haggard face. Around her, the battleground lay littered with unconscious men and women. Only two of the welcoming committee were still mobile, one of them grappling with Morgen, the other one, the bird-woman, charging Nyx. The leader held a sword in her hand and, unlike the man on the ground, she held it like she knew how to use it.

It made little difference. Nyx's grip on the staff never slipped. Chaos shuddered through her veins, lending power to strikes and blocks, her blows numbing the bird-woman's arms. Nyx watched the woman tire, watched her falter. Then Nyx lunged, rapping fingers and wrist with precision strikes from her staff.

The woman's hands, nerveless, dropped the sword. Nyx knocked it out of reach with the low end of the staff; on the return swing, she brought the other end of the staff down low, sweeping the woman's feet from beneath her.

The woman went down hard. Nyx was on her in less than a second, a leg on either side pinning the woman's arms, her bo staff across her throat, slowly cutting off air.

The woman bucked weakly beneath Nyx. Her face turned blue-red and the gasping, choking sounds she made were truly awful. An inner part of Nyx cringed away from those sounds, but black-veined hands continued to hold the staff down on the woman's throat.

"*Nyx.*"

Someone shook her shoulders, tugged futilely at her wrists.

"Nyx, stop."

More tugging, fingers digging into pressure points that *should* have turned her fingers numb, made her drop the staff.

"Aw, *shit*. Please don't kill me."

The slap hit Nyx squarely on her unadorned cheek, connecting with a sharp sting that the chaos inside her liked not at all. The Harvester responded with a tingling that felt like amusement.

Nyx forgot about the woman, rising fluidly to her feet, staff still in hand, rounding on the new threat.

Morgen stood with his hands raised. "Nyx, it's me. Morgen."

Nyx hesitated. Her cheek ached, an answering anger roiling inside her, driving her forward, only… *Morgen*. She *looked* at him, the haze of anger clearing. She remembered laughter, brown eyes flashing as he flirted with Evra. Remembered hands tugging her back from chaos.

"That's right," he said, soothing. "We need to find Evra. And Kaden, remember?"

Evra. Kaden. Evra would be getting sicker by the hour, and Kaden…well, gods only knew where he was if he'd been on *this* planet the last four years.

Nyx shook her head fiercely. The throbbing in her right cheek dissipated, the blackness in her veins receding until her skin once again looked normal.

But it isn't. Normal. What had the chaos thorns done to her?

Worry about it later, she ordered herself. Right now, they needed to get what they'd come for and get off this planet.

Nyx put the bo staff away with some difficulty. It wanted to stay in her hand, and she wanted to let it. She shrank it down and slipped it into its loop, exchanging it for Veritas, pulling the small dagger out of her boot sheath. She walked over to the shuddering woman, who was hunched over on all fours trying to choke down air. When Nyx approached, the woman scuttled away like a crab, shuffling backwards.

Nyx caught her behind the head, dragging her back and pressing Veritas to the woman's throat. Nyx's hand trembled, but it was *her* hand, *her* control, even if the fear in the woman's eyes made Nyx feel inhuman.

She pressed the tip of the dagger down, just enough to draw a couple drops of blood. The woman whimpered. *She's probably done a lot worse to end up here, and worse since to the people who arrived after her,* Nyx reminded herself.

Yes, another part of her answered, *but what you did to her was just as bad.*

"A woman came through this Station not long ago. What do you know?"

"I don't know nothin' about that."

The blood on Veritas's blade turned black.

"You're lying to me." She applied a little more force to the knife, resisting Veritas's urging to press further. Already another trickle of blood eased onto the blade. This trickle Veritas drank down, blood disappearing into metal.

Nyx felt the blade's satisfaction beneath her hand and suppressed a shiver. "No one has died here yet," Nyx said, slipping Morgen a look. "That can change."

Playing along, Morgen stepped up beside Nyx, sword in hand.

The bird-woman gritted her teeth. "Fine. My gang wasn't on watch when the other bitch came through."

"Who was?"

"It doesn't matter. They don't have her. She took 'em all out, wanting to know about some kid that came through months ago."

Nyx watched the blood on Veritas turn from black to a steady blue, indicating truth. "And what did they tell her?"

"I don't know."

Blood ran from blue to black.

"You're lying to me again." Drawing on every cheesy film she'd ever seen involving interrogation, Nyx got up in the woman's face. "I *hate* being lied to."

Veritas bit in deeper, expressing its satisfaction.

The woman squirmed. "Look, these guys, they thought they knew the kid she was asking about. Girl got dragged through a few months ago with Mad-Hand Rogers."

Blue.

"And where is the girl now?"

Silence.

"Where?"

"She got picked up by Warren's Cartel not long after she got here. Word is they sold her to the Lord of the Far Hold."

Lord? Hold? Nyx supposed on a prison planet you had to give yourself airs, since no one else was going to do it for you.

"Sold? For what?"

The woman gave a derisive snort. "What else? Concubine.

Word is he likes 'em young. Not too picky about the gender, either. We don't get much young around here. When we do, they all go straight to him. No one else pays better."

Nyx swallowed the bile burning its way up her throat. "Where is the Far Hold?"

"Half a day that way." The woman jerked her head to Nyx's left.

The landscape was empty as far as Nyx could see, the same hot, desert-like terrain they stood in now.

"It won't do you any good. Newcomers don't get into the Hold. Not walking free, anyway."

Blue.

Morgen stepped forward. "How fortunate we will have a seasoned, respected local to vouch for us, then."

The woman frowned, a wrinkle appearing between her brows. "Yeah? Who?"

Morgen smiled. It would have been comical to watch understanding dawn on the woman's face were it not for the remembrance of where they were and why.

Nyx pulled out Gleipnir, bound the woman's arms behind her, and checked the sun's position in the sky, almost directly overhead. "Come on. If we move now, we can make it before sunset."

The woman's eyes widened, but she kept her lips pressed firmly together. Nyx sheathed the dagger, catching sight of her Guardian tattoo as she did. The outer edges of it were sprinkled with hairline fractures, the ink just a little faded from the rich colors of the tattoo's center. She rubbed her thumb over the outer edge and a pang ran through her chest.

Griff. Had her travel on the ley lines disrupted the bond? And if it had, how long did Griff have?

She let Morgen handle the prisoner watch and trekked off in the direction she'd chosen to dub east. The sooner they found Kaden and Evra, the sooner Nyx could get back to her Avatar.

17

Nyx's first mistake was in equating "half a day" on a foreign planet to the same amount of time half a day constituted on Earth. Her second mistake was in being dressed for winter. The Station was currently around fifty degrees Fahrenheit in the daytime, and significantly colder at night.

Here, the sun beat down upon them like Phoenix in late July, one hundred and twenty degrees of relentless heat that had Nyx peeling off her sweater, grateful she always wore a tank underneath. Fortunately, she didn't tend towards sunburn, though she thought the rays out here might put that tendency to the test.

In six hours the landscape hadn't changed a sliver, hardpacked, mud-brown dirt beneath her boots, stretching on in every direction as far as the eye could see. Large formations of onyx rock were the only features to break the landscape's monotony, not a single bush or tree in sight. Every now and then Nyx caught sight of small, lizard-like creatures scurrying from one rock formation to the next, but they never stayed in the open for long.

Her feet ached, swelling from the distance and the heat. Sweat had long ago soaked her shirt and dried on it, making it a crusty, unpleasant thing. Wanting to distract herself from her own pointless self-pity, she brought up a problem she'd been turning over in her mind for the last few miles.

"Morgen?"

"Hmm?"

"How do you plan on finding Kaden? I mean, we know where Tamrin likely is, so we know where Evra is, but once we find *them*..." Nyx trailed off. "It's a big planet. We don't even know if he's—" The words stuck in Nyx's throat. She cleared it and forced them out. "We don't even know if he's still alive."

"Well, with that kind of optimism, how could we *not* find him?"

"I'm serious, Morgen." To underscore her point, Nyx stopped walking.

Morgen stopped three steps later and really looked at her. "Hey, now, don't fret, little Guardian. If there's one thing I know about Kaden, it's that he's a tough bastard. Going to take more than one little prison planet to put him down."

"So you think he's alive?"

"Guaranteed."

Bands Nyx hadn't realized were constricting her chest loosened. "And as to finding him?"

Morgen shrugged and started walking, Nyx falling into step next to him.

"If there's a second thing I know about Kaden, it's that he's a glory hound. Not intentionally, mind you, he doesn't *seek out* the glory, it just comes to him because of that infernally irritating do-gooder nature of his. People sort of gravitate to him, you know?"

Yeah, I know.

"Which means, really, that I expect to find him smack in the middle of one trouble or another with a horde of admiring followers. Can't imagine he'd *want* followers from the lot to choose from on this planet, but I expect he's got them anyway. Burden of being a born leader, you know. We ask around, ask enough people, and someone'll know something for the right price."

"Is that price a fist in the face?"

Morgen laughed, a melodic, deep-throated sound. "Depends on the person."

They walked in silence a few paces and then Morgen asked, a little too casually, "How well did you know him?"

Nyx's heart skipped a beat. Her hands clenched into fists that she forced, finger by finger, to loosen. "Not well. Not very well at all."

She picked up her pace, even though her feet objected, and kept it up until Morgen called a rest by a pile of onyx rocks stacked twice as high as her head. She didn't argue about the break, tired as she was, just sank gratefully against a rock, a small moan of relief working its way out of her throat.

The bird-woman smirked. "Not used to hoofing it, pretty girl?"

Nyx tossed her a smile and didn't answer. *You never win with people like her.*

Nyx slipped her pack of endless bread, cheese, and water off her back. The water consisted of a canteen that never went dry, and she'd have passed out hours ago without it. The bread was a tiny loaf, the cheese a triangular hunk. Both were wrapped in waxed paper, and every time she broke a piece of either off, the originals failed to diminish in size. It wasn't as if the original grew back what was torn off, it was as if nothing happened to the original at all. She tore off more food than they all needed trying to watch how it happened, until Morgen made her stop.

She was halfway through her own rations when she noticed little dust clouds swirling around her feet. Which might not be too abnormal on a desert planet, except she couldn't feel any wind.

"Morgen?"

"Hmm?"

"Was there any native life on this planet before prisoner occupation?"

"Some."

"What kind?"

"The kind you don't want to meet," the woman answered, a chuckle on her lips. She stepped back, resting her hip against a rock.

The movement looked casual enough but Morgen followed it warily, followed the woman's eyes as they flicked down to the clouds of dust swirling about Nyx's feet.

Unnatural, to have dust clouds without wind. Unless…

Morgen tackled Nyx the same instant tentacles burst through the ground beneath her feet. Pale and fleshy, they were a near-match for octopus tentacles, save for the wicked, chitin-like spikes adorning the ends.

One long tentacle snaked out, wrapped around her ankle, and tightened with machine-like strength.

The pale tentacle pulled at her, tugging her toward a sea of others that waved and snapped. She grabbed onto Morgen's waist and dug her heels into the ground.

Both slowed her progress, but the tentacle still dragged her, pulling them both inexorably toward the main body of the crea-ture. Morgen pulled a long knife from its sheath and drove it into the ground, jerking them to a halt.

Firmly anchored, Nyx kicked and flailed. The tentacle around her ankle refused to budge. It grew tighter, the pressure ratch-eting up the rest of her leg. Nyx's leg strained at ankle and hip, her shoulder sockets groaning as she clung to Morgen. Skin around the pulled areas burned, threatening to tear.

Too much pressure.

Nyx let go of Morgen. The tentacle whipped her forward five feet, and the loops that held her bo staff broke as the creature dragged her body across sunbaked earth. Sensing its prey captured, the beast retreated deeper into the hole, pulling Nyx with it.

She fumbled for a weapon; dagger, trapped against her ankle. Sword, too long to pull in close quarters. Staff, useless in this scenario.

"Nyx!" Morgen ripped the long knife from the ground and hurled it at her.

She reached. The hilt glanced off her fingertips and the knife clattered to the ground. She scrabbled, grabbed it, and heaved herself up, slashing at the tentacle and praying to any gods who might be listening that she didn't cut her own foot off by accident.

The blade glanced off the tentacle like a table knife off solid rock. She hacked again and again, a small cut in the thick skin and a droplet of clear, viscous fluid her only reward.

The hole loomed nearer, less than a foot away. Nyx gathered herself, putting everything she had into a final strike. As the blade whistled through the air, a sharp bite flared through her cheek. Chaos shot through her veins and strength flooded her just long enough that when the blade hit tentacle, it cut clean through.

Nyx shuddered to a halt, her foot kissing the lip of the hole while the creature screamed, making a noise Nyx had always imaged an angry pterodactyl would make. Tentacles flailed in the air, whipping wildly. She threw herself flat to the ground.

All at once the tentacles retracted. Nyx jerked her feet back from the rim as they slithered by, but a tentacle brushed against her leg, knocking Veritas loose and sweeping it into the hole as the beast disappeared.

Panic flooded her—if she lost Veritas her Station would never unlock—and she lunged for the hole, diving in headfirst, waist resting on the rim as her upper half went down.

Darkness and the smell of something dank and viscous greeted her. She blinked rapidly, eyes adjusting just enough to make out a labyrinth of underground tunnels. A few more blinks, a little more time to adjust, and she made out the blurred shape of the dagger, nestled in a small groove straight ahead.

Nyx stretched, willing her fingertips to lengthen the scant centimeter needed to reach the blade. She wiggled her hips forward, teetering precariously on the hole's rim, and stretched farther. Her fingers brushed the dagger's hilt. She fumbled it toward her, a small moment of relief as she grasped it in her hand.

Then a roaring like rushing water sounded in the tunnel and a bulbous head, its mouth a circle of vicious, shark-like teeth, tunneled at her. She scrambled back, the frantic fervor of the movement too much for the delicate rim she balanced on. The edge of the hole gave way, tumbling her down, straight at the creature.

A foul rankness hit her as the creature's maw opened, the scent of decades of rot and ruin spewing forth as it roared. Nyx fumbled, yanked the dagger up, and plunged it deep into the soft, bulbous flesh surrounding its mouth. The creature screamed again, sulfurous heat and slime spattering Nyx's face.

It snapped at her as a hand clamped tight around her ankle and hauled her up. The creature's maw snapped shut on empty air, close enough Nyx felt the brush of a fleshy mouth against her cheek.

She was dragged roughly over the lip of the hole, then back another five feet for good measure before the hand let go of her ankle. Nyx's face kissed open air and she scuttled away on instinct, slamming into Morgen with enough force she knocked them both to the ground.

She clutched Veritas to her chest like a prayer and buried her head in Morgen's shoulder. He smelled like cinnamon and spice and the older brother she'd always wanted.

"Thanks." The word came out muffled against his shirt, her sides heaving much more heavily than his.

"Oh, no problem." He patted her shoulder. "Hey, Nyx? Don't take this the wrong way, but for a nice, quiet girl, you attract a lot of trouble."

Suddenly aware she lay on the ground, and the creature had come from *beneath* the ground, Nyx scrambled to her feet. "What the hell was that thing? Will it come back?"

The bird-woman, who had watched the pitched battle with

an air of detached amusement, slapped her hands against her thighs, cackling. "*That* was a Draken. And no. Nothing much gives 'em trouble round here, so they aren't very used to pain. Tend to run from it. You gotta be some kind of crazy, diving in there after a damn dagger."

"Yeah." Nyx wiped foul-smelling Draken blood off the blade and slipped the dagger back into its sheath. "Some kind of crazy." But if she'd lost that dagger, the Station would never come out of lockdown. She thought of Griff and a shiver of guilt flickered through her.

"Watch for the dust," Nyx said, thinking back to the casual way the bird-woman had stepped back right before the earth had exploded. "That's how she knew the Draken was coming."

"Clever girl." It didn't sound like a compliment.

Nyx retrieved her bo staff. The loops that attached it to her were broken beyond her ability to repair, so she wrapped them around the staff into a kind of hand grip and proceeded to use the staff like a walking stick, hoping the cloth would interfere with the weapon's desire to meld itself to her hand.

Why did I think it would be a good idea to take dangerous items to a dangerous planet?

She grinned at the bird-woman, motioned her and Morgen onward, and started singing "On the Road Again" in as obnoxious of an off-tune voice as she could. She'd never had much singing talent, so it wasn't difficult to manage.

18

Nyx lost her enthusiasm for being on the road again several hours later. She had spent most of those hours staring at a wall in the distance, a massive structure formed of the onyx rock that littered the landscape here. Only within the last hour had it actually appeared to draw any closer.

Time not taken up staring at the massive structure had been spent trying to ignore the back-and-forth stings and pulses of the chaos thorns and the Harvester, and trying to discern why she felt so certain the two were talking to each other. It didn't seem like a *good* thing, all this communication between two things she didn't understand.

The Harvester grew heated, so hot it should have burned Nyx's skin, but didn't. She snuck a surreptitious glance at it only to find that the spherical space inside the interlocking rings, empty for as long as Nyx had been in possession of the necklace, was glowing with a brilliant gold light, bright enough that looking at it hurt her eyes, like trying to look straight at the sun on a cloudless day.

Not a single ray of light escaped the bonds of the interlocked rings, and when Nyx tucked the Harvester back behind her shirt, afraid that Morgen or the bird-woman would see it, the light did not show beneath the cloth.

The bird-woman stopped walking and Nyx realized they were at the base of a long, steep rise. Atop that rise stood the distant wall she'd been staring at for the last few hours of their journey.

The bird-woman held out her chained hands. "Once we move past this point, the watchman will be able to see us. Wouldn't want them to think I'm a prisoner."

Nyx looked at the woman, pulled Morgen back six steps. "Do we really think relying on her to get us in there is a good idea? She *knew* that Draken was underneath me."

She's a convict sentenced to life on a prison planet. It's hardly shocking she was hoping you'd get eaten.

Morgen snorted. "She'll double-cross us as soon as she gets the chance, but it doesn't look like we have another way inside. That wall's at least fifty feet high. We don't have the equipment to scale it or the manpower to get us out of a tight situation if we get caught."

"Aren't you supposed to be an elite soldier? Your best plan is to let the double-crosser double-cross us?"

"No, little Guardian, my *best* plan was to come here alone, without a deadline. I would have pretended to be a fellow prisoner. I would have been crafty and careful and built alliances. Instead, we need to find Evra before she becomes delirious and loses the only item that can get us off this planet, and I have an amnesiac Guardian as my sidekick."

"It's not like I have trouble remembering what's happening right now," she muttered.

"No, but you're so worried about Evra and that fading tattoo on your arm that you're distracted."

"I—"

"Which is understandable, but it doesn't help us. So, yes, currently my best plan is to let the double-crosser double-cross us, because we need to get inside the Far Hold as soon as possible. If you have a better idea, I will happily consider it."

Nyx did not have a better idea.

"What happens if we get separated?"

"I will do everything I can to prevent that. I *am* half-Siren. If you want to help, try and act vulnerable, or something."

"Act vulnerable?" Nyx repeated. Had Morgen lost his mind?

"You remember that hypnotizing effect I mentioned Hidden are supposed to have? When I was researching the Hidden, I read that it's like a defense mechanism. Your kind tend to be lovers rather than fighters, so maybe being in distress brings it out."

Seriously?

"Should I bat my eyelashes and cry piteously about how life is so unfair and why is no man around to save me?"

"Could you?"

"No. Let's just get this over with."

Returning to the bird-woman, Nyx removed Gleipnir. They crested the long rise together and Nyx was unable to escape a sense of awe at what people could build, even in a place like this.

The onyx wall towered above them. It possessed no visible flaws or weaknesses, only a gate and a watchpost above. The closer they came, the more Nyx appreciated the futility of looking for a chink in the Far Hold's armor. Even if it *had* one—and by the looks of it, she doubted it did—there was nowhere to hide in the surrounding landscape, nowhere the watchman could not see them.

The woman approached the gate with a practiced swagger, hand on the crude sword Nyx and Morgen had returned to her for appearances' sake. She stopped two feet from the gate, Nyx and Morgen a foot behind her, and tapped her scabbard against the iron bars, twice.

The gate towered above them, reaching as high as the wall. The iron wasn't smoothly wrought, but rather patched together in uneven rows, and the stars alone knew what power had smelted it together. Impressive in its crude massiveness, it sent shivers rippling through Nyx's spine.

A guard appeared at the gate, a leering grin breaking across his face when he saw the bird-woman. "Kiara, you old hag. What brings you to the Far Hold?"

Old hag? Nyx put the woman at thirty-five, at the oldest. A bit worn from rough living, but hardly hag-worthy. Then again, how old did a person live to be on a place like this? Maybe thirty-five *was* old by Arkadia's standards.

"Got a couple to enter in tonight's fights."

"Cutting your timing a little close, K."

"Yeah, but they're good, and they're fresh."

Silence. Then, "The girl don't look like much of a scrapper."

Kiara hooked her thumbs into her belt. "She took down eight of my Station guard." Kiara turned her head and spit a long stream onto the baked earth. "By herself."

The guard looked Nyx over, skeptical. "And then you took her down?"

"We came to a deal of sorts."

The guard spit to his right. "I'll bet you did. All right, we'll get 'em in. But ain't nobody getting paid until we see how they do. Rumor is the lord's itchin' for a good fight."

Kiara shrugged. "They'll do just fine. Gives me time to make sure you pay the going rate, too."

The watchman chuckled and the iron gates swung open, their movement slow and catchy, marked by screeches and a terrible groaning. Under cover of the noise, Nyx stepped up next to Kiara. "How exactly do you intend we get out of this fight?"

Kiara laughed. "Oh, I don't. You wanted into the Far Hold? You're in. You wanted to see the lord? Winner of the fights has dinner with him." Her gaze flicked between Nyx and Morgen. "Of course, there is only *one* winner."

"Morgen?" Nyx's voice pitched a little higher, a fact that wasn't lost on Kiara.

The older woman smirked, but there was a flicker of…something in her face, and her words came out softer than anything else she'd said. "You don't look like you were made for this world, pretty girl. But then, most of us weren't. My advice? Die quickly, or throw your past to the wind. You won't survive by holding on to it."

Morgen stepped up beside her. "We'll figure it out, little Guardian. Just keep it together."

Easy for him to say. How many worlds had he traveled to? How many times had he been in similar situations? Worse situations?

Despite his earlier assurances, Nyx felt her panic rising. Morgen was an elite *soldier* for the stars' sakes, of course he wasn't worried. What the hell was she? A bored girl with no past, no future, and a couple decades of martial arts experience she had never expected to actually use.

Nyx blinked. *Two decades? I've never thought in concrete numbers before. Two decades. But that would mean I started training when I was…five.*

The chaos thorns in her cheek pulsed and memory swept away the scene before her, overlaying it with a green-fielded valley. A man with long silver hair tied loosely at his neck sat on his knees in front of a very young Nyx. Her…father?

"You understand why this is important? Your mother and I, we won't always be here to protect you. You must be strong. You must be fast. You understand?" His voice flowed, smooth and rich like strong coffee, and though little Nyx did not really understand, not at all, she nodded.

"Good." He held his hands up, palms facing her. "Then hit me."

Little Nyx made a fist, careful to wrap her thumb around her fingers just-so as she'd been taught, and clumsily drove her fist into her father's palm.

Memory disintegrated, gave way to someone shaking her. Morgen.

"You sure the girl ain't sick, Kiara? I don't want a repeat of last year."

"I told you she ain't sick."

"Then what the hell's going on with her?" Nyx looked at her hands, realized her veins were pulsing black, normal, black, normal.

"She bought spell enhancements off a dark warlock on Abaddon. What the hell do you think landed her here? They trigger when she's angry."

"Yeah." Nyx played along with the story Kiara had crafted for her. She hadn't come all this way to lose her chance because she was suddenly being assaulted by *memories*, of all goddamn things. "And you piss me off."

The guard, an unwashed man with scars riddling his body and a look on his face that made Nyx think he wanted her out of the fights because he had other things he'd like to do with her, laughed.

Kiara joined in. "See, what'd I say? She's gonna be great."

"Nyx?" Morgen asked, voice low and worried as they passed through the gate, into the welcoming reception of a full contingent of guards.

"You know those memories I don't remember? I just remembered one."

Morgen was quiet for a spell as they walked, not into the Hold, but into an outer area leading to an interior wall and gate.

"If your memories *are* Hidden and not gone, it's possible the chaos thorns are having a deleterious effect on the Hiding. Though the specifics of Hidden magic are largely unknown, it belongs to a family of magic that is predicated on knowing the nature of a thing. In this case, the thing is *you*.

"Magical theory suggests chaos, bonded to you as it has, introduces an element that alters your nature. The Hiding, designed for the original you, would slowly begin to unravel, and—why are you looking at me like I sprouted a second head?"

"I thought you were a soldier."

"I am."

"And all soldiers can spout magical theory focused on what is apparently a small subset of magic?"

"No, I'm special."

Nyx stared at him.

"Look, the warrior ways were not my first calling in life. I like magical theory. I read a lot. When Kaden went looking for your mother, I read a lot on the Hidden. Didn't have much else to do, being unemployed and planet-bound."

"Knowing what you know of magical theory, then, do you think my mother is alive?"

"If she *is* what's blocking your memories, then yes. A Hidden's works don't survive their death."

Nyx contemplated that as they were escorted toward the inner gate, unable either to temper her hope that somewhere out there she had a living connection, or reconcile it with the knowledge that if she did, her mother had in all likelihood destroyed her memories and abandoned her.

Remembering what Morgen had said about her being distracted, she pushed the thoughts aside and focused on the present. The land to either side of the path they walked was divided into evenly spaced rows of plants that Nyx assumed were edible because they looked like farm rows, but she couldn't be certain because she'd never seen a one of them before in her life.

The rows were tended by haggard-looking souls whose better days were long behind them. Still, one of them whistled softly to herself, and Nyx wondered at that. She wondered at the order, too, of armed guards escorting her to what she had little doubt would turn out to be a city.

Morgen caught the look on her face, interpreting it correctly because he said, "Complete anarchy never works. Even in a place like this, people need *some* order if they're going to survive. If no structure exists, people simply make their own."

The inner gates swung open. Nyx took a deep breath and followed Morgen into the Far Hold.

<h1 style="text-align:center">19</h1>

The city rang with the hum and buzz of activity that marked all cities, albeit this one carried a distinctly medieval feel. Nyx trod the path of rough, uneven stone that ran between crude structures, most of them cobbled together out of mud and vegetation that had been pressed and dried to form a sheet-like material.

The nicer structures were made of the same onyx stone as the wall, but every building without fail shared the same roof, made of a thatched, black straw-like material resting on a latticework built from white poles. Nyx edged closer to the buildings, wondering where the white poles came from when every other building material here was so basic.

They passed a small hut, its resident nowhere in sight, and Nyx sidled close enough to get a good look. Close enough to see a skeletal hand hanging down the corner of the hut's roof. Bones. The houses were built from human *bones*.

She saw them everywhere, after that. A door made from femurs lashed tightly together, a circle of skulls forming a fire ring, even a laundry line made from bones and black straw.

Nyx saw loiterers, scrappers, pickpockets, and laborers. She didn't see any children. She might have been able to imagine this was any other medieval city were it not for that notable absence. The youngest person she saw looked at least nineteen.

Scooting close to Morgen, Nyx ducked her head. "There aren't any children here?"

Morgen's mouth pressed into a grim line. "Only those here by accident. All of the prisoners are sterilized off-world before admission."

"Oh." Maybe it was a kindness—certainly a prison planet was no place to bring a child into the world.

"Though mind you tell Evra," Morgen said, shifting from somber to mischievous in the space of a second, "that since I wasn't technically sentenced here, they didn't get around to the sterilization part with me, so I can bless her with as many little Amazon children as she wants."

"I'll be sure to mention it to her." Nyx had a hard time picturing Evra with kids.

The guard escorting them paused in front of a low building that reminded Nyx of a longhouse, the building built entirely of the black straw that had formed so many of the roofs she'd seen. A harsh and sour smell wafted from it, like rancid meat. Guards ringed the door, then flanked around the entire perimeter of the building.

Behind the building towered a ring of bone and straw bleachers, the stands already packed with people. She noticed a narrow chute leading from the building to the stands.

Guess that's where the fights take place. Which gave her a pretty good idea of what—or who—was inside the building and why so many guards were posted around it.

Every inch of Nyx's body told her the building before her was no place she wanted to enter and yet the man led them in, the contingent of guards at their backs pressing them forward.

The source of the smell became apparent once Nyx's eyes adjusted to the building's dim interior. The room was packed with people in various states of filth and degradation. Some were cleaner than others, but every one of them could have done with a bar or three of soap. On the less fortunate souls, clothes were barely present, hanging in tatters off spindly shoulders.

Crudely made weapons were everywhere—in hands, hanging from scabbards, tucked into boots, and were those...? Yes, those were sharpened shards of bone woven into one woman's hair.

Scars marred the flesh of them all, ruining faces, adding lines to arms and legs. In the center of the room, four people grappled with each other over a molding hunk of cheese. The prize went to a man whose tongue shot out like a frog's, four feet long, and snatched it away.

In the corner, a man with lank, greasy hair heaved himself on a squirming, green-skinned woman who didn't look much older than Nyx. Nyx looked away, drawing a belt of laughter from their escorting guard.

"Don't worry, little girlie, it's your first fight. We never throw you fresh things in with the rabble on the first night. Over here's for you."

He led them along the perimeter of the room to a row of cages that lined the wall. Nyx studied the other fighters as she walked. Some of them, those who cared enough to notice her and Morgen's entrance, came flying at them, snarling like ravaging animals. The guards kicked them back, booted toes digging into ribs and bellies.

The ravaging, half-feral ones drew the attention first, but Nyx realized she'd made a mistake in thinking they were all half-starved. It was just that the better fed, better dressed, and better equipped individuals stood apart from the rest, in corners or against the walls. They looked contemptuously upon the rabble in the middle, none more so than the nine-foot-tall, stone-skinned giant at the far end of the row of cages. He leaned against the wall, shoving pieces of meat into his mouth and spitting out the bones.

The guard caught Nyx looking at the giant and grinned. "He's the favorite to win tonight. Never leaves his opponents alive." His grin widened at the flicker of fear that crossed Nyx's face. "Consider yourself lucky, girlie. He's in the same building as you. Means you won't be fighting him in the first rounds."

Of course, Nyx thought, there would be another building like this one, on the other side of the arena. Otherwise you could never put all the fighters together in a building like this—if they knew they'd be facing each other later, they'd kill each other off in *here* first. Though she suspected they probably did that to some degree, anyway.

The guard stopped in front of a cage and opened the door. Nyx wanted no place in the cage. She wanted no place in the *room*. She looked to Morgen. He nodded. Nyx walked into the cage, trying not to let her fear show as the guard locked it tight behind her, a sealing spell of some sort on his fingertips. He did the same for Morgen in the cage next to her.

"You know how the fights work, girlie?"

Nyx shook her head.

"Fights start after sundown. Newcomers are in the first rounds. You ain't gotta fight to the death, but the crowds like it. You win the tourney, you get dinner with the lord and your freedom. You lose, you're dead or back here." He leaned in close to the bars, his breath hot and sour. "And you only get the first night in the safe cage. You come back, you're out there with the rest of 'em."

The guard leaned back, pulling out a wrinkled piece of yellow paper and a nub Nyx guessed served as a pencil. "An' I'll be needin' your names and origin planets." At their blank stares, the guard shrugged. "Lord likes to have 'em before the fights start."

"Nyx, Earth." The guard's eyebrows rose at the planet she named, but he recorded it down and turned expectantly to Morgen.

Morgen rolled his eyes. "Andrew, Earth. Mind telling us who's fighting first?"

Nyx felt the same *something* in his words that had wrapped

around her back in the Den when he'd tried to influence her. It settled onto the guard, sinking in, and he didn't seem to notice, a slightly glazed look coming into his eyes.

"Newbies and ladies first." He grinned at Nyx, and she didn't like anything she saw in it. "Hope you're more than you look like. You get to fight an Amazon."

Relief flooded Nyx as the guard tucked his list into his pocket and left.

Evra. Of course she was here. She would have wanted the quickest way into the Hold—and to its lord—that she could get.

"Andrew?" she asked.

"What? If you can't roleplay on a prison planet, when can you? And this is perfect. Have Evra drag the fight out. The longer the better."

"Okay. What are you going to do?"

Morgen grinned. "*Andrew* is going to start a riot. I happen to be quite persuasive, as you may have noticed. Once I have the place in an appropriate uproar, they'll shut the fight down. I'll sneak out, grab you and Evra and Influence a guard to take us to this lord. We get Tamrin and go from there."

"Okay, right." It sounded like a good plan. Thank goodness she wasn't going to have to *actually* fight someone as a spectator sport on a prison planet.

"Hey, Morgen? What would your plan have been if I *wasn't* conveniently fighting Evra in the first match?"

Morgen just grinned at her.

20

Nyx clenched the bo staff tight in her hands as the guard led her out of the room and into the narrow, enclosed chute she'd seen from outside the building. At the end of the chute they passed through a door that opened into an arena that could have been straight from the UFC, only it looked more medieval and was three times as large—presumably to provide room for all the expected sword and weapon swinging.

Tall posts were set at each corner of the large octagon and a netting of fine metal wire affixed to the posts ran the perimeter of the arena, locking the competitors in. The crowd seethed and pulsed, a living entity in its own right. People packed into the bleachers and crowded into the standing room surrounding the net, faces pressed right up to the wire.

Spectators ran the gamut from well-dressed and well-equipped to barely having enough rags to cover the important bits, which told Nyx two things: admission to the fights was free, and this was *the* place to be if you lived in the Far Hold.

Nyx stared at the people—milling, chatting, watching. Like this was a normal event in a normal place. She went cold and sweaty at the same time, her palm slipping on the staff in her hand. Her heart skittered behind her chest, off-beat and pattering as if it were no longer a part of her.

A noise like roaring wind whipped past her, though the air around her stood perfectly calm. The guard pushed her through a gate and into the cage. Nyx tripped over the threshold, stumbling.

The crowd erupted into laughter.

They don't matter. You're fighting Evra, it's fine.

Realizing she still wore her pack, she struggled out of it and set it carefully against the cage. On the opposite side of the ring, a guard led Evra into the arena, and a little of the tension went out of Nyx's shoulders. Despite everything, she'd been worried it would be someone else, or that some other Amazon had ended up in the Far Hold's fights.

Then Nyx *looked* at Evra. Sweat shone on every exposed slice of the Amazon's skin, running down the warrior's face in rivulets. Her eyes stared blankly out, the whites a jaundiced shade of yellow. Her hair, normally bound back with careful attention, hung in lank pieces about her face.

Evra clutched her longsword before her, its tip resting on the ground, holding her up. No recognition crossed her face when Nyx approached.

So this is what fever delusions look like.

A gong sounded behind Nyx, and she didn't have to be a local to figure out what that meant. Evra hefted the sword and charged straight at Nyx. Despite the sweat pouring off Evra's skin and the glazed-over sheen of her eyes, she moved swiftly, her grip steady on the sword.

Nyx stood frozen, watching Evra come at her as if the scene played in slow motion, the sound muted. Less than six feet separated them when the world snapped back into regular time.

Stumbling back, Nyx brought the staff up just as Evra closed the gap between them, the force of the Amazon's charge channeling into her blow. Sword met staff with a chime-like ring of metal on metal and the impact drove Nyx to her knees.

The crowd roared.

Nyx's world narrowed to blocking sword swings and trying to get Evra's attention. The former was making her arms go numb and the latter was having no effect.

"Evra. It's Nyx. Please stop."

Evra paid as much attention as if Nyx were giving a lecture on the virtues of lemon-water. Nyx suspected she could have stripped naked and done the hula and Evra wouldn't have noticed. The Amazon fought like a programmed, empty shell, striking with accuracy and force, but no light of thought burning behind her eyes.

The only upside to this fight was that it seemed the memories Nyx had accessed earlier had given her a boost of confidence in the martial department. So when Evra faltered, Nyx slid staff against sword and brought both around in a circular arc that ripped the sword out of Evra's hands. Then she managed to sweep the Amazon's feet, leap atop her, pin her arms, and press the staff against her throat.

"For the love of the stars, Evra, you need to snap out of this."

In response, Evra snapped at *her*, snarling like a dog gone rabid. The crowd cheered, chanting something in unison Nyx didn't care to make out, but suspected was along the lines of "Finish her."

The sharp clang of bells rent the air, a horrifying screeching noise that sent the crowd around them into a mad scurry to desert the stands. Were the bells the result of Morgen's riot?

Nyx wanted to drop the staff, to reach up and cover her ears, but she didn't. If Evra made it up, Nyx wasn't confident she could put her back down.

Evra, too, snarled at the sound, but after the tenth clang of the bells, she blinked. Nyx hadn't seen Evra blink the entire time they'd been in the arena.

"Evra?"

Another blink, a slight relaxing of the Amazon's muscles.

"Evra, it's Nyx."

Evra blinked rapidly. Her eyes remained a horrid, jaundiced color, but they looked human again. "Nyx?"

"That's me. If I let you up, are you going to try and kill me?"

Evra thought about it, shook her head.

"Okay, then." Nyx stood and stepped away. The Amazon pitched and rolled fluidly to her knees, looking around her as if seeing the arena for the first time.

"Do you know where you are?"

"Arkadia. I gained intel my sister was in the Far Hold, but I could only get in by competing in the fights. They put me in a cage. After that, everything went dark. Then I woke up and you were holding me down and—" Evra scrambled to her feet, stumbling a little. "Holy stars, what are you doing here? *How* are you here? Are you mad?"

"Am *I* mad? You stole from a Guardian's Den and came to a prison planet while degenerating from a magical malady and you want to know if *I'm* mad?"

"So you just came after me? Alone?"

"No, I brought Morgen."

"You brought a wanted criminal as your backup to a prison planet?"

"Well, of course it sounds bad when you put it like that."

"What other way—" Evra cut off, her and Nyx both spinning to the right as footfalls echoed across the arena. Evra retrieved her sword, stepping back to Nyx's side as a woman walked toward them, the long braid of her red hair trailing in the slight breeze. She wore black from head to toe, one gauntleted fist resting on the sword at her hip, lean muscle rippling beneath smooth skin.

"Which of you is Nyx?" Her voice rang out, musical but strong. It reminded Nyx of someone, but she couldn't think who.

Nyx and Evra looked at each other, then turned to the woman and said, in unison, "I am."

"I do not have time for this." The flame-haired woman drew her sword. She advanced two steps, during which time Nyx raised her staff to a defensive position and Evra hefted her sword.

The woman stopped. She tilted her head to one side, cracking the bones along her neck, a show of controlled frustration if ever Nyx saw one.

"You appear to be in distress." Flame Hair indicated Evra's hand—it trembled slightly as she held her sword. "This would be easiest if Nyx simply came with me."

Nyx looked the woman over. She was well-fed and well-dressed, and better outfitted than anyone else Nyx had seen on this planet.

"Where exactly are you supposed to take Nyx?" Nyx asked.

Flame Hair tossed her head. "The Lord of the Far Hold wishes to see her."

Nyx and Evra shared a long, confused look. Hope stirred in Evra's eyes, but for once she let Nyx do the talking. "We happen to wish to see the Lord of the Far Hold ourselves. Take us both and you won't have any trouble."

"My orders are only for Nyx."

"Lady, you will never figure out which one of us is Nyx. And as bad as she looks," Nyx indicated Evra's trembling, "I guarantee she can still kick your ass halfway across this piss-hole you call a city. So do yourself a favor and take us both."

Flame Hair stood, grip tightening and relaxing, tightening and relaxing on her sword hilt, a fine muscle feathering along her jaw. The alarm bells continued ringing at steady intervals, and though Nyx didn't understand what they meant, she guessed they factored into the woman's decision-making.

"Fine. Both of you. Let's go."

Nyx didn't move. "Both of us, and Andrew." She had a feeling he was still "roleplaying" his new name as the great riot-leader of Arkadia.

The look Flame Hair gave Nyx could have superheated a glacier. "Who the fuck is Andrew?"

"Friend. In that building over there." Nyx pointed at the

building, just in case Flame Hair didn't get it. "Cage four. You want us, we want him."

Flame Hair didn't *quite* growl.

"Time's a-wasting." Nyx drummed her fingers along the staff, nonchalant.

Flame Hair put two fingers to her mouth and let out a high, piercing whistle. Twenty-three seconds later, by Nyx's count, a guard appeared. "There is a prisoner in cage four. Andrew. Bring him to the lord's chamber."

"Yes, sir!" The guard clapped a fist to his chest and darted off.

"Let's go."

When Nyx hesitated, Flame Hair turned that smoldering gaze on her. "Andrew is coming. You will receive no more concessions from me. Come, before I change my mind and decide I *do* want to waste the time putting you both on your backs."

The tingling from the spikes in Nyx's cheek meant Nyx wasn't *quite* afraid, but she knew warning signs when she felt them. She shared a brief glance with Evra, retrieved her pack from the far side of the cage, and they followed Flame Hair out of the arena.

"Andrew?" Evra whispered.

"Morgen is roleplaying," she responded, with as straight a face as she could manage.

21

Nyx felt the difference in the city's ambience as they moved down the main road. It wasn't just a lack of wandering people, but the feeling in the air itself, tension hanging thickly. The still-ringing bells kept Nyx on edge, heart beating insistently against her chest, and she had a feeling they weren't related to whatever riot Morgen had or had not managed to start.

Aside from the bells, everything was utterly, inexplicably silent. The tension and the bells proclaimed imminent danger and yet the world around her waited. Beneath it all, Nyx couldn't shake a new question, a new fear—why did the Lord of the Far Hold want to see *her*? She had wanted to see him, of course— theoretically, they would find Tamrin at the Hold—but finding him this way, being summoned, *fetched*…it made no sense.

It was a surprise, and experience had taught her surprises were bad more often than they were good.

Nyx wanted to ask what the lord wanted with them, how much farther it was to the Hold, but the set of Flame Hair's shoulders kept Nyx silent. They rounded a corner and her eyes fell on the Far Hold's Keep. A cliffside towered in the near distance, paths and doors carved into its onyx facade.

The paths were worked eight stories up the cliff, as high up as feasible given the rocky monstrosity's steepness. Nyx saw a couple areas where passes had caved in, or where new doors were to have been hewn but these, too, had collapsed. A field of spikes had been laid into the ground, extending about ten feet out from the base of the cliff.

Gauging the distance, Nyx figured they were about five-hundred yards out from the Keep. She risked a glance at Evra. Sweat poured off the Amazon, soaking her clothes through and leaving Nyx to worry the woman would desiccate before they reached the Keep. Evra's entire body shivered, gooseflesh pimpling her skin, but she stolidly rejected Nyx's two attempts to support her.

Damn pride's going to get her killed.

By the time they reached the stretch of spikes, Evra was wheezing like an asthmatic racehorse. Each spike rose two feet taller than Nyx's head with barely a foot and a half of space between each spike, every one of them plunged into the ground at random.

Nyx halted, looking for a path through. Flame Hair didn't waste a second, slipping her lithe frame between two spikes, winding her body through the tangle so skillfully that the sword at her hip didn't clang against a single spike.

Evra followed, slipping through with equal skill, even if her hands occasionally grabbed a spike for support.

Nyx shook her head and slipped the pack off her shoulders. Holding the pack in front of her like a shield in one hand, bo staff in the other, she followed the two women into the spikes. She did not quite manage the grace of Evra and Flame Hair, though she found a rhythm easily enough, twisting hips and sliding along in the narrow spaces between the spikes.

She did not manage to keep the bo staff from clanging against every fifth or sixth spike. When she emerged on the other side, half a minute after the other two women, they were eyeing her with twin frowns of disapproval, as if Nyx were a discredit to the entire gender.

Why couldn't I have remembered one of my dad's lessons on stealth? Nyx shrugged her pack back on under the watchful glare of those higher and mightier than she. *Surely he must have taught me a thing or two about stealth.*

She took a moment to revel in the phrase *my dad*. She'd never been able to think it and affix a face to it before.

Nyx felt immense relief when Flame Hair led them to a doorway at ground level instead of to one of the outer paths leading up the cliffside. People with power tended to think having their quarters high above ground gave them extra magisterial import. Nyx thought it just made a building more difficult to escape in cases of emergency. At least the Lord of the Far Hold wasn't a complete idiot.

No, she thought, *he just has a predilection for young children.*

"Why does the Lord of the Far Hold want to see Nyx?"

No response.

"I mean, where did he even hear her name?"

"If I answer you, will you stop talking?"

"Yes."

"He heard it when his tournament master informed him of the fighters in the first round and asked me to bring her to him."

"And you just do whatever he says?"

"When it suits me, yes."

Flame Hair led them down a maze of corridors until Nyx was certain they were actually at a subterranean level. They rounded a corner and she spotted two guards flanking the only doorway Nyx had seen so far that actually *had* a door. They had passed several breaks in the walls that led into rooms, but none of those breaks had had an actual door.

At Flame Hair's approach, the two guards snapped to attention so fast Nyx thought it a miracle their necks didn't break.

Flame Hair didn't slow, merely flicked her hand out in a gesture that apparently meant, "Open that door," because one of the guards scrambled to do just that. Flame Hair breezed through, Nyx and Evra following in her wake.

Once inside, Flame Hair pivoted on her heel, addressing the guards. "You are dismissed."

"But, sir, the bells."

Flame Hair did not speak. She did not have to. She raised her chin, ever-so-slightly, that smoldering fire in her eyes, and the guard who had dissented swallowed nervously. He held out for two more seconds, then clapped his fist to his chest, shouted, "Yes, *sir*," and made off as fast as he could down the corridor, the second guard hot on his heels.

Flame Hair shut the door, giving Nyx time to look about the room. Nyx had expected skulls and weapons and drudgery for decoration. Maybe a man cowering in a cage in one of the corners. Instead she found…comfort. Simplicity. The room felt like the living room of any house might, albeit a fair bit larger than most living rooms.

Stone benches topped with cushions were scattered against the walls. Rugs that looked like they were made out of scrap clothing that had been woven together still managed to be pretty, covering the floor from wall to wall. She even saw a few books and wondered where they had come from.

Then again, if a person knew they were going away for life, Nyx supposed some of them might have the foresight to tuck away some reading material.

The thought almost made her snicker. Almost. She strayed a few feet, and when Flame Hair made no move to object, Nyx wandered along the edge of the room. The layout, the sparse decoration…something about the space felt familiar.

Nyx felt the arrival of a new presence in the room even before she heard the sharp catch of breath that pulled her gaze off the furnishings and drew it to the far wall, where he stood in the room's interior doorway.

His hair, pale gold, hung longer than the spiky cut she remembered, and he had drawn it back at his neck with a strip of cloth. A few more lines were etched into a face too young for them, giving a harder edge to what had already been a hard face. And those eyes, green like broken glass and just as sharp, looked into hers like the world had ended.

She felt a little like she had the first time she'd met him, when the fact that he could notice her when no one else did had startled her so badly she'd almost fallen into the lake she'd stood beside. *Would* have fallen in, if he hadn't caught her. She'd been stunned and surprised, hopeful and a little desperate, and absolutely tongue-tied.

She felt a little like that now, and she didn't want to. She didn't want to be the woman who had looked at him and thought the universe had finally given her something good, because everything else in her life had been shit. She didn't want her instincts relaxing, telling her that she was safe because *he* was here.

He wasn't safe. He never had been.

She finally managed to untangle her tongue.

"*You're* the Lord of the Far Hold?" What was it Morgen had said? *I expect to find him smack in the middle of one trouble or another with a horde of admiring followers.*

A flicker of emotion passed across Kaden's face and then was gone. He nodded, once.

A noise of pure rage, more animal than human, came from behind Nyx, and too late she remembered just what kind of person Evra thought the Lord of the Far Hold was.

22

Nyx moved without thinking, faster even than Flame Hair's intervening movement, whipping the bo staff up in front of her. She ran, but Evra had a head start, and after a few steps Nyx gave up on catching her outright and instead threw herself into a slide, momentum bringing her in between Evra and *him* just as Evra's sword came down.

The sword met Nyx's upheld staff with a clang that echoed off the walls. Evra's eyes widened. She didn't move, her full weight bearing down on the sword, down on Nyx, who pushed back.

"Get out of my way," Evra growled.

"I think this is all a misunderstanding." Why was she even bothering to defend him? He was perfectly capable of defending himself.

"He has Tamrin. *Move.*"

"No. I know what you've heard, but it can't be right. I know him." *No,* she corrected herself, *you* thought *you knew him.*

"Tamrin? Is that what this is about?"

The voice behind Nyx startled her, sliding over her in dulcet, honey tones. She had always thought his voice was far too soft to match the rest of him. She *felt* him smile behind her, the one he smiled when he'd figured out a puzzle.

"Ah. You must be Evra." He whistled, a low, simple melody and was answered by the sound of quick footfalls.

"Kaden?" A girl's voice, a little frantic. "Is everything—"

The voice cut off the same instant Evra whipped her sword back into its sheath and ran. She collided into a girl who could have been a younger version of Evra herself, enveloping her in a bone-crushing hug.

Tamrin stood only an inch below Evra's own considerable height. The girl's blonde hair was pulled back in a braid identical to the one her sister usually wore, and the muscles ripping along her arms, though not *quite* as impressive as Evra's, nonetheless told the world in no uncertain terms that she could handle herself.

Evra pulled back just far enough to put her hands on either side of Tamrin's face and check for visible signs of damage. Upon not finding any, she glanced uncertainly from Tamrin to Kaden and back.

"I heard..."

"It's a ruse," Tamrin said. "Things don't end well for kids here. We usually get sold to the brothels or the mines, and it's a hand-toss as to which one is worse. Kaden wanted to protect us, but no one seen to have any human decency could maintain a hold on this city.

"So he lets it be known he has certain *tastes*." Tamrin's mouth curled in disgust. "The prices he pays ensures no one bothers selling kids anywhere else. He has never touched any of us, I promise."

Evra finally wrapped her head around her sister's well-being and swept Tamrin into another quick embrace. Looking over the girl's shoulder at Kaden, she spoke words Nyx hadn't thought the woman capable of. "Thank you."

Kaden's lips parted slightly again, then closed, and he just nodded.

"And thank you, Guardian." Tamrin looked at Nyx. "For helping my sister. She doesn't ever think she needs any."

That brought a smile to Nyx's lips. "You're welcome."

"Guardian?" Kaden swore and grabbed her arm, pulling her to him and running his free hand over the raised ridges the tattoo made along the underside of her forearm.

Nyx cocked an eyebrow. "Didn't you know? You told Morgen the Guardian would change."

"Anyone with eyes could see the Guardian would change. Sena was done. I never considered her replacement might be you of all people."

Never considered… His words wormed into her, slow in their initial effect, until at long last they caught hold. They destroyed the last shred of hope she'd clung to. She'd thought that if he knew she would become the Guardian, become a part of this world, he could still have an explanation for everything that would matter.

That possibility gone, she was left with the undeniable truth: she *had* only been a means to an end. He had made her trust him, extracted a promise from her she couldn't break, and then he had left her with an object likely to get her killed.

He'd abandoned her without a second thought and he had never expected her to be the wiser about any of it.

The thorns in Nyx's cheek flared with heat again, heat that told her, as if she didn't already know, that she was pissed. "Take your hands off me."

If she hadn't known better, Nyx would have said the look in his eyes was hurt. He held on a moment longer. Then he met her gaze and carefully, pointedly, let her go.

Nyx flexed her wrist, rotating it in a circle as if it burned. The action brought her tattoo to her attention. The fracturing in the outer lines was more prominent, and it had begun eating away at the inner layers, too. What would happen if those cracks worked their way to the center? If parts of the tattoo faded completely? How long did Griff have?

"Nyx? Are you okay?" Evra's voice, quiet.

"I'm fine." Irritation bit beneath her skin. "Why does everyone keep asking me that?" Her skin prickled painfully and Nyx rubbed at her arms. The blackness spread through her veins again, highlighting the vessels against her skin.

A rap sounded on the door. A guard entered the room with Morgen in tow. Flame Hair dismissed the guard in less time than it took to draw breath, eyes widening when she saw Morgen.

Nyx rounded on Morgen. "Tell them. Tell them I'm fine."

He glanced at the faces in the room, finally coming to rest on the black lines that traced along her arms, and looked somewhat at a loss for words.

Panic swelled in Nyx's chest, rising until it flooded her lungs, until she couldn't move, couldn't breathe. She choked, coughing, wheezing, trying desperately to take in air, but though she breathed it in, it felt like nothing made it into her lungs.

A wave of dizziness swept her and her knees gave out, ground rushing up to meet her. Before it could, Kaden was there. Nyx didn't see him move. He was on the other side of the room one instant and the next his arms were beneath her, halting her descent with a gentleness that shouldn't have been possible from such a hard person.

Nyx hacked again, her vision fading to a pinprick as her body starved for breath.

Kaden's arms wrapped around her, strong and gentle, pulling her against him. Words wrapped in honey murmured in her ear, soothing, pushing the darkness, the binding tightness, back until she could breathe again.

Little by little, the world came back.

"What happened to her?" Tamrin asked.

"Panic attack," Kaden answered. "She gets them, sometimes."

I used to get them.

She hadn't had one in years, and it made this one all the more shocking. Gradually she became aware of Kaden's legs on either side of hers, her back pressed up against his chest and his arms wrapped around her. He didn't smell like the cedarwood soap he had used when they lived together, but he still smelled like *Kaden*.

Nyx was tired, and she wanted nothing more than to forget the last four years and snuggle against him, to bury her face in his neck and pretend they were not where they were.

She didn't, but she didn't move away, either. Not right away. Not even when his fingers brushed gently across the thorns embedded in her cheek.

"What happened here?" he murmured.

Nyx tried, but the words wouldn't quite come out yet, and she was forced to look at Morgen.

"Ah, right." Morgen shifted, uncomfortable under the weight of Kaden's expectant stare. "Well, you know the first ley line trip can go a little rough, and uh… Well, see the thing about it is—"

"What. Happened?" Kaden growled.

Morgen sighed. "Our little Guardian here brushed up against a chaos pocket."

"She *what*?" Kaden said, at the same time Evra flatly stated, "That is not possible."

"Look, I know how it sounds. I wouldn't believe it myself if I hadn't seen it. She was *there*, her face brushed up against it, and then somehow she just…pushed herself back."

"There is no *pushing* against a chaos pocket," Evra argued. "Movement in ley space is difficult enough for a trained traveler, and *no* traveler has ever escaped a pocket's gravity."

Kaden looked at Morgen, his arms tightening slightly around Nyx. "And would you care to explain why she is *here*?" His voice ran like ice, the opposite of Flame Hair's fire. "Taking her on the ley lines was dangerous enough but then you brought her to a prison planet? We cannot *leave* here, Morgen."

Brought me here? Like I'm a piece of luggage? Nyx wiggled until Kaden got the message and let her loose. They rose to their feet simultaneously.

"No one *brought me* anywhere. Morgen wanted to find *you* and I wanted to find Evra before magical karma kills her. We struck a deal."

Whatever further argument they might have had was interrupted when Tamrin rounded on Evra. "I do not know what magical karma is, but I was right. You *are* sick. What is it?"

Evra kept her mouth firmly shut.

"Oh, for stars' sake," Nyx said. "She signed a magically-binding contract with Sena to remain as the Station's assistant for a year. She broke it when she came here. Griff says she's suffering from fever delusions."

"Who is Griff?"

Nyx spared Kaden a glance. "The Avatar of my Station. Now, since I'm not a complete idiot and I did not come to a prison planet without a way off it, can we please get out of here before Evra dies?"

"You have a way off?" Flame Hair moved half a step forward, her eyes feverish with hope.

"I know of a way off," Nyx said carefully. She didn't like the interest with which Flame Hair was now looking at her. "What I *don't* know is anything about you."

"Easy, little Guardian." Morgen put a careful hand on Nyx's shoulder, and she realized her hands were curled into fists. "Nyx, this is Maruca."

"You know her?"

Morgen nodded. "Me, her, and Kaden go way back. Like, cradle way back. She wasn't sentenced here. She disappeared around the same time Kaden was sentenced." Morgen frowned, looking at Maruca. "You followed him here?"

"Yes, she did," Kaden said. His voice was hard and his eyes were on Morgen's hand, settled on Nyx's shoulder.

Morgen followed Kaden's gaze and removed his hand.

"I wasn't going to let you suffer this alone," Maruca said.

Nyx glanced at Maruca, then Kaden. The sharp stabbing behind her chest was, she decided, most certainly acid reflux.

"We all leave, then. I trust someone here knows the quickest way back to the Station?"

"If we cut through the Bergen Swamp we can make it in just under eight hours." Kaden gave Maruca a meaningful look. "We would need a rather large distraction to slip through the swamp."

"Understood." Maruca walked to the door.

"Hold it there, Ruca," Morgen said. "You two going to fill us in?"

Maruca's molten voice filled the room and Nyx wondered how one ever compared with that kind of intensity. "Bergen rules the territory we need to cross through. He has been wanting to take over the Far Hold for over a year now. I have been acting as a double, slipping him scraps of information and gaining quite a bit of my own in the process.

"If I tell him I have found a way into the Hold, he will not waste any time in moving on it, leaving the swamp mostly unguarded."

Nyx looked at the faces in the room, each calmly accepting this explanation as if it made perfect sense.

"You're going to start a *war* as a *distraction*?"

"Yes." Maruca's voice was perfectly even, a little disdainful. "You do not understand these people. War will come anyway, in time. And I might remind you that Kaden set the alarm bells off to get *you* out of the fights." Maruca did not bother to conceal that she thought Nyx hardly worth the effort. "If we do not give these people a war, they will simply turn on us."

Maruca looked over Nyx's shoulder at Kaden. "I will go. Gather everyone and head for the Devil's Rock. You can hide from Bergen's forces there and I will meet you as soon as I am able to slip away from him."

Everyone—aside from Nyx—barely gave a head nod to Marcua leaving the room to go start a war.

"What if something happens? She's going to infiltrate an army of *convicts*. What if they figure it out?"

Kaden dismissed the concern. "Maruca can handle herself."

Oh, great. Maruca can handle herself. You think I'm an idiot for even coming here, but Maruca can handle herself.

Nyx's gaze drifted from person to person. She invariably found herself met with concern, pity, or some mixture of both.

They think I shouldn't be here. They respect Tamrin more than me and she's all of fifteen.

A flicker of black pulsed through her veins.

They think I'm dead weight.

Against her chest, the Harvester flashed hotly. The sudden desire to find out what it could do, if it could be used, struck her. If she wielded the kind of power something called the Harvester of Worlds no doubt commanded, they would respect her *then*.

Its warmth flared, and she knew if she pulled the pendant out, that light like the sun would be shining within the overlapping spheres. All she'd need to do was give it permission, and it would—

"Little Guardian?" Morgen touched her shoulder and she jumped.

Give it permission? Was she insane?

"Can I talk to you for a minute?" She grabbed his wrist and tugged him off to the other side of the room, as far away from everyone else as she could get, ignoring the weight of Kaden's stare tracking her every movement.

"That thing I'm Hiding," she whispered. "Can it, I don't know, influence its possessor?" She felt stupid even asking.

Morgen's eyes rounded and he leaned in closer, his voice barely audible. "Please tell me you didn't bring it with you. *Here.* To a prison planet."

"However this Hiding/promise thing works I can't—I can't take it off." She had tried numerous times over the years. It never ended well. "I've had it for years and it's never made me want to use it before."

Morgen winced. "You've had it on *Dead* Earth for years. Where its power is significantly muted."

"So it *can* influence me? Morgen, what the hell is it?" Her voice rose in pitch alongside her panic. "What does it do?"

"I don't *know*, little Guardian. Trust me, I looked in every record and history book I could find and it doesn't exist. The only people talking about it are conspiracy theory nut jobs who think it literally destroys worlds."

"So what do I do?"

"At its core, all magic is will-based. Complex magical artifacts will have a will of their own, a desire to carry out their intended purpose, but they need a wielder to do that. Whatever you want at any given moment, it will try to convince you it can give you.

"Recognizing what it's doing is half the battle. Your will just needs to be stronger than the artifact's."

"Oh, is that all?" It was only called the Harvester of Worlds. Surely its will was easily surmountable, with an insignificant name like that.

Morgen gave her shoulder a reassuring squeeze. "It will be all right, little Guardian. You can do this."

She closed her eyes and took a deep breath. He was right. She could do this.

She *felt* Kaden's approach, even before she opened her eyes and found him standing a foot away.

"What?" she snapped.

"Something I should know?" His voice was low, controlled, and Nyx finally gave herself permission to actually look at him. His eyes bore the haunted, wary look of a caged animal, even if he *was* at the top of the food chain in that cage.

Even the way he stood was different from how she remembered. He'd always held himself with a certain poise and readiness to act, but now he stood on a razor's edge, as if the slightest provocation would snap the hair-thin control on his temper.

Given that, she probably should have been more careful with her words, but since he was the progenitor of her current problems, she didn't feel like walking on eggshells around him.

"Nothing that concerns you."

Nyx savored the surprise that flitted across his face. Clearly, he'd spent too much time here with everyone jumping to do his bidding. Stars knew Maruca seemed only too happy to shout, "Yes, my lord," whenever he so much as blinked.

He recovered from the shock soon enough. "I am responsible for the safety of six children. If there is a problem, I need to know about it."

"There is no problem."

He glared at her. When the power of his masculine stare did not produce further explanations, he changed tactics.

"This way off Arkadia. What is it?"

"Also none of your concern."

"Nyx." Her name rolled off his tongue in one carefully controlled syllable. "If I don't know the particulars, I can't guarantee that nothing goes wrong."

"The only particulars you need to know are these: get me, Morgen, and Evra to the Station, and we can all leave. No issues, no problems."

"Morgen?"

Morgen opened his mouth.

"Uh-uh," Nyx ordered, "zip it."

Morgen looked between her and Kaden and finally gave Kaden an apologetic shrug.

"Sorry, man, but she does kind of have the power to turn me into the All Council when we get back. I'm shoring up goodwill."

Kaden's jaw clenched. "Fine. I hope your goodwill sustains you if we end up trapped on this rock for the rest of our lives." He stalked over to Tamrin and started issuing orders.

"Yes," Nyx said, "because stars know any part of any plan that doesn't receive his personal oversight is doomed to eternal failure."

Morgen gave her an odd look. "You know no one talks to him like that, right?"

"Yeah, well, I do." In point of fact, she never had talked to him that way before. There had never been any reason to because they had never argued about anything. They'd never had anything to argue about. They'd just been…drifting.

She wasn't drifting anymore.

23

Kaden drew on black paper with a thin stick that left white marks. Nyx watched as he drew a large oval, then a line leading from it to a smaller circle, then a line leading from the small circle to another small circle.

"This is the Far Hold, where we are now." Kaden tapped the thin stick to the oval. "Maruca took an underground tunnel that lets out here." He tapped the upper-right side of the Far Hold oval, where the line led to the first smile circle. "She'll be taking this path to Bergen's swamp." He tapped the circle. "The tunnel entrance is unguarded and it's how she will be getting Bergen's forces into the Hold. It's also how we're getting out."

He gave them each a pointed look. "We need to exit the tunnel and reach the Devil's Rock before Bergen's forces do. Too early and Ruca will not have time to distract Bergen's patrol guards. Too late and we risk running into his entire force on its march here."

He drew a crescent shape on the map. "Once Bergen and his men pass this point and Ruca gets them inside the Hold, she will loop back and meet us at Devil's Rock. We will go on to the swamp entrance together. Bergen will not leave it completely unguarded, but almost all of his people will be concentrating their efforts on the Hold.

"Once we are through the swamp, the Station is maybe a two hour trek, here." He tapped the final circle, indicating the Station. "Any questions?"

Nyx frowned, looking at the map. From the position of the Station to the Hold, going through the swamp was clearly the fastest route between the two. "Why didn't my guide take us this way when she led us here from the Station? She's a freelance type so I'm guessing she has arrangements with Bergen like she does with the Far Hold. Looking at this map, I'd say she took us this way." Nyx put her finger on the map and drew an arch from the Station to the Far Hold that left a wide berth between them and the swamp. "Why?"

"The swamp is not the safest of places."

Was anywhere on this planet safe?

"Does it have something worse than Drakens?"

Kaden's head snapped up. "You saw a Draken?"

Morgen laughed. "I wouldn't say she saw one quite so much as it almost carried her off to its underground lair. She took a good chunk out of it. Don't think it'll be bothering anyone any time soon."

Nyx sniffed. At least Morgen didn't think she was useless.

Kaden did not appear to find the situation nearly as funny as Morgen. He fixed Morgen with a glare that had him tamping down his happy-go-lucky grin, and continued in a serious voice.

"Drakens are not pleasant, but they are solitary hunters. The denizens of the swamp are not. Most of the indigenous life there is small and shy, and I doubt we will see any trace of it. The Meerkin are another story.

"They are approximately the size of a Morabeast—"

"And in Earth species that would be what?" *Housecat? German shepherd?*

Kaden considered, a small frown line appearing on his forehead. "About the size of a grizzly bear, but leaner."

Great. Now must be the part where he tells me they hunt in packs, are extremely difficult to kill, and move with the stealth of ninja-trained assassins.

"Meerkin hunt in groups of three to five. Their exterior is covered in plates of interlocking chitin. It is similar to snakeskin, only near-impenetrable, making them extremely difficult to kill."

Two out of three. Nyx didn't even bother contemplating the weirdness of chitin scales. What was with this place and its bizarre array of sea-like land creatures?

"Their hearts are more centrally located than other creatures. Instead of the chest area it is more here." He indicated a place corresponding to the soft underbelly of most four-legged creatures.

Nyx guessed Meerkin underbelly was all chitin-scales.

"You will have to slip in between the chitin scales and twist," he demonstrated, "to make the kill. If we are lucky, we will not encounter the Meerkin at all. If we do, we likely will not know it until they are on top of us. They are nearly impossible to hear, even if you are listening for them."

And three for three. For once, being right brought Nyx no joy.

Maybe it was the casual way Kaden had said, "Make the kill."

Fighting itself, Nyx loved. She loved the adrenaline rush that came from a sparring match, loved the danger demanding that she forget everything and clear her mind, focus only on the threat in front of her. Maybe it was a product of the childhood she was only just beginning to remember—maybe it was just who she was—but she *lived* for that.

Killing, on the other hand…she didn't like that.

Evra looked over the map, a frown tugging down the corners of her lips. "If the swamp is so dangerous, why do we not loop around? Take the path Nyx and Morgen followed here? A few hours would not be such a great deterrent."

"The sand wastes are impassable at night." Kaden looked at Nyx. "You saw *one* Draken. Imagine hundreds of them beneath the sand. In the day they are mostly dormant. At night, they hunt." His thumb hooked into the necklace he wore, and Nyx realized it was made of Draken teeth. "I figured that out the hard way."

"Aren't we in the middle of the sand wastes right now?"

Kaden nodded. "The ground beneath this area is riddled with marachite deposits. It dulls the Drakens senses and they will not tunnel near it. That is why the Far Hold still exists. The route from here to the swamp has been artificially planted with buried marachite to make the path safer, but the Drakens map their areas and they know the path's limits. Step off it, and we may not be safe."

On that cheery note, Tamrin re-entered the room, five sleepy-eyed children following in her wake. The first of the lot looked about fourteen, a mousy brunette whose default emotional setting appeared to be "terrified." Nyx immediately dubbed her Mouse.

The next three kids looked between twelve and seventeen, two girls and two boys. The two girls had light purple, pearlescent skin and slightly pointed ears. They were not identical, but bore an unmistakably familial similarity.

The girls all stood away from the oldest boy. It was a subtle distance, one Nyx thought might even be subconscious. He was seventeen, maybe, with dark brown skin and black hair grown a little long around his face. Nyx saw nothing that would make the others shy away from him. Indeed, with his hunched shoulders and downcast eyes, he appeared to be trying to make himself look smaller. Invisible.

The last and youngest of the group, a sandy-haired boy of maybe eight, came in trailing a lump of misshapen cloth with two buttons sewn onto it. Nyx guessed it was the prison planet's attempt at a stuffed animal.

When the boy saw Kaden, he broke into a run and threw his arms around Kaden's leg. He couldn't pronounce Kaden's name, the syllables not all quite coming out.

"Kade, why are we up?"

"We are taking a trip."

"But it's bedtime."

"Normally, it is." Kaden knelt, bringing him to eye level with the boy. "But this is a special circumstance. Do you like staying here?"

The boy thought about it, shook his head so hard Nyx was afraid he would scramble his brains.

"We have a chance to leave, but it is very small chance. It means we must be awake now, and you must do everything Tamrin tells you to do. Can you do that, Tobi?"

Tobi nodded.

"Good. Then go join the others." Tobi ran back to the group and took the mousy-looking girl's hand. Nyx thought it comforted Mouse more than Tobi.

"We are going out through the tunnels, just like we practiced. Pair off and *stay with your second*. Understood?"

The group nodded. None of them complained. None asked how they were leaving. Every single one of them simply paired off and did as Kaden instructed.

They might be kids, Nyx thought, *but they're prison planet kids.*

Kaden led the way, Morgen filing in a step behind him, as if this was old times. For them, Nyx thought, it probably was.

The children went next, Nyx following behind them with Evra and Tamrin after her.

Kaden pulled a rug aside, revealing a thick metal ring he grabbed and pulled, lifting a section of the floor. He slipped through and the rest followed. When it came Nyx's turn, she slid down, dropping onto a rounded tunnel floor, the top just barely high enough for her to stand if she ducked her head. The children would have no trouble with the height but the taller of their group, like Evra and Tamrin, were going to have to crouch.

Tamrin pulled the door closed after them, plunging them into total darkness. Nyx wondered how they were going to see— lighting flaming torches in an enclosed space would eat up all the oxygen, besides which, she hadn't seen any torches. Of all the modern technologies Nyx could have brought, why hadn't she thought of a flashlight?

Kaden's voice, whisper-soft, filtered through the tunnel. "Lana, Fari, do you think you could help us out with some light?"

The two girls giggled, and then they began to glow. It was subtle at first, gaining strength until the tunnel was bathed in soft purple light, the sisters two brilliant beacons at the center.

Nyx watched them in wonder. "They're beautiful."

Nyx didn't realize she'd spoken out loud until Evra, her voice as awed as Nyx's, said, "They are Luminescents. They rarely leave their home planet. They sleep above ground during the day, soaking the sun into their skin. At night they slip into the ocean's depths, reflecting light to see by as they mine for the minerals they sell."

Evra's tone darkened, her voice soft enough it did not carry beyond Nyx's ears. "Their species does not produce children easily. Their young are cherished above all else. The loss of these two must have hit them greatly."

Nyx hesitated, then asked the question that had been bothering her since she first saw the children. "How do kids end up here? I mean, I understand how Tamrin came here, but accidents like that couldn't have brought *six* children here."

Evra grimaced. "Prisoners are not technically allowed to bring anything with them to this planet. But if the criminal is wealthy or well-connected enough, some Enforcers can be bribed to look the other way."

Nyx looked at Lana and Fari, glowing brilliantly, hands clasped together, their soft giggles still echoing through the tunnel. "And some of these prisoners…they choose to bring *children*?"

"On a planet where no one can have children? Yes, they are a lucrative commodity."

Nyx didn't really feel like talking after that.

The tunnel narrowed significantly, until Nyx's shoulders brushed the walls as she walked. In some places she had to turn sideways in order to slip through. The tunnel widened and narrowed without rhyme or reason, the heaviness of the earth pressing down on them from above. Nyx found the weight of it oddly comforting, like being wrapped in a tight cocoon of blankets, and when they reached the end of the tunnel she was one of the few not letting out an audible sigh of relief.

The exit was a rough hole above them, a little higher than Nyx's head. Kaden leapt out nimbly, reaching in to help Tobi, then Mouse—whose actual name was Lauralyn—up.

When he reached down for her, Nyx shook her head and took two running steps; her right foot pushed off the ground, then her left off the side of the tunnel wall, propelling herself up. She grabbed hold of the rim, momentum and upper-body strength pulling her out of the tunnel.

Evra and Tamrin managed the exit more easily, the two of them tall enough to practically step out. Evra faltered on her second step above-ground and Tamrin steadied her. The pallor of Evra's skin had worsened, now tinged a grayish-green, and she sweated heavily enough to soak her clothes straight through.

Nyx stopped, slipping her pack from her shoulders.

"We need to keep moving," Kaden said.

"She needs a minute."

"We don't have a minute."

"I'm fine," Evra said. To prove her point, she started walking.

Nyx glared at Kaden, who turned away and slipped back up to the front of the group. Nyx hurried after Evra, digging out the waterskin from her pack as she went and shoving it at the Amazon.

Evra pushed it away, shaking her head. "You'll need that."

Nyx shoved it back at Evra. "It'll refill itself once it's back in the pack.

Evra looked understandably skeptical.

"I took it from the Den," Nyx explained.

Evra took the waterskin but didn't drink. "What is the cost?"

"If you drink from this for three days without another water source you become unquenchably thirsty and drink yourself to death."

"Oh." Evra put the waterskin to her lips and tilted it back, drinking until she drained it dry. She wiped her mouth and handed the skin back, giving Nyx a small smile. "If we are still here in three days, I will be dead. So nothing to worry about."

Nyx shook her head and put the waterskin back in her pack.

The Luminescent girls had ceased glowing, the stars above shining clearly enough to see by. The stars formed constellations Nyx had never seen before, and the moon among them shone a pale yellow, three-quarters full. Not far from it she came upon a second moon, glowing nearly as brightly as its twin. A shadow moved across the first moon, something winged and wicked, a piercing cry rattling the night sky.

They moved at a fast clip, one far too brutal for an eight-year-old to maintain for long. When Tobi pleaded for them to slow down, Kaden merely fell back and scooped him up, then returned to the front and continued on as effortlessly as if he hadn't just added sixty pounds to his carrying weight.

The openness of the landscape, the lack of anywhere to hide, grated unpleasantly against Nyx's nerves. She felt uneasy, only growing more so when she heard a noise in the distance like the dribble of hard rain.

Nyx stepped alongside Evra, voice low. "What is that?"

Before Evra could answer, Kaden's voice came back from the front of the line, tight and clipped. *"Run."*

Kaden slid Tobi onto his back and *ran,* the rest of the group falling in behind him. Nyx wondered about the kids' ability to keep up, but it soon became apparent that running was not something they lacked practice in. Rather the opposite.

The not-quite-rain sound grew louder, closer, until Nyx recognized it for what it was. Marching. Not far. Certainly not far enough for her and the others to get out of sight. The landscape was too open, too barren, and Nyx didn't see how running was going to fix that, unless…they crested a hill and *there*, a large, rocky formation just ahead, a little to the right.

The formation was in a large crescent shape—so long as the approaching force passed on the outer side of the curve, she and the others would be safely hidden on the inside curve.

Kaden increased the pace and the group matched it, Nyx's leg muscles beginning to twinge and burn. Just ahead, Lauralyn kept pace, her stride full and even. From the determined, almost joyful expression on her face, Nyx guessed running was the only part of the group's training sessions she excelled in.

Kaden and Tobi reached the rocky outcropping first, followed by Morgen, then Lauralyn, then Lana and Fari. Evra and Tamrin reached it next, slipping behind the outcropping just ahead of Nyx and disappearing from view.

Kaden waited at the edge of the rock, keeping watch as, one by one, his group made it to safety.

Nyx was twenty paces from them when Kaden went dead still, his gaze trained on something over Nyx's shoulder. One person, she realized, was missing from the group ahead of her, and she did not hear his footfalls at her back.

Nyx looked over her shoulder and her stomach flipped.

24

Nyx didn't stop to think, she just turned back and ran to the boy on the ground. Kaden darted after her, on her heels in seconds but Nyx was closer. One thick, fleshy tentacle wrapped around the boy's abdomen. His fingers were dug impossibly deep into the earth for stability, the only thing keeping the Draken from dragging him underground.

Nyx remembered the force those tentacles wielded, saw the strain reflected in the boy's eyes. If he let go, the Draken would pull him below ground faster than Nyx or Kaden could reach him. If he held on, the tension might well rip him apart.

Panic blossomed behind Nyx's chest. She pulled her sword from its sheath and sprinted, closing the gap between her and the boy. She fell to one knee, sword whistling through the air in an overhand strike. The thorns in her cheek pulsed and flared, black limning her veins, and metal met tentacle with all the force her chaos-strengthened body could muster. The impact jolted up her wrists, her arms, all the way up to her shoulder, the blade sinking halfway through the Draken's tentacle.

The creature screamed, tentacle flailing wildly and for one terrified moment she thought she'd only succeeded in getting the boy killed faster. She hefted the sword to strike again when the Draken dropped the boy, retracting the injured tentacle and disappearing beneath the ground.

They run when they're injured, the bird-woman had said.

Only the Draken wasn't the problem anymore. The problem was the army marching toward them, the sound of their footfalls so close and heavy they must be just on the other side of the hill.

Kaden dropped next to Nyx as the boy rose to his knees, pulling his entrenched fingers from the ground. As he did, one-inch claws retracted, smoothed down into normal-looking fingernails. He stood but collapsed immediately as his leg buckled, the flesh around the ankle angry and swollen. Kaden lightly touched his fingers to the skin and the boy let out a string of growled curses.

"It's broken," Kaden said, his voice flat.

On the other side of Devil's Rock, a line of figures crested the hill. It was only a matter of time until they were seen. Not enough time to make it to the rock. Not without leaving the boy.

She met Kaden's eyes. No way in hell was she leaving the boy.

We're going to die. The thought settled into her with a certainty she'd never felt before, not even when the Kumir or the Draken had had her, because then she had been fighting. Acting. She could take no action here. She could only sit and watch and wait for death to find her.

That's fucking bullshit. She was not going to sit here and die like some helpless damsel waiting for someone to rescue her. Think. There had to be something they could do, some tool at their disposal, some way to hide—

Hide. Of course.

"Give me your hands," she whispered. She didn't know if physical contact was necessary, but given she had no idea how her power worked, she wasn't taking any chances.

Kaden and the boy looked at her like she was insane.

"Give me your hands," she hissed, "and I *promise* that I will keep us hidden."

The look that came over Kaden's face said he understood her well enough. Understood, too, that she knew exactly what he'd done when he'd given her the Harvester. But he took her hand. The calluses along his fingers and palm were rougher, thicker, than she remembered.

Since Kaden had, the boy took her hand too. Morgen had said a promise was enough to make her magic work. She hoped to hell he was right.

"Whatever you do, don't move." She gripped their hands and thought, as hard as she could, *Safe. I promised to keep us safe, keep us hidden. I always keep my promises.*

She repeated it in her head, a mantra she refused to stop thinking, and on the third repetition she felt something stir inside her, a cool wave unfurling. She couldn't stop a little gasp as it enveloped them, couldn't stop the rush of emotion that came as she felt like she'd finally found some integral part of her she hadn't realized she'd been missing.

Bergen's army flowed over the hillside, Maruca marching at its head next to the man Nyx assumed was Bergen. Maruca held her head and shoulders back, her face a blank stone mask. Clad entirely in black, her red hair gathered in a tight braid to mid-back, she looked like a harbinger of hell, the marching steps of the army sounding like a drumbeat that heralded her coming.

Maruca's eyes flicked sharply left, widening as her gaze landed on them, and for one heart-stuttering moment, Nyx thought she had failed. But Bergen's gaze never wavered, and when no one in the shuffling mass of people turned a head to notice them, Maruca turned her gaze resolutely ahead.

Maruca could see them, but the others couldn't.

Because I promised to keep them safe, and Maruca isn't a threat.

Bergen's horde followed behind him and Maruca, fanning out wide enough that where Maruca had passed them at fifteen feet, the nearest of the men came within six inches of them.

Nyx repeated her mantra, her promise, furiously in her head, terrified to even breathe. She kept her gaze downcast, found herself staring at her fraying Guardian tattoo. She thought of the sad, half-insane creature she'd seen in Arkadia's Station and wondered again if that was what living without a Guardian did to an Avatar. Was Griff even now sinking into the depths of an insanity he might never recover him from?

A black weight settled onto her, drawing an answering flare from her thorn-riddled cheek, and she barely noticed when Bergen's horde finally left them behind.

She had abandoned her Avatar. Had she really thought that just because no one could tell her *why* a Guardian wasn't supposed to travel that it wouldn't have consequences?

What did I think I was doing here? Did I really think I could help? I barely kept us hidden and—

"*Nyx.*"

She jolted back to the present. The sound of footfalls was distant now, the dust settled on the ground. Kaden crouched in front of her, his hands clenched on her shoulders, peering into her eyes.

"I'm here," she said.

"You weren't." Kaden's hands eased their grip. "What's going on?"

Nyx didn't bother trying to pass herself off as fine this time. She'd been spiraling ever since she got to this planet. Her thoughts were darker, her attention shot, and welling up underneath it all was a ball of rage growing steadily larger and less stable.

She reached up and brushed her fingers across the black thorns. "These seem to be having an effect on me."

"Then we will get them out," Kaden growled. He reached for the thorns, but she stopped him, drawing his hand away.

"Don't you think I tried that?" She reached into her pocket and retrieved the tiny thorn Morgen had pulled out of her cheek.

"It came out."

"Yes. I made Morgen take this one out. He said he'd never heard anyone scream like that before."

Kaden's lips pressed into a thin line.

"I may not be fine, but I'll be all right. And we have bigger problems." She nodded at the boy. "He can't walk on that. Do you have anything we could use to make a splint?"

"No." Kaden considered the boy's ankle. "But I may have something else." He walked rapidly to the crescent rock and Nyx looked over at the boy.

He was hunched over, inspecting his ankle. Up close, Nyx saw faint markings on him, thin stripes a touch darker than his brown skin, barely noticeable. They patterned across every inch of him Nyx could see, from arms, face and neck, to the battered ankle, like tiger stripes.

Beautiful.

The claws were out on his hands again, though not quite as long as before.

He caught her looking and the stripes blended seamlessly back into his skin, the claws retracting. But his eyes, when he looked at her, were all feline, as was the snarl in his voice.

"Yeah, I'm Tiagren. Wishing you hadn't saved me?"

The harshness caught Nyx by surprise, and it took her a moment to find her voice. "I don't know what Tiagren is. Or why it would make me regret saving you."

He half-barked a bitter laugh. "Yeah, sure."

When Nyx said nothing he did a double-take, feline eyes scanning her face. He blinked once, lazily, just like a cat. "You really *don't* know. You grow up in a Shiskin hole or something?"

"I don't know what that means, either." Nyx shrugged. "I grew up on Earth." *I think.* "I'm sort of new to all this. My name's Nyx." She held out her hand.

"Kalvar." He ignored her hand. "You saved my life so let me do you a favor. Don't be nice to me. They won't appreciate you for it." He jerked his head toward Devil's Rock. "No one will."

Nyx studied him, surprised at the steadiness of his voice, as if he were stating a simple fact. At last, she said, "Kaden doesn't seem to have a problem with you."

Kalvar laughed, and Nyx heard genuine fondness in it this time. "Yeah, well, Kaden is odd as a blue-feathered fen in midwinter. No offense," he added hastily. "I get you two are…you know."

"Oh." Nyx glanced away, saw Kaden walking back to them with Tobi, of all people. "No, we aren't."

They sat in awkward silence until Kaden and Tobi reached them. Kalvar took one look at Tobi and said, "No. Absolutely not. Are you insane?"

"It's the only way," Kaden said. "We are on an isolated planet. What happens here no one ever need speak of."

Kalvar shook his head. "No way. It'll ruin his life. Just leave me, I can make it back to the Hold or something."

"You will not make it ten feet on that ankle. And even if you did, the Hold is about to be in the middle of a war. You would be dead in a matter of minutes. Or worse."

Kalvar didn't answer.

"Do you really want to spend the rest of your life here? You will never get another chance to leave."

"I won't do this to Tobi."

"It is not your choice to make." Tobi's voice came out distinctly more adult than an eight-year-old's voice had any right to sound. Nyx looked into his eyes and saw the weight of centuries blazing behind them.

"You don't understand," Kalvar pleaded. "You're too *young* to understand."

"I understand more than you think." Tobi gravely handed his misshapen stuffed animal to Kaden. "And I am Shaman."

Kalvar's eyes widened. He scrambled back but Tobi struck out, his little hands grabbing Kalvar's broken ankle. Power blossomed around them, strong and strange and wondrously terrifying. Tobi's eyes brimmed with ancient knowledge, and as she looked into them Nyx had the unsettling thought that in *this* moment, Tobi was not the only person looking back.

Kalvar bit back a cry, writhing as bones shifted back into their proper places, the angry red swelling receding until the skin turned once more smooth and unblemished.

Euphoria and pain filled Tobi's face, then faded as the power he wielded faded with it. For a moment, the other presences inside him lingered, and when the boy turned to Kalvar it was not his voice, but many, that spoke. "Do not blame yourself, young Tiagren. The Shaman answer the call, and the call runs deep, more so in those who touch the Congregation as strongly as this one does. We understand he seems young to you. But we are always with him. We guide. We protect. His time is not done. It is only beginning.

"Shamans are often used, and with little respect. Your own kind experience much of the same. If you wish to do something, do not show him your sorrow. Show him your gratitude. It will likely be the only time he is ever given it."

The voices faded and Tobi's eyes normalized, their brilliant glow dissipating. He didn't appear to remember the conversation between the Congregation and Kalvar, and when he looked at the older boy his eyes filled with a mix of apprehension and concern.

"Are you all right?"

Nyx watched the battle raging in Kalvar's eyes. She didn't know why, but she knew he thought allowing Tobi to heal *him*, specifically, had ruined the boy's life. But the Congregation's words lingered in Kalvar's ears and the look on Tobi's face was that of someone who had done a good thing and expected it to be punished for it.

Kalvar took a deep breath. "I'm fine now. Thank you."

Tobi's eyes widened, his young face showing a mix of exhaustion, fear, and happiness all rolled into one strange, confused expression.

He's too young for this, Nyx thought. *For any of this.*

"You are welcome," Tobi said, his words grave, his face shy. He took refuge in retrieving the lump of a stuffed animal from Kaden.

"Maruca's back."

How Kaden knew that when his back was turned on the direction Maruca approached from was a mystery to Nyx. The woman loped toward them at a brutal pace, strong legs eating up the ground in long, graceful bites.

She must have kept that pace the entire time to reach the Hold and double back here so fast.

Despite that, when Maruca reached their group her breathing was strong and even, the barest quickness of it the only indication of her previous exertion. She ignored Nyx, Kalvar, and Tobi, her fury directed at Kaden.

"Explain. You were out in the open for anyone to see. You could have been killed. You *should* have been killed."

"But I was not. Everything worked out."

"*Barely.* Kaden, I can't—" She floundered. When she regained her voice, it held only a trace of her former panic. "After everything we have lost, I *cannot* lose you too."

"Hey." Kaden put his hands on Maruca's shoulders and pulled her a couple inches closer.

"You will not lose me, understand? We are this close to getting out of here." He held his fingers half an inch apart. Then he smiled. "Besides, it's not your job to protect me, Ruca."

Maruca's face twisted into a wry mimicry of his smile. "Of course it is. *Someone* has to keep you out of trouble." She turned on Nyx, her expression decidedly less pleasant. "What happened?"

Of course. Kaden's here, Kalvar's here, but somehow this must be my fault.

"It's my fault," Kalvar said. "I got snared by a Draken."

"You *what?*" Maruca dropped to a crouch next to Kalvar. She tilted his chin up, inspecting him for signs of damage. "You are all right."

"Thanks to Nyx. She saved my life, Ru, you should ease up on her."

Nyx restrained laughter at a seventeen-year-old giving a

woman like *Maruca* orders, but then the impossible happened. Maruca's eyes softened.

"Perhaps." Maruca's lips quirked up, ever-so-slightly. Standing, she turned to Tobi. "I suspect you helped as well?"

Tobi nodded.

"Thank you. And do not ever speak of it again." The harsh lilt of Maruca's voice shocked Nyx. Tobi only nodded, as if this was expected, maybe even a relief.

"We're an hour out from the swamp," Kaden said. "Ruca, how are we looking?"

"Bergen is suspicious. The coup seems too easy and he does not trust me completely. I would be very surprised if he did not send a contingent back this way." Maruca calmly pulled Kalvar to his feet. "We should move."

They moved out, and Maruca never asked how Nyx had managed to hide them all. Either she already knew—a possibility Nyx didn't care for, didn't like the idea of Kaden telling Maruca anything about her—or she simply didn't care.

25

The contingent Maruca feared turned out not to be one Bergen sent to double-back, but one they stumbled directly on top of. Nyx felt the difference in the ground beneath her feet—the spongy give in the earth, as if she walked on a mat—a split second before that ground erupted, dirt and sand flying into her eyes.

She stumbled back, blinking against grit, the hard grains rasping against her eyelids, and saw them. At least a dozen men and women casting off crude tarps that had been buried lightly under the sand, spitting out the long tubes that had reached to the surface, allowing them to breathe beneath the earth.

Nyx's first thought was for the kids. She whirled, blinking rapidly, willing her vision to clear. When it did, she saw Tamrin and Evra herded the children together, pushing them back, away from the fighting. One of the men broke after them, sword in hand.

Heat flashed from the chaos thorns and Nyx *moved*, bo staff in hand, the distance between her and the man melting away. He hefted his sword. Rather than meet it, Nyx dropped into a slide and whipped the bo staff into the backs of his legs, chaos-black flashing through her veins as the staff struck.

Nyx morphed the slide into a roll, tumbling out of the way as the man fell, *hard*. Nyx rolled to her feet at the same time a third party entered the fight. Kalvar flipped the man onto his back, dark brown tiger stripes flashing prominently along the boy's skin. His fingernails extended into black claws and he tore the man's throat out in one vicious, efficient swipe.

Kalvar looked to Nyx, blood dripping from his claws, his canines extending over his bottom lip, eyes wild and gold and wholly feline. Nyx met Kalvar's gaze, listening to the last gurgle of blood in what was left of the dying man's throat, and thought from the defiance she saw in Kalvar's eyes that he *wanted* her to hate him, that it was the reaction he was most comfortable with.

Nyx lifted her chin. "Help Tamrin and Evra protect the others."

His upper lip curled briefly at the order before he obeyed it, darting back to join Evra and Tamrin in forming a protective ring around the younger children.

Nyx stood, poised to dart in either direction, unsure if she would be more useful protecting the children or joining the battle, when she realized it didn't matter.

Kaden, Maruca, and Morgen moved in perfect rhythm, their actions the flawless coordination born of years spent training and fighting as a unit. Most of the attackers were laid out on the ground and those still standing were not escaping the three ex-Enforcers.

Maruca and Morgen worked the fringes, each movement precise, each blow falling exactly as intended. Deadly and beautiful as they were, it was Kaden that Nyx couldn't look away from.

Where Maruca and Morgen danced between the blades, Kaden floated. He did not step so much as glide, did not strike with the blade so much as the blade seemed to move through the air of its own volition, smooth and steady and deadly.

Nyx watched the fight as if it were a Bolshoi ballet, her attention caught on each turn of foot, each pivot. When the finale came and the world quieted, when Kaden slipped his sword into its sheath and turned in her direction, a shudder went through her.

He stilled when he saw her, hand resting on the pommel of his sword, and ridiculous as it was she felt, for a small moment, the rest of the world slip away from them, felt the intervening years disappear, as if for *now* they were just two people who had once shared a connection.

Her lips parted slightly and she felt the need to say something, anything, but no words came. Kaden looked at her as if he stood on the verge of a decision, but before he could make it, Maruca and Morgen fell in at his side. The world came to life again between them, and the moment for Kaden to decide or Nyx to speak disappeared.

Kaden signaled to Tamrin and the group moved on in silence, skirting the fallen bodies and no one much looking at anyone else. It was a relief, to Nyx, when they came in sight of the swamp.

"We shouldn't be surprised," Kaden said. "Bergen isn't stupid. He would know any attempt on his part to take the Hold would be an excellent chance for another group to move on the swamp."

Nyx stared at the entrance to Bergen's swamp and, more importantly, at the three guards stationed outside of it.

The terrain had become increasingly populated with vegetation the closer they drew to the swamp, first with patchy grasses, then bushes, then the copse of trees they now hid behind. In fact, Nyx could really only tell where "trees" ended and "swamp" began by the presence of the guards.

After a minute or so of staring, in which Nyx could only assume the others were strategizing, Nyx felt obligated to point out the obvious. "There are only three of them."

"She is so *cute*," Maruca snickered.

Nyx restrained the urge to punch the other woman. "What did I say now?"

"Those three are Bergen's most dangerous assets." Kaden crouched beside Nyx, leaning in next to her, close enough she could breathe in his scent, feel his breath on her cheek.

"See her?" Kaden pointed to the woman standing at the swamp's entrance. "That is Amalee. She is a Siren who has trained her voice very well to do one specific thing: scream. She opens her mouth and your brain tries to melt out of your ears."

"And that," Maruca said, pointing to the beefy man standing next to Amalee, "is Jaren. He is one-tenth Hydra. The purebloods are all extinct, but he has enough in him to regrow pretty much anything you cut off. We are not even sure if he *can* be killed by traditional means."

"And that," Morgen chimed in, pointing at the final member of the trio, a lanky man with powder-white skin, "is Chinshi. Not only is he quite handy with that mace in his hand, but those fangs in his mouth are poisonous. One fang contains ten times the amount of poison needed to kill an average person in under thirty seconds."

As if on cue, Chinshi yawned, revealing a fine array of fangs.

"You seem to know a lot about them."

Maruca snorted. "We ought to. We put them here."

"I see. I don't suppose they were arrested for tax fraud?"

"They attempted to assassinate the head of the Council at a Universal Peace Banquet. They almost pulled it off, too." Maruca watched Jaren, hatred limning her features.

"We stopped the assassination," Morgen said, "and as reward we were given the delightful task of trailing them all over the bloody universe for the next eighteen months. I never wanted to see the inside of my crappy Enforcer quarters so much in my life. All though," Morgen brightened, "the *women* on Prisma Sari were worth the entire escapade."

Nyx cocked an eyebrow. "And here I thought you were in love with Evra."

"Quite in love. A man can remember his past experiences and still be blissfully content with his current and future monogamy."

"Uh-huh. So how did you catch these guys last time?"

Maruca sighed. "It was anticlimactic, actually. The Prisma Sarians are the descendants of the Fates. Time runs in their veins. *Using* that power is the highest taboo in their culture, but one pretty young thing was so enamored of Morgen here—stars above only know *why*—that she gave him a vial of her blood as a parting gift."

"That's…sweet?"

"It was stupid. If her people ever learn of it, they will likely kill her. Still, when we finally found those three, her blood bought us the time to hit them with enough Zarian-grade paralytic toxin to knock them out for a week." Maruca shook her head. "We fought them eight times on six different planets and the time we actually caught them, they never saw us coming."

Maruca sounded bitterly disappointed. Morgen and Kaden looked equally morose.

Nyx raised her eyebrows. "Well, since I'm guessing none of you have Prisma Sarian blood or paralytic toxins on hand, can't we just, I don't know, sneak in?"

Kaden shook his head. "There is only one path through the swamp and Bergen lost over three-hundred men clearing it. Some of us might make it through off-path. There is no chance that all of us will."

Nyx cursed. "Why does Bergen even want this place if it's so damn dangerous?"

"This is where the blackthatch grows," Kalvar answered. "Anything else you try to build with here rots after a few weeks. Freelance groups used to brave the edges of the swamp, come out with a load of thatch and sell it. Now Bergen has a stranglehold on the market."

Something in the flatness of Kalvar's voice, the way his hands curled into fists…

"You know Bergen?"

Kalvar nodded, one sharp, angry movement. "He's the one who brought me here. Paid to have a boy sent with him for currency. But Tiagren don't make good pets in the manner he intended." Kalvar grinned, his claws slashing out. "So he found other uses for me instead."

"I'm sorry," Nyx said, softly.

Kalvar shook his head. "It doesn't matter now. Ru got me out. First thing she did when she infiltrated his camp." Kalvar's eyes lingered on Maruca, warmth and gratitude and the world's largest schoolboy crush burning in his eyes.

It was equally obvious to Nyx that Maruca was completely oblivious to it. She ruffled his hair fondly and said, "You would have gotten yourself out, kid. I just sped things up a bit."

"Not to interrupt fond memories," Morgen said, "but might we get back to the trio of problems on our hands?" Morgen looked Nyx over with a speculative eye. "What do you have in your bag of tricks, little Guardian?"

Nyx shrugged the pack off her shoulders and sifted through the contents. "Not much that looks useful to the current problem. Self-replenishing food and water. Endless rope. Some wooden flute-thing Griff insisted I take…" *because he said Morgen would find it useful.*

"The flute," Morgen said. "Does it have gold etchings on the side?"

Nyx rolled it over in her hands. "Yes."

"Let me see it."

Nyx held out the flute. Morgen accepted it reverently, like a fanatic touching a holy relic. He raised his eyes to Nyx's, his fingers gently cupped around the wood.

"I'd heard it was in Earth's Den but… do you have any idea what this is?"

"A badly-made flute?" The wooden tube was not straight and

smooth as flutes ought to be, but instead gnarled and twisted at odd junctures, the finger-holes crudely carved and of varying circumferences. It was a little under two feet long, and the only nice thing Nyx could say for it was that the gold etchings—whatever language they were in—were pretty.

"Not a flute. *The* flute, the one belonging to Piper himself."

"Wait." Nyx rubbed at her temples. "The *pied* piper?"

Morgen nodded. "He is not quite as your Earth stories portray him, but yes. They say Piper carved this from a limb of the last Bariboam tree. Its structure amplifies a Siren's power."

And Morgen is half Siren.

Morgen twirled the flute through his fingers like a baton. A second twirl brought the flute to his lips.

"Morgen, Griff said it was dangerous. Shouldn't you—"

Too late. Morgen stood, revealing himself, revealing *all* of them, to the trio guarding the swamp's entrance, and blew across the flute.

Sounds drifted across the night air. To call them mere music would be to cheapen them irreparably. Notes flowed out in rich, honeyed tones, coating the air with a sticky sweetness that captured Morgen's song and sang it back, blending anew with each fresh note he created.

At first, the melody only soothed, a lullaby of incomparable strength. The tension in Nyx's shoulders eased, her muscles turning supple, ready. She came to her feet, as did the others in their retinue, standing behind Morgen.

The trio guarding the entrance stood frozen in their first steps. Jaren's face had gone completely slack, the carefree contentment of a child. Chinshi's face bore open confusion. Morgen changed a single note in the song and the confusion fled Chinshi's face, the worried lines melting into a contentment twin to Jaren's.

He plays a note for each of us, Nyx thought. *And how easily we are all bound.* It should have infuriated her, the honeyed control a single note held over her, but the song stole even anger from her.

Only Amalee, full Siren, resisted. Her visage was a mask of fury, the utter stillness the song commanded broken by the subtle twitching of her little finger. Nyx sifted through the notes, each of them steady, each of them strong, until, *there*, that one. A harsh note, higher than the rest, warbled, trembling in the air like an opera singer's vibrato.

Then the note shattered. Amalee opened her mouth and screamed.

Her voice was a wailing, hungry thing that bathed the air in acid fire. Nyx dropped to her knees, clapping her hands to her ears, but it did no good. Amalee's scream filled her, Nyx's hands useless to block the sound. Pressure filled her head, swelling, until she feared her brain would burst out through eyes and ears, would crack her skull like the popping open of a can of refrigerated biscuits.

Morgen's fingers flew across the flute. His pursed lips shifted oh-so-slightly and a second melody joined the first, two songs he kept simultaneously alive. The new tune did not attempt to control Amalee; rather it counteracted the scream issuing from her lips. Where Amalee's voice scalded and pressured, Morgen's song buffeted, sweet and cool.

Bit by bit, the pressure behind Nyx's eyes lessened, sliding out until none of it remained. Still, Amalee screamed, and all it would take was a slip of Morgen's fingers, a lapse of his concentration, for that blinding pain to return.

Morgen's song wrapped around Nyx like a physical thing, deflecting the equally physical wrath of Amalee's voice, and Nyx felt as if she stood on the shore of the ocean, a tidal wave crashing upon her and yet failing to cause injury.

Amalee strode toward them, her hand ripping her sword from its sheath. Two notes in Morgen's song shifted, releasing Kaden and Maruca from the invisible ties that had held them still. They charged Amalee before the Siren reached Morgen, and though her scream carried no ill-effects to them, Amalee was clearly an expert swordswoman and, for a time, she fended off both Kaden and Maruca.

Then Amalee slipped. Maruca's parry ripped the sword out of the Siren's hands, and the blow of Kaden's sword hilt rendered the woman unconscious, her voice falling silent.

Morgen dropped the second song once Amalee was out. The first song held strong, though sweat dripped from his forehead, into his eyes and along his cheeks. He walked boldly to the swamp entrance. Nyx and the others followed, whether by their own volition or the song's, she could not honestly tell.

They stepped onto the narrow path that led into the swamp, scraggly, misshapen trees curling around and above them. In between the trees grew tall grasses, thorny plants with poison-orange flowers and everywhere, everywhere, the black straw-like plant that could only be blackthatch.

26

The path beneath Nyx's feet was not a solid thing, not entirely. It gave and bounced, like walking on a rope bridge or a waterbed. If she stood still too long her feet sank beneath the surface, yet once she moved the ground sprang back up as if her weight had never been upon it.

Once the last of their group drew inside the swamp's borders, Morgen released the notes that held them. Nyx woke as if from a daze, her arms and legs and movements somehow more *hers* than they had been only moments before.

The two notes Morgen still held shifted in tune and tenor. Jaren and Chinshi's eyes slipped closed and they crumpled softly to the ground. Morgen released their notes and for a brief, singular moment, all was quiet and still.

Morgen inhaled deeply. When next he blew across the flute the notes were new, and they were many. These notes—indeed the entire song—felt different, and it was not until she saw a rustling in the swamp that Nyx realized these were not notes for human, or even alien, ears, but for those things that *felt* rather than heard music.

A great groaning shook the earth as trees lifted their roots out of the dirt and slid along the land, roots slithering like serpents to carry the trees to the entrance of the swamp. The trees planted themselves at that entrance, so close together that a slip of paper would not have fit between their enmeshed trunks. Roots burrowed back into the ground.

The grasses and blackthatch and the thorny poison-orange flower plants came next, weaving between the trees, crawling vines wrapping around trunks until Nyx and the others stood behind a living wall of vegetation, five feet thick and growing thicker.

Still, Morgen played, and still, the plants came. Nyx and the others stumbled back, deeper into the heart of the swamp, the Luminescent girls growing frightened and bathing the dark features of the swamp in sweet lilac light.

Morgen did not retreat, the wall growing faster and thicker and closer to him, small vines springing up around his feet, curling around his ankles and inching up his legs.

Nyx stepped up beside Kaden.

"He's lost control of the song." She recognized the burnt-out fever of Morgen's eyes, the mechanical way his fingers held the notes and his lips blew across the flute's opening. He looked as Evra had looked in the arena.

"Morgen."

Morgen gave no indication he'd heard Kaden. The song continued, faster, more frenzied.

"Morgen, stop." Maruca, this time. She walked toward him, speaking his name. The plants did not allow her more than three steps, wrapping around her ankles and rooting her to the ground. Maruca pulled her dagger and sliced through them. She cut quickly and managed another step forward, but only one. The plants came back two-fold and she was forced, the next time she cut herself free, to retreat back to where Nyx stood with Kaden.

"What happens if he doesn't stop playing?" Nyx asked.

"Aside from getting trapped in his own living artwork?" Maruca paused, considering. "At the rate he is burning through power, he will be dead within the hour if we cannot stop him."

"What do we do?"

Maruca flicked her hands out, as if she'd simply been waiting for someone to ask.

"We get him *out*."

She knelt and pressed both hands to the ground, fingers splayed wide. She closed her eyes and spoke, words dripping from her mouth like molten fire.

Kaden reached for her, obviously recognizing the words she spoke and what they meant. "Maruca, don't."

She already had.

Tendrils of blue flame sparked from the edges of her splayed fingers, slipping outward. Where they touched, plants crumpled. The tendrils of fire slid straight for Morgen, plants curling up in their wake as Maruca burned a path.

Nyx sidled up next to Kaden. "How is she doing that?" She asked it in a whisper, afraid somehow that if she spoke with too much volume, the words would break Maruca's hold on the power.

Kaden was silent for a time, and just when Nyx thought he wouldn't answer, he said, "Maruca is an energy mage. She's manipulating the plants' energy and turning it back against them, killing them."

"Could she do that with a person?"

"She could. But to manipulate it in such a way, she has to overcome the innate desire all things have to live. Her will has to be stronger than theirs. The will to live in most creatures is very strong. It is simpler, and easier, to use a sword."

Nyx dwelled on this while she watched the blue flames dance closer to Morgen. Their progress had slowed, and the vines were creeping back in along the edge of the path Maruca had cleared. They died when they touched those flames, but it did not stop the hordes of others from trying to reclaim the space.

Sweat broke out on Maruca's forehead.

"Kaden? Why didn't you want her to do this?"

"With Piper's flute, Morgen's power is too much a match for hers. She could burn out as easily as Morgen."

Nyx saw the truth of it as she watched Maruca's flames battle the onslaught of vegetative growth, watched her progress dwindle, every effort now engaged in holding the path she had already cleared. Sweat rolled off her in rivulets, tunneling across her face, down her shirt.

Kaden knelt beside her, a snarl on his lips, his hand on his shoulder. "That is *enough,* Ruca. It is lost."

Maruca's eyes flicked open, flames burning fiercely in the depths. "I have to try."

"You have tried. *Look.*"

Maruca looked. The vines piled atop each other, trying to climb *over* the light, and Maruca raised the flames into a wall, her body shuddering as she forced more effort from it.

"I made you a promise." Kaden said, his voice soft. "I promised you would we leave this place. Together. If I'm going to keep that promise, you have to stop."

Maruca turned and looked into Kaden's eyes. She held his gaze, and she held the flames. At last, she looked away, curled her hands into fists and called the power back, flames vanishing into her fingertips.

The vines fell in mad hordes upon the empty space, a sea of growth filling the barrenness in seconds. The vines growing up Morgen's body encircled him up to his waist. He looked half-man, half-plant, and wholly mad.

Maruca rose to her feet, tension in every muscle. "We cannot leave him here."

Against Nyx's chest the Harvester pulsed. Her hand rose of its own accord, seeking the chain, the pendant, around her neck.

It practically purred against her skin, as if she'd made a particularly good decision.

Yes. The Harvester could drive the plants back, could free Morgen, could—

No. She had no idea what the Harvester could do, much less what it *would* do, if she let it. Will, *her* will, had to be stronger.

But it was hard, so hard, to watch the vines encompass Morgen —laughing, mischievous Morgen, who felt so much like an older brother—to know that if they kept going he would be lost, and it would be her fault for letting him take that damned flute.

If she allowed the Harvester to work for a spell, long enough to free him, could she bring it under control again? As if it felt her wavering, the Harvester flared eagerly against her palm.

A fresh wave of vines slithered by in answer to Morgen's call. Nyx noticed how they bumped against her feet, against Kaden's and Maruca's, but carefully skirted Evra, and it was that observation that gave her the strength to pry her hand loose of the Harvester.

"I think we should let Evra try."

"What?" Evra croaked. She leaned heavily on Tamrin and she did not look much better than Morgen.

Maruca eyed Evra critically. "If he actually likes her and he is not just being *Morgen*…" She drummed her fingers against her biceps, flames sparking from the tips. "She *might* be able to reach him."

"Will you try?" Kaden asked.

Evra looked distinctly uncomfortable beneath the group's gazes, but she pushed herself off Tamrin and walked to the front of the group, to the space where path met growing sea of vegetation, muttering to herself as she went.

"You know, in my parents' time a suitor walked barefoot over hot coals, or something equally reasonable, to prove their interest in a partner. Now? Now I have to see if his magical Siren-song plants try to kill me.

"Morgen?" Evra called. "I am coming to you. If your plants attack me, I will be cutting something important off you later."

A trembling went through Morgen's body, like the shaking from silent laughter, and it gave Nyx hope.

Evra lifted her foot, let it hover over the thickly blanketed vegetation covering the ground. The plants hissed and coiled and then, grudgingly, cleared a small space for Evra's foot. Evra placed it in the space provided, then lifted her other foot, the plants clearing aside once more with hissing reluctance.

Plants moved and Evra walked, until she stood just behind Morgen. He gave no indication he knew she stood behind him, but when she placed her hand on a bare patch between his shoulders, the plants ceased their growth.

But he continued to play, the wall of vegetation growing denser and wider, pressing Nyx and the others deeper into the swamp.

"Morgen?"

A trembling in the notes, a brief shuddering of the vegetation, as if the lightest of earthquakes had set the trees to rustling.

"Morgen, stop this foolishness and let it go."

The notes held steady, like the sustain pedal on a piano had been held down, but the notes no longer flowed anew. Morgen's fingers froze stiff over the holes along the flute's stem, the muscles in his throat clenching.

Evra slid her hand over Morgen's shoulder, down his arm, until her hand covered his.

"Let it go, before it burns you to nothing, fool." With a lack of gentleness that suited her character, Evra pried one of his fingers off the flute. The plants winding around him stilled.

Morgen's chin dipped, and he seemed to notice his body for the first time, to notice the plants covering him. He put his finger back where Evra had moved it from and began to play once more, a different song.

Plants uncoiled and fled his body, slithering off him like snakes returning to the ground. The plants cleared a path back to the group, not unlike the one Maruca had attempted to forge in flame. Morgen took in one long, shuddering breath and the song ceased, the stillness flowing in its wake eerie for the music that had come before.

Morgen stood frozen, lips and fingers still pressed against the flute until Evra reached up and drew it away.

Once the flute was out of Morgen's hands, he turned to Evra, his skin drawn tight and ashen-gray. His legs buckled and he fell to his knees on the thick floor of vegetation and pressed his forehead against Evra's thigh, his entire body trembling.

After a moment, Evra leaned down and whispered in Morgen's ear, speaking too softly for her words to carry past him. He laughed, a rough, barking noise that sounded like a mix of genuine amusement and a shaky grasp on sanity. But he pulled himself together and stood, and if the old glint of mischief wasn't quite back in his eyes as he walked to the group, Evra at his side, who could blame him?

Evra passed the flute to Nyx, who sequestered it in her pack while Morgen watched it disappear with an addict's longing.

The children watched Morgen with wide eyes, as if he might be a god or a demon and they weren't quite sure which would be safer. But they snapped to attention when Kaden gave the order to move, falling into a double-file line, the Luminescent girls glowing softly to lighten the swamp's dimness.

Nyx took a moment to drink in the whole of Morgen's creation—a wall of trees and vegetation packed fifteen feet deep into the swamp, frightening in the power that had created it and yet hauntingly beautiful all the same. Then she turned and followed the others deeper into the swamp.

Rather than taking his customary place beside Kaden and Maruca, Morgen filed in next to Nyx at the very back of the group, Evra and Maruca walking just ahead. They walked in silence, until the silence grew heavy and Nyx broke it.

"You know you're a little scary, right? I mean, that was

awesome and you probably saved our lives and all, but you're still scary."

Morgen mustered a shadow of one of his trademark grins. "Little Guardian," he said, slinging an arm over her shoulders, "you don't know the half of it."

27

Nyx wanted to be home with a ferocity that hurt. She wasn't even sure when she had begun to think of the Station *as* home—maybe it had only happened over this trip— but she missed her room, the bookstore, the kitchen, even the portal room. It was, all of it, *hers*.

If anything has happened to Griff... She pushed the thought aside.

Nyx kept her eyes on the trees, certain she saw shadows flickering through the winding limbs, movement there one second and gone the next, the prickling hairs on her nape telling her the shadows were not simply her imagination.

She kept her hand on the hilt of her sword, watchful. When they rounded a bend in the path and she spied an opening ahead, only the people in front of her kept Nyx from sprinting for it.

She was so focused on the spot that she didn't realize the group had stopped until she ran straight into Evra's back. For once, the Amazon did not turn to scowl. Her head was canted, listening.

The prickling on Nyx's nape grew to a painful pitch, culminating when the shadows she had seen descended abruptly from the trees, flowing out from every side of the swamp.

They stepped into the light, and Nyx named them. *Meerkin.*

Only these Meerkin were not in a small group as Kaden had said they hunted in. They flowed as numerous as ants, first fifty, then one hundred, then on until Nyx no longer had a hope of counting their numbers. They reflected the Luminescent girls' light, the purple a soft sheen on the bronzed chitin of their scales.

They were, each of them, the size of a bear, though in all other aspects they were more cat-like. Pointed ears tipped forward, obsidian claws peeking out of chitin-plated paws.

Meerkin eyes glowed in the trees all around her. Nyx whirled and found glowing eyes at her back, as well. The thorns in her cheek pricked painfully, her senses flaring to life. The smell of the Meerkin wafted to her, a spicy, burning scent that belonged to neither swamp nor forest.

The armed among Nyx's group had their swords out. Nyx tensed, hand on her bo staff, waiting for the Meerkin to attack. They did not. They held a perimeter around Nyx's group, waiting with the perfect stillness and perfect patience of cats.

Waiting for what?

Nyx shifted to the right, peering between the people in front of her. Her cheek prickled again and she felt a change sweep through the Meerkin. Not fear…respect.

The Meerkin grouped nearest to Kaden stepped back and to either side, creating a living hallway through which a solitary Meerkin walked. He stood twice as tall as the rest of his pack, like some primal Meerkin god. Age was written in the careful, rambling-lumber of his gait, and though it looked as though each step caused him pain, he bore it well.

The large Meerkin came to within a foot of Kaden and stopped, settling back onto his haunches, his face easily of a height with Kaden's, even sitting. He flicked his rough, chitinous tail over his front paws and exhaled long and slow, his breath ruffling Kaden's hair.

Kaden remained perfectly still, not even blinking. Kaden and the Meerkin faced off, each silent and unmoving, for one minute. Then two. Then three. Then the ancient Meerkin nodded, satisfied. When he spoke, Nyx could not tell *where* his voice came from, for his lips did not move, and yet she knew it was his voice she heard.

"You may put your weapons away. For now, my kin will not attack."

Maruca looked to Kaden. After a moment he nodded and slipped his sword back into his sheath, Maruca and the others following suit. Nyx tried to lean on her staff as if it were more of a walking stick than a weapon, hoping not to give offense—she had not let go of it for some time, and it now appeared to have no intention of letting *her* go.

"What do you want of us?" Kaden asked. "Your kind are not known to hold their claws."

The Meerkin's tail twitched angrily, but when he spoke his voice was calm. "I have come to speak with our human kin among you."

Kaden shared a look with Maruca. "I do not know of whom you speak."

"The night-haired girl, she who has been touched by chaos."

Every face in the group turned to look at Nyx.

How do I get myself into these situations? "I don't guess any other women here brushed a chaos pocket?" she whispered to Morgen.

"I don't think so, little Guardian."

"I was afraid you'd say that."

Nyx took a deep breath and made her way to the front of the group, the others shifting aside to let her pass. When she reached Kaden he made no effort to let her through. She attempted to walk around him but his hand shot out, holding her back.

"You do *not* have to do this." Kaden spoke low, his eyes never leaving the Meerkin before him.

"Look," Nyx said patiently, "I think if he wanted to hurt me, he could have done that by now. I'm tired and I want to go home. Let's just see what he wants."

Kaden let his hand linger on her arm a moment. "For the record, I do not like this."

The control freak leader of the prison clan does not like a decision not being his. Noted. But he let her go and Nyx walked forward.

The ancient Meerkin might be of a height with Kaden, but that put him several inches taller than Nyx, and she had to crane her neck to look up at him. He brought his face down to hers, so close the wet tip of his nose touched hers. He sniffed, moving from her face to her hair and then, apparently satisfied, drew back.

"Greetings, little one. My name is Vorex. I am the eldest of my kin and I speak for us all."

"Uh, hi. I'm Nyx."

Vorex waited.

"I don't think I speak for anyone here but myself."

The stone-like whiskers on Vorex's face rippled softly in silent laughter. "You humans have strange ways. Very well, Nyx Who Speaks for Herself, our seers told us a time would come when one who was kin but not of our kin would travel through this land, and here you are."

Nyx hesitated, but Vorex offered no further words. "I'm sorry," she said, "but I don't know how we are kin."

"These make us kin." Vorex reached his paw up to brush the thorns in Nyx's cheek. Nyx gasped. Vorex had an opposable *thumb*. He ran it gently across the chaos thorns and his paws— fingers?—would have felt human if Nyx had closed her eyes, were it not for the rough paw pads covering them.

Vorex twisted his neck, exposing the gap in his interlocking plates of chitin. In those gaps, obsidian thorns littered his skin.

As soon as she saw the thorns, Nyx felt the Harvester become aware of them too, felt it ready itself to speak with them, as it had spoken to her own chaos thorns. She placed her hand over her chest, covering the Harvester and willing it to silence. To her surprise—and intense relief—it obeyed.

Focusing on the Meerkin, she managed an, "Oh. I see."

Vorex smiled. "For a long time, we did not. It eluded us who could walk this swamp and be our kin but not our kin. But our seers have never led us astray and when our sentries spotted you, they understood. They woke me from the Long Sleep, that I might speak with you."

It was clear Vorex expected Nyx to know what the Long Sleep was, and be impressed that he had awoken from it simply to speak with her.

Nyx decided faking it was better than asking him to explain. "I'm honored that you would come. But what exactly is it you want from me?"

Vorex bent down, bringing his face once again to eye-level with hers. "We want you to lead us home."

Blood thundered through Nyx's ears. "What?"

"The seer told us when kin of our kin came through the swamp, she would lead us home." At Nyx's confused expression, Vorex asked, gently, "Do you know how my people came to this planet?"

Nyx shook her head.

"Our homeland is called Kyvren. It is a place of fire and stone. Most would consider it harsh, but it is the birthplace of my kind, and we loved it fiercely. One day, one of our younglings came across a structure on our land where before no structure had been. He brought the Elders, and within the structure we found a creature like no creature we had seen before. He looked similar to your kind, though he was shorter and much rougher.

"He told us his kind were dwarves, and that the structure was a Station. That soon many others like him would come through it. His people came, and they claimed they wanted to live among us in harmony, to exchange goods and ideas.

"They were strange to us, these creatures from beyond the

stars, but they were not unkind, in the beginning, and so we allowed them to stay. They showed us improved methods for tunneling into the rocky mountainside where we made our dens, and in return we showed them how to fish the chitin-ore out of the shallow edges of the firepools without harm. How to smelt the chitin-ore into armor that would allow them to venture deeper into the firepools to fish out the larger ore deposits.

"This was our mistake. We did not recognize the avarice of the dwarves. They mined the chitin with unsustainable ferocity. They hoarded it until we ourselves could not fish enough chitin to make armor for our young ones.

"We appealed to the dwarves to mine less, or to give us of their stockpiles, that we might protect our young from the coming fire rains. They sneered at us. They told us that that which they had mined belonged to them. If we wanted it, we would have to buy it from them.

"Imagine, purchasing what had always been freely available to us from people we had allowed to come to our world. Still, to save our young ones, we would gladly have paid, but we had nothing of value to the dwarves and they knew this.

"When the fire rains came that spring, many of our young ones perished for lack of armor. We do not bear young easily or quickly, and their loss was felt terribly. My own daughter perished in these rains. She was barely six months."

Vorex paused, the memory of that loss fresh on his face.

"I'm sorry," Nyx said, and meant it.

Vorex smiled a sad smile. "You are. The dwarves were not. We licked our wounds through the remainder of the spring, mourning our losses and plotting. The Elders decided unanimously that the dwarves must leave. We approached them at summer's advent and told them they were no longer welcome on Kyvren. They could leave in peace, or we could force them out, but leave they would.

"They refused. War broke out. We had tooth and claw but we had never fought a war before. They had weapons. Axes and swords and they were vicious. They decimated our populations, and if we took many of their kind with us, we did not take enough. Where once we had been twelve dens, each den many thousand strong, we were reduced to a few thousand, and clan heritage no longer mattered.

"The dwarves threw back at us that choice we had offered, telling us we could leave or die. They had no right to offer it—Kyvren was ours, by birthright—but we had so few young left, and we feared the extinction of our race. The dwarves told us their rulers, the All Council, were offering us a home on a new planet called Arkadia.

"We agreed to leave. The dwarves emblazoned we Elders with a spell to guide us to our new world, and so it was that we first stepped onto a ley line." Vorex paused, deep lines of sadness etching his face.

Shyly, Nyx reached out and brushed her fingers against the obsidian thorns in Vorex's neck. "And you got lost in the chaos pockets?"

"No, little kin of ours. Chaos blocked the line, and the spells within us prevented us from reversing course. Those who could overcome the compulsion we urged to turn back, though whether they made it safely to Kyvren, or what fate they faced there, I cannot say.

"The rest of us either could not or would not turn back, and we entered chaos. It…consumed many of our number. It infected the rest of us, and only once the pocket had been drained dry into us and the path cleared were we able to complete our journey.

"We arrived here only a few hundred in number, and we were not the same. These thorns…" Vorex brushed a paw against his neck. "They fused our armor with our bodies. It became a living part of us—even our young are born this way now. And if the protection is not so bad, I miss the softness of fur, the comfort of removing armor to curl into a ball with my loved ones.

"I tell you this not to evoke your pity, but to make you understand what has been taken from us. We have been tricked, slaughtered, exiled, charged, and dropped on a planet where the galaxy sends its living refuse. All for the crime of having a resource the All Council desired."

Nyx worked to swallow around the tightness in her throat. She turned to Kaden, found her vision blurry and swiped angrily at her eyes.

"Did you know about this?"

"I—"

"Did you *know*?"

"It is not the version of events I was led to believe. The All Council's histories paint the Meerkin as an inherently vicious race exiled to Arkadia to prevent them from spreading war to the galaxy." Turning to Vorex, Kaden bowed low. "My apologies, Elder. I can see in your face that what I have been told is not true."

Vorex bent his head, sniffing Kaden's hair. "You are sincere in your words. That is rare, for your kind. I will accept the apology for your ignorance on behalf of my people."

Kaden nodded and straightened.

"So, kin who is not of my kin, will you lead us home?"

"You intend to return to Kyvren?"

"It is our home."

"How long ago were you sent here?"

"Over three-hundred and twenty circuits of the Anigar."

Nyx looked to Morgen.

"About nine-hundred Earth years. It is an unprecedented age, even for a Meerkin."

Nyx swallowed her disbelief. "Who lives on Kyvren now?"

"Dwarven mining families. They ship the chitin out to the Council's armormasters."

"And how long do the dwarves live?"

"A couple hundred years at most, why?"

Nyx turned back to the Meerkin leader. "Vorex, you under-stand that none of the dwarves who drove you out remain alive on Kyvren? That those who live there now may not even know what happened to you?"

Vorex's paws curled, obsidian claws slipping out. "They still live and breathe and take what is not theirs. And their lives are born of the spilled blood of my kin. I will not suffer them on Kyvren, not after what their ancestors have done."

"You would slaughter them?"

Vorex drew himself up, angry. "We are not like *them*. The dwarves will be given every opportunity to leave."

"And if they don't?"

"Then we will use more forceful measures. I cannot promise no harm will come to them. I cannot promise none of them will die. But we will avoid killing, if at all possible."

"It could take years to drive them out, with such an approach."

"Years we have. And if I dislike what chaos has done to our race, at least our young will be born with armor. That which drove us out before will not do so again. We are no longer soft, we Meerkin."

Vorex settled back, waiting.

"And if I refuse to take you, what will you do?"

"I would not force you, little kin. You and your group are free to leave, if you so choose. If you refuse, then you are not the one our seer foresaw. We will wait for her, instead. We are good at waiting."

Yes, they are, Nyx thought. "I think—" The collective hush of Meerkin tensing hit her palpably. "I think you have waited long enough. Let's go home."

The Meerkin broke out in joyful cries, half-yowl, half-hyena-yip, the forest alive with the sound of a dream centuries-old coming true.

Vorex was the only one who did not give noisy voice to his joy, and Nyx thought it was because he was oldest, and had seen hopes come and go the most.

"We need to get to the Station you came here through," Nyx told him. "It's about a two hour walk from here."

"I remember the place. We will be there within the hour, for tonight my kin will carry yours."

At his words, Meerkin streamed out of the swamp. This delighted the children and made the adults shift in discomfort. Tobi squealed loudest of all the children, immediately running to the smallest of the Meerkin who had come forward. Boy and Meerkin spoke quietly for a few moments. Then the Meerkin knelt and Tobi scrambled onto his back, just like the big cat was a pony.

The other children followed Tobi's suit, talking with a Meerkin and then clambering gracelessly onto his or her back. Kaden, Evra, and Morgen went last, looking about as comfortable climbing onto a Meerkin as if they had their hand stuck in a shark's mouth.

"As for you, little kin, you will ride with me." Vorex knelt. When Nyx hesitated, a hurt look flashed across his face. "I would not harm you."

"It isn't that," Nyx said truthfully. She stepped in, close to his ears and spoke softly, so her words would not carry. "Walking pains you. I saw it when you walked in. I would not add to that pain."

Vorex relaxed. "It is always painful at first, arising from the Long Sleep. But my bones are awake now, and you will be as a feather on my back."

A very heavy, human-shaped feather, Nyx thought drily. But she slipped onto his back, amazed at the fluid suppleness of the chitin scales covering his body.

Vorex's whiskers twitched, as if he could read her thoughts, and he said, "Hold on."

Before Nyx could ask *where* she was supposed to hold, Vorex shot down the path, ten powerful strides carrying them out of the swamp. Nyx clung to him with her legs, leaning low over his neck, and only once she was confident she would not fall off did she risk a glance back. Meerkin bounded behind them, numbering in the hundreds. The Meerkin who carried her friends followed directly behind Vorex, a sea of Meerkin following after.

Settling into the rhythm of Vorex's run, Nyx relaxed her grip, and let the night wind of an alien planet blow through her hair.

28

Nyx's joy at the night's ride dimmed as the Station came into view. A clenching tightness took hold in her chest and refused to subside, leaving her anxious and restless.

They came to a stop before the Station and she slipped off Vorex's back, the other bi-peds following suit. The humans, Vorex, and two other Meerkin entered, but the Station was too small to allow any others—without its Guardian, it was crippled, unable to alter its fundamental state.

Nyx doubted the Station's Avatar had any control over it at all.

She searched until she found the Avatar's glowing eyes. He cowered in the same spot she had last seen him, all but hidden in a dim corner. Nyx dropped to her knees and held out her hand, as if he were a dog or cat she was trying to befriend.

He whined, high and fearful, and though the look in his eyes said he wanted to come to her he shuffled backwards, scuttling until he pressed himself into a corner.

"Nyx." Kaden's hand pressed against her shoulder, urging her up. "You cannot help him now. And we should go."

She could hear what he hadn't added. *Before something happens. Before we're stuck here.*

Nyx let him pull her to her feet. "Where is the portal?"

"Over here." The Luminescent girls, Lana and Fari, were obligingly glowing, and through the dim purple light Nyx followed Morgen's voice until she spotted him, standing next to a portal very much like the one in her Station, only the silver posts and orbs here held no sign of life.

"Evra?"

"I am here, Nyx."

Nyx hurried to her. Evra reached into the folds of her cloak and pulled out the silver-blue orb of light that had spun so brightly in Nyx's Den. Pressing it into Nyx's hand, Evra told her, "You had better open the doors. I cannot, in this state."

Nyx cradled the orb to her stomach. It hummed beneath her touch, cool against her skin. Nyx looked at Evra. "Will you—will you make it back?"

Evra smiled. "Do not worry, Nyx. I have seen my death and this—this is not it."

The scary thing is, I can't tell if she's joking or not.

Tamrin came and put her hand on her sister's shoulder. "I will make sure she finds her way back."

Nyx nodded. Heart pounding, she carried the Opener of Doors to the portal. The deep, thrumming hum began in the floor beneath Nyx's feet, the silver orbs atop the six pillars spinning, slowly at first, shaking off the dust of centuries of disuse, then spinning faster, with ever-increasing frequency until they spun with such speed that at first glance they once again appeared stationary.

"I'll need to go last," Nyx realized. "To keep the door open."

Kaden looked to Maruca. Something inscrutable flickered across her features, but she nodded. At her assent, Kaden turned to Nyx. "It is best if our group goes together. We will wait for you."

"And I, too, will wait." Vorex's rumbling voice brought a smile to Nyx's face.

For as little as I've known you, she thought, *I will miss you.*

"You should go, Vorex. Take your people home."

"Korven!"

One of the two Meerkin inside the Station scrambled to Vorex's side.

"You are our seer. You have never been to our home but you know how to find your way. Lead our people home, Korven, and I will greet you at the end."

"Yes, Father." Korven's whiskers trembled but he approached the portal, the cosmic ooze in the center responding to his nearness. Nyx could feel the Opener of Doors holding back the layers of the spell the All Council had placed to seal the portal. The Opener hummed and burned in her hands, stretching like a cat awakened from a long nap, its power spreading out, lazy but strong.

Vorex went to the Station's door and opened it, Meerkin filing in, stopping in a line behind Korven. Korven bent his head to the black lip of the portal, sniffing. Then he stepped onto the platform, cosmic ooze swelling over his paws, inching up as he sank into it lower, lower, until it covered him and he disappeared.

The first Meerkin followed after, then the next, and the next.

It would take an hour, Nyx thought, maybe longer, for all of them to go through. Already her fingers ached, and she understood the Opener, for all its usefulness, was as dangerous as the other objects in the Den. It exacted a price for its use, and Nyx prayed she could pay that price as long as she had to.

Vorex returned to her side, calm and stoic for someone who had waited several centuries to return to his home. "I would have a word with you, little kin. In private, if I may."

Nyx nodded and Kaden and Maruca fell back to a respectful distance.

"I am the last of my kin still alive who has set paw on our homeworld. The rest of those who passed through the mists of chaos with me are long-dead. I tell you this because I wish to warn you of how they died, that you may avoid such a fate.

"When we arrived here my kin and I were stressed. It was understandable, given the circumstances, and we acted out accordingly. But soon our actions went beyond what was understandable. We argued constantly. We fought and found our emotions ruled by tides of anger foreign to us. Still, it was not until several fights ended in bloodshed that we calmed enough to look for an external source to our rage.

"Even in the past, when our clans battled for supremacy, we did not murder our own kind. It did not take us long, once we cooled enough to logic, to deduce that these thorns were the source of our problems.

"Naturally, we attempted to remove them."

Nyx winced. "Yeah, I tried that myself."

"You did?" Vorex rounded on her. "How many did you remove? Do you still have them?"

Nyx blinked, surprised by the force of his response. "Just one, on account of the pain. And yes. Why?"

Vorex relaxed. "I apologize. I did not mean to alarm you. As we removed the thorns, we did not realize—" Vorex stopped, shook his head. "My kind do not show our age much. We feel it in our bones, more than it shows on face or fur. Those who had some of their thorns removed felt weaker, tired. We thought it was only the pain of the extraction, a temporary side effect. But without fail, every single Meerkin who had their last thorn removed died.

"So our elders banned the removal of the thorns despite their harsh effects on us. It was not until many years later that our seers were able to unravel the truth. These thorns," Vorex brushed the thorns in Nyx's cheek, "they are connected to your life-force, now. Their removal hurts so fiercely because you are ripping out a piece of your life."

Nyx's heart stuttered. "I tore out part of my *life*?"

Vorex nodded.

"How much?"

"I am afraid I do not know, exactly. We think perhaps the

outer thorns pull less than the inner, but we had no true means of testing the theory."

"Oh." Nyx put a hand to her stomach. Morgen had pulled out an outer thorn. But how much had she lost? A few months? A few years? A decade?

"They can be restored," Vorex assured her. "The life-force extracted remains inside the thorn. If you replace it, it will become a part of you once more."

Nyx let out a long breath. "Does it hurt?"

"Yes. Not quite as much as the removal did, but yes."

"How many did you have removed?"

"Fourteen."

Nyx swallowed. "And replaced?"

"Twenty-nine. These are mine." Vorex tilted his neck, revealing the thorns on the left side. "And these are not." He tilted his head the other way, showing a new cluster of fifteen thorns. "These were given to me by our Elders. When our seer saw you coming, he also foretold many centuries would pass before your arrival. The Elders believed I had the best chance of surviving long enough to lead our people home. So they gave of their own lives to ensure that I would survive." His voice sounded bitterly against the Station's walls.

Gently, Nyx reached up and brushed her fingers against the thorns. "You didn't want this."

"To steal the lives of my friends? My mentors? To live an unnaturally long life, long enough to watch my children grow old and die around me? No, I did not want this. But you have lessened the pain, little kin. I had begun to think the Elders' sacrifices were for naught, but you have proven me wrong. And now, when I die, it will be on my home soil."

"I'm sorry that you waited so long for me."

"Do not be. It was not the point of my tale to bring you sorrow. I only wished to warn you from removing the thorns, and to prepare you. The emotions the thorns cause are powerful, erratic, and their effect will worsen with time. You can learn to control them, but you must *want* to do so. They give a heady power, a feeling of invulnerability, when you are in their grip, but they will use you to your own detriment. Remember that, little kin, and be safe."

"What *are* they?"

"If I knew, little kin, I would tell you. The most I can impart is that they are a wrongness in this universe, a thing that should not exist in its current form."

They sat in silence after that, thinking and watching the Meerkin depart the Station. When only twenty Meerkin were left, Kaden approached her.

"Re-entry is going to be difficult for us, since the Station is closed. We will have to enter through the opening Evra made in the Den, and that involves pulling ourselves out of the ley line when it is still running full-strength.

"Morgen is going to go first with Evra. They have both traveled extensively, and having seen the opening they are best suited to finding it first. The rest of our group will travel in pairs, each novice paired with someone who can find their way to Earth's Station. Morgen and Evra will watch for them and pull them out of the line."

Nyx nodded. "Sounds like a solid plan."

"I'll travel with you."

Nyx looked into the spinning blue depths of the Opener. It was that, or look at Kaden. "You should travel with Maruca. I can handle myself."

"You nearly died on the way here."

"Yes." Nyx reached a hand up to touch her cheek. "But I was trying to leave, then. Now… I'm the Station's *Guardian*, Kaden. It will let no harm come to me on my return."

Nyx felt the truth of the words in her bones, in the steady ache that had been drawing her to the portal ever since the Opener brought it to life. Refusing the portal's call wore on her, and she knew that the second she stepped into the line, her

Station would bring her home. It wanted her back and it would not be refused.

"Maruca is taking Kalvar through," Kaden said, finally.

Nyx said nothing.

"We'll travel together, Nyx. However much you may dislike it."

Nyx swore she saw a flicker of hurt on his face, present for the briefest moment and then gone.

The last of the Meerkin slid beneath the portal's cosmic ooze. Vorex turned to Nyx and gave her a small bow. "It will be many years before my homeland is stable, and still more before we allow any outsiders to visit. But when that day comes, I hope you will travel to see the beauty of my world."

"I would like that," Nyx said. "And if it is within my power, I will." The knowledge she would likely never be able to leave her Station again weighed heavy on her. "You gave me knowledge to help with my problems. Let me do the same for you. The person who runs the Station on your world, where the travelers come through, he is called a Guardian. He inhabits that position because he is bonded to the Station's Avatar, but he can choose to pass that bond to another.

"Convince the Guardian to give the bond to one of your kin. Then, the Avatar can teach you about how the Station works. You can shut the Station down to new Arrivals and still be able to send the dwarves off-planet. It will give you control again."

Vorex nodded, his face grave. "We will do as you suggest, kin who is not of my kin."

"And Vorex?" she added, thinking of Griff. "Whoever becomes your Guardian…tell him to be kind to his Avatar. Tell him…tell him to give the Avatar a name, if it professes no name of its own."

"I shall see it is done as you ask. Take care, little one, for I will be saddened if your face never graces my vision again."

And that's the problem with aliens, Nyx decided, as Vorex stepped onto the platform, *they're so damnably well-spoken.*

Kaden came up beside her in that quiet way of his that let her know he was there without startling her.

"It's time."

Nyx watched Morgen drilling the younger members of the group on the importance of staying with their travel partner at all times. When he was satisfied with their retention of his message he slung Evra's arm over his shoulder and they hobbled to the departure deck.

Evra looked sallow and worn, a single thread of her former self. Nyx was glad she was going through first. When the last strand of Evra's hair disappeared beneath cosmic ooze, and Lauralyn and Tobi were stepping onto the platform, Nyx heard a voice that was more like a whine.

<Please>

"Do you hear that?"

"Hear what?" Kaden tensed, hand on his sword hilt.

"That voice."

It came again, higher pitched.

<Please>

Two glowing yellow eyes crept forward in the darkness and an image appeared in Nyx's mind of the Avatar-creature disappearing into the cosmic ooze of the portal.

"Hold this." Nyx held the Opener to Kaden.

Kaden made no move to take it. "Nyx, if you're hearing voices—"

"I am *trusting* you, Kaden. Take it."

Kaden held out his hands and Nyx dropped the Opener into them. She watched the wonder flash across his eyes as it touched his skin, then she left him to find another pair of eyes in the corner of the small room.

The closer she came, the darker the corner grew, until all she could make out was the Avatar's eyes.

Kaden's voice rang out after her. "Nyx, I cannot see you."

"I'm fine. He's just scared."

"He?" Kaden's voice sounded oddly strangled.

<Not scared…Ashamed.>

Nyx crouched, squinting in a futile attempt to see through the darkness.

"What do you have to be ashamed of?"

An image in her mind, a tall man with skin like leaves and a raised tattoo on his arm of a wolf-like creature. A man in a robe, driving a knife through the leaf-man's gut while the wolf-creature snarled and threw himself at an invisible barrier that kept him from the crime.

The robed figure shoved the man off his knife, stepped backwards onto the departure platform, and disappeared.

"They killed your Guardian."

The Avatar whined.

"I'm sorry. I can't image what it's been like living here alone all this time." Or how painful. An Avatar without a Guardian—only madness lay in such a direction. The Avatar in front of her was proof enough of that.

He crawled forward on his belly, slunk low, whining. His fur was matted and chewed-up, doing little to cover the sharp edges of bones poking out of his skin like the exposed beams of a sunken ship. He shivered and trembled as he came nearer, his muscles straining in the monumental effort it took him to move.

<Take me>

He spoke haltingly, as if he hadn't spoken in so long he was no longer sure he used the words correctly. An image flowed into Nyx's mind, a still-shot of the portal, the wolf-creature on it.

Nyx reached out with her free hand and gently stroked the Avatar's matted fur, sadness welling inside her.

"If I take you, you will die."

A low whine.

<Yes. But…>

Images again, a wolf running across an open field, through forests, hunting, playing, sleeping, the wind ruffling his fur.

"But you will be free," Nyx whispered.

He whined, long and low, a million sorrows in the sound.

"Okay," she whispered. She hooked her free arm around him and lifted him up. He didn't weigh much—maybe ten pounds, though his frame indicated he should weigh much more—and she clutched him to her side, the one-armed hold unwieldy. She was as careful as possible but, even so, she was fearful a slip of her fingers would shatter fragile bones.

He whined and pressed his face into her stomach. His fur smelled dank and rotten, the hot breath of his exhales wafting up with a sulfurous stench.

She carried him back to the portal. On the deck, the two Luminescent girls were just slipping under the cosmic dust, the last of their group save her and Kaden.

"Do you have a name?" Nyx asked the Avatar.

<I did…once. I do not remember anymore> He dropped his head fully onto her shoulder as if the act of thinking, of interacting, had tired him beyond measure.

Kaden's eyes widened as Nyx approached, her mangy bundle cradled carefully against her.

"Nyx, what are you doing?"

Nyx lifted her chin. "I'm taking him with us."

"You cannot."

"I wasn't asking your permission."

"If you take him with us, he will die."

"I know." Nyx's throat clenched, but she refused to let it alter her voice. "But he's earned the right to choose his own death, don't you think?"

Understanding and pity bled into Kaden's eyes, but he didn't waver. "You do not know what it will do to the Station if he leaves."

"Actually, I do." Nyx's eyes fell to the tattoo on her arm, drawing Kaden's gaze to it. It was the symbol of her bond, maybe even the root of it. It was the thing that *made* her Guardian. She felt it in her bones, in a way she had felt nothing else she could remember. "It will destroy this place. Collapse it, and over time its ley line will unravel, an unmaintained road leading nowhere."

Kaden took a step toward her. "Nyx—"

"No one else will ever be able to come here. No more wrongly-sentenced prisoners, no more *children*. Can you look me in the eye and tell me that's a bad thing? What *your* Council has done here, *that* is a terrible thing."

The Avatar shook.

Kaden's face—his skin, his eyes, his lips—took on the smoothness of steel. "I was only going to say that I am glad no one else will come to this place. And as for *my* Council, well, they rule the *universe*, Nyx. You have never had to answer to that kind of power. Your planet is a singularly unique place in that, outside of Earth Between, the Council holds no political sway in your world.

"If you seek to blame me for their actions, I would remind you I was young when I became an Enforcer. We all were, Morgen, Ruca, and me. If the actions of youth are not blameless, I would like to believe they yet carry a certain naivete."

He met her gaze, unflinching, and it was Nyx who looked away first. She took a firm grip on the Avatar and stepped onto the portal's platform. "What's done is done," she said softly. "And I need to go home."

Kaden stepped next to her, his gaze on the staff in her right hand. "You might want to put that away."

"Unfortunately, I don't seem to be able to."

Kaden frowned. He juggled the Opener to one hand and touched a fingertip to the silver staff. A flicker of power slipped from him to the weapon.

"I think," he said, "it might accept a new master." He closed his fingers around the metal and power flooded from his hand, arcing through the staff like current through a wire. It did not *quite* burn her own hands but it wasn't pleasant, and when her fingers uncurled it was not of her own volition. No, it was as if the staff were throwing *her* off, rejecting her.

"How did you do that?"

"Weapons that attach themselves to people typically go after those most likely to use them with frequency. I have a much longer history of violence than you. I suspected it would leave you, if I asked it."

Asked it. Of course. Just ask the bloody staff if it wants to leave. "Isn't it just attached to you now?"

Kaden shook his head. "I haven't had it long enough. It should be safe enough, in my care, until we return to the Station."

His left hand still held the Opener of Doors, and he offered it to her now. She didn't want to take it back, if only because she wanted both hands to hold the Avatar. But the Opener was her responsibility, so she settled the Avatar more firmly against her, and took it back.

Kaden slipped an arm around her waist. She let him because it was the only reasonable spot for him to hold onto and—given her previous encounter with a chaos pocket—she wasn't going to reject a guide on this trip.

Nyx took a deep breath and they moved fully into the portal. Now that return was certain, now that they were going *back*, she let loose the panic that had been building inside her ever since she realized what traveling the ley lines as a Guardian meant. It blossomed in her chest, a harsh flower made of thorns and fire.

She studied the Guardian tattoo, its cracks and fading spreading dauntingly far across the canvas of her arm. She had to get back to Griff. Before he was driven mad like the Avatar she carried.

The ooze crawled over her ankles and waist, up her shoulders, her chin, caressed her lips. It pulled her down, down, until, for a moment, she saw nothing. Then, ever-so-gently, it dropped her into the molten river that was the ley line and, for the second time, Nyx felt the ecstasy of being unmade.

29

The world shattered, rearranged itself and shattered again, scattering into whorls of light and color of uncontained being. Nyx was struck again by the feeling of traveling great distances while standing still, of being suspended in time as the universe flew past.

The beauty of the ley line flowed about her, soft and golden, its mist embracing her like a lover, and though the experience was as she remembered, it was not quite as disorienting as her first trip. She was aware of her hands holding the Avatar and Opener, was aware that they were *her* hands, if it still felt unnatural to have a body in such a place.

She was not, truth be told, certain that she *did* have a body, only certain that her mind could not survive the thought of not having form. However it was that she held on to the Opener and the Avatar—with hands, with thoughts—did not matter so much as the fact that she *did* hold on to them.

They passed by the chaos pockets with their strange magnetism and dancing colors, and Nyx felt the rush of adrenaline, but nothing else. Chaos did not call to her this time. She felt a pulse of warmth where her cheek would be and realized that perhaps chaos did not call to her anymore because she was *part* of chaos.

It was Kaden who twitched, who responded to the hypnotic call of those masses lining the sides of the ley line. But it was only a single twitch. How many times had he traveled these lines, how many planets, that it took only a moment to return his focus to the path ahead?

Nyx heard a sound—an anguished, fearful noise—and in this place of unbeing it took her a moment to recognize the sound for what it was. A scream. Ahead of them, a girl screamed.

Kaden gripped her waist tighter and Nyx saw the pockets along the ley line blur as she and Kaden slipped past them faster, felt the coolness of the golden mist slip over her face with greater frequency, as if she held her hand beneath a waterfall.

He's controlling our speed.

Eons flew past them and when Kaden slowed their approach Nyx did not *see* the battle, she felt it. She recognized Maruca and Kalvar, Lana and Fari, even though she couldn't see them in any real sense like she could in the physical world. Instead, she saw their essences, each one unique and familiar to her.

Four other essences, unknown to her, lingered in the mist. Their voices boomed out as one, silent and audible at the same time, a voice in her mind rather than in space, much as the Avatar's voice had been.

<You are engaged in unauthorized travel in the company of known criminals. Surrender immediately. Give yourself over to the Council's mercy and you may yet be spared your life.>

They're only talking to me, Nyx realized. *The others can't hear them.* And as she recognized the truth of it, she recognized another. These weren't Enforcers. They were Councilors.

Against her chest, the Harvester *burned*. It clawed at her, tendrils of rage stealing her attention, turning her vision white-hot, and she understood that she was not the only one to recognize the Councilors for what they were. The Harvester, too, had recognized them. And it was completely, undeniably furious.

Kaden's pressure on Nyx's waist brought her focus back to the things around her, and she answered his unspoken question.

<I'll be fine. Go.>

He released her and his presence leaped forward. Nyx watched his essence unfurl, and saw how a battle unfolded between unmade beings.

Threads of light swirled and moved, darted and dodged. Every now and then a cord of threads would strike out from one entity, reaching for another. Sometimes they connected and Nyx saw pain as color, angry purples and dark blues, like storm clouds flickering across unmade flesh.

She wanted to help but her hands were full. She feared letting go of the Avatar. She felt him fading, bit by bit, even as she clutched him to her chest. If she let him go, here, in this place… what happened to those who simply ceased to be in this space of non-existing existence?

She would not risk his passing here.

Against her chest the Harvester pulsed like a second heart, beating with a silent intensity that forced her own heart to match its rhythm. Even had she wanted to look away from the events unfolding in front of her, she did not think the Harvester would let her.

She followed Kaden's and Maruca's movements as they spun and struck, and she warned them as blows approached from the back or side. Speech here was mere thought, and thought was only heard by whomever she wished to hear it.

Kalvar caught on to what she was doing and sent her a thought. <Watch Kaden. I will guard Maruca.>

Nyx agreed and, as the fight went on, she grew hopeful. Maruca and Kaden fought like twin demons, their essences so perfectly matched they were nearly identical, and Nyx knew that probably meant something, but she dared not take the time to contemplate it. She directed Kaden's movements like she had her fingers on a video-game controller, falling into a rhythm, a surety.

<Left. Right. Spin one-hundred and eighty degrees. Duck and turn.> Her fears became trancelike, expectant.

Without warning, one of the Councilor's essences broke from the group. He did not attack, moving instead away from the battle and taking Nyx's focus with him.

What is he doing?

For one brief moment she hoped he signaled a retreat. Then she saw his true aim, and her blood curdled.

<*Kaden*. The girls.>

Too late.

Kaden spun.

Too late.

The Councilor's essence reached Lana.

Kaden lunged.

Too late.

A cord of threads shot out from the Councilor's essence, plunged into Lana's, grabbed hold and *ripped*.

A scream rent Nyx's mind. Lana's essence pulsed purple, then blue, then thundercloud dark, cycling over and over like an octopus's chameleon camouflage.

Then her essence went black, crumbled to dust and hung in the air, a macabre mist of death. Next to Lana, Fari's essence spasmed once, violently, turned black and disintegrated.

Dead. Lana and Fari were dead.

The voice screaming inside Nyx's head did not stop. How could Lana scream, even after death?

She can't, Nyx realized. *I'm the one who's screaming.*

The Councilor's essence near the girls' death mists flushed a sweet lilac, and a lancing instinct in her gut told Nyx the essence felt pleasure.

Anger erased reason. Nyx thrust the Opener into her pocket —it suddenly didn't matter that it was too large in the physical realm to *fit* in her pocket, because it did, now—and ripped her sword from its sheath. She didn't try to walk or run. She *flew*, past Maruca and Kalvar, past Kaden who now looked as if he ran in slow motion, his hands still reaching for Lana.

The Councilor's essence moved, but to Nyx's eyes it moved as if through a mass of quicksand. Her sword came up. She brought the blade down, an angry slash from the left top of the essence diagonal down to the bottom right.

The essence's scream filled her mind and Nyx flushed with a pleasure of her own.

The Harvester fluttered against her skin, signaling its... approval? But as the other three Councilors flocked to their injured member, approval was replaced by a fresh spike of anger. Anger, and a demand. The Harvester's voice—if what Nyx felt could be *called* a voice, for it did not speak in actual words— trembled through Nyx, making one clear, unmistakable demand: *Unleash me.*

Nyx hesitated, her hand going to her chest not quite of her own will. One of the Councilor's essences moved to strike, but as it turned to face Nyx, the injured essence trembled violently, and the Councilor turned from her.

The Harvester pushed its will at her. Nyx pushed back, staying her hand mere centimeters from touching the Harvester. Before her, the three uninjured Councilors locked onto the injured essence, dragging it away down the ley line.

Nyx watched as they disappeared, fury etching her essence chaos-black, wishing she was foolhardy enough to give the Harvester its way.

A presence—Kaden—drifted up beside her.

<Nyx, we have to have go.> His attention, as he spoke, was on something just behind her.

She turned and noticed them, then, the chaos pockets converging on the space where she floated, and she understood that they were the true reason the Councilors had fled.

The chaos pulsing through her grew stronger at the approach of those swirling pockets. Even the Harvester seemed to respond to them, as it had responded to the shards in Nyx's cheek, and she knew Kaden was right, only, how could she leave? Lana and Fari had *died* here. She didn't even have a body to send to their family, to let them know…

<They are responding to *you*, Nyx. To your anger. We have to leave. Now.>

Nyx shoved her sword into its sheath. She reached out and grabbed a handful of dust from the first cloud—Fari—and tucked it into her right pocket. She reached for Lana's cloud, tucked the mist into her left pocket.

<I'm ready.>

Kaden took her arm. A chaos pocket floated beside her, prickly mold-like exterior close enough for Nyx to smell its dank odor.

Then they were moving again, speeding through cool, golden ley mist. Just ahead, the ley mist shot straight up where it should not, and a tendril of essence threads floated down. Morgen's hand, reaching for her.

Nyx grabbed for him and Morgen yanked her and Kaden out of the ley line and into the darkness of her Den.

30

Nyx felt the wrongness the instant her knees thudded to the Den floor. The Station—*her* Station—pulsed erratically, an anemic heart rate tripping, stuttering, confused and angry. The only light in the room came from the Den's glowing artifacts, giving it the mad-scientist feel Nyx had first associated with it.

The floor beneath her trembled, shaking tables and sending objects crashing to the ground. The source of the quake huddled in the back corner of the Den, wings covering his face.

Griff.

He was the size of an elephant, but things were...wrong. Stray feathers littered the ground around him, piled two inches high. His fur was matted and tufted, his muscles hanging oddly beneath his skin, as if they were not *quite* attached the way they ought to be.

A single feather fell from his wing. Nyx peered through the space where the feather had been. Griff's glasses were gone and the eye looking out at her shone bloody and red.

Nyx picked herself up. "Morgen, Evra, lead the others out of here."

"Little Guardian, I think—"

"Now, Morgen." She threw all the force of her Guardianship into the order. "My Avatar is not safe."

As if on cue, Griff made a guttural noise, half-scream half-wail, and thrashed. His hind feet kicked a bookshelf, knocked it over. It collapsed onto its neighbor, bookshelves falling like carefully placed dominoes.

"Nyx." Kaden's voice.

"Get out. Now." The whole of Nyx's attention was focused on Griff.

"I do not think that is possible." He spoke with a calm surety that chilled her and she turned, seeing what he saw.

Only the chaos of her Station, only the abject horror of seeing Griff in a state of madness, had made Nyx miss them. They ringed the Den in a tight-packed circle, just enough room between them to allow a blade held at the ready.

Each face was lightly dusted with freckles, sun-kissed auburn hair pulled back into identical braids. All perfectly the same height, all dressed in tall boots and matching leggings and tunics. Each set of eyes were a brilliant hazel, ringed in sunburst gold and utterly devoid of emotion.

Kumir.

Breathless, Nyx counted. Stopped counting when she hit twenty. Ten would have been too many. Evra and Morgen were exhausted. No doubt Kaden and Maruca were, too. And then there were the children to think of, and the fact that the room grew more unstable by the second.

How the hell had they gotten in here?

Only the how didn't matter right now. They could not hope to fend off twenty Kumir.

She knew it for truth by the look on Kaden's face, the look of hopelessness on it that, for all their trials on Arkadia, had never crossed it there. But he tightened his grip on the hilt of his sword and she knew, *knew,* that no matter the impossibility of success, he would fight anyway.

This time, when the Harvester warmed against her chest,

when she felt the power welling within and it promised it could help her, she did not deny it outright.

Nyx pulled the chain from beneath her shirt, cupping the Harvester in her hand. Light shone feverishly inside the overlapping rings that formed the sphere, the pendant itself humming against her cupped palm.

Nyx felt its eagerness, its *need*, and hesitated.

As one, and without warning, the Kumir surged forward.

Nyx looked at the kids, huddled within the protective circle of Morgen, Evra, and Maruca. She looked at Kalvar, not quite child, not quite adult, his Tiagren claws out.

She looked at Kaden, his face grim, his grip firm on the hilt of his sword, and decided right then and there that no one was killing him before she had the chance to sit him down and ask *What the hell?* in no uncertain terms.

Nyx took a deep breath, and gave the Harvester permission.

Power exploded outward from the sphere, beams of light brighter, stronger, more brilliant than the sun. She closed her eyes. She had to. Even behind the relative safety of closed eyes the light reached, sending prisms of color flashing on the insides of her eyelids.

Nyx couldn't see the Kumir, but she could hear them. Where she had watched them lift their swords as one, she now heard them scream as one. She forced her eyes open, squinting against the harsh rays of light. It took a moment for Nyx to understand what she saw, and even then she understood it only in the way a child might see water boiling and be able to relate that they had seen it, yet be unable to explain the scientific mechanism behind *why* the water boiled.

The Kumir were unmade; it was as if the light splintering through them ripped apart the very fabrics of their beings, separating them into whatever component parts a person could be broken down into. Hair and skin dissolved, laying bare the fat and muscle, the organs and vessels which, once exposed, became paper-thin and disintegrated into dust.

Once gone, only a blackened, human-shaped shadow limned the bones and this—this the Harvester pulled to itself and drank down, sucking shadow into the glowing depths of the rings that contained its light. Shadow melded into light in the way of two substances that will not mix, the shadow making small swirls and pockets of dark in the expanse of light.

With nothing left to sustain them, the bones of the Kumir dropped to the Den floor with clanks and clatters, as bleached-white as if they had lain years beneath the desert sun. They were whole only a few seconds before crumbling into a fine, powder-white dust.

In Nyx's hand, the Harvester *purred*. She felt its satisfaction at the intake of the shadows. Felt, too, its continued hunger, its attention turning from the inanimate bones of the Kumir to the others present in the room. The light, which had dimmed to a soft glow at the influx of shadow, began once more to build.

No. Nyx closed a fist around the Harvester, stuffing it back behind her shirt, heart racing as it fought her, its power demanding to be set free. She dropped her hand from it. As it slid down against her chest, its influence dropped, its light no longer visible beyond the bounds of her shirt.

The cessation of the Harvester's light restored her ability to see with normality, revealing to Nyx near-identical looks of horror on the faces of everyone in the room.

"Little Guardian, what *was* that?" Morgen's eyes were rounded wider than should have been possible.

She was spared the necessity of answering when the room's undulations made clear that, Kumir or no Kumir, they still had a problem. A heavy desk slid across the floor. Kaden leapt over it nimbly, its trajectory just missing the rest of the group.

Griff roared, a metal-toned, anguished cry that pierced Nyx's heart.

"Morgen, get everyone out of here."

He didn't argue with her. Neither did Maruca.

Kaden did, his gaze trained on Griff. "Nyx, he is not safe."

"No, he is not. I left him to an unknown fate, once." *To find you.* "I will not leave him to another." Gently, she pressed Arkadia's Avatar into Kaden's arms. "Make him comfortable."

Kaden did not immediately accept the bundle. He met her gaze, challenging. Nyx did not waver.

At last, Kaden set Nyx's bo staff on the floor and closed his arms around the Avatar. He nodded to her once and carried his bundle to the exit.

"And Kaden?"

He turned.

"For the sake of everyone here, shut the door behind you."

Fifteen seconds later, the Den's door clanged shut and Nyx was alone with her Avatar.

"Griff?"

The mass in the corner trembled. Nyx approached slowly, picking her path between fallen objects, careful to avoid touching anything. She stopped a foot away from the griffin. He eyed her warily between his feathers, none of the gentle, scholarly griffin she remembered left in his face.

"Griff?" She stretched her hand out tentatively. Her fingertips brushed the edges of his wings and he exploded. He thrashed, wild, beak snaking out and nipping her skin, a bright spot of blood welling up, running in rivulets down her arm.

Stubbornly, Nyx reached for him again. She yanked her hand back just in time to dodge a second strike of his beak. Griff launched into the air, feathers raining down as his wings struggled to keep him airborne. The high ceiling grew higher, wider, accommodating his drunken flight. He careened and tumbled, hitting walls, his dragging hind feet knocking over tables.

He's losing control of the Station.

The room had grown to the size of a cathedral, the ceiling so high Nyx couldn't actually see it. Griff disappeared for entire minutes into the crackling darkness at the top before plummeting down, screeching and flailing, and only just gaining traction enough to avoid crashing into the ground.

The walls undulated, writhing and twisting. The floor grew spongy, reminding Nyx of the swamp, and around her everything had turned the charred black of coal. Items flew off tables, slamming into walls and shelves. Nyx ducked them as she could, but she had already taken four hits, one of those from a metal candelabra that opened an inch and a half long gash along her right temple.

A copper vase flung itself at her as she dodged a book, the vase slamming into the backs of her knees, knocking her to the ground. She lay there a moment, dazed, sinking into the spongy floor and remembering Griff as she had first seen him—housecat sized, spectacles in place, confident and in supreme control of everything around him.

Remind him who he is. Remind him what *he is. He is the Station's Avatar. He controls it. He just has to want to.*

"Griff? I need you to settle the room."

Nothing.

"Griff, you need to settle the room." The room shuddered, fighting to find stasis, trembling, objects frozen in midair for one, two, three seconds. Then the spell shattered and objects whizzed back and forth, the walls undulating faster than before. Nyx sank into the floor with alarming speed.

From across walls and rooms, the voice of Arkadia's Avatar came to her. <Exert your will. The Bond exists because the Avatar does the Guardian's bidding. Force him to do yours, and you will restore the Bond.>

<I… it isn't right to force him.>

She had argued against Evra, against Morgen, against everyone who had treated Griff like a thing, a possession. She had insisted he was a person. If she *commanded* him, she was not treating him like a person.

<Maybe not. But he will die if you do not. You must make your choice.> His voice faltered and faded, and then was gone. *He* was gone. Nyx allowed herself a moment to mourn his passing. More than a moment, she didn't have.

Nyx pushed to her feet, swallowed her own fear and self-loathing, searching for the place inside her where she felt the remnants of the bond. She immersed herself in it, took hold of it, and commanded her Avatar.

"Griff. You will land, *now*."

He moved so fast the air whistled around him, his wings tucked, neck stretched out in a forward dive. Ten feet from the ground he pulled his nose up and flung his wings wide, landing before Nyx with a *thump* that shook the entire room.

Anger burned in blood-red irises and he fought that place of connection they shared, where she held him when he did not want to be held. Guilt gnawed at her. She almost released the connection, but a tingling on her arm distracted her.

The griffin tattoo, cracked and faded, was mending. The open spaces in the griffin's tail filled in, colors gaining vibrancy. Hind paws and legs followed suit, but there the mending ended.

Nyx renewed her hold. "Griff, settle the room."

Storm clouds shadowed his eyes. His tail thumped once, rattling the table next to him. The objects in the room settled to the ground, crashing around her. Beneath her feet the floor solidified, raising her up. The walls quivered, then became fixed.

The tattoo knitted itself back together over the griffin's hindquarters.

"Return to the room to its previous size."

Another thump of Griff's tail, not so heavy this time, his eyes a shade less red. The ceiling lowered, the walls drew close, and the room became a room once more.

The tattoo knitted together over the griffin's shoulders, down his legs, only a small circle in the chest and the griffin's head left unhealed.

"Griff, put the room to rights, everything back in its place."

Tables screeched, dragging along the floor to reach previous positions. Items flew to tables, to shelves, opened drawers and slid into them. The great bookshelves righted themselves with creaks and groans, books filing onto the shelves. Lights flickered on.

The tattoo knitted up over the griffin's head. Only the circular patch in the chest remained broken.

Griff stumbled. The red had bled completely from his eyes and in the new light he looked haggard and gone. Feathers continued falling, his wings like some skeletal creature's. The muscles moved oddly on his body, and he was still that charcoal color all over.

But Nyx looked into his pretty golden eyes and saw *Griff*.

"Nyx, I—I am sorry."

Nyx dropped her hold on their connection and ran to him, flung her arms around his eagle's neck and buried her face in what was left of his feathers.

"This is *my* fault. Everyone told me Guardians don't travel. I went anyway and now look at you."

"I told you to go," Griff said, gently.

"And I shouldn't have." Nyx drew back, a shower of feathers following in her wake. Griff was mostly skin and bones, now, fur and feathers littering the floor around him.

"You *should* go now. You must, before I am lost again."

Nyx ignored him. "I'm not going anywhere, you're getting worse."

She looked at the tattoo. Before her eyes, the center faded until it was barely visible, spreading slowly outward, destroying the areas she had only just repaired.

"Griff, you need to do something. Change the walls, or redecorate, or *something*."

Griff gently laid a talon on her arm, covering the tattoo. "It will not work."

"It has to."

"If you had just left here, perhaps it would. Your efforts have brought my sanity back, and for that I am grateful. But too much damage has been done and the blame is mine. You see, when you left, Nyx, I tried to follow you."

Nyx stumbled back. "Why would you do that?"

Griff smiled, weary, and Nyx caught a glimpse of something ancient beneath his eyes. She wondered, suddenly, just how old he was.

"How could I not? I have lived lifetimes, Nyx. Some of those with Guardians I was very fond of, others not so much. But none of them sought to treat me as their equal. You gave me something I never thought to have again. A friend.

"So I thought to follow you. To help you."

"What happened?"

"I am tied to the Station in much the way I am tied to you. When you entered the ley line, our bond severed, and if an Avatar is only half-alive without a Guardian, he or she is yet still alive. When I tried to enter the ley line, it sought to sever my connection with the Station. Before I pulled back, it partially succeeded, and without *that* bond, I am dead.

"I am unraveling, Nyx. And because of my attempt to leave, the Station is unraveling with me. You need to go. Get your friends out, before it is too late."

"No." Nyx shook her head. "I can't, I *won't*. How do I fix this?"

"You cannot. But you will live on without me. Of the two of us, only I am tied to the Station. Fear not for your own life."

"I'm not worried about *me*. I'm worried about *you*. There has to be a way to fix this."

Griff did not answer. He blinked at her with ancient, soft eyes, telling her she sought a solution that did not exist.

In Nyx's peripheral vision the walls undulated, stripping themselves of the constraints of physics. *No, I won't run. There has to be a way.*

"Griff, how were you—" *made* "—how did you come to be the Avatar?"

Griff groaned, settling onto his side in an effort to disguise his failing strength. "It is of no matter. *Leave*, Nyx."

The floor softened. Griff sank into it while Nyx hopped from foot to foot to stay aloft.

"No. Look, you were *made* into this, right? So if whatever did this is coming undone, I just need to know what that was so I can *redo it.*"

"You cannot, Nyx. Only the Council knows the magic they used to bind me to the Station's Heart. It is that Heart that is dying now. Do you understand?"

"Yes," Nyx whispered, slipping her hand into her pocket, fingertips brushing against a small, cool object. "I understand."

The Station's *Heart* was dying. And a dying thing needed life.

"Good." Griff groaned, settling further onto his side. "Then go."

Nyx turned and ran over soggy ground, tripping as objects only just returned to their places began spilling onto the ground once more.

Nyx ran faster. She threw herself at the ladder, landed on the third rung and clawed her way up. She had the presence of mind —barely—to drop the pack, the Opener, and Veritas back into the Den where they belonged before she emerged into the Station's library. The ominous creaking of shelves greeted her. She recognized the sound as the stacks falling soon enough to understand what was happening, too late to do anything about it.

Nyx yanked her feet back as a bookshelf fell hard across the Den's opening. Around her, the stacks swayed and trembled like branches in a storm.

Nyx ducked her head protectively beneath her arms and *ran* as whatever will holding the stacks upright snapped and they fell around her. The sharp corners of hardcover books broke skin. Spines struck with bruising force. They pelted and tripped her, tore her shirt, flew past the protective covering of her arms and opened gashes on her cheeks, her forehead.

An entire shelf slipped free of a bookcase, slamming into Nyx's side. She fell, books raining down on her, burying her in ink and paper and stories she would never have the chance to live. She shoved L'engle's *A Wind in the Door* and *A Ring of Endless Light* out of her way. She struggled over Zelazny's *Chronicles of Amber*, ignoring the pain in her side that might or might not be a broken rib, and pushed herself to her feet again, boot landing squarely atop Mercedes Lackey's *Arrows of the Queen.*

Nyx shoved off, left side throbbing as each step jarred her body, as she made it out of the stacks and into the kitchen area.

At least, the kitchen *should* have been where she stood. Instead, Nyx found herself in an early nineteenth century study, complete with leather armchair, oriental rug, decanter of whiskey and—she shuddered—more bookcases. At least these shelves appeared secured to the walls.

She spied a door on the opposite side of the study, ran and pulled it open, found herself in a rustic, log cabin-style room with animal furs spread out on a dirt floor and a fire burning in the corner. A wooden rocking chair was the only piece of furniture.

Nyx ran through every door she found, through parlors and ballrooms, living rooms and libraries, crafting rooms and theater halls. It wasn't until she ran into an island room, sand on the floor, an ocean-blue pool in the center and cases full of island jewelry, that Nyx fully understood what was happening.

The island, this is how the Station looked when Sena lived here. Nyx bent down, picked up a fistful of sand and let it trail slowly through her fingers. The Station was flipping through its past incarnations, all the rooms it had ever had, all the ways it had ever looked.

Sand dripped between the cracks in Nyx's fingers, frustration growing at her inability to go where she wanted. She needed the Station's *Heart*, the one thing that, though its décor might change, could never cease being what it *was.*

Then it came to her. *The portal.*

The last of the sand grains slipped through Nyx's fingers. She closed her eyes and listened for the deep, thrumming hum that had called to her the first time she had been in the portal room.

She had thought it had been the stars calling to her then, the ley lines beckoning her to travel them, but what if she had been wrong? What if that thrumming, that *beating*, belonged to something else entirely?

Eyes closed, Nyx's ears strained. At first she could only hear the gentle lapping of water on sand, the faint breeze that should not but did blow in the small room.

She waited, unmoving, listening *past* the close sounds until she heard a different one, a low, sweet thrumming that sounded as if it came from the other side of the world.

Nyx did not open her eyes, terrified that if she *saw* she would no longer be able to *hear*. Blindly, she followed the sound. She followed it through the pool, water splashing up to her knees, hands held out in front of her to keep from banging face-first into walls.

Her hands found a door, opened it. She walked in, banged her shins on what felt like a coffee table and cursed. She stumbled through more doors, banged her shins on more tables as she moved towards that deep, hypnotic Heart.

Nyx knew she had found it when she stood outside a door that pulsed with energy, the thrumming so loud it vibrated in her bones, resetting the beat of her own heart so that the two beat together. The synchronicity of it frightened Nyx, made it difficult for her to tell the difference between herself and the Station—difficult to tell if there *was* any difference at all.

Nyx opened her eyes, opened the door, and strode into the portal room. The silver posts sat in their customary hexagonal pattern, orbs spinning lazily atop them. This part of the room remained normal. The rest...

The walls writhed and shifted, flipping between scenes like a madman flipping through projector slides. The walls were a forest, a beach, a library, a desert. On and on it went, the flash of images straining Nyx's eyes. Sometimes the walls were multiple things at once, forest bursting out of a sandy beach, bookshelves carefully placed atop desert plains.

The Heart. She needed to find the Heart, and soon, if the rate at which the floor rotted away beneath her feet was any indication of Griff's state.

Nyx's heart still beat in time with the thrumming running through her veins. It tugged at her, intoxicating, and she relaxed her self-control, stopped resisting. It wasted no time, pulling at her eagerly, dragging her to the opening between two of the posts that formed the portal.

Does it want to save Griff too? Does it want anything at all, or does it simply exist, some strange, space-age symbiote?

It pulled her down, drew her fingers to the cosmic floor between the silver posts. Nyx panicked, fighting the force reeling her in. Her back and neck tensed, every muscle popping as if she strained against a two-ton mass.

She couldn't slip through the floor. If she entered the ley lines again Griff would be lost to her forever.

The force yanked her down, thrust her arm into the cosmic ooze of the floor. Nyx thrashed wildly, a dolphin in a net, a lion in a cage, her struggles as painful and futile as those of any trapped animal.

Unexpected coolness spread through her arm, her shoulder, her neck. Up, up, pervading her consciousness until she became aware of another entity showing her that *here*, at the portal, a Guardian alone could take two paths. One, yes, led to the ley lines. The other led beneath and above, around and yet between, to a place existing in neither time nor space and there, *there*, Nyx saw what she needed.

Nyx closed her eyes, let go, and entered a freefall through the cosmic floor. She coughed and sputtered as the air turned into something viscous. She held her breath until her lungs burned and her head threatened to burst and then she *breathed*, pulling liquid coolness into her lungs.

It burned as she drew it in but the pressure in her head dissipated. Her fall ended abruptly as she landed on a soft mass of moss that covered purple vines as thick as saplings. They formed the floor of a circular room, the walls of which she could not see. The space felt infinite.

The room chilled her, icy air biting at her skin. She rubbed her arms. How did the vines manage to grow in such an environment? There was no sunlight here, no warmth.

Maybe they like it that way.

<We do not like it. But it is all we have.>

Nyx jumped, twisting in midair, searching for the speaker of the words.

She saw no one.

You think I'd be used to voices in my head by now.

"Are—are you the Station?"

<We are of the Station.>

"Are you its Heart?"

<The Heart is here.>

A faint glow drew Nyx's gaze to the center of the room. A ropy pedestal of vines grew waist-high. Perched atop the pedestal was a formless mass, seething and shrinking and then growing, changing shape at unknowable whims.

<The Heart is here,> the vines repeated. <We are it, and it is us, and yet we are separate. Alone.>

Nyx watched the mass twisting and changing and thought looked like a scream sounded.

"It's in pain."

<Yes. The Avatar is all we have. Our anchor, our eyes. He sought to leave us. For you.>

Anger raged beneath the voice, a harsh streak of resentment, and Nyx wondered if the Station hadn't brought her here to kill her. The vines shifted at her feet and her pulse panicked, heart rabbit-kicking behind her ribcage.

The voice laughed in her mind, and Nyx found she preferred laughter to be free in a room, where it resounded off walls and not off the corners of her mind.

<You need not worry. We will not harm you.>

Nyx did not *quite* believe them. "I came to help."

<You cannot help. The Avatar's bond to you is stronger than it is to us, and soon we will be utterly alone. You have helped enough.>

The vines slithered around Nyx's ankles, and it occurred to her that this being, whatever it was, might have a definition of harm quite different from her own.

"You must have thought I could help. Why else would you bring me here?"

<Why, to ensure we would not be alone.>

Nyx tried to move but her feet were stuck fast, anchored in layers of vines. "You can't keep me here."

<We can. We will.>

"Griff is dying. The *Station* is dying."

A momentary pause, a rustling of vines that was acceptance. <And now we will not die alone.>

"I can *help* you. Please. How long has Griff been here for you? How long has he been your eyes?"

<Since the dawn of what we now are.>

"He didn't know what would happen when he tried to follow me. This is my fault, not his. Let me fix it."

<But he left us once, to go after you. You may choose to leave again, and if you do, the Avatar may choose to follow you. Then we will be dying again, only we will not have you here.>

Nyx struggled against the vines. "I won't leave again. I promise."

<You are mortal.> The vines hissed, angry. <To be mortal is to be fickle. Unknowable. You may mean your words now, but the emotions which led to you to leave us once may one day call you to leave us again. Your promise means nothing.>

Nyx slumped, knees landing on the soft vines that crawled over them, over her legs, up her waist. She couldn't let Griff die. He was her first friend, her first *true* friend.

If he died, if the Station died and she managed to get out, where would she go? Back to bills and evictions and applying for low-level retail jobs? She was *someone*, here. She had purpose, and if wanting to stay at any cost meant she was weak and foolish, well, better weak and foolish than utterly useless.

Nyx gathered her courage, fought down the panic, the *finality*, of what she was about to do. "I can make my promise mean something. Griff is bonded to you, to the Heart, yes?"

<It is so.>

Nyx fumbled in her pocket, pulled out the chaos thorn and held it up. "This thorn holds a piece of my life. Its essence. Years. I was told I could give it to another, if I chose. I believe life will restore what is broken in you. If you let me give it to you, let me save Griff and the Station, I would agree to bind myself to you as Griff is bound. My promise would mean something then, wouldn't it?"

The vines did not respond immediately. They quivered around her legs, her waist. It felt to Nyx like excitement, and she was not sure she liked the way it felt.

<You would do this?>

"On three conditions. One, it seems Griff cannot leave the area immediately surrounding the Station. If I am to be bound, I need freedom to wander all of Earth Between *and* Earth, no restrictions."

The vines quivered. <This condition is acceptable. And the next?>

"Ten times. I want to be allowed to leave Earth. Go other places on the ley lines, ten times."

<Not possible. We are dying because you chose to leave. You leave again, we die again.>

"I don't think that's true. You need *an* anchor. You have Griff, already. When I join with you, you will have two. Only one of us need be present to sustain you."

A pause. <True. But our Avatar nearly went mad at your departure, at the bond between Avatar and Guardian unraveling. An insane Avatar is not much of an anchor at all.>

Nyx had expected this argument and come up with a solution. "This thorn, it came from these." Nyx brushed her hand across her cheek. "If I take one and give it to Griff, he will have a part of my essence that the ley lines can never unmake. He will not suffer the effects of my departure again."

The vines laughed, low and soft, echoing off the corners of Nyx's mind. <Girl-child, you do not understand what those 'thorns,' as you call them, take from you. Or what they give to others. You would be a fool to give one to the Avatar. Twice the fool to give one to *us*.>

Nyx shrugged. "Then I am a fool. Do you want to live, or not?"

The vines seethed. <Your third condition?>

"Griff. I want him to have the freedom to wander Earth and Earth Between as well, *and* I want you to let him travel. Ten times, like me. If you have me as an anchor as well, only one of us is needed here at a time. Let him go. He's earned it."

The vines deliberated, rubbing against each other like a fly cleaning its legs. <Six. You may each travel six times, each duration no longer than one week.>

"I think—"

<Six times. Take the offer, Guardian, or stay here and die with us.>

The room is shrinking, Nyx realized. It encroached upon her, shrinking towards the Station's Heart. When it reached the Heart, the Station would die.

"I accept."

<Excellent.>

A new tattoo cropped up, this time in the webbing between the thumb and forefinger on her left hand, an elegant, stylized number six.

<And Guardian? Should a trip take longer than a week, it will count for the next one. Fail to return, and you will not like the consequences.>

The vines wrapped around Nyx's waist and legs, pushing her up, out, flinging her at the Heart that writhed and twisted. Nyx hovered over the Heart, held aloft by the green and purple vines, and fought the nausea twisting her insides into knots.

Gripping hold of the thorn, she shoved it into the amorphous mass. At the same time, a tiny green vine, no wider or longer than a sewing needle, pierced the flesh on her hand, wriggled deep, and disappeared inside her.

Nyx screamed in unison with the vines.

It felt as if the needle-vine grew within her, stretching alongside veins and sinews until it covered every inch inside her, a second-skin beneath the one she had always known. The foreignness of it burned. She clawed at her skin, digging *beneath*, fingernails drawing blood, scraping away chunks of skin until the green vines twined further up her body and gently restrained her hands.

She was aware of the vines now in a different way than she had been before, felt them moving as if they were a part of her though they were not attached to her body.

Blood dripped from her arms, splashing across the vines and Nyx felt the blood land on them as if she *were* the vines.

The room stopped shrinking. Instead, it spun outward, appearing to Nyx as infinite in its expansion as the universe itself. The Heart sat on its pedestal, a calm, steady pulse replacing its earlier writhing.

Beneath that calmness a cold, ancient anger burned. Nyx felt it in her bones, in the foreign layer beneath her skin, as she had only grasped it on the surface before that needle-vine pricked her skin.

Sweat dripped from her forehead and she shivered. "What— what *are* you?"

The vines chuckled. <You only *now* think to ask? We are that which should not exist, but does. A half of a whole, a sundered being.>

"That doesn't tell me anything."

<It tells you everything. You simply do not understand.>

Nyx longed to claw at her skin, but the vines held tight around her wrists.

<Do you hate us? Do we revolt you?>

Slowly, Nyx shook her head. "You scare me."

<That, Guardian, is the first sensible thing you have said. And now, it is time for you to go.>

The vines lifted her up.

"Wait." The vines halted. "Griff. What happened to him? If you won't tell me plainly of yourself, tell me how he came to be here."

<Why should we?>

Nyx groaned. Talking to the vines was like dealing with a herculean-strength toddler. They were utterly stubborn and had no sense of social norms.

"I saved your life."

<For selfish reasons.> The vines paused, waving at each other in that way Nyx suspected meant they spoke to each other where Nyx could not hear. <Still, you did.>

So the vines told her of Griff, and Nyx wept, feeling her tears drip off her cheeks, feeling them again as they splashed onto her vines below.

<We are not ungrateful for what you have done for us. But it is time for you to go. The ley lines hum, the Council comes, and your illicit friends are above in plain sight. We must admit, we are *most* interested to see how you will make your way out of this.>

The vines lifted her up and yet down, between and around, until she burst through the portal, coughing up cool not-liquid into her hands. She stared, horrified, at the black ichor coming out of her lungs.

31

Nyx wrapped her arms around herself, shivering, her hair hanging in wet, ropy strands around her face. She looked up into an array of puzzled faces staring at her with varying mixtures of concern and horror.

One face moved toward her: Kaden, a small bundle still held in his arms. Arkadia's Avatar. Dead. Nyx was glad Kaden still held him, glad he hadn't tossed the Avatar aside like refuse.

Kaden reached out, took hold of her elbow with his free hand and pulled her off the portal platform. He cupped her face in his hand, turning it left then right, as if looking for a difference he felt but couldn't quite see.

"What happened?" he asked, voice soft.

Nyx shook her head. The memory of the black ichor swelling out of her lungs made her gag, and she couldn't speak.

Since she couldn't, Kaden did. "The Station was in chaos. We roamed for what felt like hours and when everything settled we were *here*, just in time to see you coming up out of there." He pointed at the portal.

"Station was dying," Nyx coughed, "had to—" She broke off as the now-familiar deep thrumming of the portal filled her bones, heralding the arrival of travelers, and she recalled the Station's warning.

"The Council is coming. You need to hide."

Fingertips rose from the cosmic dust and she knew it was too late. They could run, but what if the Council searched the Station? Searched Earth Between?

I need to hide them, she thought, and this time, with the Council involved, she didn't trust her ability to think *We're not here*, to keep them safe. The Station responded to her need, quickening.

I'm bonded to it. Like Griff. Griff made the Station rearrange with a blink. How difficult could it be? *Back. I need them all back against the walls.*

The floor rippled and moved, responding, carrying Kaden and the others to the edge of the room as if they stood on conveyor belts. A trickle of warmth dripped from Nyx's nose, trailing down across her upper lip.

"Nyx, what are you doing?" Kaden walked forward. Nyx urged the floor to send him back. The Station did not respond immediately so Nyx added a physical motion, her hand moving back, guiding her intentions. The floor carried Kaden back and the warm trickle running from her nose increased.

"Hiding you. Whatever you do—all of you—don't make a sound."

In the portal, the hand Nyx had seen coming up in the center was further along, revealing an elbow, an arm.

I need a new wall, a false wall.

The Station shuddered. Nyx lifted her arms and her wall burst through the floor, reaching to meet the ceiling just as the first face broke the surface of the portal's platform. Black cosmic dust sloughed off the body, revealing a face diagonally bisected by a fresh, angry cut. Rage prickled in the thorns on Nyx's cheek, flushed through her.

You killed Lana. And Fari. You killed them, and I cut you.

Black hair slipped straight and obedient past the man's

shoulders. He stepped off the platform, lithe and graceful and far taller than she. He was dressed in garments that were not *quite* robes. What material they were made of, Nyx couldn't say, but they made not the slightest whisper as he walked, long, taper-thin fingers slipping out from the edges of the flowing sleeves.

The architecture of his face was perfect—high cheekbones and olive skin, eyebrows arched aristocratically over slanted eyes of slate gray. He held perfect posture without any apparent effort to it, shoulders back and head lifted. The only marring to his perfection was the slash across his face, and even that seemed not to matter so much.

Nyx felt she understood, now, what harsh beauty was, because she was staring at its embodiment.

The man stopped two feet from her, eyes sparking with anger to the sword strapped to Nyx's side, as if he knew it for the one that had marked him.

He doesn't know. Nyx forced herself not to take a step back, to remain as relaxed as possible, hands loose and not clenched into fists. *We were pure essence on the ley lines. Even if he suspects, he has no proof.*

The man did not speak, waiting as, one by one, three other forms arose from the platform behind him, each similarly garbed and bearing the same pristine, chill manner. The second man out could have been the first one's twin, save the absence of a scar, and that he looked slightly older.

The woman who stepped off after him stood shorter, though the difference in height did nothing to diminish her. Her posture claimed ownership of all in her vicinity. Almond-shaped, hazelnut eyes set into rice-milk skin surveyed the room, surveyed Nyx. Full, plum-colored lips shifted slightly, a small moue of disapproval. Her hair, braided into dozens of thin cords, matched the color of her lips and seemed to move as if each braid were a limb, reminding Nyx of nothing so much as the myth of Medusa.

The fourth and last member of the party stepped out, tall and regal, her skin as pale and harsh as alabaster. Soft, wild curls framed a face born to be a poet's muse. Her elegant hands twitched and curled, fingers fluttering about, as if she were playing an invisible piano or weaving a multitude of threads. She took her place next to the others, the four forming a solid line.

Nyx, bedraggled, bruised, and bleeding, stared into the faces of four of the most powerful people in the universe, and attempted a welcoming smile.

The woman with the plum-colored lips spoke, her voice eerily reptilian, the cords of her hair shifting, snaking over her shoulders.

"Greetings, Guardian Nyx. I am Alora. This is Jevryn." She held her hand out, indicating the unscarred man. "Kiev." The man Nyx had scarred. "And Koral." The poet's muse. "We are of the All Council. I am sure you are at no loss as to why we are here."

Nyx recognized the voice as the one from the missive-box she had first received. She also recognized the promptings of a trap in Alora's open-ended statement.

If they need me to implicate myself, they don't have any proof. If they had proof, they would take her now. They had suspicions, ones they hoped she would confirm for them.

Nyx had never been a very good liar—the anxiety of the attempted deceit rarely outweighed the benefits for her. Still, she took her words in mouth and gave it her best.

"Of course, I'm so glad you're here, but...how did you know he escaped?"

Alora and Kiev shared a look, Nyx's gratitude at their arrival clearly not a reaction they had prepared for.

"He?" Alora asked.

"Morgen Drahl." Nyx furrowed her brow, doing her best to look confused. "He *is* why you're here? I captured him, as your missive requested, but he escaped through the ley lines. I hadn't even managed to message you yet."

"The access to your Station is closed off to all but the All Council. Morgen Drahl could not have escaped through this portal."

"Oh, no, he didn't. I left him in the Den. It was supposed to be the most secure area—I'm still really new at this—and he cut a hole through the floor and jumped into the ley stream."

Kiev took a step forward, fury etched across his marred face. "And you allowed this to happen?"

"Allowed?" Nyx didn't have to feign her outrage—it bubbled to the surface, hot and ready. "I have been a Guardian for *three days*. You sent me after a man who, by your own admission, is highly dangerous. I'm not a cop, I'm not a soldier, I'm not trained for this. I didn't even ask for this job.

"I mean *look* at me. Does it look like I just let him walk out the door?" Nyx wiped the blood running from her nose.

Alora shared a look with the others, all four blinking rapidly in perfect unison. Nyx wondered, a sinking feeling in her gut, if they shared some form of telepathy.

"Your Station shut down entirely. That means an object was removed from your Den. How do you explain this?" A strand of Alora's hair rippled, skittering over her shoulder.

Nyx shrugged, wiping her bloody hand on her pants. "I had a criminal in my Station. Criminals bring trouble. Having the Station impervious to outside entry seemed like a good idea."

Jevryn's eyes flickered over Nyx. "Do you mean us to understand that you removed an item from your Den with the specific *intention* of closing off your Station?"

"It's the truth."

"Is it?" Kiev stepped in, addressing the question not to Nyx, but to Koral. The eyes of the poet's muse narrowed. She stepped forward and circled Nyx twice, looking her up and down.

"This one is difficult to read." Koral circled again, her fingers twitching like mad. "Something about her blocks me, Kiev. I cannot verify the veracity of her words." Koral paused. "Not without a *deeper* look."

Pounding rattled the wall behind the All Council, fists beating in panicked, rapid strikes. Nyx froze, waiting for Alora and the others to turn, to dismantle the false wall and find not one, but two wanted criminals and a host of other individuals impossible for Nyx to explain.

No one moved. Koral continued to study Nyx with the mortician's eye for a cadaver, her head slightly tilted at an angle that made Nyx think she conversed silently with the other Councilors.

Nyx stood with locked knees, watching the Councilors blink in unison and failing to understand why disaster had not yet struck. The beating of fists behind the wall was so *loud*, unless... unless it *wasn't*.

Nyx listened, realizing she did not hear the sound of strikes echoing in the room, did not hear them rattling the false walls. Nyx knew fists flew at that false barrier because she *felt* them; the wall was a piece of the Station she had created. She was connected to it.

After a moment of concentration, Nyx could even tell that it was Morgen and Kaden who pounded on the wall, and that Kaden's blows were the more panicked of the two. She wished they would stop. They would only succeed in bloodying their knuckles, and she didn't need their panic to know that whatever Koral meant by a "deeper look" would not be good.

"Are you certain that is necessary?" Jevryn asked. He tilted his head down, studying the floor as if it held a particular fascination for him, black hair falling over his shoulder in a soft, silk curtain.

Kiev made an impatient noise. "Drahl is unaccounted for. The Arkadia system has been breached, the effects of which include an entire *race* of imprisoned peoples now waging war on one of our most valuable planetary assets. Arkadia's Station has been shuttered, we have no idea how many prisoners may have escaped, and you wish to waste time asking what is *necessary*?"

Jevryn lifted his head, cocking a brow. "I am merely suggesting we not obliterate a young woman's mind for no stronger reason than your wounded pride and broken face, brother."

Kiev growled, the sound like rocks tumbling over sand.

"Enough," Alora snapped. "A consensus must be reached for a deeper inquiry. Jevryn?"

"She is a Guardian, however new she may be. They cannot leave their Stations."

"You mean they *do* not," Kiev corrected.

Jevryn shrugged. "I would be quite impressed had she managed a ley line trip three days into her duties here. I would also expect this Station to be in chaos. Since it is clearly not, I see no warrant for a deeper inquiry."

"Koral?"

"She hides *something*." The muse's eyes spat sparks. "It is reason enough for me."

"Kiev?"

"Stations can be patched. Jevryn's touching words are not enough to convince me she should be spared."

"A Station may be patched," Alora conceded, "but Avatars always show the effects. Let us see the Avatar and judge by his condition." Alora looked expectantly to Nyx.

Nyx swallowed. "What are you guys *talking* about?"

Look terrified, she ordered herself. Not hard to do since Jevryn had so casually used the phrase *obliterate a young woman's mind.*

You don't know anything about Arkadia, Nyx reminded herself. *You don't even know what it is. You don't know about Meerkin or escaped prisoners and you will not open your fool mouth and get yourself killed.*

"Sniveling is not very becoming." Koral's fingers stretched toward Nyx, a viper's smile on her crimson lips.

"*Koral,*" Alora snapped.

Fingers stopped a hair's breadth from Nyx's temple.

Alora smoothed her voice. "Guardian Nyx, you will summon your Avatar."

"What? I don't understand what's going on. Shouldn't you be looking for Drahl? And what the hell is Ar-cady?" Nyx asked, deliberately fumbling the pronunciation of the prison world.

"It is not necessary that you understand. All Stations and their personnel answer directly to the All Council. You will summon your Avatar because we have asked it of you."

Nyx's gaze leapt from Koral to Alora to Kiev, stopping last on Jevryn. The man who had tried to reason with Kiev on her behalf gave no indication he would intervene for Nyx any further. He stood, unyielding as a statue, no warmth slipping from his demeanor.

Nyx swallowed, resisting the urge to wipe her sweating palms against her jeans. "Of course. I'll call him."

Nyx closed her eyes and held the certainty of her death close like a lover. Held it close, because she had been calling to Griff ever since the All Council's arrival. Plea after silent plea had been met by a wall of silence from her griffin.

I failed. Whatever bargain she'd struck with the Station had been too little, too late. Griff was gone and soon she would be gone too. Nyx called him again. The best way to act as if you were doing what you had been told was to actually *do* what you had been told.

Griff, if you can hear me, I need you. Please come. She repeated it over and over, pleading.

Griff did not come.

"I think we have our answer," Kiev murmured.

Alora waited one second. Two. Three. Then she nodded to Koral. The muses' hand snaked out, fingertips adhering to Nyx's temples like they were lined with super-glue. Her fingernails extended, narrowing to needle-thin points, and slipped through skin, drilling into Nyx's head through bone and marrow, past blood and tissue, ripping through the physical to get at the *thoughts*, the *mind*, the things that made Nyx, *Nyx*.

Nyx screamed. She clawed at Koral's hands while inwardly she fought to keep those fiery needles out of her thoughts, out of *her*. The more she fought them the deeper they dug, scarring, scoring, *scratching*.

Fire spread through Nyx's body, twisting and antagonizing, Koral's fingertips pressed deep into the soft flesh at Nyx's temples, pushing fire needles further inside.

Nyx felt her walls breaking. She shoved everything she had into shoring them up, and just as she was certain they would break, she felt the faintest flicker of an outside power bolstering her.

She didn't have time to wonder who or what was coming to her aid. Koral's needles pressed further, voracious, reaching for every truth Nyx sought to hide, and she knew the trickle of power aiding her would not be enough to hold her cracking walls together forever.

Then the needles just…stopped. Koral's hand ripped free and Nyx crumpled, as if the muse's fingertips had been the only thing holding her upright.

A shadow fell over her, followed by the fluttering of large wings and a roar that shook the Station's foundation. A black talon settled on the ground in front of Nyx, a barrier between her and the All Council.

"Griff." Nyx couldn't hide the relief in her voice. She scuttled back, pressing herself against Griff's hind leg, burying her face in black lion's fur.

Her head *hurt*. The inside was raw and grainy, as if its contents had been scraped out, examined, and then shoved back in with no finesse or care for where things were supposed to go.

Griff's wing settled around her shoulders like a blanket.

"What is the meaning of this?" Griff's voice boomed, thunder rumbling off canyon walls.

"Avatar." Jevryn actually bowed, a short, sharp inclination of his head. The others did not. "We must apologize."

"Must we?" Kiev's eyes glittered. He stepped forward, ignoring Griff's warning hiss and the snakelike movements of the griffin's neck. "Explain your absence, Avatar."

"Explain your torture of my Guardian, *Councilor*."

Nyx wished they would stop talking. Each word dropped in her mind like little coins in an empty cathedral, echoing and splintering for eternity. Chills racked her and she shivered, only managing to stay upright by clinging to Griff's leg.

Koral's eyes blazed. "You dare to question *us*?"

"I will do more than question if you have damaged her."

"Insolent creature. We *made* you. You exist because we will it. I could unmake you in an instant."

"*Enough.*" Jevryn stepped between Koral and Griff. "The girl's Avatar is here and in full control of his faculties. This is the proof you requested, is it not, Kiev?"

Kiev's eyes, cool and inscrutable, did not leave Nyx's disheveled face. "And why did it take her Avatar so long to respond? An Avatar's link to its Guardian is instantaneous, is it not?"

Jevryn looked to Griff and there was…*something* in his eyes. Something almost tender. "Avatar?"

Griff thump-thumped his tail, floor rattling at the impact and sending spikes of pain through Nyx's head. "I was engaged with the Station. As you know, when an Avatar connects with its Station, the call of its Guardian is not immediately recognizable."

"How convenient," Kiev purred. "For what need did you communicate with your Station?"

"Morgen Drahl escaped our custody today by way of a direct patch into the ley lines. My Guardian feared your displeasure, so I offered to try and track Drahl's path on the ley lines by direct communication with the Station."

"If this is as you say, why did your Guardian not inform us of it when commanded to call you?" Koral asked.

"I didn't—" Nyx coughed, a deep rattling in her lungs, blood bubbling up into her mouth. She spat it to the side, watching Alora's lips curl in distaste. "I didn't know he wouldn't be able to hear me while he talked to it."

Griff's wing rubbed her shoulder, reassuring. "My Guardian is new. She has learned fast, but she can hardly be expected to know such esoteric details so early in her appointment. Had I been aware you were coming to us, I would have informed her of it."

"What did your investigation tell you, Avatar?" This from Alora, her braids writhing and twisting together.

"I believe Drahl traveled to the Arkadian prison planet, though how he managed passage through its Station, or for what purpose, I cannot say."

Kiev looked to Alora. She shook her head, once. His lips drew back in a silent snarl, but he did not move.

"Take better care with your tasks in the future, Guardian. The Arkadian prison planet was breached mere hours ago. Several criminals escaped, some of them believed to be heading towards this Station. Though your rather...*unusual* choice to lock down your Station from within means it is unlikely they are here, we will need to perform a full search."

Too tired to argue, Nyx only nodded.

"A full search includes the Station's Den," Kiev said. "Earth's is in possession of the Opener of Doors, is it not?"

"It is," Griff answered.

"And I trust that item is not missing?"

"Of course not."

"I should hope, for your Guardian's sake, that that is true." Kiev waved Koral and Alora to the door, pausing to look back at Jevryn, who hadn't taken a single step.

"Are you not coming, brother?"

"The three of you are more than capable of handling a search. I will stay here. It would not do for something untoward to happen to the Station's Guardian while you are...searching."

"Do you not trust me, brother?"

Jevryn's lips curled up into a mockery of a smile. "Of course not. I know you."

Kiev returned his brother's smile. "And I know you. Enjoy talking with your pet, little brother." Kiev turned on his heel and walked out.

32

Nyx was too tired to puzzle out what Kiev meant by "pet." Acid bathed the inside of her skull and she fluctuated between forcing her eyes wide open and squeezing them shut, unsure which was more painful.

Jevryn took a step toward her. Griff curled his wing tighter around her, a warning rumble low in his throat. Jevryn stopped, letting his hand fall to his side.

"Do you truly think I would harm her, Arradin?"

"Griff. My name is Griff. And why should I believe you would not? You harm all you touch, Jevryn A-Morridahn."

Jevryn blinked and his lips pressed into a thin line. He looked away, briefly, before his gaze returned to Griff. "The pain of Koral's fire lasts for days. You know this better than anyone. Would you let her suffer when you know I can take that pain from her?"

The seconds stretched by in silence.

"Look into my eyes, Arradin, and tell me honestly that you believe I would harm her."

Griffin stared at the Councilor for a long, slow stretch. Abruptly, his head jerked and his wings twitched, as if he did indeed see a literal answer in Jevryn's eyes.

"Understand that your intervention will earn you nothing from us. Certainly not my forgiveness."

The corner of Jevryn's mouth quirked up bitterly. "You once made it quite clear to me that nothing I do can ever earn that. What I offer her, I offer for myself, Arradin."

"Griff."

"Very well, *Griff.*"

"Why would you offer this now?"

The rise and fall of Jevryn's shoulders was too aristocratic to be merely considered a shrug. "I have my reasons. They are selfish ones."

Griff lowered his face to Nyx's. "It is your choice."

Nyx coughed, the rattling in her lungs moving deeper. "You know him?"

Griff shook his head. "Once, I thought I did. I was mistaken. However, I do not think—" He paused, looking between Jevryn and Nyx another time before continuing. "I do not think he would harm you."

Another cough rattled its way up Nyx's throat. Fever flushed her body and a fresh wave of fire scored her skull. She looked up at Jevryn. "Take it, if you can."

He crouched in front of her, his eyes searching hers before he took her head in his hands. His fingers were surprisingly gentle, and his gaze held something that looked like regret. From his right hand slipped blessed coolness. It eased into the burning cotton of her brain and pushed the fire from her body. The touch of his power felt comforting, almost familiar, and if it hurt him at all to take her pain, Jevryn A-Morridahn didn't let it show. He took the rattling cough from her too, but there he stopped.

"I am sorry. But anything more and they will notice."

Jevryn took six steps back, returning to his place by the portal as Alora and the others re-entered the room.

"Your Station has been cleared, Guardian." Alora sounded neither pleased nor displeased by this fact. "And the regrettable flaw in design that allowed Drahl to escape your Den has been rectified. Failure to report any information regarding Drahl or his known associates will result in your immediate removal as this Station's Guardian."

Alora nodded at Kiev and the two stepped onto the platform, sank into cosmic ooze and disappeared. Their absence had a palpable lightening effect on the atmosphere.

Koral knelt at Nyx's side, whispering past the screen of Griff's feathers. "There is something *about you*, Guardian. I do not know what you hide. Rest assured I will find out, and when I do, you will regret having kept it from me."

"*Koral.*" Jevryn's voice was a warning, and the muse stood and walked to the platform without a backward glance, swallowed up into the ether like Alora and Kiev.

On the cusp of the landing, Jevryn paused. "Nyx. I speak to you, because I know *he* will not listen to me. You have become a Guardian at a difficult time. The Council is in unrest, and you have managed to center yourself in the middle of that unrest.

"Alora has accepted your story for now, but tides shift, and you may yet find yourself in difficulty again. I owe Arradin—Griff, as you call him—a debt I can never repay, nor would he accept any payment from me. So I offer that debt to you instead. If you find yourself in difficulty again, and you wish to tell me what really happened here today, then take this—" he pulled a sapphire ring from his left third finger and did not toss it to her so much as levitate it across the room, letting it drop into her outstretched palm, "—speak my name to it, and I will come.

"I cannot promise you any outcome, but I will do my best to give you guidance."

He stepped onto the platform then, cosmic dust slipping over his feet, up his ankles. When it reached his shoulders, just before he slipped beneath it, Jevryn winked at her and added, "The scar does wonders for my brother's visage."

Nyx watched him disappear, face blank, unsure whether to laugh or cry or howl to the heavens the glory that she was still alive. She looked down at Jevryn's ring. It was shiny and black, with a red stone set into the middle and little rivulets of red etching out from the stone. It looked suspiciously like a man's wedding ring, and the way he'd spoken to Griff...

"So, uh, you two have history?"

Griff refused to look at her or the ring. "I was not always an Avatar, Nyx. I was once a person who made mistakes."

This much, the Station's Heart had told her.

"And Jevryn was one of these mistakes?"

"It was a long time ago, Nyx. And frankly, it is none of your business."

Ouch.

Nyx undid the clasp of the chain around her neck and slipped Jevryn's ring onto it, feeling it slide down to clink against the Harvester of Worlds. It seemed fitting, somehow, two dangerous things together. She settled the chain back under her shirt as Griff gently picked her up in a talon the size of her entire body and deposited her on a bench that had not been in the room seconds before.

"I told you to take the others and leave." Griff's voice still rattled the room, thundering through walls and floor, though it held none of his previous anger. He took up as much space as a baby dragon, and his being shadow-ink black from fur to feathers added to the wow factor.

"You did." Nyx took a deep breath, bracing for the rattling cough before she remembered Jevryn had taken it from her. The rest of her body still ached and protested at every movement, and she winced as she shifted on the bench. "I didn't listen. I like your new look, by the way. It's very impressive. You know, in a feudal warlord sort of way, but still."

"Nyx." Griff brought his great head down to level with hers, his beak almost touching her nose. "What have you *done*? The Station was dying. Now it is not, and now it *hears* you."

Nyx shrugged. "Maybe it wasn't dying."

Griff drew back his head, looking down at her. "I know when the Station changes, Nyx. I control it." He pointed at the false wall. "I know that wall should not be there because I did not make it. You did. The Station was *dying*. It did not die, and now it answers to you. So I will ask you again, *what did you do?*"

"What I had to. I saved your life."

He clenched his beak, twisting his neck to the side, bones cracking. "Did it ever occur to you that perhaps I did not *want* to be saved?"

Hot breath blew Nyx's hair back, the walls rattling. Griff's anger filled the room, hanging heavy and leaden in the air. *Good thing there aren't any windows in here. I think his voice would break them.*

"Why would you say that?" Nyx's throat tightened, tears pricking at the backs of her eyes. She was so *tired*, and now Griff was angry.

"I am eternal, Nyx. I have been here for millennia, and I will be here for all the conceivable ones to come. Do you know what it is like, to know you will never feel death's release? It is madness. The Station's death, as awful as it was, was my only freedom."

The words made tattered shreds of Nyx's heart, pain flaring from the thorns in her cheek, rattling her emotions further.

"Is it so hard?" She hiccuped, a bead of saltwater escaping her left eye. "Am I so horrible to be stuck with?"

I guess I shouldn't be surprised. People always leave me. My parents. Kaden.

Griff's face softened and the tension drained from the room. Shadows fled and Griff shrank, not much, but more to the size of a horse. He reached out, one knife-sharp talon carefully wiping aside the saltwater trickling down Nyx's face.

"Nyx, you are the only Guardian who has ever thought to treat me as a person and not a convenience. I did not flee to death's arms to escape *you*. But understand that however tolerable, even joyful, time may be while you are here, you are not as I am."

I wouldn't be so sure of that, anymore.

"Some day you will hand the mantle to a new Guardian, and when that day comes, I will still be here. This is my prison, Nyx. I can never leave."

"I'm sorry. I didn't know."

"How could you?" Griff gentled. "It is not your burden to bear. But now I fear for you. For what you have done so that the Station lives, and answers as you bid it."

"I did what I had to." Nyx repeated. *What I thought I had to.* "I made a deal. For both of us. You won't be stuck here all the time, not anymore."

"What do you mean?"

Nyx reached up, chose a thorn in the outer ring of the whorl of thorns in her cheek and ripped it out. She couldn't stop the scream, didn't try. It tore out of her throat of its own volition, acid-dipped blades flaying into already sensitive nerves.

She didn't remember falling off the bench, but when she forced her eyes open, she lay on the floor, Griff's lion hind-foot three inches from her face. A wave of dizziness swept her, black dots dancing in her vision. She fumbled, almost dropped the thorn. She grasped it more firmly and, with a monumental effort, sunk the thorn into Griff's hind foot.

Electricity jolted up her arm, numbing it up to the shoulder. Then the black spots dancing in her vision grew larger, merging into one seamless canvas of black, and her head hit the floor.

33

Nyx dreamed, but the things she saw did not feel like dreams. She dreamed of Griff lying at the foot of her bed, tail flicking while in her window the sun rose and set, rose and set, repeating this cycle thrice more. She dreamed of Kaden and the others in the kitchen, exhausted and bingeing on food. She dreamed of Evra and Tamrin sparring with Maruca and Morgen in a large room that looked like a gym, dreamed of Lauralyn and Tobi playing in the clearing behind the Station.

She dreamed of Kaden, sitting alone in a small, dark room. It had no window in which a sun could be seen rising or setting to mark the passage of time. He stared into nothingness, oblivious to Maruca knocking on his door.

Nyx woke, rubbing crusted sleep from her eyes, her throat dry and painful. A glass of water appeared on her bedside table and though drinking it down was almost as painful as the dryness in her throat, she managed.

Griff lay on the floor at the bed's foot, as he had in her dream, his eyes closed in sleep. The room had grown to accommodate the horse-size he maintained, and his fur was still jet black. She tried to slip quietly off the bed, but the instant her bare feet hit the floor she jumped, an involuntary movement that tortured her bruised body, and she let out a squeak of alarm.

Griff jolted to wakefulness, wings flaring out majestically, his wild eyes landing on her.

"What's wrong?"

"Nothing," Nyx stammered.

"You screamed."

Nyx didn't think it qualified as a scream, but Griff looked like he was on the verge of panic so she didn't argue.

"I, umm…my floor is feeling my feet on it. It's *weird*."

"Oh. Yes, that happens when one is bonded directly to the Station." Griff paused, tucking his wings alongside his body. "Nyx, *how* are you bonded directly to the Station?"

So she explained. Once she started, the words wouldn't stop tumbling out, in a mismatched jumble about chaos and Station Hearts until Griff calmly asked her to begin at the beginning, and the entire tale from Arkadia on came out. When she finished, Griff was quiet, his golden eyes staring out the window.

"Are—are you mad at me?"

"No, I am not angry. I am worried. Despite the length of my time here, I do not know what the Station *is*, what its Heart is. But I know that however foreign it may seem to us, it does feel. It has memories and sometimes, when it slips deep into stasis, it dreams those memories and I catch glimpses of them.

"The All Council believes that the Avatar, bonded directly to the Station's Heart, may be susceptible to some influence from that Heart. It is why the Stations have both Avatar and Guardian. The Avatar is a buffer between Guardian and Station, allowing the necessary control over the Station while the Guardian remains free of the Station's influence."

Remembering the pulsing darkness, the foreign otherness of that place beneath the portal's surface, Nyx well believed it *could* exert such an influence.

"If the Council thinks it could influence us, they must think it wants something."

Griff nodded.

"What?"

He shook his head. "I do not know. But I believe the Council does. I believe they fear it very much, and will do everything in their power to halt it. Which is why you must try never to attract their attention again. You have altered the Guardian bond, opened yourself to the influence the Council fears.

"If they are ever given cause to inspect that bond, to learn of the change…they will not allow it, Nyx."

His words had a horrible finality to them.

"You mean they'll kill me," she said flatly.

"Yes, Nyx. In a heartbeat."

Nyx leaned back against the bed, every muscle in her body aching. "And they can do that? Just kill me, without fear of repercussions?"

She didn't need the dip of his beak to know the answer.

"Try not to worry too much. The Council has many things to occupy their time, and this Station, in particular, is at the bottom of a very long list."

"So when do we get a new one?"

"I beg your pardon?"

"All Council. How long is their appointment for? Is it like a four-year term, or—" She trailed off at the look on Griff's face.

Gently, he said, "There is no appointment. The All Council that is, is the All Council that *was*, and near as I can tell, they are the All Council that ever will be."

Nyx's heart thumped heavily against her chest. "They're immortal?"

"In a sense. Do you know what a Nexus is?"

Nyx shook her head. Griff's spectacles, which had been gone since he'd turned black-furred and large, reappeared. Nyx smiled. Scholar Griff was back.

"You are sitting on one. Within a Nexus, time is fluid. Broken.

Suspended. It is why I do not age, why the Guardians, while they are inside these walls, do not age. The All Council, too, live on a Nexus, and they rarely leave it. Having lived so long, they fear death above all else."

Nyx's stomach turned over as the implications sank in. She'd understood, on some level, that when she'd bound herself to the Station it was for the rest of her life. Maybe she hadn't had the time to really let it sink in, but she'd understood it.

She had also thought that life would be finite. The possibility of it not being so, of her life stretching out, unending, while everyone she knew lived and died around her…

Griff gently rubbed a talon between her shoulders. "We will find a way to undo it, Nyx."

"I don't—I don't think it will *let* me."

That cold, eerie voice echoed in her mind. *You do not understand what those 'thorns,' as you call them, take from you. Or what they give to others. You would be a fool to give one to the Avatar. Twice the fool to give one to us.*

And yet…and yet she couldn't regret it. Griff was alive. The Station, whatever it was, was alive. *She* was alive. She'd spent the last seven years drifting through her life as if she lived in a foggy half-world, unable to connect with anyone, to really live. Eternity scared the hell out of her, but if she had to live it somewhere then this place, here, with Griff, was the one she would choose.

And though it wasn't a pleasant thought, clearly she could still die by physical means, if it came to that.

"You have time, Nyx. Time to figure it out."

Indeed she did. Maybe Sena was right and, given enough of that time, she would come to view the Station as a prison rather than a haven. But for now…for now eternity was a distant concept, one she couldn't fully wrap her head around, a problem that could wait for another day. She had more pressing ones at present.

Such as, "How am I supposed to avoid the All Council's

attention with a band of prison planet escapees living in my Station?"

"You may wish to discuss the finer points of that with them. They cannot leave via the portal without being tracked, and even should they be willing to risk it, their departure would inevitably implicate you, and I will not allow that.

"Now that the All Council has sealed over the ley line access in the Den, there is no other means of leaving via this Station."

It brought up a question that Nyx had not had time to be properly curious about before now. "Griff, if travel via the Stations is trackable, how did the Kumir get here?"

"If anyone knew the answer to that question, we could put a stop to the Kumir."

Nyx frowned. "How did people travel between planets before the ley lines were created?"

"Portal magic. It can only be come by via the Shadow Market these days, and if that is how the Kumir do travel it is a very expensive means of transport for them."

Nyx rubbed at her eyes. She wasn't going to solve a decades-long mystery just by thinking about it. Especially right now.

"Nyx, I must ask. What is it, exactly, you have done to me?" Griff slid his left hind foot forward, a tiny black thorn just showing between the fur.

Nyx drew a deep breath and explained. When she was finished, she added, "You can leave, now. Only six times, but still…"

Griff didn't say anything.

"I—I'm sorry." She stroked the embossed number six running across her hand, and wondered if she'd made a decent deal or a terrible one. "I know it isn't much—"

"No. It is too much."

"I just—I just wanted you to have something. Some choice."

"I am grateful, Nyx. I never—" His eyes sparkled with a wet sheen. "I never dreamed I might see my homeworld again. Truly, you have given me something impossible, and I cherish it.

But I would not have chosen this at the expense of years of your life."

Nyx shrugged. "I live on a Nexus, right? Do a few years in a thorn even mean anything?"

"We'll find a way to undo it," Griff repeated, but she wasn't sure even he believed it.

But she just answered, "I know. I should take a shower. And go talk to everyone." She really, really didn't want to talk to anyone. "I just need to know—we're good, right? You and me?"

"You are my Guardian, Nyx. The one I would choose, if such a choice were given over to me."

Downstairs, Nyx walked past rooms that hadn't been in the Station before she slept—a small meditation room, a large room that looked mostly like a jungle, a playroom full of puzzles and stuffed animals—until she came to the gym she'd dreamt of. Inside, Evra sparred with Tamrin, working on hand-to-hand. On the other side of the gym, Maruca and Morgen drilled with swords, moving together with the kind of ease and fluidity born from years of camaraderie.

She's good, Nyx thought. Then, *I wonder if I could take her. Kaden always said I was too good.*

But that brought back memories of sparring *him*, sweat slicking her arms as they traded punches until they wound up on the ground, laughing, her mouth on his.

Why am I too good? she'd asked.

Because you fight like I do.

At the time, she'd thought he was complimenting her. But Evra also thought Nyx fought too well.

I fight like an Enforcer. That's what Kaden meant. And she'd learned those moves from a man with silver hair.

Who were you, Dad? The memory of her child-sized fist flying into his palm.

Evra spotted Nyx in the doorway and halted her bout with Tamrin, an upraised palm quelling the younger Amazon mid-punch. At Evra's shift in attention, every face in the room turned to Nyx. Stillness filled the room, the walking-on-broken-glass kind of stillness, and it took Nyx a moment to name the odd tension in the room: fear. They were afraid of her.

She remembered flesh dissolving off bone, shadows flying into the Harvester, bones crumbling into dust. She found Morgen's eyes. When he didn't look away, she cleared her throat. "Morgen, could I talk to you and Evra? In private?"

Nyx led Morgen and Evra into a small study next to the gym that, near as Nyx could tell, had simply appeared because she had need of it. The door had barely whispered shut before Evra rounded on Nyx.

"Are you all right?"

Nyx had not been prepared for the ferocity of Evra's concern, but something loosened in her chest at having it, and she hadn't realized just how worried she had been that after the affair with the Harvester, Evra and the others might want nothing to do with her.

"I'm...all right," she said cautiously.

"Griff wouldn't let us see you. He blocked your room off from ours. We tried to find you for a couple of days but..." She trailed off, eyes flicking down, then back up to meet Nyx's. "He was angry. With me, especially, and I do not blame him. Nyx, what I did... stealing from the Station, from *you*, I can offer no apology that would be adequate to—"

"Evra, you're an idiot." Nyx cut the Amazon off, pulling her into a hug—or at least a close approximation of one, since Evra stood stiff as a wooden statue during the entire affair. "The next time you go off on some hair-brained rescue mission would you just ask for my help?"

"I—what?"

"*Ask.*" Nyx stepped back. "It's this thing normal people do when they need help. Instead, you took off on your own and I had to work with the brainless wonder over there to bring you back."

Morgen's eyes danced with laughter. "This brainless wonder got you there and back again, didn't he?"

Nyx grinned. "Yes, but if I'd had to listen to you moon over Evra's beautiful eyes one more time, I might have wished for the sweet release of death."

Evra rolled those eyes, a faint blush creeping into her cheeks. "You are not angry?"

"I was," Nyx admitted. "But I get it. Tamrin's family. And I wouldn't wish that place on anyone."

"No. She does not discuss it much, but…it is good that Kaden found her. I am not sure what condition she would be in, had he not. Nyx, I truly am—"

"We're cool, Evra. Really."

Evra drew her brows together, a wrinkle forming between them. "I am quite warm, actually, and I am not sure what that has to do with this conversation."

Nyx laughed. "It's Earth slang. It means things are good between you and me."

"That makes no sense."

"I know. Loverboy here took all the Enforcer slang classes. Maybe he can explain it."

Morgen gave a flourishing half-bow. "I should be happy to assist you in understanding the strangeness of Earth English's many sayings, fair lady Amazon."

"Thank you." Evra's voice had ice in it, and she shot Nyx a withering look that had Nyx working hard not to burst into laughter.

Then the Harvester pulsed hot against her chest, and Nyx sobered.

"I'm glad you and I are all right, but that isn't why I wanted to see you." Nyx took a deep breath, plunged ahead. "Morgen, when are you guys taking the Harvester back? After what it did —what I *let it* do—to the Kumir, I—"

Morgen swore. "*That's* what happened to the Kumir? You used the Harvester?"

Nyx frowned. "What did you think I did to cause that?"

"Mystic Guardian powers? Weird Hidden abilities I don't understand?" Morgen threw up his hands. "Anything but used the bloody Harvester of Worlds. Did we not have an entire conversation about *not* using it?"

"I didn't see another way out of the situation. You said it was will-based so I thought I could stop it. And I did."

"Well, yes, but—"

"You said Kaden wanted me to keep it Hidden until you could use it to clear your names. How long do you think that will take?"

Morgen looked distinctly uncomfortable. "The plan was to clear our names, sure. It's just…"

"Just what?"

"Well, that was all sort of Kaden's plan. And maybe he knows something I don't, but I can't quite see how having it's going to help us clear our names when the All Council thinks we stole it in the first place."

"Oh." Nyx slumped into the chair that appeared conveniently behind her, grasping for any answer that did not end with the Harvester being her permanent possession. "The Councilor who tried to steal it—Alistair?—what did he want it for?"

"The same reason powerful people want anything, I'd guess? More power? I'm sorry, little Guardian, but I don't have all the answers."

"So you're saying I'm stuck with it," she said flatly.

"You could leave it in the Den," Evra suggested.

Nyx shook her head. "Of late, the Den doesn't seem to be as safe as it's touted to be. The All Council can search it whenever they want." Who knew, if she tossed it in there, maybe it would light a giant signal beacon all the way to All Council headquarters: *Harvester here.*

"You don't have to keep it, Nyx. Saddling you with it was

never fair in the first place." The corners of his Morgen's lips tugged down. "Especially since you didn't know what you were taking."

"If I don't keep it, who does?"

He hesitated. "You could always send it back to the Council. There are ways it might be anonymously returned. They've presumably had it for centuries, to no ill-effect, and some, at least, would no doubt be watchful of Alastair after its return."

Nyx considered it. She wanted nothing more than to be rid of it. But she'd seen what the Council had done to the Meerkin. She'd seen their prison planet. She'd seen what they would have done to her, what they *had* done to Griff. And now, she'd seen what the Harvester could do.

Of the councilors she'd met, only Jevryn seemed even remotely feeling and, as he'd clearly hurt Griff badly at some past point, she wasn't feeling kindly disposed towards him, either. Which left the option she didn't like.

"I'll keep it, for now, but will you keep looking? Into what it is? If we can, I don't know, destroy it without it causing problems?"

"I'll look, little Guardian." Morgen didn't sound hopeful that he would find anything. "Stars know I'll have plenty of time on my hands."

"What are you guys going to do?" The thought of them leaving en masse, of the Station being suddenly empty was a pain she hadn't counted on. "You know you can stay as long as you need to, right?"

"Little Guardian," Morgen grinned, "I hope you like having roommates, because none of us are going anywhere anytime soon."

The tightness in Nyx's chest eased.

"There is something, though," Evra said. "The youngest two children, Tobi and Lauralyn. They have no families to return to. I will find a way to get Tamrin home, and Kalvar is old enough to make his own decisions, but the younger two... We cannot appeal to the usual institutions for misplaced children. They would trace them back to Arkadia and we would find ourselves in new difficulties.

"Griff said they are welcome here for the time being, but they cannot grow up inside a Station."

Inside a Station, Nyx thought, *they wouldn't grow up at all.*

They needed somewhere to go, somewhere they would be wanted.

"I might have an idea, but I don't want to say until I'm sure. I need to go down to Earth Between."

"Would you like me to come with you?"

"That's all right. I need some time to myself. Do me a favor, though? Don't say anything to Tobi and Lauralyn yet? Not until I know?"

"Of course."

Nyx got halfway out of the Station before footfalls pounded after her.

"Guardian, may I have a word?"

Maruca. Nyx stopped, waited while the flame-haired Enforcer caught up and proceeded to stare at her for some time.

"It is Kaden," Maruca finally said. "He has not left his room since we arrived. He will not let anyone inside, not even me."

"What do you expect me to do about it?"

"Talk to him. He might listen to you." The words came out tinged in no small amount of bitterness.

Nyx folded her arms across her chest. "You don't like me very much, do you?"

Maruca tossed her head. "I do not know you. I know Kaden came to Earth to find the Hidden, leave the Harvester with that person, and return home. Instead, he stayed with you. For three years, he stayed with *you.*"

Get your timeline straight, honey, I only had him for two.

"When I finally found him on Arkadia," Maruca continued, "he was broken. It took me a long time to convince him to rebuild himself, and I never wanted to see him like that again.

But now he is in that room, and he has not come out, and I blame you for that." Maruca took a deep breath. "So, no. I suppose I do not like you very much. But I love Kaden."

Of course you do.

"He is my brother, and so I would ask even you for help, if it meant fixing him. I would ask that you try."

Nyx looked into Maruca's eyes, green broken-glass eyes, so like Kaden's. Traitorous relief swept through her as the familiarity and trust between Maruca and Kaden cast itself in a new light.

Nyx caved. "I don't think it will do much good, but I'll try. I have something I have to do, first, for the kids, but after, I'll talk to him."

Relief showed itself in the sagging of Maruca's shoulders. "Thank you."

Nyx watched Maruca float down the hall, trying not to think about just how frightened she was at the prospect of talking to Kaden when there was no one else around to be a buffer between them, no urgent matter needing handling to keep her from having to *actually* talk to him.

34

Nyx passed the sign welcoming her to Earth Between, feeling something was different about the place. When she passed the mottle-skinned harpy hawking potions and merely gave a pleasant nod, skirting deftly to the side of the con artist, Nyx realized what the difference was: this place didn't feel *strange* anymore. Magical, wondrous, bizarre, yes. Surely no better words described the top-hat wearing man sporting iridescent reptilian scales for skin who, when passing her on the street politely tipped his hat with claw-tipped fingers and said, "Good day, mademoiselle Guardian."

But foreign? Other? These words did not describe her world.

She entered the Warlock's shop, relieved to find she was still disappointed by the lack of dust. She hadn't changed *that* much.

She walked up to the counter, noting the rusted Swiss army knife had sold in her absence, and the bowl of Snickers bars labeled, "Earth Dessert Bars. Delicacy" had been replaced with a sign reading, "Earth Nutrition Bars, 35 Universals." The bowl was empty.

Nyx shook her head, rang the desk bell on the counter. Instead of Ankira, Diana danced out. She was resplendent in midnight blue silk, her flowing pants rustling sweetly as she walked, the blouse leaving her arms bare. She looked as beautiful and sophisticated as ever, but Nyx could only wonder just how many knives the woman had hidden inside her silks.

Diana smiled her polite politician's smile. "An honor to see you again, Guardian."

"Please, just call me Nyx."

"Nyx, then. Have you found your way to more trouble already?"

"No. I'm not here on official business. Sort of the opposite, actually. I was hoping I could talk to both of you. In private?"

Diana hesitated. "Ankira is not..." She looked away, and when she looked back a dark sadness welled in her eyes. "We attempted the pairing yesterday. It did not take. It was our last chance and she is not taking it well."

If the look in your eyes is any indication, you're not taking it too well, either.

"I understand. I wouldn't ask, if it weren't important."

Diana drew her lower lip behind her teeth, considering.

"I will see how she is." Diana vanished up the shop's back stairs, reappearing a few minutes later. "We will see you."

She flicked her fingers at the door and Nyx heard the lock slide home, the gold lettering on the doors changing from "Open" to "Out. Back in one hour."

Nyx followed Diana up the narrow wooden stairs and into the cheery yellow kitchen with its dozens of thriving, potted plants. The Warlock sat at the kitchen table, a cup of tea grown cold between her brown hands. Dark circles hung beneath her eyes and no trace of her cheery demeanor lingered.

"Nyx." Ankira's greeting attempted warmth, but the words came out hollow. "Please, have a seat. Would you like some tea?"

"Yes, thank you." She said *yes* more because she thought it would help the Warlock to have something to do than because she actually wanted tea. Nyx slipped into a chair while Ankira poured golden liquid from a cherry blossom patterned teapot into a delicate porcelain cup.

"Thank you."

Ankira nodded, reclaiming her seat while Diana stationed herself behind, one hand on Ankira's shoulder, a comfort and a protection.

"The truth is, I've come to ask you a favor." Nyx stirred the golden liquid, watching the straggles of tea leaves swirling along the bottom of the cup. "But I have to ask that, no matter your decision, you never speak of what I tell you today. Can you promise me that?"

The two shared a look, then Ankira nodded. "You have our word."

"Okay." Nyx took a deep breath and told them, as best she could without incriminating herself, everything she knew about Toby and Lauralyn.

By the end, Ankira's lashes were trembling. "We heard Arkadia had an outbreak but...children?"

"They had the best luck they could have had, in such a place. They found their way to someone who didn't belong there either, someone who took care of them. And then they found their way here. I can't alert the Council. They have nowhere to go and the Station, refuge as it is, is no place for children."

"No, of course not."

"I understand what I'm asking of you both. I know my timing must seem indelicate, and I know you wanted children of your own, but—"

"We'll take them." Ankira's hand gripped Diana's so hard her knuckles bled bone-white.

Even as Nyx's heart leapt, she spoke caution. "They are not normal children. They are likely angry and screwed up and who knows what else. I—I don't know if they would ever be able to love you the way you want. Maybe you should take some time, think it over."

Ankira looked up at Diana. They shared a long silence and Diana nodded.

"You do not have children because you need to be loved,"

Ankira said. "You have children because you need to love *them*. We would be honored to have them."

"Okay." Nyx let out a breath she hadn't realized she was holding. She had been so certain they would say no. "Would you like to come down to the Station tomorrow afternoon to meet them?"

Ankira nodded. They settled on a time and Nyx walked back to the Station, feeling heavier than she had when she'd left, and for entirely different reasons.

35

Nyx stood on the third-floor landing, staring at the doors lining the hallway. She knew which door she needed—she felt the pulse and flow of the Station as a living thing inside her, intimate and frightening. She knew Kaden lay just behind the farthest door, sitting in a corner in darkness as he had in her dream that had not been a dream.

The door closest to Nyx opened and Kalvar stepped out, his hair disheveled and an absent, wounded look on his face. He spied Nyx on the landing and the corners of his lips pulled up a bit.

"Hey, Nyx. Have you seen Maruca?"

"I think she's in the kitchen." She could *feel* Maruca in there, and she sincerely hoped Griff could teach her how to block out the Station's senses. Feeling so many things happening all at once was disorienting in the extreme.

"Thanks."

Nyx nodded, staring down the hall at Kaden's door. Kalvar surfaced from his inner musings long enough to follow the trajectory of her gaze.

"He used to talk about you, you know."

Nyx's fingernails made little half-moon indents in her palms that didn't *quite* draw blood. "Oh? What did he say?"

Kalvar shrugged. "Just talk. I don't think he ever thought he'd see you again."

Nyx nodded. Kalvar ducked his head, drawing back into his inner world as he trudged down the stairs in search of Maruca.

Nyx marched down the hall and banged on Kaden's door. She banged a few times, waiting in between sets, but nothing. He didn't answer even when she called his name, though she felt him stir a bit. She tired of the unresponsiveness soon enough, and it took only a sliver of thought to pull the deadbolt from its pocket in the doorframe.

Unhindered, Nyx twisted the handle, pushed the door in.

The hallway light, filtering in through the one foot of open space, traveled across the room, illuminating a small swath of bed, a foot and a knee in crossleg position, a lean stretch of torso, shoulder, a third of a face.

One illuminated green eye squinted at the light, at her. Kaden's voice, usually honey and whiskey, came out a dry, flat rasp. "N—You. You aren't here."

"Of course I'm here. Your sister is worried about you."

"Ruca." A smile ghosted across Kaden's lips. "She would be." He shook his head, shook the smile away. "But she isn't here, either."

Nyx frowned. "She's downstairs. You came here with her. To the Station. With *us*. You remember?"

"Of course I remember."

"Good, then—"

"Of course I remember, but it wasn't real. Never is. And it ended the same as it always does. You died."

"I'm not dead, Kaden, I'm right here."

"You die every time," he continued, "and then they bring you back. And just when I start to believe it's you this time, really you, you ask where it is, and I *know* it isn't you."

You had him for three years, Maruca had said.

But I didn't have you for three. I had you for two. So where were you in the year in between?

Softly, "They didn't send you straight to Arkadia when you left me, did they?"

Kaden lifted his chin, the sliver of light partially illuminating his face making him appear distorted, deranged. "You haven't tried that tactic in a long time. Asking me what I already know, thinking if I answer enough I'll slip up and tell you what you *really* want to know. It's a bit pathetic, really."

Nyx shrugged. "You think I'm a figment of your imagination. What harm does it do to tell me?"

Kaden weighed it, rolled it over. "If I tell you, like you want, will you let me rest?"

"Sure," Nyx played along.

Kaden's eyes narrowed. "For how long?"

Nyx swallowed, tapping her fingers on her biceps. "Eight hours."

She could tell by the look on Kaden's face it was too generous an offer, and she scrambled to correct it. "Eight hours *if* you tell me where you think you are now and why."

Kaden's shoulders slumped. "We're in the Council's Psionics compound. I'm here because they want to know where the Harvester is and you—*you* are just an image the Mindwitches pulled out of my brain to get me to tell *you* what I will not tell *them*."

He studied her, as if she were a particularly good rendering of an actual human being.

"I guess I can't be blamed for letting them dredge you out of my memory. For seeing your face. Your body. The way you walk, the way you talk. They're burned into me. But I never gave them *you*. Not even your name. Not where you are. And thanks to you, I can't tell them what they want to know, because I don't *know* where it is."

"Kaden—"

"You said you would let me rest, if I told you."

"I know what I said, but you aren't *there*. Your sister is worried about you and, *dammit*, I'm worried about you. So just snap out of it."

"You won't leave me alone?" His eyes blazed, raw hatred burning in their depths, and Nyx reminded herself it wasn't *her* he was looking at that way.

"Fine, then I'll make you. Touch a Mindwitch's Construct long enough and it deconstructs." He spoke the last in a sing-song voice, as if repeating a jingle he'd learned in school.

He blurred off the small cot, faster than Nyx thought a man who'd mostly been sitting immobile for days should be able to move. His body slammed into hers, drove her back, pressing her up against the wall. He drew her hands up, pinned them to the wall above her head, and crushed his lips to hers, no gentleness, no care. He kissed her like a dying man, drowning in her lips, her mouth, and she felt her body respond, electricity igniting a fire low in her belly.

If he can have his delusions, so can I.

Nyx closed her eyes and kissed him back. She kissed him until a low moan welled up in his throat, until he brought his hand down to cup her face, thumb stroking her cheekbone. He pulled back, and when he opened his eyes they held a clarity that filled her with relief.

"Nyx?"

She didn't trust herself to speak. She nodded, her nose brushing lightly against his.

"Shit." He sprang away from her as if her touch burned. "I'm sorry." He touched his fingertips to his lips. "How long?"

"Five days. So Griff says, anyway, I just woke up. What— what happened to you?"

Kaden shrugged, the tense set of his shoulders belying the supposed casualness of the movement. "I thought you died. Griff wouldn't let me see you."

You die, and they bring you back.

"And that made you think you were back in—" she searched for the term he'd used "—Psionics?"

"I watched you die a thousand times, a thousand ways, Nyx. Thousands of stories for why I was with you again, and some of them felt so real." He swallowed, hard. "It made more sense to be back in Psi than it did to have actually seen you."

He took a step toward her. "Nyx, I—"

She stepped back, lifting her hand, palm out. "Maybe now isn't the time."

Not after you kissed me like that. Like I meant something.

"You need a shower, and Maruca was worried enough she asked *me* to talk to you, and she hates me, so for the stars' sakes go see her."

"Nyx—"

"And then you need to sleep for real, not the tortured crap you've been doing in here, and—"

"*Nyx.*"

"I *did* almost die, Kaden. Several times. And you and Evra and everyone else here may be used to that, but I'm not. I have chaos shards in my face, my Station almost fell apart around me, and I nearly got brain-mauled by a crazy immortal *bitch.*

"And you know what? None of that's even what's eating me alive right now. You know what is? Morgen telling me you came here when you did to find the last Hidden. *Me.*"

"Nyx—"

"*Don't.* I would have done anything for a shred of information on who I am, who my parents were. Anything. And the whole time we were—whatever the hell we *were*—you knew more about me than I did."

Some small part of her brain told herself to stop, told herself she'd come here to bring him back to reality, not vent half a decade's worth of frustration on a man barely clinging to sanity, but she couldn't stop.

"So congratulations. You got what you wanted. The

Harvester's Hidden and you've been upgraded from inmate to wanted fugitive. Life's grand. I hope you got what you wanted from me, Kaden. Because you aren't getting anything else."

She turned on her heel and left the room, the weight of his gaze burning into her back.

36

Nyx sat out front of the Station by the griffin fountain, the sun warming her skin, her pants' legs rolled up and her bare feet plunged into the clear blue water. Her Avatar had not yet seen fit to return to a smaller size, and Nyx lounged against his side in companionable silence, her eyes closed, relishing the stillness of the afternoon.

She felt the Station's front door open. She knew who it was, but she looked anyway. She avoided meeting Kaden's eyes, swearing in Farsili. It was Morgen's native tongue, and she had coaxed most of the good words out of him.

Is it too much to ask for one hour of peace?

She had expected the Station to feel empty with the kids gone. Ankira and Diana had come down to collect them a couple days ago. The kids had been angry about it when Nyx first told them, so steadfast in their devotion to Kaden, Wonderful Hero of Ages, and all that. But Ankira and Diana had visited several times, spent time with them, and after a while some sensible part of the kids' brains realized that Kaden wasn't a parent, he was a —Mercenary? Soldier? Warlord?—Enforcer, and they had nowhere else to go.

Nyx had checked in on them that morning. Meek Lauralyn

had, against all odds, attached herself to the deadly Diana, and Toby had been busy mixing potions for the Warlock. They had seemed, if not happy—and she suspected happy would be a long time in coming—at least stable.

Ankira and Diana had been positively glowing.

Kalvar stayed on at the Station. He was almost of age, he'd pointed out, and Lauralyn was terrified of him. In short, he didn't really fit in anywhere. He ran errands for her in exchange for his keep because, as he put it, "I am *not* a scoffer."

Scoffer, apparently, being the Tiagren word for freeloader.

Nyx had given him the job because she'd thought it would make him feel better, but he'd turned out to be invaluable. With the Station reopened, Nyx had spent most of the last four days dealing with the flood of angry travelers whose itineraries had been delayed due to the Station's closing.

Kalvar carried luggage, dispensed directions, flashed his charming, boyish smile at the ladies—who tended to be charmed despite his being Tiagren. Nyx worked up the courage one day and asked him about that.

"Oh, people don't mind a Tiagren so long as he's in his proper place, serving them. That's where most of us work, service. And in some circles it's quite in fashion to have a Tiagren affair, so long as it's properly short."

Nyx frowned. "So you're telling me it's like crushing on the pool boy?"

"If I knew what a pool boy was, sure."

Nyx kept her outrage to herself and resolved to find a history of the races, and learn just why everyone seemed to think they could treat Tiagren like second-class citizens.

She noticed, afterward, that the wealthy ladies in particular seemed quite fond of tipping Kalvar, and she suspected he now had more disposable income than she did.

She really had to ask Griff when—or if—she got paid.

The mist she'd pocketed of Lana and Fari had turned back to two purple locks of hair that Morgen had arranged to send back to the Luminescent homeworld. He'd said the package wouldn't be traced back to Earth, and since he had every reason to make sure Earth stayed as uninteresting as possible, she believed him. She'd written a note to send with it, and Nyx could only hope it reached the girls' parents, and that it offered more comfort than it did hurt.

Against her back, a warning chirp-growl emanated from Griff's throat, and Kaden stopped ten feet away from the fountain. Nyx sighed and glared at her watch. Twenty minutes. She'd had twenty whole minutes to herself.

Kaden took another step and Griff's growl turned borderline-roar.

"It's all right, Griff."

"You do not wish to speak with him. I can tell."

"Yeah, well, I didn't really want to spend four days dealing with uptight travelers, either."

"Your point?"

"Sometimes we have to do things we don't want to do. I'll be fine, Griff. You worry too much."

Griff rose, robbing Nyx of her excellent backrest. He paused as he passed Kaden, rumbling. "If you harm her, Enforcer, I shall be displeased."

Nyx rolled her eyes as Griff loped off. "He's been all big, scary, black griffin since the near-death thing and whatnot." It was the closest she would bring herself to an apology.

Kaden nodded, as if she'd said, "Nice weather we're having," or, "Got any big plans this weekend?"

"Do you mind if I join you?" He indicated the fountain ledge opposite her.

"Could I stop you?"

"You could, if you wanted." He shoved his hands into his pockets. It would have made most men look smaller, less threatening. It didn't really work on Kaden, considering his biceps were the size of small tree trunks.

He dressed like he had when they'd been together, the

foreign, off-world clothing replaced by pale, well-worn jeans, a black t-shirt stretching across his chest. He'd taken her advice in the showering department and someone—Maruca, she suspected—had cut his hair. Not too short, just enough it didn't get in his eyes and looked casually wind-tossed.

Men.

Nyx held her hand out to the spot opposite her. "By all means."

He rolled up the bottoms of his jeans, perched on the edge of the fountain, and slipped his feet in. He looked painfully normal, not at all like the tense, blood-stained man she'd found on Arkadia, even if he still wore his Draken's-teeth necklace.

She wondered how much of his calm demeanor was real and how much of it was a battle-mask he hid behind. Once, she could have told you his mood just by listening to him breathe. Now she wasn't sure.

Nyx closed her eyes, listening to the sound of water trickling from the stone griffin's mouth. The travelers coming and going over the last week had meant Kaden and the other very wanted fugitives had been confined to a closed-off wing of the Station, and the reprieve had been useful for regaining her bearings.

She'd gotten a taste of what it could be like here—Arrivals and Departures when they came, running the bookshop and coffee counter when they didn't. She complained about the high volume of travelers, but they were half-hearted complaints.

How could she mind overmuch when she could watch a Dresidian's tentacles quiver in excitement at the purchase of a bonafide Earth novel (Nyx had steered her to Mercedes Lackey's *Oathbound*) or watch any number of faces morph into delight— or on rare occasion confusion or disgust—at the sip of a first latte?

They had coffee off Earth, Nyx had found out, and they did a lot of interesting things with it, like using it to marinate Saruvian Lizard eggs, or encrust broiled Mana fruit, but it appeared Earth held the trademark on steaming milk and pouring it over espresso.

Some days, it was good to be an Earthling.

Other days, you had your insanely lethal fugitive ex-boyfriend opening his mouth to ruin the pleasant, awkward silence you were pretending not to share with him.

"On a scale of one to ten, how mad are you?"

Nyx blinked. How mad was she? *Mad.* Like she was a housewife or something and he was a businessman who'd stayed out too late drinking when he'd told her he was at work and now she was *mad?*

Well, she was mad enough now that the only sound she managed out of her mouth was, "Mrmph." She shook her head, tried again. "Why?"

She had eight-billion whys. Let him pick which one he wanted to answer.

"I never expected you to get mixed up in all this. I knew the Guardian here would change, soon, but I never thought it would be you. When I heard your name on Arkadia, my heart almost stopped."

Nyx was quiet for a moment, then held out the arm with her Guardian tattoo. "You didn't expect this?"

"Of course not."

"Then what, exactly, did you think would happen when you left me?"

"I knew you would be angry." He rubbed his thumb over the scar running from his elbow to his wrist. "It would hurt. You would move on."

And there it was, in clear, concise, dispassionate language.

She laughed. "You were all I had. And I told you everything about me, so you knew that. You knew it killed me every day, not knowing who I was, *why* I didn't have anyone. Two *fucking* years, Kaden? You watched it eat at me for two years and you could have told me everything in ten minutes."

"And you would have believed me? If I'd started talking about other planets and magic before you'd seen the Between?"

"You could have brought me here. You could have given me a choice."

"I couldn't risk bringing the Harvester out of Dead Earth before you agreed to Hide it."

"Right. Because it is all about *you*, after all. *You* needed the Harvester Hidden, *you* couldn't take the risk."

Kaden's jaw clenched. "No, it isn't about me. What happens with the Harvester affects a great deal more than you and me."

"You don't even know what it *is*. You don't know what it does, and you left me with it anyway."

"You were safe enough with it in Dead Earth. Especially after you Hid it."

"If I'd stayed in Dead Earth *I'd* be dead right now. That's where not knowing anything got me. I tried so hard to leave I nearly killed myself. Where would you and your precious plans be if that had happened?"

"I did what I thought was best."

He was never going to apologize, she realized. Maybe, if she pushed him, he'd say something along the lines of, *Sorry you went through all that*, but he would never apologize for what he'd done. Because he still didn't think he'd done anything wrong.

There was only one other thing she needed to know.

"Why did you stay with me?"

"What?"

"Why stay? Why make me think we had a relationship? I've seen the Enforcer skill set. I'm sure you could have extracted the promise you needed."

"Do you think I would do that?" His voice was too level. She felt the tension vibrating off him, as if he wanted, *needed*, to punch something. "Do you honestly believe I could torture an innocent woman?"

Nyx shrugged. Amazing, how steadily her heart beat, how calm, when across from her Kaden threatened to explode.

"I don't know. Is it any crueler than making me believe you loved me? All just to hide this?" She drew the Harvester from behind the collar of her shirt. "You never said those words to me. Two years and you never said it, not until the night you asked me to promise I would keep this safe."

Silence.

"You knew if you said it, I would promise."

"Yes." Tight, clipped.

A curious numbness spread through Nyx's veins, ice crawling up around her heart and forming a protective shell.

"It doesn't mean it wasn't *true.*"

Nyx pulled her feet from the fountain and put more distance between them. "I would say that, too, if I were a wanted fugitive whose ability to stay hidden depended on someone I used and betrayed."

He stared at her, lips pressed into a thin line. She stared back, waiting, some small part of her still wishing for him to say something, anything, that would make it better.

He didn't.

"The painting, Kaden. The one I bought you. You took everything else with you. Why did you leave it?" She hated herself for asking, hated herself for needing to know.

He gave a short bark of laughter. "I didn't take anything with me, Nyx. I destroyed everything. If anyone came looking for me, I didn't want them to trace my life here back to you. But I couldn't bring myself to destroy that. So I left it for you."

"Oh." The word came out small in her throat. It didn't mean anything. Not really. "All I saw was that the only thing I ever gave you was the only thing you didn't want."

She turned and walked away, the Station growing a wall of rose briars in her wake, curtailing pursuit. He didn't get to see her pain—pain was something you let others see when you wanted them to know how much they'd hurt you, when you wanted them to fix it.

She didn't want him to know. There was nothing he could do

to fix it. She didn't want to know whether he'd meant it when he'd said it was true he'd loved her. She wasn't sure which would be worse: that he'd never loved her at all and those two years had been a complete lie, or that he had loved her and he'd still done what he did.

37

Nyx slipped into Kaden's room and gently set the painting on his bed. It had been two days since the fountain, two days she'd spent moody and withdrawn, staring at that damn painting any time she was in her room. She couldn't keep it and she couldn't throw it away. She'd given it to Kaden once, she might as well give it back to him.

But standing in his room, she couldn't help but run her fingers lightly across the canvas-painted boats, couldn't help but let it bring back memories she didn't want.

We should get a boat. Kaden's arm around her waist as they looked through the street festival's art stands, his gaze lingering on the painting of ships.

A boat, Nyx echoed. *What would we do with a boat?*

His answering grin, half-crooked, heart-stopping. *Live on it. See the world. Make love on the open sea. The options are limitless, really.*

Uh-huh. We can't afford a boat. She couldn't afford the painting, either, but she'd snuck back later and bought it anyway. Watching his eyes light up when she gave it to him had been worth it.

She thought it had been worth it. It had felt so real, every moment she'd spent with him.

Nyx saw a slight flicker in the shadows to her far right, a change so minuscule she wouldn't have caught it if she hadn't already felt someone wander into the space which had previously been empty.

"You may as well stop skulking in the shadows. I know you're there."

Kaden stepped out of the shadows, his brow furrowed.

"How did you know?"

Because I felt your boots on the floor. Because I'm bonded to a sentient alien building and it's freaking me the fuck out.

She shrugged. "Just did. You know women don't find stalking attractive, right?"

"I was not stalking."

Nyx raised one eyebrow. "So you were blending into the room for practice?"

Kaden raked his hand through his hair. "You *are* in my room," he pointed out.

"Fair enough."

He took a hesitant step forward, then another, and another, until he stood a foot from her, looking at the canvas painting.

"I never considered what it might look like to you. That it would hurt you that I left it." He waited, but she didn't say anything. "Why did you keep it?"

"Because I loved you." No point in denying the obvious.

"Nyx—" He stepped forward, stopping when she moved away.

"It doesn't mean I do now. You held all the cards, Kaden. And you used all of that to manipulate me into doing what you wanted. And maybe I understand why you did it. Who knows, maybe it was even the right thing to do."

She'd felt the Harvester's power, after all. She'd seen what it could do.

His eyes measured her. "But?"

"But however good your reasons, you *hurt* me. You used me and I—I don't know if I can forgive that. And you don't have the right to ask me to."

"I know. But you can't tell me you don't feel anything for me." He stepped close to her, brushed his thumb softly across the sensitive spot along her jawbone. "You still shiver when I touch you."

His lips were so close and it was unfair how quickly her body forgot the reasons her mind gave it to say no. She *wanted* to believe he'd actually missed her. That he'd loved her. That he still did. But he'd let her live in the misery of believing that no one in the world cared for her, then made her believe that *he* did, and when it was convenient for him, he'd left her without any explanation at all.

"Sex is easy, Kaden. And if you want to push it, I'll probably fuck you." Stars knew he hadn't lost any of the magnetism she remembered. "But it's not what I want. And you don't need to bother."

His hand fell away. "Bother?"

"With trying to forge an emotional connection so I won't kick you out. You and the others are welcome here for as long as you want. Frankly, it's just as dangerous for me to have the All Council find you on Earth as it is for you."

Probably more so, for her, because she couldn't run if it all went sideways.

"I'm sure we can manage to coexist until you all decide what to do."

With her new connection to the Station, avoiding him would be a practically nonexistent problem, and given enough time she would stop feeling…whatever the hell it was she was feeling.

"If you need anything," she continued, "let Griff know, he's more than capable of accommodating any requests."

She was halfway out the door when he said, "Viktor Hawthorne."

She stopped, raising an eyebrow in question.

"Morgen said he told you about your mother. She came to Earth with an Enforcer named Viktor Hawthorne. I don't know if he's your father or not."

"Thank you." Her fingers twisted on the doorknob. "This doesn't change anything between us."

A shadow of a smile ghosted his face. "I know."

"Then why tell me?"

"It's the only thing I know. The only thing I can offer you. Because it may not change anything, but I *do* care about you."

He stepped into her space again and she let him, pretending her heart wasn't beating faster, her breath wasn't catching in her chest.

"I didn't stay with you for two years because it was the only way to get what I needed. I stayed because I wanted to. And I have missed you every day since I left."

She closed her eyes and the truth came out. "I missed you, too. But I didn't even know you."

"You knew the important parts. I never lied to you. I just didn't tell you everything."

"It's the same thing, Kaden." So like him, to not understand the distinction. "And regardless, we aren't the same people we were then. You're different. I'm…very different. We don't really know each other."

"Then maybe we should get to know each other again," he murmured. He was too close, the scent of him washing over her, his physical proximity trying to convince her brain she was years in the past, when she'd still thought things between them were real, and simple.

"I don't know, Kaden. I'll think about it."

She stepped out of the room, closing the door behind her before anything could happen that she would regret. Before she could become any more confused than she already was.

She didn't need to know what to do about Kaden right now. He wasn't the most important thing in her life anymore. He wasn't the *only* thing in her life, anymore.

Viktor Hawthorne. Elena Fortuna. She had names, and a time-line, and they might not be much in the grand scheme of the universe, but they were more than she'd had before.

She had a *chance* of finding out where they were, of why her mother had Hidden her own memories from her—why they'd left her here with nothing—and that chance brought a smile to her lips.

She made her way downstairs to the kitchen, where she could feel Evra was perilously close to destroying her espresso machine, arriving just in time to grab Evra's wrist mid-air. She grunted at the effort of stopping the Amazon's fist before it connected with the top of the espresso machine.

"Hitting it will *not* make it do what you want."

"You cannot know that," Evra growled.

"Here. You sit there." Nyx indicated a seat on the far side, putting the bar between Evra and the espresso machine. "I'll make your cappuccino."

Evra eyed the machine haughtily. "Fine. I want extra of the foam." She stalked to the indicated chair and sat down. "You look...happy?" She spoke the last word as if it were a mortal sin.

Nyx filled the portafilter with new espresso grounds, tamped carefully, and twisted the portafilter into the machine. "More... hopeful, I would say." She watched the shots pull, dropped the steam wand down into the milk, listening to the hiss and gurgle as it frothed.

"That is charming. Hope does not pay the bills, no?"

Great. Why did I think Morgen should teach her Earth sayings? "No. But last time I checked, your salary was paid in full."

"True. But I am as bored as a two-drink whore in a chapel full of clerics."

"Well," Nyx considered, "there's always the chance more Kumir will show up."

Evra's lips twitched. "Do not tease me with things I want and cannot have."

Nyx grinned, pouring the steamed milk over the espresso

and scooping out a healthy dose of foam. "You never know. We still don't know who sent them."

"I think we can well guess."

"You still think it was Alastair?"

"Who else? Kaden and Morgen thwarted his plans to take the Harvester from the Council's vault. It makes sense he might hire Kumir to follow Morgen, hoping Morgen would lead him to it. Since the Council has lost track of Morgen, it is unlikely Alastair would send Kumir here again."

"Well, here's to hoping he's thorough so you don't die of boredom." Nyx plunked the cappuccino down in front of Evra. "Can I ask you something?"

Evra took the cup, a new coffee addict's delight in her eyes. "I suspect you are going to anyway."

"Why are you still here?"

Griff, after five days of poring over Evra's contract, had finally found a loophole, and the Amazon was free to leave whenever she wanted.

Evra shrugged. "It is interesting here."

"You just said you were bored out of your mind."

"You are infuriating, you know this?"

"I'm told it's one of my best qualities. So what gives?"

Evra's fist curled, tensing to punch something, then relaxed. "I stole from you and caused you a great deal of difficulty. Despite all that, you helped me. I have not known anyone who would do that for me, before." She shrugged, as if the answer meant nothing, which told Nyx it meant a great deal.

"Yeah, well, I don't know many people who would nearly kill themselves and fight through a prison planet, even to rescue their sister." Nyx leaned her head right, then left, bones popping.

Evra shivered. "I *hate it* when you do that."

"I know." Nyx grinned. "Wanna be friends?"

Evra considered, then asked, serious, "We do not have to hug, do we?"

Nyx let out a short bark of laughter, a rippling sound that carried through the Station. "No, we don't have to hug."

"Then, yes, I accept."

"It's not a marriage proposal." Nyx turned thoughtful. "Although, I think Morgen has one of those in mind for you."

Evra scowled. "He has mentioned something of it, along with three children and a white picket fence. I do not want three children. And I am not sure what a white picket fence is, but I do not want one of those either."

Nyx kept her face carefully neutral. "No, of course not. So. You're bored?"

"Unbelievably so."

"Great. Now that we're friends and all, do you want to go on a quest?"

"A quest?"

"Yeah."

"What kind of quest?"

"I need to find my parents. I think—I think at least my mother is still alive, and I've been getting these patches of memory back. I want to know what the hell happened to me."

Evra's eyes glinted at the possibility of adventure. "You wish to find someone who should theoretically be impossible to find?"

"Yes."

"That sounds delightful."

"Great." Nyx smiled, leaning back against the countertop. She both felt the countertop against her skin, and felt skin against her countertop. The two-way sensation was odd but not entirely unpleasant, and she was growing more accustomed to sorting out the information the Station sent her.

"Are you all right?" Evra frowned. "You have that look again."

"I'm fine."

"Hmm. Look, are you sure you do not want to give up this whole Guardian bit and join the Mercenary Guild? It is quite lucrative and we could see many places."

Nyx smiled. "Thank you, but no." She looked at Evra, feeling utterly at home. She closed her eyes and saw through the Station's senses instead, feeling Kaden and Kalvar up in their rooms, Griff prowling through the Archives. She felt the wind caress the Station's outer walls, felt the roots of the plants curling deep into the Station's soil. It was strange, feeling a sentient building's every touch.

Strange, but amazing.

"No," she repeated, "I quite like it here."

She was Nyx Fortuna, Guardian of Station 27, location Earth Between, and she wasn't going anywhere.

WANT THE STORY BEHIND HOW NYX AND KADEN MET?

The bonus prequel story to Guardian of Chaos is available exclusively to my newsletter subscribers. You can get it for free by signing up for my newsletter at:

https://michellemanus.com/newsletter/

If you enjoyed the book, it would be beyond super awesome of you to leave a review at your retailer of choice. Reviews really are the best way you can help support authors.

Thanks so much for reading!

ABOUT THE AUTHOR

Michelle lives in a desolate land with a dark wizard, a unicorn, and a feline overlord. Despite certain stereotypes you may be familiar with, the dark wizard is not holding her captive, nor does the unicorn require virgin riders. The feline overlord, however, may well be evil.

She holds dual BAs in English and Philosophy, which has gotten her about as far as you would expect it to in life. Despite all evidence to the contrary, she's still desperately holding out hope that in an alternate reality she's a sword-wielding princess.

You can find Michelle on her website: www.michellemanus.com or her social media. Stop by and say hi! The virtual world is way cooler with friends.

facebook.com/michellemanusbooks
x.com/MichelleManus
instagram.com/michelle.m.manus

ALSO BY MICHELLE MANUS

The Aspect Society Trilogy

Siren's Song

Valkyrie's Call

Truthfinder's Promise

The Nyx Fortuna Series

Guardian of Chaos

Guardian of Shadows

Guardian of Madness

Guardian of Torment

Guardian of Defiance